The Eternal Forest

The Eternal Forest

by

George Stanley Godwin

"To my wife, Dorothy"

Edited by Robert S. Thomson

Rthomson@islandnet.com
www.godwinbooks.com

GODWIN BOOKS

VANCOUVER • BRITISH COLUMBIA • CANADA

The Eternal Forest

Copyright © (no. 433781) Robert Stuart Thomson
Godwin Books, Vancouver, Canada, 1994

ISBN 0-9696774-2-1

Printed by Hignell Printers, Winnipeg, Manitoba
Cover design, text formatting: Sherwood Graphics, Surrey, B. C.

For information write to:
GODWIN BOOKS
P.O. Box 4781, Vancouver, B.C. V6B 4A4
Tel. (604) 682-5605 Fax. (604) 682-5640
To order copies by mail please see p. 320.

Canadian Cataloguing in Publication Data:

GODWIN, GEORGE b. 1889.
The Eternal Forest

Previously published as: The Eternal Forest under western
skies.
ISBN 0-9696774-2-1 (bound). – ISBN 0-9696774-X (pbk.)
PR6013.O27E8 1994   823'.912   C94-910780-8

Includes:
Introduction by Mr. George Woodcock
Illustrated biography of George Godwin
Notes on the text
Extracts from George Godwin's *Journal*

Editing, design, biography, notes and photographs:
Robert Stuart Thomson
Godwin Books, Vancouver, B.C. V6B 4A4

Critics' reaction:

I

"A S SOON as I read George Godwin's long-neglected novel, *The Eternal Forest*, I had an extraordinary sense of *déjà vu*. I had "been there before" even if the times and places were different. (. . .) I arrived, like him, as an English chechako or greenhorn in a British Columbia village. It was not, like his Ferguson's Landing, in the Fraser Valley in the 1910s, but on the southwest corner of Vancouver Island in the late 1940s, yet the circumstances were strikingly similar. (. . .)

So I can vouch in a special and rather intimate way for the authenticity of the central plot line of *The Eternal Forest*. Even the thoughts of the Newcomer, so often strange and inflated and even slightly hallucinatory, are those of a man exhausting himself in solitude under the beautiful indifferent eye of Nature. I know because I shared them. (. . .)

The conflicts that are essential to *The Eternal Forest*, between small farmers and exploiters, between peasants and speculators, between a rural largely subsistence economy and an urban-based one, between individuals and corporations, between Europeans and Asians, are all subsumed in the great central conflict of the book between the forces of the natural world exemplified in the forest and those of material progress, exemplified in the city, where people are destroyed or sometimes, as in the case of the Anglican parson, mysteriously regenerated. (. . .) What interest us most in *The Eternal Forest* are the portraits of human beings struggling and sometimes by sheer wilfulness succeeding against both the villainies of corrupt men and the ever-returning, ever-encroaching power of the bush."

— *George Woodcock*

II

"*The Eternal Forest* pulsates with the vitality of the bush – ruggedness, the frontier and struggle. It captures the spirit of the times when European emigrants, mainly British, responded to the call of a new life in the Canadian wilderness . . . The clash of the genteel English with the harsh but beautiful reality of the forest.

Godwin's talent is to define the everyday lifestyle with descriptive phraseology. He is a keen observer, a naturalist who sees everything: the sweat, the very trickles, the colours and the sounds of all around him . . .

The Fraser Valley is captured so well when it rains: 'The trees dripped with water that had not fallen as rain and the trampled undergrowth soaked the Newcomer as he worked: the humid earth squelched under his heavy boots; the branches of the trees wiped wet fingers across his face.' "

– John A. Cherrington

III

"*The Eternal Forest* can best be described as 'The Great Fraser Valley Novel.' (. . .) It realistically depicts the erosion of rural, community-based life in the Valley by Vancouver-based capitalism. (. . .) Rich in empathy and controlled insights . . ."

– Alan Twigg, Vancouver and Its Writers

IV

"I must confess I was quite moved when reading this novel. It is a genuine report from the turn of the century, and reflects then-contemporary ideals and prejudices. As such, it is of real importance to the history of B.C."

– Dr. Sandra Djwa
Head, English Department, Simon Fraser University

Contents

The Eternal Forest

Introduction by George Woodcock

As soon as I read George Godwin's long-neglected novel, *The Eternal Forest,* I had an extraordinary sense of *déjà vu.* I had "been there before" even if the times and places were different. A whole generation after Godwin came to British Columbia and turned his experiences and observations into fiction. I arrived, like him, as an English *chechako* or greenhorn in a British Columbia village. It was not, like his Ferguson's Landing, in the Fraser Valley in the 1910s, but on the southwest corner of Vancouver Island in the late 1940s, yet the circumstances were strikingly similar. I came from England with very little money to a self-contained little society of loggers, fishermen and small farmers into which I was admitted with kindness and condescension, like the Newcomer, the unnamed hero of *The Eternal Forest.* Like him, and like Godwin who himself settled in the Fraser Valley and gave it up, I and my wife cleared our bit of land with more ardour than skill, built ourselves a house and spent all our money, so that in the desperate end, and before selling out, I was, again like the Newcomer, earning our scanty living by manual labour for cash or sometimes for barter – a salmon, a halibut, a haunch of bear!

So I can vouch in a special and rather intimate way for the authenticity of the central plot line of *The Eternal Forest.* Even the thoughts of the Newcomer, so often strange and inflated and even slightly hallucinatory, are those of a man exhausting himself in solitude under the beautiful indifferent eye of Nature. I know because I shared them.

But *The Eternal Forest* is more than a semi-autobiographical novel about a man enduring and recognizing reality. It is also the collective portrait of a little community of settlers along the banks of the Fraser, too well-established to be classed as pioneer, but still permeated with the insecurities of a frontier life largely dependent on natural resources.

The copy of *The Eternal Forest* I have seen is undated, but there is enough to suggest that it was written during the years immediately preceding the Great War. This was the time when, belatedly, something of a literature was beginning to appear in British Columbia. The Cariboo gold rush of the 1860s had evoked surprisingly little in the way of fiction, and at the end of the nineteenth century attention tended to be concentrated farther north in the Klondike which produced a considerable literature. But in the early years of the present century a number of still interesting novels of British Columbia life began to appear. In 1908 there were Morley Roberts' *The Prey of the Strongest* and Martin Allderdale Grainger's excellent novel about coastal loggers, *Woodsmen of the West.* In 1909 appeared Frederick Niven's *The Lost Cabin Mine,* and these are merely examples of a larger body of work.

The Eternal Forest cannot have appeared before the early years of the next decade, for we know that George Stanley Godwin and his wife Dorothy arrived from England via Calgary in 1912 to settle in Whonnock, a cluster of small farms on the Fraser River close to Ruskin (which Godwin called 'Carlyle'). There, like the Newcomer, he bought land, painfully and inexpertly cleared a fragment of it, ran out of money and took to labouring work to survive, turning his dress trousers into work pants. We also know that Godwin was back in England in 1916 to enlist in the Canadian army, though he already suffered from the tuberculosis that should have made him exempt.

However, the Great War in no way figures in the novel, where the Newcomer's reason for abandoning his holding is not presented as patriotism, but sheer exhaustion of the will without the hope of anything better until he escapes. This suggests that the period of the action lies between 1911 and 1914, and it seems likely that *The Eternal Forest* was written in Canada as well as depicting experience there. It was published undated by a small New York firm of Appleton, later absorbed into the conglomerate Appleton Century Croft, and this gives a strong hint, for in the early part of this century there was virtually no publishing industry in this country and Canadian novelists regularly printed their books with New York houses. Had Godwin waited until he returned to England to launch his book he would surely have sought out an English publisher as he did for the quite numerous later books of his freelance career. So we can perhaps take 1914-15 as the possible date for publication.

The dominant line of *The Eternal Forest* is of course the effort and failure of the Newcomer to build a satisfactory life on his recalcitrant patch of forest. But, for this reader, the portrait of this protagonist is rather like a sculpture almost at the final stage but with the features still incompletely determined. A name would have anchored the character more securely in our minds. (He and his wife do not address each other even by their first names.) And the rich subjectivity of his reaction to the natural world might have been more sharply defined by a clearer reaction on the part of his neighbours than their tolerant and slightly disdainful disregard of him.

In contrast are the sharp sketches of these characters themselves, borrowed or adapted, one assumes, from real life. Individually they are representatives of the various strains of belated immigration that came together in the Fraser Valley under Ottawa's boostering of the 'Last Best West,' i.e. British Columbia and the northern prairies after the great central wheatlands had been mainly taken up by homesteaders.

Except for the old Indian chief Jim, regarded with mixed pity and contempt in the fashion of the time as the representative of a dying culture, they have all come from somewhere else, from the American states, from England, from Scandinavia. The model of industry is the Swede Johansson who alone among the settlers finally conquers his fifty acres at great cost to his family. The Olson family prospers on its versatility, as salmon fishers, farmers, loggers, prospectors. The English are represented at one end by the feckless remittance man Bob England and at the other by Old Dunn, a self-educated Yorkshire miner who, like many of the working class English who came to the West Coast about the turn of the century, is imbued with vaguely socialist ideas. His particular Guru is the American Henry George, whose *Progress and Poverty*, advocating a single land tax as the solution to social injustices, was popular among older proletarian radicals at this time.

Between these people of various European strains there is no racial antagonism, and the Italians who maintain the CPR permanent way (the actual track and its bed of broken stone), are regarded with tolerance as happy and child-loving. On the other hand even the Newcomer shares that fear and dislike of Asians which was so widespread at the time, permeating even the labour movement. The Japanese were regarded as intrusive and intent on taking over the province in one way or another. The Chinese and the Hindus (really Sikhs) were resented for their price cutting, in labour and produce. They were talked of in ways that would offend the ears and eyes of the present politically correct age, but in preparing this edition the integrity of the original has been considered of prime importance. This was how most people – even generally decent people – thought in those days. In this sense *The Eternal Forest* is the portrait of a time as well as of a place.

Europeans and Asians alike were caught in the economic problems of the era, and particularly of the boom-and-bust cycles that set in after the CPR was completed in the late 1880s and land became a commodity and a matter of politics and speculation. At the time Godwin wrote of, the land market was particularly volatile because two new railways, the Canadian Northern and the Grand Trunk Pacific, had entered the province, caused their booms and their waves of speculation and were now on the downward slope towards bankruptcy. But in the Fraser Valley the CPR remained unaffected, resented as in the prairies as a rapacious manifestation of corporate power.

The oil craze that also ripples through *The Eternal Forest* had hit western Canada in 1910 with the discovery of traces of oil and natural gas just over the border in Alberta. Ever since then there have been speculations about oil in the Fraser Valley. Coincidentally, a few days before writing these lines I was driving near Whonnock, the fictional home of the Newcomer, when I noticed, placed by local environmentalists in the fields, notices calling on people to protest against the possibility of oil drilling.

The conflicts that are essential to *The Eternal Forest,* between small farmers and exploiters, between peasants and speculators, between a rural largely subsistence economy and an urban-based one, between individuals and corporations, between Europeans and Asians, are all subsumed in the great central conflict of the book between the forces of the natural world exemplified in the forest and those of material progress, exemplified in the city, where people are destroyed or sometimes, as in the case of the Anglican parson, mysteriously regenerated. In apocalyptic phrases at the end of the book, Godwin poses the great eternal conflict between the constantly changing city and the eternal implacable forest.

The eternal forest would witness in the fullness of time the city's passing, its decadence and death. The forest, invincible and cruel, would claim back its own and stand triumphant in the land, rooted fast in the shattered masonry of a forgotten city.

Today, at the end of the century in whose early years George Godwin wrote *The Eternal Forest*, we are in fact lamenting the disappearance of the forest through clear-cutting. Yet only a few years ago at the height of the Cold War, the destruction of the cities seemed all too possible. Godwin's final pronouncement is in keeping with the neo-nihilistic early twentieth century mood of writers like Jack London, who taught the implacable indifference of the natural world to human aims and needs. Yet what interest us most in *The Eternal Forest* are the portraits of human beings struggling and sometimes by sheer wilfulness succeeding against both the villainies of corrupt men and the ever-returning, ever-encroaching power of the bush.

George Woodcock
June, 1994

Acknowledgements

Godwin Books of Vancouver, Canada, would like to thank the following for their assistance in bringing *The Eternal Forest* back to life.

Dr. Eric Godwin (George Godwin's eldest son) for many photographs of the Godwin family and much useful biographical information concerning his father.

Mr. George Woodcock for his encouragement and helpful suggestions.

Mr. Ted Staunton of Sherwood Graphics, Surrey, B.C. for many constructive ideas on design, layout and language.

Dr. Gloria Burima for her encouragement and many excellent suggestions.

Rev. Stephanie Godwin (George's sister Maud's daughter) of Woodstock, New York, for information on the Godwin family.

Mr. John Cherrington (author of *History of the Fraser Valley*), for his historical suggestions.

Ms. Judy Fraser and Ms. Fern O'Brien for proofreading.

Mrs. Jill Jahansoozi (George brother Dick's grand daughter) of Victoria, B.C. for a photo of Dick Godwin.

Mr. Guy Cribdon, History Division, Vancouver Public Library, for excellent research advice and leads.

Ms. Laurie Robertson, Historical Photographs, Vancouver Public Library.

Thanks also to:

Prof. T. Barrett, Classics, UBC.; Ms. Anne Carol, Vancouver City Archives; Mr. Micky Hambleton, blacksmith, Fort Langley; Mr. Bryan Klassen, Curator, Langley Centennial Museum; Ms. Cindy Lee, Public Affairs, CPR, Vancouver; Dr. Gwyneth Lewis, Classics Dept., Langara College; Ms. Cathleen Nichols, Avian Research Dept., UBC; Mr. Allen Soroka, Librarian, Law Faculty, UBC; Prof. Warren Stephenson, English Dept., UBC; Mr. Colin Stevens, Curator, Burnaby Village Museum.

Foreword

A short biography of George Godwin
(1889-1974)

Recognition and fame, fickle things! George Godwin was an incisive thinker, a poet of nature and a master stylist. *The Eternal Forest* is an impressive novel. Why did such a novel go out of print soon after it was first published in 1929? And who was George Godwin?

Most of what is known of George Godwin's early years comes to us from Godwin family recollections and from Godwin's *Journal,* a personal notebook which he started in Calgary in 1911. From these two sources we learn that James Godwin, George's father, was born in Fareham (Hampshire) in 1845. James moved to London in the economically depressed 1880's and made a fortune as a wholesale meat merchant in Smithfield Market. Cancer took James in 1893 when George was only four.

George's mother, née Elizabeth Free, was born in Swansea in 1849. Her family was of East Anglian and Huguenot origin and tended to produce clergymen and lawyers. It also produced at least one writer: the Reverend Richard William Free, who penned several fiery books on missionary work and church politics in the early twentieth century. Elizabeth Godwin died in 1911.

James and Elizabeth Godwin had eight children. In descending order: Bert, Margaret, Donald, Ted, Maud, Dick, George and Connie. Judging from the *Journal,* George's early years at the family summer home in Reculver (near Margate) were carefree and wild: swimming in the ocean, boarding yachts and spying on their occupants, climbing dangerous cliffs. This anarchic idyll came to a close rather late (age eight!?) and Godwin was sent off to boarding school, first to Glenrock in Sussex (which he liked) then to Saint Lawrence College in Ramsgate, Kent, which he loathed.

Lonely, homesick, and bored with the teaching, George escaped into his own world of books and read voraciously. It was here that he acquired that formidable appetite for knowledge which was to prove so useful in his writing career. He also learned to endure hardship if he must do so in order to remain loyal to his principles. He writes in his *Journal* that he was quite prepared to accept being caned weekly if this was the price he had to pay for continuing to neglect the official programme of studies. This is the same fortitude shown by the Newcomer of *The Eternal Forest*. It is likely that Godwin did not finish his final year at school and the "family council" decided to send him (and his elder sister, Maud) off to Dresden for a few years.

In Germany Godwin studied at a state school. When he returned to England he took a job in a London-based German bank. However, the drudgery of banking was ill-suited to a lad of his intellectual abilities and restlessness and it was probably about this time that Godwin began to consider starting a new life in Canada.Certain details in *The Eternal Forest* suggest that Godwin, like his contemporary, Grey Owl, was profoundly disenchanted with the pettiness and snobbery which were often rife in the genteel England of his social class. Surely things would be better in Canada!

Wanderlust was no stranger to George's siblings: elder brother Dick had settled in Samoa. Elder brother Donald (the editor's grandfather on his mother's side) had settled in Coquitlam, B.C. and this might have induced George to set his sights on Western Canada.[1] Godwin was already studying law by this time but he interrupted these studies to marry and emigrate to Canada.

---

1. There is a street in Burnaby named after Donald Godwin.

In 1911 George married Dorothy Purdon, the daughter of a Belfast physician. Soon the young couple were off to Canada with five hundred pounds sterling to stake them. For some reason they chose to start their new life in Whonnock (the 'Ferguson's Landing' of *The Eternal Forest*), a farming/logging community about 25 miles upstream from New Westminster (see map). There the Godwins bought and cleared land, and had a house built on it, all of which is described in *The Eternal Forest.*

Carving a clearing from dense forest and then trying to cultivate a small, sloping plot proved to be hard, financially unrewarding work. Local historians of Port Haney/Whonnock have observed that almost everyone who tried to make a living by farming in that area at that time failed.* The Godwins soon depleted their 500 pounds sterling, their first child (Eric) arrived, and their 'farm' was failing miserably. Their timing had been unfortunate: they had arrived in 1912, at the end of the big boom years. They also found they could not compete economically with the Chinese, the Japanese or the Americans. In short, they discovered the harsh reality behind the façade of the Canadian Government's bland, misleading slogans ("Last Best West," etc.)

By 1916 the Godwins decided to return to England. The decision must have been a difficult one (for George at least; we suspect that Dorothy couldn't wait to get back to the comforts of England) because this sojourn in the rain forest had yielded some benefits. It had provided an opportunity for Godwin to test his mettle and clarify his values by exploring a society very different from England's. Perhaps he also learned to appreciate the advantages that England had to offer. Doubtless the Newcomer speaks for George when he says to his wife:

"When we came," he plunged on, wrinkling his forehead and floundering for the right words to convey the problem as he

saw it, "when we came, we were little, weren't we? I mean our outlook on life was petty and overlaid by the things that don't really count at all.

"I don't think that in England I ever thought straight, really, though sometimes I tried to. Life was overlaid with so many small things that the great issues were all in shadow. But out here one can see great principles at work. Life sticks out. You know what is real and vital."

Living among rustics at the edge of the bush gave Godwin plenty of time to reflect upon some big questions: Why would a beneficent God permit nature to be blindly cruel? Why did the Canadian and B.C. governments allow unfair competition in the market place? Why did scam-artist oil and property promoters go unpunished? In brief, what was Canada's future and was it worth linking his own family's destiny to it?

*   *   *

Back in England (1916), George signed up with the Canadian Infantry. At first he was rejected because of poor eyesight, but he memorized the eye chart and got accepted. He was gassed in France and sent back to England. As a result of the gassing he contracted tuberculosis (like the Newcomer) and spent at least a year in a sanitarium. In the early 1920s Godwin finished his legal studies and was called to the Bar. However, the practice of law was not to his liking and characteristically he chose a more difficult course: that of freelance journalist. (This is doubtless the "quixotic" streak mentioned by the Newcomer.) Godwin was to write some twenty books covering a broad spectrum of interests: mysticism, faith, healing, politics, economics, history, law, criminology, agriculture, husbandry, literature (see the list of his books on page 318).

In short, George Godwin spent most of the rest of his life in England, raised a family of five children (Eric, Monica, Bill, Tony and Geoff), wrote his twenty books, and finally passed away in 1974 at the ripe age of 85. He rests in the churchyard of Leatherhead in Surrey.

The Eternal Forest was originally published by Appleton (New York City) in 1929 and soon came to be classified as "out of print." Who knows why? Therein must lie an interesting mystery. In preparing this new printing Godwin Books has taken the utmost care to respect the integrity of the original edition. We have limited our editing to improving the punctuation, revising a few unreadable passages that were, strangely, never edited in the first place, and toning down a few of the offensive and derogatory names which some of the characters in *The Eternal Forest* use when referring to people of 'ethnic' origin. However, nothing essential in the 1929 version has been changed.

In addition, we have added several things of interest: an introduction by Mr. George Woodcock, a biographical outline, a map, a Table of Contents (of our own devising), photographs, notes and excerpts from the *Journal*. We felt that the historical photographs would conjure up the look and feel of the pre-World War I era and that the juxtaposed modern (1994) snapshots would help the reader to visualize the places and people mentioned in the book and appreciate the spectacular changes which Vancouver and Port Haney/Whonnock have undergone.

Coming fresh from afar, George Godwin (like De Toqueville before him) saw things with the clear, objective vision of the outsider and it is this vision that makes the book so interesting, at times so uncannily reminiscent of our own times. For such reasons we are pleased to bring back to life a book which will add something unique and vital to Canada's literary and historical legacy.

Robert S. Thomson, Editor
Godwin Books
Vancouver, British Columbia
August, 1994

Elizabeth Godwin (1849-1911), George Godwin's mother. Photo dates from 1909. *"And my mother, being Welsh, with Huguenot blood in her veins, would be as affected by the pathos (of these tales we read together) as much as myself. Often we would cry together."* (See Godwin's *Journal*, 3, 4).

James Godwin (1845-1893), George Godwin's father. Born in Fareham (Hampshire). *"I thought my father a hard man then (when I was three) but now, in the light of experience, I can think more kindly of him. What could a little child know of the jaded nerves and irritability of an overwrought man suffering from cancer?"* (See *Journal*, 1).

George Stanley Godwin (1889-1974). At first rejected by the army because of poor eyesight, Godwin memorized the chart and passed the test. He fought in France with the Canadian infantry. Wounded in a gas attack, he spent the rest of the war in Dorset teaching tank warfare.

Dorothy Purdon (1885-1979), George Godwin's wife. Born in Belfast of Huguenot ancestry, she was the daughter of a physician. *"A heroic woman without heroics. Prosaic, unimaginative, matter of-fact. But hardened by a vein of unsuspected steel. Something fine."* (*The Eternal Forest*, p. 158).

Dick Godwin (1887-1972), George's elder brother. Dick went off to Samoa and ran a copra plantation. *"Wilful wild Dick! (. . .) Instinctively he turned towards the open places of the world; streets and offices are not for such as he. Men like him belonged to the times of Elizabethan England."* (Journal, 2, 6-10.)

"The 'Newcomer's" house in Whonnock. 1914. That's Godwin's eldest son, Eric, romping around the yard. *"By comparison with Johansson's shack the new house in the slashing was a fine mansion."* (*The Eternal Forest,* p. 79).

George Godwin with son Eric (on the reader's left) and Geoff (on the reader's right). Eric is now (1994) a retired medical doctor; Geoff was tragically drowned during his second attempt (the first had been successful) to cross the Atlantic in a small sail boat. The photo was taken in 1960.

George and Dorothy Godwin in England in the late 1960s.

George Godwin in England. 1960s.

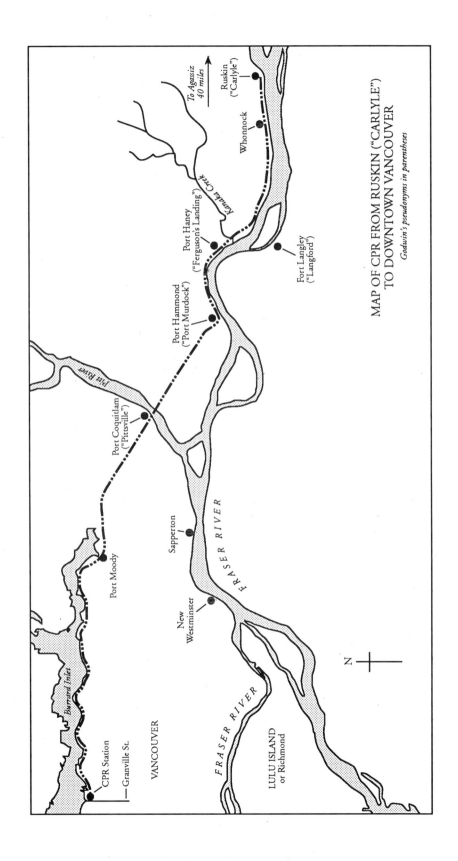

MAP OF CPR FROM RUSKIN ("CARLYLE")
TO DOWNTOWN VANCOUVER
Godwin's pseudonyms in parentheses

Ruskin
("Carlyle")

Whonnock

*To Agassiz
40 miles*

Port Haney
("Ferguson's Landing")

Kanaka Creek

Fort Langley
("Langford")

Port Hammond
("Port Murdock")

Pitt River

Port Coquitlam
("Pittsville")

Port Moody

Sapperton

New
Westminster

FRASER RIVER

FRASER RIVER

FRASER RIVER

Burrard Inlet

CPR Station

Granville St.

VANCOUVER

LULU ISLAND
or Richmond

N

Prologue

1.

In the summer of 1849 a Scots mariner, master and owner of the schooner *Maria Ellsworthy*, port of register Aberdeen, passed in fair weather up the Californian coast from Santa Barbara, sailed into that neck of land south of Vancouver Island known as the Gulf of Juan de Fuca, and came to anchor off a small wooden village that huddled at the water's edge, a solitary break in the wall of timber that stretched, north and south, along the coast.

In Santa Barbara he had been told how there was virgin land for a man's taking, a land of mineral wealth, gold, silver, copper; great waterways alive with salmon, vast forests; and a climate soft as that of southern England and more sunny.

A fellow-countryman, met casually on the waterfront of the old Spanish port, had talked of the gold that was being brought to the assay office of San Francisco from the new diggings as proof of his assertions. Captain Ferguson had listened at first without interest, but a new eagerness had grown upon him as the idea of turning settler took hold of his slow but deliberate mind. Gold did not tempt him, but he longed for the land.

He had several good reasons for abandoning the sea. He considered them as he surveyed the wooded mainland from his deck: he was newly married to a young wife who had made this voyage with him; she was pining for dry land for a particular affair of her own which called for the services of a doctor or midwife, and, last, there was her opinion that a married seaman should cast about for some way of life free from the hazards of deep water. Thus it was that the notion of deserting the sea for the security of a landsman's life had taken root in the seaman's mind and carried him forward to action.

2.

Gazing from the deck of his ship across the blue waters of the Gulf of Georgia, towards the mainland, Captain Ferguson wove his dreams about that silent vastness of standing timber. He saw himself master of the thriving homestead which he would carve out of the bush; he saw himself as the father of a brood, a patriarch, the founder of a family. Best of all, he saw himself with seven hours of secure sleep every night of the year, emancipated from the menace of the sea.

He put off in the ship's boat for the village, bought axes, peevees, saws, picks and other tackle he deemed necessary for his enterprise. He heard talk of gold and little else. His young wife, languid nowadays by reason of her condition, but joyous at the prospect of permanent dry land, watched from her deck-chair on board ship.

Next day the *Maria Ellsworthy* sailed up the Fraser River. Captain Ferguson gazed on the new land from his deck, and he saw nothing but dense Douglas fir, cedar, alder, birch, and maple, rising higher than he had believed any trees could grow, from a tangle of impenetrable undergrowth.

The river lay, wider than any river he had navigated, like a silver path through the silent land. And as the *Maria Ellsworthy*, at the apex of two quivering lines of quick-silver, glided upstream, the timber wheeled like a lock gate, and closed the pathway to the sea. It was as though the ship was sealed to the forest.

As a man will at such a time, Captain Ferguson promised his wife that he would drop anchor wherever her fancy should dictate. But the ship had navigated thirty-seven miles upstream before the little woman on the deck, eyes fixed upon the timbered bank, halloed that she had made her choice.

The *Maria Ellsworthy* dropped anchor in the shadow of the bush, and Captain Ferguson made his first landing where the Fraser flows through a great valley.

There it was he made his first clearing beside the river, and, among the giant stumps of the firs which he felled, he built a log house. Trim and neat it was, with two rooms. Behind it he built a big wood-shed, using soft and satiny cedar. A barn followed when he got his first cow, and so the first homestead of what was to become Ferguson's Landing was won from the bush.

But there are no Fergusons in Ferguson's Landing today. They have surrendered that heritage to others.

3.

The growth of the settlement had been slow, as all growth is slow where man labours with primitive tools against primeval nature. The pioneer had no means of ridding himself of the stumps, for he had no blasting powder. He waited, with a patience born of wisdom, for time to rot them; hand-grubbed the ground between, sowed red clover. In his second year he turned half an acre of clover in, and in his third went downriver to the village of Vancouver, bought an ox, and returned triumphant.

That was an event in the history of the old pioneer's life. He got his plough in: it replaced pick and shovel. His woman, again heavy with child, watched him set his coulter against the hidden roots, standing by a moment idle from her work – that work which had no definite beginning, and certainly no discernible end.

Soon he had fruit-trees, apples and cherries; potatoes, cabbages, beans, and a little patch of experimental wheat in his clearing. He was eating away the edge of the silent bush, the bush that watched his pigmy efforts and finally destroyed him with one blow. He marked with patient care the young fruit-tree's growth; it was rapid. The Fergusons throve for by instinct or by chance, Bella had chosen well.

The settlement was fecund, its humid soil enriched by centuries of vegetable decay. Other people came upriver, came alongside, asked questions of the Scot, decided to locate thereabouts "for company's sake" – company being a boon and a blessing in a new land.

At the end of twenty years there were ten families gnawing the edge of the bush; the ring of axes sounded across the silent river; the stillness of the forest was broken by the thunder of falling timber. Small geometric gaps appeared at the fringe of the bush, shrill greens of little fields stood out from the setting of sombre evergreens, giant conifers. Log cabins, set in tiny gardens, sent into the still air spirals of blue smoke; the sound of children's laughter and of children's crying broke the stillness of the bush.

Since then, through the years, the timber, silent, inscrutable, mysterious, has accepted its fate, receding like a tide from the river-bank, leaving in its wake patches of green or rich brown loam, cabins, barns, wood-sheds, smoke-houses forever emitting columns of white smoke.

And presently a narrow ribbon of road, conforming to the curve of the river, linked the settlement with Sapperton, the new village near the mouth of the river.* It was a rough trail, but one good enough to take an ox-team those twenty-odd miles once a year or so.

There was no money in Ferguson's Landing in those days: they bartered things. Being face to face with the task of conquering the bush, they recognized more clearly than the men of cities do, a community of interests. There was no competition among them, but a commonwealth of goods and knowledge. Simple men they were, thinking cleanly as they sent their keen axes into the heart of the yellow fir. They had no rivalries.

By the time old Ferguson had three cows and seven heifers, a sow, a boar, and a litter of pigs, he was a made man.

His well never failed him.

The bush, which had resisted him at first, bore him no grudge but yielded him a sustenance. He was content, a full man. He had turned seventy when he met his death.

The river, tidal at the settlement, was gorged with mighty salmon in those days. Only the Red men had ever fished those waters – indolent men who fished only for their immediate needs. They came and went, silent and furtive. Sometimes they slunk up to the settlement and eyed the white-skinned intruders. Enigmatic and curious men, they would offer pelts for whatever they coveted. They gazed at Old Man Ferguson's clearing with the rich contempt of nomadic men for all husbandry.

And Old Man Ferguson, grizzled now, fell into the way of it all wonderfully. He never once regretted his ship, the *Maria Ellsworthy,* which was as well, since she went down with all hands off the Alaska coast, as her lifeboat, smashed and washed ashore at Nome, testified. He never once felt the call of the sea but rather chuckled to have escaped its hardships and its perils. He preferred the bush as taskmaster for its harvest was more sure. In short, Old Man Ferguson had mastered his environment, harnessed it to his needs. He found life good and each evening saw him scheming the work of the next day.

In August he fished the wide river with the gill-net, the making of which had occupied his long winter evenings. With sixty fathom of net he cast across the river and brought back a harvest of silver sockeye salmon. They made winter food, salted and smoked with green alder-wood. Every

August, in this way, he laid up his store of fish, for in that month the salmon returned from their four-year sojourn in the open sea, fighting their way upstream to their spawning-places in the lakes and tributaries in the snow-capped Cascade Mountains. Old Man Ferguson had cleared some forty acres and passed the allotted span when a falling alder snapped his broad back like a twig.

When he died, Old Ferguson left five sons to inherit his holding. They had taken root. Only one had left the settlement to which their father had given his name. The rest of them married and started farms, slashing timber further back in the bush, pushing along the river's bank, building log houses.*

Thus the settlement grew. The Sappers came, driving a road through the bush a mile or so inland. And then the surveyors, with their chain-gang marking the line, so they said (though it sounded beyond belief), for the rail which was to be driven through the heart of the mountains down to the coast and Vancouver village.

Thus the shadow of civilization fell across the Valley. First the Sappers with their road, then the construction gangs with their railway.* As for the settlement, it was fast becoming peopled. But of Old Ferguson and of his sons nothing remained but the work of their hands.

CHAPTER I

1.

Twice a day the silence of the Valley was shattered by the Montreal-Vancouver transcontinental express. It shook the permanent way and filled the still air with the strident voice of its clanging bell. Sometimes – perhaps once a year – it checked its rush, slowed down, came to a stop at the little wayside Canadian Pacific depot beside the broad river.

These were great occasions for the settlement, for it meant the arrival of a new settler, and a newcomer was a big event for Ferguson's Landing.

To Tom Preedy, the station agent, whose days were divided between the depot and the cultivation of thirty acres of logged-off timberland which resisted every effort of his short arms and legs, the roaring passage of the transcontinental was a daily trial. For it came from that great world beyond the serried mountains, those giants which pushed their peaks against the eastern horizon, thrusting their eternal snows against the blue of the sky. And all that Tom Preedy loved and longed for lay beyond those relentless ramparts – London and all his particular London meant to him: warm pubs, cronies, the snug parlour behind the shop, evening papers, noise, familiar smells, movements, events, streets and faces.

Coming out of the cool of his little office, littered with way-bills, chicken crates, and meal sacks, he now stood gazing down the railway track. The bell above the door of his office had clanged the approach of the Montreal-Vancouver express, and today she was to stop.

Tom Preedy looked upon the Valley with a jaundiced eye. It lay before him with its shining river and undulating ranks of timber, somnolent and very still in the hot summer air.

On the river a blunt-nosed tug, like a waterlogged beetle, was pitting its fierce energy against the shapeless and inert mass of a resisting boom of cedar shingle-bolts. It was the only sign of life visible. It moved slowly downstream towards Sapperton, a black spot at the apex of two rippling silver lines.

The scorching metals, that reflected dazzlingly the vivid light of the sun, swept in a long curve about the river-bank, disappearing into the heart of the timber. Tom Preedy saw the first signs of the coming monster as a white plume of smoke that wavered like a flameless torch above the green of the towering firs. Presently as he stood shading his eyes, the heated metals emitted a low murmur that increased to a hum with a hint of menace. The still and lifeless air awoke and pulsed with an increasing insistence: it was like the beat of distant war drums, a beat that always carried fear into the heart of the little man who watched and waited for the coming of the express.

Then, swaying and advancing with outthrust cow-catcher like the lowered snout of a charging beast, the transcontinental thundered down the railway track and clanked, squirting water and steam, into the settlement station.

2.

Tom Preedy hated this express with a senseless hatred. Every time he watched its approach fear crawled at the back of his brain and he felt a sinking sensation at the pit of his paunch. Voices seemed to urge him to do mad things. He knew what these follies were but — he held them back from his mind, thrusting them away as they forced themselves upon his consciousness.

Experience, which had taught him little beyond the first principles of self-preservation (for his mind, capable of infinite futile regrets, was barren of invention), had taught him the wisdom of standing back when the express thundered towards him.

This train, this harnessed fury which conquered the eternal snows of the Rocky Mountains and devoured the miles of the illimitable prairie beyond, held for him a fearful fascination. Twice he had felt an imperative urge to jump with a shout of defiance towards that swaying cow-catcher. And once, when the Vancouver-Montreal express came through at night, with her single searchlight boring a hole in the darkness of the Valley, he had run down the track to meet her, waving his arms and shouting mad words at the molten comet that promised him escape from something intangible, elusive and intolerable.

And that night, lying restless beside his immobile wife, he had screamed in his sleep and awakened the worn-out little woman. Now he always stood back and stretched out one hand to touch the sanity of solid timber, the scorching woodwork of the depot.

But today she was stopping, and curiosity conquered fear.

Two passengers climbed down from the tourist coach, a white-coated negro porter swung down after them with leather portmanteaux, set them down, and stood by, expectancy written on his bland face.

"So this is Ferguson's Landing?"

It was the man who spoke. Tom Preedy looked the newcomers over. He saw a tall man in his early twenties, dressed in a tweed suit, a man with a remote manner, and a woman of about the same age, fair, pretty and slender.* Pulling the clattering baggage truck behind him, Preedy made for the rear baggage van.

"You'd better come and see all your junk is put off," he said in a tone that implied that the newcomers had served him a bad turn.

He thought: "English as they make 'em and green as grass. Do 'em good if they come and live in this God-forsaken hole – the fools!"

"And nobody to meet us," said the girl, looking around blankly.

3.

To these newcomers, whose eyes were wearied by many marvels, the Valley had streamed across their field of vision from the vantage-point of the transcontinental's observation car as a monotony of green. If there was life and activity in this vast land of standing timber it was hidden from view, a secret life remote from the cities of the Canadian Dominion.

On the southern side the wide and tranquil river moved sluggishly towards an unknown destiny from its headwaters high in the Cascades.* On the north the ramparts of green rose like a giant wave, forever suspended above the river's bank, thrusting their spiked crests against the blue skyline.

Even in the fierce light of a summer noon those vast Douglas firs seemed to hold entangled in their great trunks and outspread branches the shadows of eternal night. It was only at the foot of the steep slope that small patches of sheer green showed where man had eaten into that primeval solitude. It was all that could be seen of the settlement somnolent in the sun.

4.

An anti-climax, this arrival, after those days in a world of gold, a world that rolled out under a cobalt sky – the fecund prairie ripe for harvesting. An anti-climax after that climb up to the clouds from the Albertan foothills where, from the

LOOKING NORTH FROM LANGLEY

View of MacMillan Island, looking north from Fort Langley. Whonnock and Port Haney are just on the other side of this island. Photo c. 1910.

Giant cedar of the B.C. rainforest.

roof of the world, they saw with awe the pale mists stream like banners from the glittering peaks.

Beyond Banff they had gazed through the plate-glass windows of the dining-car over a world that reached, as far as the eye could see, into the violet haze of a far horizon. Range upon range, the mountains swept across the landscape. Like colossal monsters, crouched upon their bellies, they seemed, wallowing in the blue waters of the lakes, their blunt snouts burrowing down into the valleys, while upon their great flanks the timber bristled like some hairy growth.

It had been wonderful and awe-inspiring to creep precariously over vast and dizzy trestle bridges, sheer above the tumult of swollen mountain torrents. It had been unforgettable to creep, clinging like some monstrous beetle, along the stark face of precipitous mountain sides; to descend steep grades and roar, with clanging bell, into the dark mouths of rock-hewn tunnels bored into the mountain's heart.

After all this spectacular beauty the green, timbered settlement revealed itself with a vague sense of disappointment.

The Valley slept, green and still, in the shadow of the bush.

5.

Like most old-timers Bob England turned his hand to anything. He had spent thirty years in the Dominion, and twenty of them at Ferguson's Landing. He was one of the oldest of the old-timers, a short, thick-set man with a slow manner, a philosophical air of indifference to lack of money, bad crops, logging contracts which showed a deficit after a hard winter's work, and horses that went unaccountably lame.

He was a philosopher in his way, for he had the creed of

the Easy Way deeply ingrained in an indolent, kindly nature. And like most such men, he worked twice as hard for half as much as rewards more industrious spirits.

He was an expert in many things. He knew timber and could size up a stand of red cedar or Douglas fir and tell with uncanny precision what it would fetch as shingle-bolts or logs at the wharf at Sapperton.

He doctored horses and had a great reputation based on the preliminary certificate of the Royal College of Veterinary Surgeons which he had taken some thirty-five years earlier. He could doctor cows too, and had a pet theory about red-water fever. He claimed that it was caused by allowing the cattle to graze where there was bracken.

He was also a keen politician, *persona grata* with the mandarins at Victoria, and always reliable for a forecast of how the voting would go among the settlers of the Fraser Valley.

Last, he handled, whenever opportunity occurred, such real estate as changed hands at Ferguson's Landing. He had worked hard on his ranch and scratched from its heavy soil a bare subsistence; he had put in casual days with newcomers and reaped a decent harvest of easy dollars selling them land.

Nobody ever knew Bob England to be punctual, uncharitable, thorough, or in a hurry.

6.

Bob England arrived at the depot as the tail-end of the transcontinental disappeared in a whirlwind of dust and ashes through the rock-cut three miles below the settlement. He was dressed in high boots caked in mud which had accumulated through three winters and was now coated with the dust of a dry summer. His faded blue pants were patched

Looking north to Golden Ears Mountain from Maple Ridge (near Whonnock).

at the seat and his dingy yellow canvas shirt lacked the lower portions of its sleeves. He was smoking a corn-cob pipe and his hands were thrust deep into his pockets.

He sauntered up to the newcomers, removed his pipe, raised his hat.

"She was pretty punctual this morning," he observed casually. "You got my letter, I take it? My rig's outside, you must come up to the house first and feed and so on. Then I will take you round and show you a few places. Feel the heat? No? You will later. Valley heat is different from prairie heat, affects you differently. On the prairie the people boast of how much work they can get through in a day; here we brag about how little we can skin through with."

The casual friendliness of this little man obliterated the first impression which had been made by the deserted air of the wayside station and the querulous unfriendliness of the station agent. The newcomers climbed into the rickety buggy.

Bob England picked up his reins.

"Your first trip out from the Old Country?" he asked, adding, "It's fifteen years since I had a trip and then it cost me a packet."

He turned to the young woman at his side, with a slight twitch of humour about his heavily moustached mouth:

"I mortgaged my place to have that trip and it's still mortgaged – and it'll always be mortgaged!"

The buggy, moving at a casual pace, rattled down the dusty lane, passed through a broken gate and started the ascent of a precipitous by-path. In ten minutes it had disappeared among the standing timber.

Tom Preedy, mopping his forehead, locked up his office, and set off towards his ranch. The pulsing tug had pulsed itself round the bend of the river. The Valley slept once more.

CHAPTER II

1.

By a custom whose origin was as obscure as the origin of most customs, the ranches of Ferguson's Landing bore forever the names of the men who had wrested them from the bush. Thus, the Ferguson Place, now owned by the Ellisons (an Old Country family who had fled from the task of conquering Lincolnshire clay to grapple with the problem of becoming a bush rancher), still remained the Ferguson Place. Nobody ever thought of calling it anything else.

When he first came to the settlement, Bob England had

bought standing timber, logged it off, and finally cleared it of stumps. It was the England Place, and will be yet a century hence.

Bob England was a man who knew the country well enough not to take it too seriously. Women were scarce in those days and he had married, soon after settling, the daughter of old Ole Olson, who had settled, after many years of penury on the fjords of his native land, at the edge of the Sappers' road that was surveyed in the lifetime of Old Man Ferguson.

"When we were married," he explained to the newcomers as they sat in the kitchen which had been his original home, but now was but the log annex of a dressed-lumber building boasting three chimneys, "Hulda could not speak a word of English."

"And you couldn't speak a word of Norwegian," drawled his wife from the stove where she was dishing up the meal.

She was a big-hipped woman with placid features and deliberate movements.

"True enough. But we managed somehow, didn't we?" he reminded her.

"But I've learnt Engleesh," she smiled. "You could never learn Norwegian, not if you lived on the fjords for twenty years."

The newcomers, shy and strange to these new surroundings, listened to their host and hostess with the accommodating smiles of the polite.

It was a novelty, after the de luxe service of the express dining-car, to be eating a meal in a kitchen, and doubly a novelty to eat in a kitchen built of logs, and to be told quite casually that this was the first home of this strangely assorted couple.

The afternoon was spent in the search of "a location," and it was soon obvious that every available ranch in the settlement, save those by the water's edge, was situated upon the steep slope of a long timber bank.

The settlement revealed itself shyly in a succession of surprises. Solid timber, apparently without end, would suddenly open to reveal a clearing of vivid green, a trim house of logs or dressed lumber, and the strange anachronism (as it seemed to the newcomers) of wire fencing.

At that time, there were no less than thirty cultivated ranches at Ferguson's Landing.

"There's not a place in the settlement that you can't buy, if you want it," Bob England explained, as he led the way. "In this country anybody will sell anything for a profit. It may be something to do with the climate, or it may be something to do with the place. You can have my place if you like."

The newcomers listened, puzzled.

"What are you thinking of growing?" he asked them.

"Well, I hardly know. But I think I'll know what I want when I see it."

"Of course, since the boom, prices are a bit high," England continued. "Take Stein's Place, this place we are coming to." He indicated a trim, finished little ranch, some twenty acres in extent, with a stark shack in its centre. "Old Stein would have taken two thousand dollars a year ago, and glad to get it. Today I doubt whether he would sell for five."

"What made the boom?" asked the Newcomer. "I mean, why did prices suddenly soar? Surely there must be some relation between what the place will yield and the price it brings?"

"In England, yes, but here no. You see, in the West a periodic madness gets the people. Optimism they call it. Personally, I call it sheer cussed crookedness. It comes suddenly and for no apparent reason. Everybody boosts for the West, the Great Last West.* It's going to be a great country. They prove it with figures from the Dominion statisticians' department.* On paper they can show you just why you can't help getting rich. And people fall for it and buy, and pay anything to get land – any sort of land."

"That's understandable in a growing place like Vancouver, which I'm told was only a village forty years ago, but this is different; these are only what we'd call small holdings at home."

"No good comparing conditions in the Old Country with these," England explained. "For one thing, in B.C., you must remember, every acre, every rood, had to be hacked out from the standing timber. It makes a big difference. You can buy uncleared land for fifty dollars an acre, but it will cost you two hundred to clear it. That's why you have to pay high for a little layout like old Stein's."

"And the returns? I suppose, the amount of land under cultivation being so small, the profits are high?"

"Then you imagine entirely wrong, my dear fellow. Vancouver and Sapperton buy their fruit and vegetables from Washington State. They get it cheaper that way. If you settle in the Landing don't run away with the idea there's money in it. There isn't."

Nevertheless, Ferguson's Landing was beginning to cast its spell on the newcomers. They had decided to locate.

2.

Curiosity is the vice of all small communities and Ferguson's Landing, far from being an exception, was an exemplification of this universal truth. Allegiance to the cardinal virtues was whole-hearted, but when it came to the less picturesque of human failings, it made allowances, granting itself a little licence.

Gossip was its vice, universally condoned and practiced by every member of the community, from the Reverend Mr.

Top: Port Haney ("Ferguson's Landing"), 1908. Note the CPR in the centre and "Blanchard's" store just behind it. The store was actually called "Charlton's" but Godwin changed many names in his novel. The camera is pointing west, down river.

Below: the same scene today. Port Haney is just a memory and the town centre is now in Haney, just up the hill. Within a few hundred metres of this site you can visit Mann's brickyard, the Maple Ridge Museum and the Billy Miner Pub, named after the trainrobber in the movie *The Grey Fox.*

Corley, the Mission Church parson, to Old Jim, the Indian Chief, whose only strong views concerned his inalienable right to wear seatless pants when he came down to the store from the Indian Reservation to relate strange things, things seen and things heard, in the hopes of hearing even stranger things.

In Old Jim's case it has to be recorded that he came at the beck of rather more complex desires than those which drew the ranchmen: to wheedle from easy Blanchard, the storekeeper, just one more bottle of the vanilla essence which induced the sublime intoxication his blood craved; to post yet one more illegible missive to the Indian Agent detailing his many wrongs, or to see what unconsidered trifles might be discreetly purloined without detection.

Blanchard's store was the clearing-house for the gossip of the settlement.

3.

.

It was nine o'clock and the low mist that lay over the river in the early morning had been torn by a whiff of wind and finally banished by the sun. The river sparkled with dancing light points, lapping about the piles of the wharf as it swirled seawards.

Nine o'clock: the hour when Blanchard retired from his counter that was dark with the blood of many carcasses, and just now decorated with a large cheese upon which an army of flies billeted, a side of bacon from which stuck a long knife to which adhered soft soap, a bucket of guano-stained eggs and a pile of lard tins. Blanchard himself was in the boarded-off closet known as the Post Office.

He took his time in all things, did Blanchard. He took it in serving his customers, in measuring flannelette for petticoats, in weighing three-inch spikes, in untying the bunches of hickory axe-hafts which hung festooned from the store ceiling.

He took his time, too, in settling his accounts with the Sapperton wholesalers who supplied him with his miscellaneous wares. But it was said of him that he was equally slow to request payment from his customers. He granted to all the same thriftless latitude he demanded of others. Not that he was a good-natured man.

4.

The distribution of the settlement mail was in character. As postmaster (a political job secured by arrangement with Bob England who did the necessary whispering in such affairs and whose account, incidentally, happened to be two years unpaid) – only Blanchard could unlock those bags cast off from the hurtling transcontinental as she roared through the Valley. Not even Hanks, his lymphatic assistant, was permitted to deputize. It was a ritual, and one whereby he proclaimed, day by day, the secure tenure of his salaried office.

Therefore those alluring bags lay, grey, bulging, and inviting, in that preposterous post-office, until Blanchard, limping, sweating and smiling, casting his "Good-mornings" right and left, pushed his way through the impatient group of men that crowded the store, and dived into his closet-like holy of holies.

Every day in the year he was late, and every day in the year he murmured his polite apologies.

"So sorry, gentlemen, if I have kept you waiting – humph – calving cow, Mr. Dunn, calved at five, lovely heifer. Letter for you, Mr. Heggerty; looks like a bill from these Sapperton fruit jobbers.

"One for you, Mr. Fuller, no – two – and *The Times!* Like to see that when you've finished. Thank you very much.

"Nothing for you, Mr. Preedy. Yes, I'm quite sure; been through the bag carefully. Come and look for yourself, if you like . . .

"Hear the Johanssons have got gapes in their new Leghorn flock.* Mr. Dunn . . . Yes, he passed by this morning. His wife is sick again; he was walking to Carlyle for the doctor.

"No, can't make out what it is; looks to me like cancer – shouldn't be surprised.

"Another one for you, Mr. Heggerty, and the *News of the World!*"

So it went. Half the settlement came to the store on Old Country mail days, and on those two particular days of each week Blanchard was usually later than usual.

Yes, "Blanchard, blast the fellow," and, "Blanchard, damn his soul," was late. Late, but always smiling that disarming smile of his which seemed to say: "After all, gentlemen, I am lame. You know that."

You could not get over that smile and its implication of pathos. No, you could not. It melted even the hardest thing in those drummers who clanked in rattling Ford up the dusty road to "raise particular Cain with the goddamn English storekeeper about his goldarn account."*

"Yes, I'm afraid I am a little late, Mr. Sinclair. People here are dilatory; it's difficult, I do my best with them, but they keep me waiting . . . money all right, you know that. Cigar or cigarette? Looks like being a good year on the river. If the salmon come up strong no trouble about accounts . . . Top boat on the river last year . . . Yes, Kurt Olson fished three days and three nights . . . saw him come ashore . . . thought he was drunk . . . only drunk with sleep . . . heh-heh!"

Yes, Blanchard had a way with him.

CHAPTER III

1.

The enchantment of summer passed. Autumn murmured through the Valley. It laid chill, invisible hands upon the bush. The forest trembled. A voice, old as time and sad as death, sounded from its heart. The flaming maples stirred like giant torches, dripping gold and crimson fire, their dying leaves like great pools of blood, lay upon the ground.

The glassy surface of the river had mirrored the procession of the great galleons of the summer sky; now it shuddered into life. Shadows raced across its ruffling surface; it lived again, and, sensing its destiny, surged seawards, swollen with pride and gorged by many a head water tributary.

All set for winter, the settlement watched the new clearing on the face of the hill, the clearing of the newcomers. There was leisure now. It was a big year on the river, that year when the salmon, obedient to the mystery of the four-year cycle, came from the depths of the open waters and moved, silent and purposeful, against the tide of the river, swimming for their spawning-grounds, and paid tribute to the men of Ferguson's Landing.

The fishing boats had been filled, emptied, and filled again. At Sapperton the canneries were working overtime. And the Landing had money to spare. Even Blanchard's accounts were paid. A case of Scotch whiskey had come upriver. Old Stein saw it on the wharf – an unheard-of luxury. He spread the news. Spreading news was his passion.

Yet the passions common to most men did not touch him. This tall, lean man with the Vandyke beard, the long, lean face, sallow complexion, narrow brow and close-set eyes that gave the whole face a mean effect, lived monkishly.

A personality, certainly. The broad-brimmed felt hat,

the caped cloak hanging loosely from the tall figure, the venerable umbrella, the boots miraculously innocent of mud or dust, the whole get-up of the man revealed, yet masked, his strange enigmatic personality.

Rumour had given him countless brides, but Stein lived on, a solitary, in his little timber house set in the centre of his ten-acre clearing. The house gave the exact impression of its owner, of order divorced from comeliness, self-sufficiency without adequate justification. Its windows looked down over the timber to the river far below. In the far distance the serried peaks of the Cascade Mountains marched along the horizon.*

The little timber house watched this scene with unblinking eyes, and old Stein watched the hidden lives of his neighbours. Nothing escaped him. Stein, of course, knew all there was to know of the newcomers. He was sharing his observations with Old Man Dunn, outside the store, having just collected his home mail.

2.

"In the first place he has built his house too far back," he explained. "But you can't tell him anything. I walked across to offer the fellow advice. He was not rude, but I shall not go again. Let him learn. Oh, yes, they've money, I should say. I had a peep at their living-room. They have good furniture, very good. Oil paintings, and the settee which came up the river by boat, it is very good."

Fuller, who spoke seldom, joined them: "Did I tell you what he answered when I asked him if he had a good mattock? He said: 'What's a mattock?' I said: 'You don't know much if you don't know that,' and all he answered was: 'Perhaps not, but you will tell me?'" And Fuller grinned. A little leathery man with a head too big.

The voice of Blanchard, insinuating, mocking, with half-a-dozen shades and not one of them honest, came from the doorway where he stood in his dung-soiled ranch clothes. "I asked him if he would be wanting a good peevee, and he just looked at me – didn't know what I meant," he chuckled.

Old Man Dunn, burly, bearded, rubicund, listened. His small, shrewd eyes bored through these fellows. And they knew it and hated him. And he knew they hated him and repaid their rancour with a contempt which they found harder to bear than open hostility. They called him "The Sage" behind his back. Blanchard had invented the nickname and it stuck. In a way it was a compliment.

Old Man Dunn had started in the Yorkshire mines at nine. At fifteen he had mastered sufficient Latin to read Virgil. A good brain in a big body, had Old Man Dunn. But he was a failure – tinkering with chickens at his age.

Bob England, followed by a spaniel, late for his mail as usual, came up. He stood, sucking his pipe and inwardly cursing its perversity – which was, in fact, his own, for he never cleaned it.

He too could tell a story or two of the newcomers. "I went up from my place one evening to see how they were getting on," he said, his eyes twinkling. "I knocked at the door and butted right into a bit of England. He was sitting at one end of a big lounge drawn up to the fireplace he made Anderson build in, and his wife – pretty woman, if you want my opinion, and not cut out for this life – was at the other end. And both of 'em in evening dress! Fact! Fellow had on a dinner jacket, and she was in some filmy stuff."

Bob England indicated his stained pants with the stem of his corn-cob pipe: "And I was in these duds," he added. "Don't know which of us felt the bigger idiot. Dinner jackets in the bush, my God!"

"And reads Shelley," put in Stein. "Yes, I found a book lying beside a log when I walked over the clearing. Shelley!"

Old Man Dunn listened, puffed out his crimson cheeks, scratched his grey beard with a blackened nail, and rumbled: "I remember once, riding over the Badlands of Nebraska. My horse shied at something on the ground. I dismounted and picked up a copy of a yellow-backed book. And what d'you think it was?"

He turned from face to face, waited impressively and went on, "It was a copy of Henry George's book on the single tax idea. I sat right down and read it from cover to cover."*

But the anecdote was lost upon his audience. None of them had heard of Henry George; incidentally, none of them had read a line of Shelley.

3.

The clearing grew.

Old Anderson tramped up the muddy trail every morning with his rush tool-bag slung over his shoulder, one calloused hand swinging the lard bucket which contained the prodigious sandwiches of his midday meal. He moved slowly, planting his great feet firmly, his face wooden as the planks with which he had worked a lifetime.

"Old Anderson will build your house," Bob England had said. "Kurt Olson would have done it quicker, but he's up at Nome. Old Anderson's slower than the second coming, but he's thorough. Just leave him alone. Thirty cents an hour, and he'll reckon up the odd minutes."

"This is the plan," the Newcomer said.

Anderson looked at it casually.

"You want two bedrooms and a living-room, a kitchen, and, I tink, an attic for young chicken and junk," he announced with finality, ignoring the paper beneath his horn-like thumb.

Anderson saw a house in his head and stood it upon the earth. That was his way: a good way. He had built half the settlement. He lumbered about the clearing. "Here I will build it," he announced.

From its northern boundary, the land sloped sharply down towards the river. Below, the pattern of the finished England place lay like a piece of torn Persian carpet in little geometric sections of green, brown and russet.

They had not wanted the house there at all. They had wanted a garden, a small garden which would glow all the more radiantly because it would oppose its ordered comeliness to the clutter of the clearing, with its great uprooted stumps, its tangle of vine-maples, its felled alders.

And Anderson was pegging out the site so that the kitchen door would be right against that mighty fir stump so big that twelve men might have eaten around it! They argued it with him, pointing out that the house would be right upon their northern boundary, as surveyed.

Old Anderson listened, and when they had done, silenced their protest with a word. "There ain't no odder level site on de place," he told them, then with a hint of fatherliness: "Why did you buy dis place anyhow – a bit of hillside?"

How could they tell Anderson how they had tramped the settlement for the ideal location, and found it here? How could they explain just what this enchanted place meant to them, looking down over the Valley and the silver river to the far white mountains? Together, undisturbed, encircled by the bush, alone.

Therefore they had no part in the building of their house. Anderson built it and the Newcomer carried and fetched as he was bid. Presently he was nailing on the soft cedar shingles. A proud moment, making one's own home! And they hugged to their hearts the illusion that this half-articulated thing of yellow timber would take shape as the house of their dreams. Some sort of miracle was to happen, it seemed. This thing which rose under the hammer of the slow old man would change and become their house, would stand complete and perfect as they had devised it.

A miracle, indeed!

When the yellow boards became walls and the roof was in place, clothed in its red cedar, they realized with consternation that Anderson had made for them a house in his own likeness: it was plain, rugged, strong, very honest and very useful. The old man asserted his proprietorship by praising it, put the seal of authorship upon it by squirting a jet of tobacco juice on to the shrill new fir floor-boards.

So they settled in there in the shadow of the bush.

4.

An axe! A beautiful thing and perfectly adapted to its purpose. The product of many centuries of experience, its pedigree goes back into the mists of time, for it is the lineal descendant of that flint axe with which prehistoric man first gave battle to the forest, shouting his triumph at his crashing adversary.

Of tempered steel and seasoned hickory wood, it is balanced, adequate to its occasions. In the hands of a man it confers godlike sovereignty to him over the might of the bush. Even the plough must cede it pride of place for before there were fields, the world stood dressed in a thick garment of dark green. The axe, father of all cities, of the highways, of the farmlands.

The clearing grew. The ring of the Newcomer's axe could be heard down at the England place. "He works like a

Chechahco," Bob England remarked to his wife.* "But he certainly does go at it."

Bob was by his stable, running his hands over the fore-locks of his mare Maude. "That fellow will split his shin or carve his foot off one of these days," he was thinking. "He goes at it like a demon. Somebody ought to tell him." He straightened up his back: "He'll learn," he told the mare.

Autumn lay upon the Valley like a sadness, but the New-comer rejoiced, for with his own two hands he had done this mischief among the timber. He was learning, too. At the end of two months he had a perfect swing, driving in his keen axe-blade thigh-high, and following each stroke so that the tempered steel shaved along the surface of the wood, leav-ing it smooth and trim. He had found out how to make a tree fall where you want it, and looking around at the lying trunks, scattered like the contents of a giant's match-box, he grudged the price of knowledge. Much work he could have saved had he but known before.

Food had never tasted so good before, and every callosi-ty on his hands was new evidence of virility. The bush satisfied him, awakened the primitive man that had been stifled by the streets of cities and the ways of towns.

Anderson brought his bill up the hill and with it a sack of apples. The little house was built. It stood, yellow and naked, against the rich garment of the bush. The eye of the bush looked down upon the house, and the little house returned the stare with the truculence of youth. It was a blatant little house, new and crude and unadorned. It had no outward graces.

But inside it was beautiful; they had made it so. They were settled in now, settled and learning things.

There was no reason why, the day's work done, they should not dress for the simple evening meal.*

5.

They heard the wind stir through the bush, and saw the Valley shudder into shadow; they watched the dark clouds scud across the low vault of the sky until the mountains were wiped from the horizon. The trees dripped with water that had not fallen as rain and the tangled undergrowth soaked the Newcomer as he worked; the humid earth squelched under his heavy boots; the branches of the trees wiped wet fingers across his face.

Far below, on the floor of the valley, lay the river, dim and swathed in wreaths of mist. The bark of a dog, unnaturally clear, ascended to him, ripping a hole in the stillness. The silence became the receptacle of sound, the bush awoke and spoke; its voice, for all the moisture, seemed parched and dry.

When the breeze died, a sigh shuddered through the forest. The scudding battalions of the skies halted in their forced march against the mountains and set an airy camp above the bush. And to the Newcomer it seemed that from the waiting forest pennants of amorphous vapour writhed upwards beckoning with fantastic arms.

Then the rain came, and from the heart of the bush he heard a million hidden drummers beat a mad tattoo of welcome. The great drops fell slowly, one by one, and the waiting branches caught them, holding them cupped, suspended.

The forest trembled ecstatically at the rain's touch, glistened like a polished stone, and a million jewels winked from the gloom. From the ground, the humid smell of the aged earth, evocative, eerie, came to the worker's nostrils, the odour of death and decay, cleansed by aeons of time.

So the sounds of the forest grew, and swelled to a passionate thrumming. He looked up and saw a sable canopy descend, slowly, like the drop curtain of a fabulous theatre. Night fell, and the forest became inscrutable, a voice calling from the darkness, and this darkness was the death and end of light, the gloom of uncreated worlds.

Out of this blackness he saw a single yellow eye, unwinking, watchful. The hidden drummers beat upon their drums, the darkness pulsed with sound. The eye watched. It was the window of the yellow house and it seemed to put to him a question whose answer no man has ever heard.

CHAPTER IV

1.

The Newcomer worked upon his clearing, and his mind took its leisure, roaming the fields of memory and fancy as he toiled.

The shadowy world of the Roman Empire, the many-coloured pattern of history. What was the good of it?

A slave, setting up his bake-house to bake the bread of liberty; and, once set free, casting envious eyes upon the patrician caste forever closed to him.

A Roman father claiming the *patria potestas* over the dead body of his son.

A patriarch guarding the sacred fire, the *sacra* of his House.

The clamour of the Roman mob, and the smouldering eyes of the glittering *praetor* resisting the appeal to the *Lex Talionis.*

The hot dispute of the citizens over Riparian rights. The judgment and the written scroll.

The Caesar in the Capitol.* The twelve wise jurists turning at their Emperor's command to the task of compilation, remote fashioners of the twentieth century's shape, destined to work for the centuries to come, a thousand, five thousand years.

The *Institutes* of Justinian.* Parallel columns. English and Latin. Dry reading.

The tree shivered at the blows and the worker stood back as the column swayed.

The high-roofed library in the mellow light of stained glass oriel windows, listless readers, the silent-footed attendant, a figure from a world of dreams passing an enchanted life forever carrying books into which he might never look until the curse upon him was lifted.

The rumble of the Thames Embankment beyond the green of Temple lawns, hooting newspaper vans, taxis, hurtling trams, shouting newsboys.* The quick life of the swollen river; pastel-tinted barges, slow and aimless, guided by amorphous Charons; bustling tugs bent on business; sinister police-boats with blue-uniformed men in them. And, on the Surrey side, the huddled warehouses, wharves and factories elbowing against each other, pressing back with their feet in the water where once dense forests stood.*

Under these tall trees, with the Valley far below, that world of London now seemed as distant to the Newcomer as that other world of old Rome.

He leaped upon the fallen giant and set about lopping the branches.

How much better the axe! Two hours of Justinian merely left one where one was, with a dream added to the storehouse of memory. Broken pictures of the past, fragments of useless learning. That was all.

But the axe lived; it lived and talked. Why even those old Romans paid it supreme tribute, setting it up as their symbol, the glittering core of the Roman *fasca*. It meant force without anarchy; it meant discipline and conquest.

The axe paid cash and asked not for credit.

"The quick life of the swollen river; pastel-tinted barges, slow and aimless, guided by amorphous Charons; bustling tugs bent on business; sinister police-boats with blue-uniformed men in them. And, on the Surrey side, the huddled warehouses, wharves and factories elbowing against each other, pressing back with their feet in the water where once dense forests stood." (p. 33). London, England, 1910. The Surrey docks are to the right.

2.

The shirted figure, bare-chested, lithe, swung the axe. And the axe spoke: a tongue of living wood spurted from the wound in the tree's side, the tree vibrated, passionately resentful. The bush watched.

The alders were felled easily because they were young and their green and grey mottled bark, beautiful as the skin of snakes, concealed a soft, sappy wood. They reeled under the blows, groaned, swung drunkenly, and spun earthwards. With bent and twisted branches they throbbed for a moment like living things feeling the agonies of death, and came to rest.

The giant Douglas firs were no such easy game. Their corrugated trunks, fluted from base to summit, symmetrical as Corinthian columns, soared up into the sky and spread branches like great dark and velvety fans against the leaden sky.

Against these, even the axe lost sense of power: it became a pigmy tool wielded by a pigmy hewer. For these are the mighty ones of the bush, the worker told himself, the aged fathers of the forest. They have looked upon the Valley through the centuries. Fire has not destroyed them, nor the wind that tears at them, nor yet the silver-frost that weighs their outspread members with tons of frozen water, until they shine, silver bright, like trees of glass.

They have conquered the elements, he considered, and now comes man, equal conqueror, to lay them low.

Yes, to the Newcomer the bush spoke. It gave peace to his mind and satisfaction to his soul.

3.

Old Man Olson sat upon the chopping-block in the big wood-shed. He was whittling wood with a large pruning-knife with a hooked blade. He was doing that and thinking of his son Kurt – Kurt, the strongest of them all. Little Kurt, his youngest. He loved him better than the rest. Aye, Kurt was the clever one. What was there he could not do with those clever hands of his?

Sitting there, with his great boots comforted in a carpet of chips, the old man had an open field of vision across country, for the Olson ranch stood beyond the crest of the Valley facing the hinterland, and the woodshed was open on one side so that big logs could be passed in easily from the tail of a cart, or a rig of a neighbour could be housed there for a night conveniently.

Six foot three inches he was, and bent. His thin, wiry body was wrapped in a patched Mackinaw. He wore three pairs of thick woollen socks. His ruddy face was the colour of bronze and from it sprouted strong white hair. But the old man saw neither the drenched, clipped clover of the orchard that sloped down gently to the road beyond, nor the apple-trees that stood, all symmetrical, in straight rows. They looked like toy trees from a Noah's Ark, with their bowl-shaped branches, carefully trained by early pruning.

Aye, Kurt was the clever one, and he would be coming back from the North, out of the Yukon. That was good. He would be about the place again, big, powerful, gentle, with his queer high-pitched voice, so thin, coming out of that deep chest.

Old Man Olson was very old and no one expected much of him. There was his age, they said, and then his loins had peopled half the settlement: the old fellow was a grandfather many times. An old man like that, he should be given a thought now and then.

Old Man Olson kept to his own. He never opened his mouth when strangers came but sat and looked at them without curiosity out of his deep-set blue eyes that glittered beneath white bushy brows. Only among his own people did he talk. For he had come to the West too late to pick up a strange tongue. He spoke only Norwegian.

In summer the old fellow spent his days in the sun, sitting beside the kitchen door smoking his long Norwegian pipe with the china bowl. A lonely time with the boys out working about the place, ploughing, seeding, planting spuds, pruning those trim trees, manuring; or away back in the bush for long days taking out shingle-bolts, bringing the wagon down the hill, swaying under its chained load; fishing for salmon in the river.

And the women. Too busy to bother with an old man,

what with calving, cooking meals for the men, helping in
the orchard in their great white sun-bonnets, milking, cleaning stables, getting the children off to school, getting them
to bed.

Aye, it's lonely for Old Man Olson when the orchard is
white and the sun sits in the sky over the settlement. He likes
best the winter when things are quiet about the place and he
can drowse beside the crackling iron stove in the over-heated living-room, smoking his long pipe, spitting every now
and again, comfortable, with the nice smell of his people
about him, and the stove warm to his long thin legs.

So he will sit for hours looking about him, saying little
but following the talk, approving the oleographs – King
Haakon and his Queen – the pretty calendar, gift of Blanchard, the fret-work frames with the carved beavers, the
bright vases, the slowly moving Mission rocking chair.*

When Kurt came they would have music, too. He played
the concertina, played it beautifully, any tune you could ask
for. Was there anything that boy could not do, anything at
all?

Old Man Olson sat there in the woodshed whittling and
thinking. And the rain, keeping up a steady drum upon
the cedar roof, dripped down and became a busy little river
scurrying along with little alarmed ships that were only chips
after all.

Kurt was in his old father's thoughts very often now. Love
gave the old man vision: he knew the boy was fretting. It
would be a woman: how could it be otherwise? But what
woman?

He whittled more slowly, pondering the riddle.

4.

Blanchard stood in the shadows of the counter cutting up

a side of bacon by the light of an oil lamp set on an empty biscuit tin. The rain beat upon the store windows and churned the river. Rainy season weather, and more to come. Hanks, his assistant, was tying up parcels of goods with incredible slowness, his tongue sticking out of his mouth as a child's will, breathing heavily, as though the effort were too much for his fat body. Ranchers idled about, waiting to buy, lingering for gossip.

Blanchard was cutting bacon. But when these fellows went he would throw off the bluff and limp through to the dirty little low-ceilinged back room where the invoices of years hung from the walls by their spikes like dead and withered chrysanthemums. This was Blanchard's office where he slept on hot summer afternoons, or warmed himself with whiskey in such wet winter weather. There he played the wheezy gramophone with the discoloured tin horn when an overdue account was paid up, and on such an evening as this, unlocked the little cupboard where he kept his whiskey, taking a nip, standing there alone, with ears alert for that fat fool of a Hanks.

Blanchard was cutting bacon: at least, that was his ostensible occupation. But he was chiefly occupied in listening to the talk. This evening hour, when the men tramped in from their ranches in the bush and waited in the store for the *Vancouver Daily Province* (which came up on the Agassiz local) was the idle hour of talk, the clearing-house of the settlement's news and tattle.

After a long tramp through the rain, two, three, four, or even five miles, the warmth of the store, and the light, and the sight of familiar faces, were welcome enough.

Talk came round always to the old theme – whether this was God's own country, or just the dregs of creation, no man striking a middle course, but each speaking from the bitterness of failure or the easy optimism of success.

"It stands to reason that you get a reaction after a boom like we've had," Bob England was saying.*

He touched on the shadow of the depression which was already stealing across the Valley like a paralysing sickness, filching the green dollar bills, laying an embargo on the cheques from the mills at Sapperton, slamming down the price of produce, sending up the price of wheat, meal and bran.

"You can't have it both ways," he argued. "Six months ago any of you fellows could have got out with a big price. But you waited for prices to go a bit higher – and they didn't."

The accusation, addressed to the silent group of shining figures that still dripped circles of water upon the boards of the floor, was made in the accents of defence. Everybody there knew that in every transaction which had taken place at Ferguson's Landing, on every sale of wild land or cultivated ranch, Bob England had picked up his easy commission.

Money for walking around the Landing with easy marks! Easy to be philosophic with a wad salted away, quite easy! That was how they felt and thought to themselves.

It was Old Man Dunn who spoke first. His bronzed face was obscure in the shadows of his great sou'wester. Only his iron-grey beard was distinct, moving up and down.

The Sage was going to speak, and, as usual, he would fire a lot of stuff nobody could make head or tail of!

"A boom is bad economics," he asserted in his terrific voice. "A boom means a mortgage on the future of the country. You take the money for work that's not yet begun. And some time in the future some poor beggar comes along, pays your unearned profits and sets in to earn 'em himself. He pays for the work you didn't do and then does the work himself."

A smile flickered across Blanchard's face. Sententious old fool! Lets his wife do all the work and wears out his pants reading books.

But Blanchard's thoughts were well masked.

Old Man Dunn had resumed his indictment of the profit-grabbers, the land-sharks whom he was always cursing as the country's evil.

"Here's an example – that young English fellow up behind your place on the hill, Bob England. What in God's name can he do with that land?"

A murmur of agreement greeted the challenge.

"Alder bottom."

"Yes, but peppered with damn great first-growth fir stumps that'll cost fifteen to twenty bucks apiece to blow out."

"The soil's no good there either." The last speaker, Heggerty of the ferret face, became confidential. "Why two years ago, in August, Johansson nearby couldn't get a mug of water from his well, no, sir."

"Damn shame, I call it."

"And the slope of the layout is such that you couldn't plough on it. The team would fall off onto Bob's place."

"Look at the land around the Landing: It's only forty years since you could have it for paying to register your deeds. I recall young Ferguson telling me that his old man claimed that he could have owned most of the Valley if he had taken the trouble to take it."

"That's true, too."

"Even two years ago you could buy decent bush land for two dollars an acre. Look at it now. Stuff that won't grow an artichoke fetching a hundred dollars an acre."

Bob England had listened to the speakers, sucking his pipe in silence. It was easy for them to talk that way, but he had a mortgage on his place. He had needed the money. He consoled himself with the easy logic of people who choose to deceive themselves and silence doubts.

"After all," he said, "if I didn't happen to be the agent for most of the Vancouver real estate men here, one of you fellows would jump at the chance to take over from me."

Like most little men, Bob England felt the urge to impose himself physically. He had been sitting on a sack of potatoes. He got up and swaggered like a cockerel.

"Why don't you do something about our road, Bob?" It was Heggerty who spoke, the only man present without the protection of oilskins, standing there in a patched mackinaw that was starting to steam.

"Why don't you make it so we can get a team in and out and earn a bit with our cedar? As it is, there I am, five hundred bolts cut, and no way of getting them out."

He was the poorest man in the settlement and it was said that his children (he had eleven) often went hungry; that his wife was dying of consumption; that he was a fool. But it was even worse than that: he was that unforgivable thing, a failure.

A man, you might say, with a right to be indignant against the world, against life, against the government in particular, or anyone who represented it in even a remote and inferior capacity.

Bob England did have government connections and Heggerty held him with wide, accusing eyes. Heggerty had spoken in an aggressive manner, without heat, but with that cold, dangerous wrath of a man who is hard driven, and his words sounded to those others like an indictment of Bob England.

Wasn't Bob England the road boss? Wasn't he the fellow who got the letters from the Department at Victoria? When the Minister came up the Valley, didn't he hump up that hill to England's place and feed with him? Didn't Bob England have the say-so? Didn't everyone know he was the Party Man who passed the word about the voting?

"Hell!" Heggerty gave expression to the bitterness of his thoughts as he considered his wrongs.

Bob England met Heggerty's eyes without wavering. He did not answer at once, but cocked his dark head and cupped his hand to nurse the fizzling point of a sulphur match. It wavered up, dispersing evil fumes; he sucked the living flame into the bowl of his pipe until his face glowed with the reflected light. But his eye was on his critic.

"The grant gave out, Heggerty, that's why your place is without a road. No money, no road work, you know that."

His shrewd, fearless glance challenged the eyes of the other. He had taken up and disposed of the unspoken accusation of graft made by a neighbour.

"When the grant's finished – well, work stops," he added laconically.

But he had by his contagious pugnacity, veiled as it was beneath that quietness which is the characteristic of men who don't understand fear, created an atmosphere of contention.

Blanchard paused, long knife in hand, scratched his head and waited. It was interesting to see how these fellows stood, one against the other. He knew what each of them was worth to a cent.

Heggerty had come back to the argument: "Ferguson's Landing never got its proper appropriation, Bob England, and you oughter seen to that." A whine had crept into his voice; his arrogance was gone.

"Up at Langford they got five hundred dollars more – and a smaller settlement, by the hokey!"*

Heggerty had now got an audience that was very different from the silent woman who would bend over the washtub as he sat at the deal table of their low log cabin and grumbled at life and the way he got treated. It was a change.

Yes, and it would be something to tell the old woman when he had trudged those five miles home, elaborating the clever things he had not said, the fine answers he had never made.

He turned towards the figure in the shadows – Blanchard, thin, remote, standing apart from the dispute.

"Wot you giving for eggs today, Mr. Blanchard?" he asked.

Blanchard looked at the speaker and his eyes flickered for an instant before the mask fell.

"Twenty cents, Mr. Heggerty; it's a poor price, but those fellows at Sapperton only give me twenty-four and I've got to handle them." Then, inviting sympathy, "Traveller up this morning from Sapperton, bad times, people buying Chinese eggs all along. Chinese peddlers selling the garden truck they grow on Lulu Island, cutting our throats." His voice trailed off petulantly. A man hard done by – an honest, simple fellow, trying his best to make a living under difficult circumstances – Blanchard.

But to Heggerty the storekeeper's eyes had said: "It's time you paid that bill of yours, Heggerty. You may have a hundred brats, but I can't keep 'em through the winter. I'm not here for my health. And as for your eggs, why damn you, I won't take any more of 'em. No, not even in exchange. You are too lazy to wash the dung off of them, and you starve your fowls so that they lay eggs like the first effort of a precocious pullet. Yes, Mr. Heggerty, and what became of those very pleasant greenbacks you got working on the road. I don't think I saw the colour of them. What became of them, eh?"

Having read these unspoken reproaches in the enigmatic eyes of Blanchard, Heggerty raised his voice like a speaker dismissing his subject in a few well-chosen words.

"Well, sir," he declaimed, a ring of braggadocio in his voice and a feigned courage he was far from feeling within. "Well, sir. I'd be mighty glad to be back in Dakota. Yes, sir! Dakota, that's a country, I'll say. Good prairie, where a man can raise a crop and go ahead at the bank. Yes, sirree!"

And Heggerty knew, and knew that his hearers knew, that in Dakota he had never owned an acre, but had been nothing better than a professional bum, and that he had made his way to B.C. by the all-tie-route, tramping the weary miles along the Canadian Pacific Railway, sneaking into empty freight cars under cover of night, being kicked off railroad property by hard-faced cops.

Having tried to save face, Heggerty picked up his sack (in the bulging end of which were the groceries which were to keep his family alive for another week) and with a "Goodnight, people," disappeared into the darkness and the rain.

A five-mile tramp in the dark, wringing wet, burdened with fifty pounds, along a trail that took you into the bush, a trail you kept missing because in the infernal dark you couldn't see the blazed trees showing faintly through the obscurity; a trail rising, rising up to that crest that loomed dark and menacing over the Valley and far beyond. A trail that led to a log house that leaked, that was too small for its many occupants, to children that cried, to a silent woman who accused you without a spoken word. Aye, a man may think many things under such circumstances.

He may, before he reaches the end of his trail, cast off even the mask of self-deception. He may look at himself as he is, a weak thing, full of absurdities and meannesses. A cowardly creature sneaking away from life into the bush.

It may do all that for a man – the darkness, the clinging penetrating wetness, the bush. Most of all the bush, because it comes alive and stalks you, stabs little fears into your heart, makes you feel your smallness, your futility, the sad shortness of your little span of suffering, of life.

5.

Blanchard gathered up the fruits of his labour (a handful of jagged lean rashers) and threw them with the gesture of one pleased to see the last of them, towards Hanks (who was standing like a somnambulist, tying parcels, an automaton with projecting tongue and laboured breath).

"Did you hear your brother-in-law is coming back?"

The speaker, a lean man with a lantern jaw and arched nose, who had listened in silence to the talk, spoke with the refined accent of English county-folk. But his black hair, his sharply chiselled features, his slow movements, gave him away for what he was – a half-breed, born in a shack of a Kanaka squaw and a Scotch father.* His name was Woods, and Bob England in his dry way used to say of him that he was the only gentleman in the settlement because he was the only man who could afford not to work.

"He should be in any time – he may even be on the local," said England. "This time Kurt's luck was out. He mushed in too late to stake anything of a claim. And anyway, the whole caboodle is a washout – there's hardly pay dirt there. He'd have done better pan-handling along with that Chinaman up the other side of the river. He makes wages anyway with his rocker – patient devil!"*

"Kurt doesn't need any man's pity," boomed Old Man Dunn. "There's a man who is really educated in the real sense of the word."

Blanchard moved restlessly behind the counter. He could stand a good deal – but not Old Man Dunn.

He knew how much those two lived on, Dunn and his skinny wife. Land sakes! How did they do it? Last month, why last month, he, Blanchard, paid them money! Fine thing, keeping store if people sold you more stuff than they bought. Nice thing!

"An educated man," continued the Yorkshireman, oracularly, "don't necessarily mean a man who has been to Oxford or Cambridge, nor yet to Durham. It's a man who can survive under most conditions. Take Kurt as an example and you see what I mean. Look at the things that fellow can put his hand to! He's a miner, a boat-builder, the best salmon fisherman on this stretch of the Fraser, an expert carpenter, a lumberjack and a farmer. And when it comes down to the social side, he can play concertina and fiddle and dance as good as any of them at the Recreation Hall. Yes, I reckon he is an educated man – in the right sense of the word, mind you – in the proper sense."

Old Man Dunn stopped speaking. He waited for comment. None came. Heads nodded, grotesquely like inverted coal-scuttles under the big sou'westers.

"Johansson's bought a cow," somebody announced to nobody in particular.

"Yes, a Holstein. Due in about a month."

"A cow, eh?" queried Old Man Dunn. "Now there's another worker for you, that Swede. A cow?"

"Where did he get her?"

"What did he pay, d'you know?"

"From Fuller. Hundred plunks."

"And a year ago," said Old Man Dunn, "he told me himself that he hadn't the next instalment on his place – that fifty-acre block of heavy clearing you sold him, Bob, at fifty dollars an acre."

"And forty too much at that."

Old Man Dunn ignored the interruption: "I never knew a man who would break his back as a hired-out man like that Swede does." There was admiration in his voice, but no sympathetic understanding; he merely marvelled at a strange and unaccountable phenomenon because he loved the truth. "He works as if the devil's behind him."

Blanchard, his voice neutral, colourless, observed in his dry way: "Johansson can pack two sacks of wheat up that trail, even in the rainy season – two hundred pound weight and a two-mile hump, mud like oiled grease."

Murmurs of incredulity came from under the inverted coal-scuttles.

"Fact," Blanchard assured them. "I've helped him take up

the load." He became explanatory. "He gets you to heave one sack onto the small of his back, he gets his arms back and over it, and then you dump the second hundred-weight on top of his arms."

A voice from the shadows: "A mule, not a man." A large globule sailed out from the shadowy corner like a disheartened comet, described an arc and ended on the floor near somebody's boot. "A bloody mule, yes, sir. It didn't oughter be allowed. An' his wife's mighty sick, yes, sir."

"How's Miss Lulu getting on, Mr. England?" asked Blanchard, to correct the atmosphere created by the expectorator. "I hear she is going to stay permanently on the Coast. Vancouver, isn't it?"

Bob England said: "I thought so, too, but I think she may be back any time now."

"Pity," said a voice from the shadows.

The coal-scuttles nodded agreement.

"That house gets pretty rough when the shingle-bolt outfit are rooming there. I reckon Mrs. Armstrong didn't ought to keep a pretty girl like that around with that roughneck bunch about."

"Too much hooch flies about in the evenings," said another voice.

The inverted coal-scuttles wagged in unison.

Blanchard leaned across the counter. His tongue, like a tiny flashing snake, moistened his thin lips; his left eyebrow lifted imperceptibly; he seemed to put a mute question, make a silent suggestion. In the highlights thrown from the hanging oil lamps he looked like a mischievous satyr.

He said: "That house hasn't a good name. Half-breeds hang about when Armstrong is away." He paused as though he had said a thing better left unspoken.

"I must be off," said a sedate voice.

A tall figure moved with a slow, stately walk to the door,

contemplated the watery darkness for a moment. It was as though he would make it plain that there was no connection whatever between Blanchard's last words and his own sudden departure. He cast a "Good-night, people," over a high shoulder and was swallowed up in a blackness that seemed to drift into the store from the open door.

There was a titter: "Put your foot in it with Woods," someone said.

"Woods be damned!" muttered Old Man Dunn. "The fellow *is* a breed and we all know it."

Blanchard coughed slightly. Woods paid cash: his wife's cash.

"As I was saying, breeds hang about that house when Armstrong is away."

Dunn paused, thinking, "That will draw one of 'em." It did. The black, shining coal-scuttles converged upon the common point which was Blanchard, standing with his elbows on the dark stains of his counter.

The voices rumbled to a lower key.

"Oh, no harm there," said Bob England. "Nothing wrong with them. Old-timers, the Armstrongs."

It was said defensively, perhaps because Bob England looked upon quarreling as bad for business. Besides, he had drunk many a bottle under that decayed, lichened roof.

Blanchard's voice, even and toneless, cut across the acquittal of Bob England's advocacy.

"You weren't here when the store murder happened, were you? Nope. Well, you know the story. They never got the fellow. He made a clean get-away. They telegraphed down the line. No go."

Blanchard paused. "Well, he was supposed to have smashed open that door."

He pointed with a stringy arm towards the oblong of the door hung with its quivering curtain of rain against the sable of the night. "But he never did. It was a put-up job. There never was a holdup man in the store at all."

Blanchard's enigmatic eyes roved from one shadowed face to another. About the thin lips of his mouth a twisted smile seemed to flicker and then go out.

They all knew this version of the unsolved murder mystery. But they liked to hear it again.

Blanchard was speaking again:

"You know what old Mrs. Hitton says? From her windows over there," he said, pointing with his left arm, "she can see the store. Well, I've heard her say myself that a minute after the shot rang out a white figure flitted from the back of the store across to Armstrong's house."

"A woman's figure?"

"Yes, a woman's figure."

Footsteps clamping mud from boots on the boards of the store steps cut across the talk. The gossips wheeled together.

"Good evening, people."

Two women stood in the doorway, the water pouring from their oilskins. They advanced into the shelter of the store, shaking the water from their heads.

One was tall, handsome, forty or so, with a firm, vigorous figure. The other was young, slim and pretty. Her dark hair was matted to her forehead; beneath it, her large eyes were very blue.

"Well, well, Mrs. Armstrong," said Blanchard, "a nice night to travel, I'm sure." Their eyes flickered in an almost imperceptible contact. It was as though there flashed between them a warning, a threat. A promise. A denial.

"And Miss Lulu, so you don't find the city so fine after all?" Blanchard's even voice was full of conventional amiability, half storekeeper, half neighbour.

"She had to cut the trip short," Mrs. Armstrong explained.

"I'll be wanting her at home. An outfit's coming in and I'll be boarding them."

The men listened in silence. It was as though they had been surprised while about some questionable business. It was as though this dominating, vital woman challenged them to question her ways of life.

Another figure had stepped into the light of the store. A giant of a man, black and glistening, but moving without a sound, like a spectre. They became aware of him with surprise. It was as though a figure had stepped noiselessly from the frame of a picture.

"Well, people."

"Why, Kurt – like a blooming ghost!"

The blond giant smiled, held up his gumboots. They saw that he was in his thickly-stockinged feet.

"Leaked," he explained laconically.

The black frame from which he had materialized became suddenly a fiery oblong: a spurt of flame and a roar came out of the night, shaking the store-house. The Agassiz local, her engine bell clanging, boomed on her way, her seven hundred mile "local" journey.

They waited for the commotion to subside. Blanchard stood erect, a smile on his lips. He was looking at the immobile figure of the Norwegian giant who stood staring with parted lips.

Blanchard's eyes shifted round until they rested on the object of the Norwegian's curiosity. He saw Hanks, fat, lymphatic Hanks, head on hand, sleeping through the din, sleeping softly like a child.

"Looks like he was a dead man," commented Kurt in his peculiar high voice.

"Ah! like a dead man!" Blanchard echoed. He gave the sleeping figure a prod.

CHAPTER V

1.

The Valley continued to grieve the death of summer. A tattered mist floated over trees and river. It was like a funeral garment from which peered forth the melancholy face of the stricken land. And the great, grey river, phantomlike, moved sluggishly seawards. The rain fell, not in great gusts and squalls, but as a curtain of water that hung quivering between sky and earth. It was autumn's requiem mass for summer, a recitative sad as death, an unchanging whisper of falling water, and the answering voice of the drinking forest.

In the cities men work throughout the year against an old age that may bring scarcity. But at Ferguson's Landing they took a shorter view: they laboured for an annual harvest which would support them through each winter to another spring. In summer the settlers worked to lay up food and fuel against the winter. Old age – they gave it no thought.

Not that winter in the Valley came with the stark threat of death with which it descends from the mountains to lay icy hands upon the prairie. The Valley winters are mild and when the rain lets up, a man may work about his place in shirt-sleeves. Yes, it is like that. Flowers will sometimes blossom when the fall of the year is long since past and the new year is at hand.

The fecundity of the Valley feeds the settler and gives him sustenance. He must take it while he can so that there is a sack of flour in the kitchen by the stove, potatoes in the pit, salmon smoked and pork butchered, salted, cured.

There must be food because there may be no money. Booms bring money but when they pass they take it away. The boom gives nothing: it merely lends, and it is an usurer, exacting a Shylock's return.

2.

But only Old Man Dunn, deep in his worn armchair by the kitchen stove, understood these things. He got his ideas from books, passing his wisdom in his sonorous voice to the miniature of a woman who bustled about tasks which seemed to have no beginning and no end.

The Dunns had drifted into Ferguson's Landing thirty years before, from Nebraska, from California, from Florida. They had been everywhere, moving about the world seeing things, only to come at last to the shadow of the bush, where the towering columns of the giant firs threw shadows upon their old farmhouse, and shadows upon their lives, too.

The old couple were like halted travellers, uncertain of their bourne, who debate: "Whither?" And, finding no answer, linger on in a permanent camp whose permanence they will not admit or recognize.

They were wanderers at the end of their road, but wanderers who comforted themselves with talk and thought of the last journey for which they saved: the Old Country. Home.

One of the oldest houses in the settlement, it was, for Ferguson himself had dug the holes that took the cedar supports upon which it stood. The shingles of its steep-pitched roof were festooned with lichen and moss, so that every winter it leaked. And every winter the old man would go out and stand in the rain, looking up. Always he boomed that it must be seen to – and returned to his chair and his books with nothing done.

Coarse green grass had sprung up in the orchard in which the house stood. The apple-trees were gnarled and knotted and twisted, eaten by parasites, yet bearing prolifically despite neglect, great crops of speckled fruit, as is the way at times.

Loganberries they had, and the great giant raspberries of the coast; huckleberries grew wild in the slashing at the rear, pushing their bushy heads out among the gorse, starring the green with their bright red fruit where vine maples sprouted.

Everything about the ranch looked sad. It was like a place left for years untenanted and forgotten. So that it was only when the tiny figure of old Mrs. Dunn appeared at the door, grotesquely capped with her husband's great sou'wester, and carrying a bucket of steaming chicken mash, that the passer-by gaped in surprise to realize that this wilderness was the habitation of the living.

3.

Old Man Dunn was opening his mail, steel spectacles perched upon his great nose. His wisp of a wife was standing at the hot stove, hands on hips, intent upon her oven. It was baking day. She baked once a week – the best bread in the Landing.

She was thinking: No, not so good as ten years ago; for if you would have good bread, light, tight bread, with crisp crust, you must have strong arms for the kneading of the dough (and Mrs. Dunn's arms were thin, like a chicken's legs without their feathers).

Good batter, the white and spongy batter through which the knife cleaves, leaving a wound that opens and gapes like a mouth. The second kneading, then loaves, the cottage loaves of Yorkshire. How many years ago?

Put it in the oven, but let that oven be hot, hot, hot for the first ten minutes, so that the batter will puff up like a balloon before it stands to tan in the glowing iron oven.

She stooped to the oven door, a cloth in her hands, the blast of heat on her face. Pans of new bread fill the kitchen with a friendly smell, and Old Man Dunn looks up from his French Revolution.* It made a man hungry.

She thought: Men were like that. Food interested them, if nothing else. Food and learning. Useless, lumbering creatures – all wants, all appetites. The loaves stood upon the white wood table, in two rows, little loaves, one for each day of the week; little loaves dark brown at their crowns, with chestnut flanks that shaded off below to yellow. Bread, the homely stuff; bread, of which one never tired.

"A good batch, Tom."

There is satisfaction in her voice.

She withdrew the probing knife; it came out clean, flecked with beads of moisture. Yes, a good batch.

4.

Kurt has changed since he came back from the Yukon. He does not seem able to settle down. Kurt, usually so quick to put into execution the clever schemes of his head, is idle, doing nothing. And he won't play, even with the children. Twice he has spanked little Ole's bottom and sent him in screaming from the wood-shed, where the sad giant sat brooding.

"Maybe you will start in on the new boat?" his brother asks him. He bears no grudge for the spanking given to his youngest. "A good engine, four horse power, I was thinking, and a bit of a cabin."

These two fish together every summer, the married brother with the brood and with the old man on his hands, and the bachelor who spends his money like water and lives with the married man.

They are famous fishermen, the Olson brothers, handling their boat with knowledge of the river, knowing every sunken snag, every danger point. Nobody knows the salmon runs as they do, those channels on the river bottom through which the salmon swim in long flashing silver columns, like an army in shining armour; nobody. They pick up their bearings by their secret landmarks – the cottonwood tree in line with the Indian Reservation Church, the cone of Mount Baker in line with the wharf shed – drop their nets at points known only to themselves, lift here or there where some monstrous, gnarled cedar root lies, capsized upon its side in the silt, its great twisted roots reaching up blindly through the water like the petrified tentacles of an octopus – an octopus in search of the nets of fishermen.*

But Kurt merely grunts. "Maybe," he says, and continues to brood.

Ole, son of Old Ole, talks it over with his wife.

"It's the goldfields," she says. "He reckoned he'd come out rich this time, 'stead of which he's lost a finger."

But it was not the lost finger, hacked off beyond Dawson with a jack-knife, that was worrying Kurt, nor yet the claim that was a washout, nor the team of huskies that died on him. No, it was none of those things. Ole and his wife could not understand. Old Ole watched, his sharp eyes following the lumbering movements of his great son. "To smack little Ole's behind: something was amiss there."

5.

'Way back in the bush Heggerty was building him a shack. He had neither the skill nor the patience to build himself a proper log house of the materials at his door. So he planned to put some of the children in the new shack to make things more tolerable.

He worked on a cross-cut saw single-handled, as did most men in the settlement. The six feet of springy steel with the upright wooden handle ate down into the trunk as he worked steadily. The saw and the man were one, working in unison. The damp smell of the bush and the sweet perfume of the new-cut wood. Cedar! Easy wood to work, soft and light, friendly.

Each four-foot-two trunk section he up-ended, there in the moist clearing, with the bush dripping still, after the letup of the rain. Into each section he drove his wedge and its clang sped into the bush like an arrow of sound. It seemed to call: "Beware! Oh, forest, man is here; man, the destroyer. Man, who eats your heart away, ravishing your loveliness."

Under those hammer-blows the blocks fell apart and lay with satiny wood exposed, each surface a perfect board for the taking, a board to be cleaved away with the thick-bladed "throw" that need only penetrate an inch to send a springy board ripping free, straight and clean and knotless, a perfect "shake," that will throw off any rain, even the rain of Ferguson's Landing.

6.

Today Johansson is a hired man. He walks three miles each morning, wet or fine, to Mann's brickyard up the line. He can do anything, that man. But his wife is sick. The doctor only shook his head when he examined her. A bad time of life, he said. And a man paid money to hear this!

She crawls about the little house at her work, slowly; she sighs and holds her hand to her back. Her homely face is yellow and set in a fixed expression of melancholy and suffering. She is thinking: And now there is the cow! A cow means more work, but the thought thrills her. A cow!

Bob England has got his case of whiskey stowed away. The team is hired out for the winter. The barn is full. There's no work about the place, barring chores, and Johansson will be glad to earn a dollar.

There's Bob in the best room, in shirt-sleeves, crushing the antimacassars, knocking pipe-ash on the patterned carpet, drinking his whiskey. A regular nuisance, he is.

In the new clearing there is no sign of life except the smoke from the chimney. The Newcomer has left his cluttered mess of felled trees. He is behind the house building a wood-shed, building it alone and learning as he goes. There is no method in his work, and every time Johansson strides across the clearing he is wanting to tell the Englishman things, wanting to help him. But he wouldn't have it thought that he is hinting for work, so he keeps his counsel to himself.

CHAPTER VI

1.

Mrs. Armstrong is busy preparing for her boarders. Her house stands not a stone's throw from the store and is handy to the wharf where the fishing boats lie moored, with the music of the slow river under their ribs. It is a dilapidated house, once white, now stained by the weather. The picket fence by the narrow road is broken here and there, the roof of the woodshed gapes where shakes have come loose and slid to the ground. The axe is blunt. There is no store of winter firewood, not a rick.

An empty woodshed near winter: the hallmark of sloth!

It was true, then, that an outfit was coming in.

Five years ago Mann, up at the brickyard, had set out to take out shingle-bolts. Ten thousand cut bolts lay under the tangled undergrowth where he had abandoned them. Bullheaded Mann, with such big ideas, always about to make a fortune, so glib and convincing with his fat laugh and fluent tongue. But somehow, always just overlooking some silly little point which brought his schemes to nothing.

He had hired men to cut the bolts, away back in the bush, and they had cut them. But he had forgotten a road, a slashed corduroy road, to drag his spoil to the wharf. His money gave out and the bolts lay damp, but sound, beneath the new growth of the forest floor. Now, practical men were coming in to take the cream off that old enterprise. There lay the logs, ready to be fetched and going for a song. Mann needed the money for his brickyard now. It only remained to make a slashing, lay a corduroy road of slender alder trunks, slimy with sap, in order to run those bolts down the steep slope on iron-shod sleds.

They would be making money, this new outfit, so they would pay well for their board.

Mrs. Armstrong was bustling about her kitchen, stirring the tainted air with her skirts, the air over-heated and sour. All her movements were vigorous, and her arms, white and round below her rolled-up sleeves, were strong like the arms of a man.

She was trying to get through a week's work in a day, after her return from Vancouver where she had been paying one of her frequent visits to her sister, the CPR brakeman's wife. She enjoyed a retrospect of that week and smiled secretly. Everything was at sixes and sevens but she was gay: men were coming.

"There's no bread," she announced. "No bread and no time to bake." The daily disaster of the feckless housewife.

She threw her words at Lulu like an accusation.

The girl turned apathetically, her voice toneless: "I'll go down to the store," she volunteered. "Maybe Blanchard got some from the Sapperton local."

She moved slowly across the room and the hostile eye of her mother followed her, a speculative eye, critical, all-seeing, unhampered by deceiving affection. The grievance was no less a grievance for that its cause was no fault of the girl's. It was the hostility of middle age towards youth.

The girl had no get-up, no spunk, and she was getting more and more useless, more and more melancholy.

"Yes, and you'd better hustle," she snapped. "And for God's sake try to show a little more pep when the men come in. We gotta make 'em comfortable. You know that. There's that crawling worm Tom Preedy, with his easy depot money, taking in boarders now. Competition? That's about it! Well, I'll show him." Her voice was vicious.

Yes, Mrs. Armstrong would show the little man, the little runt who whined about "his work" at the depot. Work!

"They say he's afraid of the trains."

"Runt," she snapped.

Let him start in with the boarders, only let him try it on. Let him put up CPR dining-car fare if he likes. Runt!

Men didn't only think about their eats; they liked a bit of fun after a hard day's work. They got it at Mrs. Armstrong's.

The tall woman contemplated the confusion of her domain: the unwashed dishes, a week uncleansed, the dirty dishcloths hanging from the double line that was festooned with petticoats and drawers; the grey ashes, fallen from the clogged stove to the iron sheeting beneath; the bucket half filled with dirty water.

But the slatternly aspect of the room had no power to deflate the spirits of this woman, at once so feminine and unwomanly. "We'll have a jolly winter," she thought. Her bright eyes glittered at the mental images that passed through her free imagination, a smile played about the corners of her full-lipped mouth. She pressed her two hands on her hips with a downward movement, inhaled a deep breath until her firm bosom rose and swelled voluptuously. In her mind the fun had commenced already.

2.

Yes, for Mrs. Armstrong the coming of the men meant a winter of jollity, a welcome break in the monotony of this God-forsaken dump. They would have laughter and music of concertinas, fiddling, and jests which would get freer and freer as the strangeness of the men wore off and coarse familiarities passed unchecked.

A voluptuous woman, Mrs. Armstrong. She welcomed admiration and, if her fancy was taken, rewarded it. She had had her adventures before. What woman wouldn't, with a man who spent the best part of the year out at the Y timber limit fifteen miles away and only came out of the bush once in a while on the snorting loco that brought the Hindus out of the saw-mill up at Carlyle, round the bend of the river?*

Sure! Her entertainment would be without frills. But she knew what was what – Vancouver had given her a wrinkle or two. She would serve her boarders' fare out with the sauce of sex. Boarders never complained of what they got at Mrs. Armstrong's. No, it suited them. They brought their own booze and after dark the sound of music and the rhythmic beat of spiked boots dancing on bare boards could be heard half a mile away.

3.

Lulu Armstrong was walking through the rain down to the store to buy bread. She walked like a cat, daintily skirting the great pools that puddled the rough road.

She had awakened that morning in her wooden bed, under the board ceiling that sloped sharply down to the low window, with the vivid memory of a strange dream etched sharply on the tablets of her memory. It was still alive in her mind, a vivid inward vision that shut out the grey world of reality before her.

A fantastic dream: she lived it again. She looked down from a high place through an unending avenue of mighty firs whose giant branches interlocked above a golden river. Like tall cliffs, they were, towering about an incandescent canyon. Nothing moved. Nor had she been able to stir, there at the terminus of the upward sweep of that grotesque avenue. She had been aware that bonds held her captive, she remembered wanting to escape – yet wanting to stand thus forever, gazing down that endless vista which passed the earth's horizon and swept on out into stellar spaces where the golden stream became a shining lance-head, and the great trees vanished in the void.

The scene had passed, fading swiftly.

She was peering into a long case in which lay a jewelled golden sword. It was slender, tapering to a fine-edged point. Somehow it was connected with the mystic avenue of gold. As she watched, it had swelled, broadened, and become a two-bladed flame of light. Then that too had faded and there before her stood the image of the avenue: a dream within a dream. The avenue motionless, eternal, a waiting avenue.

A ball of gold like a sun appeared and rolled towards her from the illimitable distance, rolled and rolled, growing bigger and bigger. Onward it had come, and, as she had watched, fascinated, fear had crawled into her heart. It would consume her in its fiery heart.

It had rolled along the golden avenue towards her through an eternity. She had feared it, yet had ached with longing to cast herself into its molten heart. It had become a mighty, blinding globe of fire, turning with slow but ruthless revolutions.

Years passed, while the fireball travelled the spaces of infinity. It had become vast as a sun poised on the rim of the sea, a monstrous disc, no longer round, a glowing disc that lost its light and became touched by shadows, shadows that drooped over its crown, and shadows that peered from behind its round face. Yes, it was a face, a face that gazed at her with wistful eyes. She recognized it; it was the face of Kurt.

Such a dream as that! A dream which followed you.

She was at the store. In that prosaic world of strangely assorted wares, bales, tubs, brooms and pitch forks, axe-handles festooned from the ceiling, cheeses and pyramids of tea canisters, she came back to the waking world.

"Can you let us have bread?" she asked.

But Blanchard had no bread.

4.

Lulu Armstrong had been a week in Vancouver when her mother followed unexpectedly. Nature had endowed Mrs. Armstrong with a burning temperament and an insatiable appetite for pleasure, excitement and constant change of scene and company; fate had made her the grass-widow of a man who seldom spoke, who never looked at her, or, looking at her, never saw the woman before him. A poor sort of man, with a taint of Red blood a generation or two back. A man who went on mad drunken orgies. An unappetizing man, whose mouth always oozed from one corner the brown saliva of the tobacco-chewer.

Lulu was to go to Vancouver to take the business course at the big school on Granville Street.

It was the local school-mistress's idea. She had said: "Don't you let her rot here, Mrs. Armstrong. Mark my words, that girl's clever. She could be a stenographer. You send her along to Vancouver. She's got a future – but not in this place."

So it was that Mrs. Armstrong agreed. The girl was to stay with her Aunt Annie, whose husband, a brakeman on the CPR, earned his one hundred and sixty dollars a month. Riches!

Lulu liked her aunt; she was so unlike her mother. A little mouse of a woman, Annie was. And Lulu liked her uncle. He made her laugh – and she seldom laughed in the house with the stained white walls. He would make her laugh even though he had but one joke. He would say every time he got back from his three-day run: "Say, Lulu, I'm fair made of gold!"

And his great mouth would open wide, displaying his gold teeth of which he was so proud. A prairie man, he was, from Calgary. A man with a sense of humour. Not subtle, but warm and kindly. He liked the dark girl. She was to board with them. "Fine!" he had said when he heard it.

Then Mrs. Armstrong came down like a whirlwind.

"Gee! Annie," she had exclaimed, as she came into the little parlour, with its prim Morris chairs and Mission sideboard, "I can't stick the winter out in Ferguson's Landing without one trip down. Put me up for a day or two. Sure, I can sleep on the couch. Anywheres. I'll put in a few movies; it'll cheer me up."

Her mother had seemed so excited, Lulu thought. She filled the room with her loud voice; in a minute her sister was doing things for her, bustling about. She had no place for this tornado of a woman, but before that magnetic, forceful will, she collapsed like a house of cards. She had been her sister's slave since she was a tiny child. She would be yet when they were both old women.

There are people like that, people who have grasped the truth that liberty and the enjoyment of the good things of life come only to those who take them by sheer force. Desire is their only monitor. They are the happy slaves of their appetites and the thought of self-denial fills them with a nausea. To such, self-renunciation is a sign of weakness. They are of the earth, earthy, creatures of primeval appetites, impulses, spites and treacheries, seldom redeemed by touches of true tenderness.

Such a woman was Mrs. Armstrong. During her stay in the city she disappeared into its heart twice – disappeared completely.

Lulu had come down to get the kitchen range going for her aunt. The Mission couch upon which she should have seen the sleeping form of her mother was empty, made up as she had made it up the night before. She had run to her aunt, thinking of accidents and such catastrophes that crowd into the chambers of the mind when danger threatens a loved one.

She had marvelled a little at the quiet way in which her aunt had taken the news. True, there had been a furrow between her soft eyes, but she had shown no sign of fear for her sister's safety. And, after noon, Mrs. Armstrong returned. She came in like a tornado, her loud voice filling the little house.

Yes, she had gone on to a cabaret with a woman friend she had not met for years. "No one you know, Annie, my child." Her hard eyes flickered from sister to daughter. They seemed to say: With babes like you a simple lie does well enough – "And so she put me up for the night . . . lives in a swell bungalow out Kitsilano way."

The second time what kept her out all night was a desire not to disturb the house. Oh, yes, Mrs. Armstrong had great faith in the capacity of the truthful to swallow lies. Experience had taught her that it was only the liar who had to be handled carefully, with craft, cunning. With them it was her

practice, wherever possible, to tell the truth. They disbe-
lieved her, which was what she wanted. She impressed truth
itself into her service; on her lips, those soft, voluptuous, but
slightly twisted lips, it lived as a lie.

Why had she returned?

Lulu asked herself that question as she walked through
the rain from the store to the hated house she never thought
of as home. Home is a place where one is alone, not a house
where men tramp in and out, day and night. Why had she
not begged to be allowed to stay in Vancouver? Why had
she weakly agreed to return to this life she hated?

And Kurt's face came up once more and all the details of
that monstrous dream.

CHAPTER VII

1.

Winter had gone from the Valley; the miracle of spring
was at hand. After his long absence the sun, benignly
warm, smiled out of a pale-blue sky like a friend returned. The
Valley, washed and nourished by the rains, sparkled in the sunshine. The whole land was emerald green. And the broad river lay like a silver scythe upon the floor of the Valley.

The annual miracle, the eternal cycle of the years; life out
of death; beauty out of desolation, through the centuries,
through the aeons.

And the great trees of the bush, they know it too. The sap
is risen in them and a new recording ring, unseen, encircles
each rugged trunk. The odours of the forest multiply. Yes,
it is the quickening to life, a universal burgeoning in the Valley, and beyond the Valley, in the bush.

At this season you may hear, close to the ground, that

ground which stirs and moves, the great heart of the earth. Mother Earth: the fecund, kindly giver of all life.

The mighty firs put forth the shrill green of their spring foliage; vividly it stands out against the sombre green of the forest's winter dress. The forest is a vast cathedral of many aisles whose pillars are those giant trees that soar straight up with interlocking branches. A Gothic cathedral, more splendid than any made by man, are these silent groves of spattered shadows; these groves that were God's first temples.

2.

The life of the settlement quickens in response to the coming of spring. From the new clearing on the hill the first fires show. The Newcomer has set about the task of burning, and plumes of dense smoke puff upwards against the wall of green, high into the still air. The ring of the axe sounds through the moisture-laden bush; the far-off boom of an explosion tells of men returning, after a winter of enforced idleness, to their battle against great stumps. It is dynamite against the forest.

From the river comes the staccato bark of gasoline engines. The men are out after spring salmon. All winter they have seen to it that their sixty-fathom gillnets were ready to hand. Their boats are like flies moving upon the river's silver scythe.

On the eastern horizon the ranks of the Cascades gleam white against the blue skyline. Far away, in Washington State, Mount Baker, the mountain of a dream, thrusts a conical head into the sky.

The sun moves across the sky, blessing the land as it goes. The earth responds to the benediction, its incense rising from the humid forest whose floor is carpeted with flowers. That pungent smell of the bush! That first smell, which stirs in man the memory of lives lived a million years ago.

3.

Old Chief Jim is sitting in the sun down on the Indian Reservation. He is sunning his spidery legs, his gaunt old body comforted by the warmth. His withered face is a map of many lines and his eyes are half-burnt, smouldering fires.

What does he dream of, this old man, this drunken old thief, this squaw-beater? Can it be that he is concerned with the past? That he is dreaming of the days before the white man came, with his implements and strange gods, and his fire-water?

Perhaps.

The Reservation is not cultivated, for no Indian Agent or admonitory priest could make of the Red man a tiller of the soil, a delver. The Red man will fish a little, sufficient for his needs, but that is all. Sometimes he will go forth with his slow and stealthy glide into the bush, carrying a pack. Then he will return silently, bearing his game upon his back.

Many things the white man has filched from him, even his gods. There is no totem at the Reservation. But there is a church, with a wooden cross from which the white paint has been washed and blistered through summers and winters.

The crucified one. He looks up at the symbol. Crucified! Not so bad, but he knew better tortures than that. Had heard them from his father. Tortures, good tortures, tortures better than a nailing to a wooden cross.

4.

The white man has taken most things from him and has brought him fear – fear of tortures, tortures worse than any he ever heard his tribe tell of, because they would go on, and on, and on.

Better far the worship of his own God.

So brooded the Old Chief, a chief with but twelve tribes-men for a following, a chief who had no seat to his pants, a chief with only an insatiable thirst for fire-water, a thirst engendered by the white man and now to be slaked only with lemon essence, vanilla, ketchup, curry powder.*

The sun wheeled over to the west and sat upon the tops of the trees like a golden ball. They stabbed it and it sank. A chill breathed over the shadowed face of the Valley and the sun was gone. From the river, from the damp grasses of the banks and from the lush undergrowth, rose the two-noted love song of the bullfrogs: *Wan-Ik! Wan-Ik!*, a sound which filled the silence of the Valley. *Wan-Ik! Wan-Ik!*: bullfrogs calling to their mates in the lush grass. Frogs, touched by the spell of spring, responding to the universal pulse of life, to the primeval law to multiply. *Wan-Ik! Wan-Ik! Wan-Ik!*

5.

Kurt had not built that old boat, but he had drawn it under the piles of the wharf, painted her a bit, tinkered with her gasoline engine, made her ship-shape. As the sun sank he slid alongside and tied up. He had fished the runs familiar to him since childhood. One cohoe, white and gleaming, lay on the slimy boards, its enamelled eyes open, but unseeing. A tiny rivulet of scarlet blood oozed from its still gills.

At first Kurt did not notice the figure looking down at him from the wharf. When he did, he scrambled out of the boat and shinned up to the low bank. From there he made his way over to the wharf where a figure was standing, dimly outlined against the evening sky.

"Why, Lulu, sure I didn't see you."

He stood, feet spread apart, took a small pouch from the

hip pocket of his canvas pants, produced a brown cigarette paper and slowly rolled a cigarette. All the while his eyes looked across the river as though he saw, there on the far bank, an object of absorbing interest.

"Guessed a little air wouldn't hurt me," answered the girl.

There was a pause. Then: "Nothin' doing on the river yet, Lulu, all I got was that feller – cohoe, a dollar at most."

So they stood, this brooding inarticulate Norseman who had done the inexplicable, smacking little Ole's behind, and this dark girl who had dreamed of an avenue of trees, a golden avenue and of a rolling ball of fire which became a face – the face of this silent fellow, this man whose words came out as though they hurt him.

"Well, I'm glad winter is done," she said, to cover with the sound of her voice the voice of her thoughts.

It had been a long winter of heavy rains.

"Fellows gone from your place?"

He asked the question casually but her quick ear caught and interpreted the emotion behind the simple words.

The sun had now sunk and night was stealing up on the Valley; the greens of the bush were now black against the hard blue of the sky. The familiar evening star shone out. The silver river had faded to grey and was now dark and sinister. It lapped, with little inky tongues, about the piles beneath their feet.

"They go tomorrow," she told him.

Simple question and simple answer. But each knew the heart of the other without the spoken word. For these two tongue-tied creatures, this man, strong and resolute in danger and this girl, gentle and yielding, were moved to the depths of their being.

Man and maid, the two forms moved into the shadows and merged.

"Lulu!"

One word, but it crumpled the defence of the girl. She answered: "Kurt," and it was like a cry from a great depth.

One word, but it burst the restraint of the man.

Behind them, its wide doors gaping black, stood the wharf barn with its store of baled straw, its potato sacks, its leaning sacks of wheat that seemed to huddle like a sleeping flock.

A rat scuttled under their feet as they moved into that friendly gloom and became one with the darkness.

Night, tenebrous night, fell upon the Valley and the shadowy land faded into an immensity of velvet darkness. Dim against the starry sky, the jagged outline of the tall firs was still visible: the edge of the sky was torn by them. The river, mysterious and cruel, flowed stealthily towards the waiting ocean.

Presently, from the west a lozenge of light travelled along the river-bank, revealing trees fantastically bleached and pursued by giant shadows. A rumble reverberated along the Valley; the clang of an engine bell leapt before it. The ground trembled with a deafening roar and the transcontinental express boomed on her way. The yellow lights of her long steel coaches winked their incredibly fast Morse, and were gone. Far along the Valley the boom died away to a faint murmur as of distant thunder. The fierce headlight of the great locomotive became but a luminous moth fluttering past the darkness of the bush. A long wailing whistle sounded from the bend. Then silence fell upon the Valley.

There remained only the monotonous note of the bullfrogs. *Wan-Ik, Wan-Ik, Wan-Ik:* down there in the wet grass, down there by the river-bank. Business of immense import was at hand.*

6.

Spring, and the rising of the sap; spring, and the first flowers of earth; spring, and the young salmon deep in the sable heart of the river, taking their first long journey into open waters from their spawning-ground high in the headwaters. The young salmon, strong and flashing, steer for the blue, salt Pacific for their four years of life, and carry in their torpedo heads the map of the ocean and the map of the rivers. These same young salmon would return after many days and, steering a true course, breathe through strong gills the waters of their pebbly native spawning-grounds, in the headwaters, in the tributaries, in the still lakes of the mountains.

A shadow like a wraith floated from the deeper shadow of the wharf house and, dividing into two silently moving parts, glided away into the night.

The song of the bullfrogs continued, monotonous, insistent; and the voice of the black tongues of the water, licking, licking, licking at the green slime of the piles.

Wan-Ik! Wan-Ik! Wan-Ik! croaked the frogs, humble instruments of the universal purpose which had worked its will on Kurt and Lulu too, there in the silent wharf house where the baled hay scented the damp night air.

CHAPTER VIII

1.

Johansson was everywhere now that it was spring. He had no time at all to work on his own place. He was out early and late, striding along with his lumbering gait, covering the ground at five miles an hour, his enormous hands swinging like clubs at the end of his long arms. A tall, ramshackle man in blue overalls, patched and weather-stained, and heavy elk-hide boots into which the ends of his pants were thrust. A man loose-jointed, held together and made strong by a nervous system of tempered steel. A man who lifted great weights by will power, and who invested every stump, every log against which he pitted his strength, with the attributes of an antagonist – an enemy to quit before whom in defeat would be disgrace.

Woods wanted Johansson up at his place to plough a patch; Bob England wanted him to clear the last five acres of his ranch so that he could clean it of roots by hand, then burn, harrow, plough, and sow in red clover. Little Tom Preedy – spending half his time in the dingy depot office, pawing his official railway forms and fretting – wanted his fruit trees pruned and wanted Johansson to do it. Stein wanted Johansson to take the end of a seven-foot cross-cut saw on a first growth fir so that he would have – long-sighted Stein! – dry wood in his shed for the winter which would come, for all this golden sun, for all this radiant warmth. Mrs. Armstrong wanted him to patch the leaking woodshed roof, and wanted him at once, having suffered the rain to come through without a murmur during the rainy season, when her thoughts were on something more enticing, with those men about the place.

Yes, they all wanted Johansson, for he was the only man at Ferguson's Landing who could turn his hand to any of the many crafts that a good peasant is master of.

These were long days for Johansson, days that began at early dawn. He would not allow his sick wife to leave her bed before sunup, but he himself was out and about, the stubble on his chin, by five, and sometimes earlier. He saw to the cow, stabled in a rough lean-to. It would turn as he smacked its flank. It was a wondrous smack, well worth that velvety-eyed beast's acknowledgment. It said: "You are my cow and I bought you. I used to dream of how I would have you some day. And I saved dollar by dollar; I chose you carefully, my beauty, and I saw many other cows before I parted with my good dollars for you. You are the half of my battle, half a man's living, you are, Cow."

But all he would say was: "Git over, Freda, git over, cloomsy. Was there ever such a cow, so stupid a beast?"

There was love and pride in those words. A cow! Milk and cream, and rich dung which gave you cabbages. Half a man's living: a cow.

Johansson did the chores out there in the patch behind his shack, the patch worn bare by his heavy boots coming and going with wood for the stove and logs for the sawing trestle. He milked the cow and cleaned her byre. He fed the chickens who were stalking now at the dung-heap.

He brought water from the well, where he had raised a rigging, upright and cross pole, weighted with a great stone at one end and with the well rope dangling free at the other. A way of saving work a little, letting gravity do its willing share. He came and went, carrying the buckets. He filled a tin tub, filled the enamel jug, filled the kettle, set the buckets down full. A little help for a sick woman. That was it.

Then the kindling for the fire. Cedar, quick to light, fast to throw out heat. And the boiling kettle, the bubbling porridge. Afterwards the tramp over the bush trail to a day of toil. Not to a day given grudgingly for hire, with an eye upon the sun on its slow westward journey. No, that was not Johansson's way. Just a day of work using every ounce of muscle, every fibre of nerve tissue. Not to please, but because that was his nature. For three dollars he gave ten dollars' value. The settlement knew it. He was a bargain – dirt cheap – so it was he had work for ten men.

Mary, his daughter, slept heavy in the profound sleep of the adolescent. She was her father's companion but he would have liked a boy, a lad to grow up and come into the place when it was fixed up as he meant to have it fixed up one day. Mary was clever. She did nothing in the little shack, that is, nothing heavy. She washed no clothes at the tub nor did she bake. She laid a simple knife and fork for each of them and put the bread upon the board: that was all. Mary was clever and she would grow to be a school marm. She was good at her books, always poring over them with her myopic eyes.

And Mrs. Johansson was proud of it – to have such a daughter. She sent all the way to Eaton's Store in Winnipeg for the girl's clothes. She selected them from the great catalogue. None of Blanchard's stuff for her!

"Our Mary is clever," she would often drawl.

2.

The Landing hummed with activity. Even Gentleman Woods did a little. His wife, who kept him, had built a great house, long and low, and very pleasant. It looked out over the Valley with a view of the mountains and the green sea of timber that rolled away into Washington State across the international line.

Mrs. Woods had said: "I'll lay the place out like a manor house set in parklands." And she hired every man in the place who was free to work, and thinned the great firs until the sloping ground looked like parkland in the making.

"Now you can manage the rest, Ted," she said. "The rest should not be too much for your heart, dear."

Woods, saturnine, gimlet-eyed, inscrutable, said: "I'll have it in grass in no time."

That was twelve years ago. And still, beneath those trees of the park which waited, the bracken raised its graceful, hated fronds. Every year it raised them a little higher. Somehow every spring Woods's heart troubled him. It was an obscure ailment which reasserted itself annually in the spring and lay fallow through the fall when little work remained to be done because of the coming rains.

This year even Gentleman Woods planned an enterprise. "My dear," he said, "I have decided to make an asparagus bed! I've looked around and found a good piece of soil. Ash, and so forth, and we'll soon have asparagus." It was wonderful the way he talked.

Yes, it was true, he had found a little patch at the back, among the stumps, where he had grubbed a kitchen garden without touching the stumps which made ploughing impossible.

About the use of blasting powder, indeed, about all violent exercise, he had firm opinions. "These roots," he would explain, his thin arms crossed on his chest, his pipe pointing, "these roots will rot in time and then one can grub them out with a mattock."

Gentleman Woods, who arranged his span of life as though he had taken on the attributes of immortality, would wait till the roots rotted away. Wait long enough, indeed, and the very forest would rot! Meanwhile, it was Woods himself who underwent that process.

3.

Everywhere the settlement hummed with life, but nowhere more actively than on Fuller's chicken ranch. It was, like its owner, plain but exceedingly efficient. The house, square and unpainted, was ugly; the land had been defaced by long, low colony-houses for the flocks of white Leghorns. White wings were everywhere – the only beautiful things in the place. From sun-up to sundown there was incessant cackling.

Most of the folk at Ferguson's Landing raised chickens: Fuller alone made them pay. He was certainly under the patronage of the deity of the fowls. His snow white birds developed none of the maladies which annually ravaged the flocks of less protected ranchers. He never had gapes or roup among his flocks; never did one of those proud pullets so far forget herself as to contract prolapsus of the oviduct. But the gods, even the gods of the fowls, are jealous gods: they exact a price. Fuller had grown every year more and more like an egg: his head was a brown egg with eyes, ears, nose and mouth. Even worse, when his little wife had her babies, they took after their father. Their little faces were like eggs, too: white eggs, too big for their little bodies.

He was busy about his incubator sheds, where the floors were a yellow carpet of teeming life. Hundreds of baby chicks, moving, scrambling, jostling.

Fuller watches them with his sharp eyes. "The survival of the fittest is the law of life," he says, "but I could never see why one shouldn't help it along. A chick that can't barge hard enough to fill its crop will grow to be a poor loafing sort of hen with no vitality."

He stoops and picks up a tender ball of golden fluff. Its little head, with its bright beady eyes, is between thumb and forefinger. It is dead. He has helped along the law. Yes, Fuller is the only man who understands chicken farming. "Those other fools keep hospitals," he says.

"At two years," he would declare, "a hen has done her job of work. Then she is ready for the crate and the Chinese dealer at Sapperton."

4.

The Reverend Mr. Corley was seen along the roads, driving the gift buggy with the staggered mare.* A figure in black, with a clerical hat and clerical collar. A man with a thin, cavernous face, full-lipped. His eyes were melancholy.

A missionary parson of the Church of England, with a little church a mile beyond the Landing. It galled him that the Presbyterians had it all their own way in Canada. He often thought about the blessing of the Establishment and wished himself back in secure, comfortable England.

A melancholy little man with grievances. "I get letters from my brother who is Rural Dean in Northshire," he told the Newcomer's wife the day he called, "and I write and tell him he little knows what pioneer work means."

He stretched his thin legs on that fine chesterfield, drank in this English atmosphere of a room, eyed the fair woman who gave him tea.

"The distances I have to cover!" he exclaimed. "Why, yesterday I drove twenty miles – enough for me and enough for Beauty, too."

Beauty was the staggered mare.

"I was out to see those Heggertys. Rough people. Having a struggle. I fear that man's an evil influence here."

That is how it was with the Reverend Mr. Corley. He was a busy man. He said it himself. "The busiest man in the Valley. I have a parish of one hundred square miles."

What he did not add was that most of those miles were standing timber that was in no need of his sermons, and offered no comforting afternoon tea.

It was the only call he made: the Newcomer's thinly veiled hostility and startling theology had nettled the little man.*

5.

The parson's wife, however, kept herself to herself. She was used to other things. She rarely left the parsonage, sitting reading in the garden or picking the berries planted by a vulgar hand. And when she shopped at the store she preserved the reserved bearing usual in Ealing.*

But the Landing, or so much of it as was Church of England, called upon her. She would receive the women in her drawing-room.

"So glad you were able to come . . ." she drawled, in the manner of the heroines of her Society novels.

There were her piano, her chintz-covered armchairs, her water-colours in trim frames, her bookcase and her photographs. A correct little room, it was, a refined little room. She sat there, a colourless little woman, suburban-bred, narrow-minded, dry, flat-breasted.

"One misses the social life, of course," she would mince at her victims, "but I feel that my husband is doing a Great Work, and that comforts one, don't you think?"

The women sat there, a trifle uncomfortably in those grand chairs, their work-calloused hands crossed in unaccustomed idleness and listened with the respect due to the clergyman's wife. They were just a little chilled.

But she was a lady, oh, dear, yes. She had photographs of a square-jawed man in naval uniform, and of another in the robes of a judge, and one in the apron and gaiters of a bishop.

"It's nice to bring the photographs of one's dearest friends with one when one comes so far from home," she suggested. And her guests, fidgeting upon their rumps, would answer: "It sure is," "You bet yer," "I'll say so," thus signifying agreement in homely phrases.

Unutterably vulgar, they were, these Ferguson's Landing women. They did not read anything, except the weekly *Family Herald and Star,* which came on the transcontinental from Montreal. They talked about disgusting ailments, mostly obstetrical, and about their men, as though they were animals to be fattened. They made their own clothes.

It all came of marrying a poor man.

That was how it was that Mrs. Corley was the only one

in Ferguson's Landing who did not know how often her husband drove down the road to the old Ferguson's Place where the Ellisons farmed. That was why she did not know how often he took Mary Ellison for an airing in his rig. A parson can do many things another man dare not do in Ferguson's Landing. One of them is to drive around with a pretty young woman, once a week, sometimes twice, and at times after nightfall.

CHAPTER IX

1.

By comparison with Johansson's shack the new house in the slashing was a fine mansion. Every time the Swede crossed the slashing he marvelled at it anew. His all-seeing eye travelled from old Anderson's house, fresh and yellow in the sunlight, to the chaos amid which it stood.

To build a house like that in the middle of a rough slashing! To spend more than a thousand dollars on a house big enough for ten – just for man and wife! To spend more than a thousand dollars on it – Stein said it had cost twelve hundred and fifty – aye, to build a house at all, when a two-roomed shack would have been enough! To build before clearing! A crazy proceeding to the experienced eye of the Swede.

But Johansson was humble in his mind; he was a simple man. He accepted the fact, completely past his understanding, that there were men who contrived to live, and to live fatly, without work. They did it by a mysterious process, the inner workings of which he had ceased to worry about.

Life to Johansson was a wresting of food from the soil. He

had seen his father do it, and in the old Swedish home he himself had learnt to labour young. At nine, he could wield a man's axe and at twelve he could put in a full day in the heavy loam behind a plough. At fifteen he could hump twenty miles and carry a man's pack.

Little time for book-learning, or for probing the mysteries of how to live without work. But there was a world beyond the bush, the wide world of Vancouver, which he had visited twice, a big bustling world where the men, all of them, wore white collars, drove fast motor cars, and ate in flash restaurants, paying a dollar or more for a meal. The Newcomer would be such a one, perhaps.

He had a friendly smile.

"Maybe, they don't need to work," suggested his wife. "I guess they're folk with money, that's it." There was no tone of envy in the slow drawl of the grey-faced woman. Envy, perhaps, implies vigorous desires for things denied. Mrs. Johansson had desires, but they were few. She would have liked to send a big mail-order to Eaton's Store in Winnipeg for clothes for Mary. Then, she longed for an American washing machine. And she would have liked to be able to sleep, and sleep, and sleep. Beyond that she had no desires.

Mary, wide eyes peering through the strong lenses of her steel-rimmed glasses, would listen to her parents' talk. She was a good girl, very quiet, and her face shone with soap. She was clever at her books, sitting through the long evenings poring over them, setting out in the morning, clean and neat, for the settlement school.

"He'll not clear that land unless someone shows him how," said Johansson.

He had come in caked with dirt and his immense boots stood beside the door, their tall tops drooped just as though the miles had wearied them as much as they had wearied the feet that travelled in them.

Mrs. Johansson stood by the stove stirring the vegetable broth that, with the bread, would make the evening meal.

"You've enough to see to without helping others," she said, "there's more than enough to be seen to on our own place."

And it was true. Johansson had fifty acres and the soil was good soil. For that reason the trees had flourished upon it, rearing up giant heads skyward, thrusting out giant branches. In girth they were fifteen to eighteen feet, those mighty trees. Remove that timber and there was a living on the land. He would be able to give up hiring himself out, become his own man, grow his own food, sell produce, save money.

He was now sitting with his feet in a tub of hot water, his great hands upon his knees. Yes, it was true enough that there was work to be done on the place, but a little every day made a difference in a few months.

And few were the days when this gaunt man did not accomplish some task after a day's work out as hired man.

It might be only a little thing, but it was done. A couple of fence-posts shaped up, pointed, tarred, and added to the growing pile; the chicken-house cleaned out and the dung cast upon the patch where there were to be strawberries (Bob England had promised him suckers for the fetching).* A few minutes of evenings in the wood-shed meant another rick of alder cut for the stove against winter. One could get work done – by doing it. It was Johansson's way. A patient man.

2.

During the winter, Johansson had worked for the outfit taking out the shingle-bolts. It had been a godsend, for without capital it is not easy to make a small holding out of bush land. A man must go slowly, working out, when work is to be had, doing as much as he can in between on his own place. He must live simply too because the land is greedy. The bush demands much from those who would wrest a living from her. Take her great trees, and she demands money: money for tools, money for blasting powder, money for fencing, money for seed.

And now the last of those bolts had gone down to the wharf, sliding and slipping on the rough alder corduroy road. Had he himself not pitched off the last bolt and heaved it triumphantly over the sill of the wharf into the chuck below?*

No money yet, but a wad to come. Enough to give him a few clear weeks to work upon his own place: he might hire Bob England's team and plough the five-acre bit. It would give potatoes for the winter.

He considered these things in silence as he dried his feet and pulled on his thick grey socks, considered them as he sat down to the table, laid with its clean red-and-white check cloth. His wife carried the bowls of broth from the stove and set them down upon the table, and the man, encircling his bowl with one arm, started to drink. His spoon was big and he made much noise.

"Mary," he said when at last he had lifted the bowl to drain the last drop and wiped the liquid from his lips, "figger out what I'll be gettin' from the contract people, sixty-five days at two dollars fifty."

Wasn't it splendid to have a girl like that? A girl who had book-learning, and who did ciphering in her head.

Both looked at the plain girl but neither saw her as such. To them, she was a superior being. They saw this marvel of their loins and wondered that they could have begotten her.

3.

The sawmills of Sapperton and Vancouver were fed from many sources. Many of them held concessions far from the railway lines; these concessions they worked with their own men, taking out the timber and running it to the river on their own spur-line, thrust through the bush to the timber limits. Others contracted out the cutting, took the timber at the wharfside, towed it down to their own mills. But any mill would give the "once-over" to a boom of logs at the mill-wharf.

The shingle-bolts which had gone down to Sapperton in that early spring from Ferguson's Landing were offered to the mill at their own wharf. With Vancouver building hand-over-fist there was a steady demand for shingles. The mill was working full time, and its circular saws screamed a crescendo throughout the day.

To the Swede, this money which he had earned working through the bad winter weather was already in the can behind the cookstove. It was money banked. He had merely to call down to the store and get it. It had been promised for today; it would come up with the mails on the Agassiz local.

He drew on his great boots again and set out. Dusk was on the bush and its shadows were deepening on the still air. He disappeared into the gloaming, walking with a lumbering gait, swinging his unlit storm lamp.

What was it Mary had said? A hundred and sixty-two dollars – and – was it fifty cents? He would buy snuff for that fifty cents. It was an unheard-of extravagance!

There was a crowd of men about the door of the store when the Swede arrived and all were talking at once. They were the men who had worked on the contract through the winter, come, like him, to draw their promised pay.

"Sons of guns, that's what they were."

"You mean we were a lot of goldarn easy-marks!"

"How the hell were we to know they were going to beat it?"

"By the Hokey! but I'd like to git that son of a gun and teach him to vamoose."

They were angry men, men cheated of money earned by

hard toil under bad conditions. They had a right to their grievance and they expressed themselves as men do under such circumstances, with varying degrees of eloquence or crudity.

Johansson pushed his way into the store. And they greeted him with the bad news. "Bilked us, they have! All that goldarn work for nothing."

"Skinned out with the dough."

"Gone across the line."

Everybody had to say his say. Nobody had anything useful to suggest. Blanchard listened, standing behind the counter, his two arms upon it. He had made those fellows pay cash for their tools and stores. He wasn't out of pocket: he felt friendly to all the world. Another man's trouble! What pleasure there is in that!

But Johansson's slow-moving brain could not take it in. He had done the work, he had performed his share in the contract. It was his money. Why hadn't they paid him? He had nothing to say because he was slow to words at all times, and disaster had always found him mute. It found him mute now. But for all his lack of words, he was smitten.

That money meant so much to him. It meant a share of spring on his own place with freedom to get on with his own work. It meant a year saved: if he went at it he would be able to get a potato patch of five acres planted and as many in clover, which meant feed for the cow next winter.

And now, so it seemed, it was gone. "There's no mail from those fellers?" he asked, but he knew as he asked the question that it was a stupid one. Perhaps that was why Blanchard smiled.

The lamentations from the men by the door broke out afresh: they were telling a new arrival of the shameless swindle, using the same oaths, curses, imprecations.

A big, burly man was the newcomer, dressed in a blue serge

suit and wearing a felt hat. His fat red face was shrewd and good-natured, his little eyes were sharp and bright. It was Mann from the brickyard, Mann whose name was none too good, a man with the reputation of a cheat and twister.

Johansson looked at him. He thought: One of those who earn without work, one of the clever ones. But what was he saying? Mann, big, fat, soft and self-indulgent, stood in the centre of a group of men with muscles like iron, men who could have picked him up and thrown him into the river without puffing or blowing about it. Mann, dominating the store by virtue of that intangible quality which makes one man master, another servant, had soft muscles but an alert brain.

His hard voice cut across the babble and the talkers ceased talking to listen.

"Well, Mr. Mann, what is it you say we should do?"

"How's that, Mr. Mann, sure, we can't be stung like this?"

"There's a law, ain't there?"

Angry voices.

To Mann, the situation was one presenting small difficulties. What fools these fellows were! Damn children, they deserved to be stung! But the world would be a hard place if there were no suckers in it! A hard place for Mann.

"No good saying what you oughter have done, fellows," he was saying. "You want to get busy now."

"Well, shoot, if it's anything we can do, we'll do it all right."

Mann smiled a superior smile.

"Telegraph a description of the two fellows who were running the contract to the Vancouver police, and say you expect they can be found on the transcontinental that pulls out at 8:50 tonight."

To have thought of that! Johansson looked at this fat fellow, this man who was said to be a bad influence on the settlement, always dead broke or spending money in lashings. That might all be true; but there it was, he had shown how to get that money. And it was simple enough – if you could have thought of it.

There was a movement from the store.

"We'll catch old Preedy at the depot, if we hurry."

Fifteen of them, they set out to send that telegram.

They were laughing and talking now. The money was as good as in their hands.

But Johansson did not go. He had purchases to make: a bit of calico to match, stay-laces, a tin of vaseline for his corns, lard, a new axe-half.

Mann was talking to Blanchard now: "And did they sting Mrs. Armstrong for their board?" he was asking.

That bland and guileless face of Blanchard!

"No, Mrs. Armstrong was in today to pay her account; she got her money all right," he said. His eyes and voice helped you to read a double meaning in his words.

"Ah, I'll go along on my way back. She will likely know something that may help those fellows out."

Blanchard shifted onto his other foot, the faint ghost of a smile came and went about the corners of his mouth: "Well, as a matter of fact, Mrs. Armstrong went down to Vancouver on the morning local," he said.

Mann considered this for a moment, his bright eyes narrowed. "In that case those fellows will waste their money sending a telegram," he said. "But if they combed the hotels down on Cordova Street, I wouldn't mind saying they'd find what they want."

And Mann turned and made his way out into the still spring night. A burly fellow he was, one who understood everything.

And Johansson, holding the calico in his great calloused hand, considered the matter. He considered it as he climbed the steep trail up to his place. But he gave it up: it was beyond his simple brain.

His wife was sitting in the chair, by the stove, rocking herself gently, as he entered. "So you got the money?" she asked.

"Huh."

That was Johansson's way: one word, where one sufficed.

The woman got up from her chair and took down from its concealed ledge behind the stove-pipe, a tin canister. She held it out to the man.

"Time you were in bed," he said, taking it from her. "You gotta kinder tired look these days. I'll fix it."

He took the canister which was their bank. The woman went.

"Time enough to break the bad news to her in the morning." Worrying a sick woman at bed-time. What was the use of that?

And Johansson went out into the woodshed and set about splitting kindling for the morning. Thereafter he fetched water from the well, took a look at the cow and a long, shrewd look at the still evening sky which was a dome of blue supported by the spiked walls of the encircling bush.

There were things beyond understanding.

CHAPTER X

1.

Spring comes early in the Pacific slope. It is a constant season without the wanton moods of tarrying winter. The warm breezes of the Pacific breathe upon the timbered mainland and the sun looks out of the clear blue sky, warm and with a promise of heat.

After the mist-shrouded winter, the watery seeding of the

skies, the Valley shines resplendent: it is as though it has come newly from the hands of the Creator.

By March the little orchards among the timber are white with cherry-blossom: it falls, and clouds of white butterflies flutter from the trees, drift with the breeze, and sink, as white shells do through water, to the green earth. The apple trees follow fast upon the cherries, and the little orchards are pink.

In the bush itself the tangled undergrowth is stirring. It has come alive. The moist earth is redolent of the pungent smells of growing vegetation: the floor of the forest is starred with the white faces of anemones. The bracken has thrust up its pale fronds through the rotten vegetation – a ghostly dwarf forest on the floor of the bush. Vine maples, with tenuous and tangled stems, writhe upward from a bed of moisture.

2.

Away back in his remote slashing Heggerty is grubbing among the stumps with a mattock. If it's but a little bit of ground it's better than no ground at all.

By the door of the shack young Joe Heggerty sits, cross-legged, a basin held between his knees. In one hand he holds a large knife. A very busy boy, cutting the potatoes, ready for father to seed. Each one must have an eye: "How else would it see to grow?" That was what his mother said. "Well, how would it?"

He watches his father as he works and the soapy faces of the split potatoes slither through his hands into the big dish.

It is little Joe who hears the sound of cracking twigs and points with his big knife to the bush. Heggerty straightens his back and stands erect, looking towards the hidden trail that winds into the heart of the timberland.

Strangers seldom come that way, for he made the trail himself, made it for his own purposes, to walk on and to pack in his junk. And these are peculiar strangers indeed: two yellow men. They come up to Heggerty with blandly smiling faces, as though he and they were old friends meeting under propitious circumstances after a long parting. Spruce little men, they are, in smart tailored suits, green velour hats and bulbous-toed American boots.

How much land has he got? Well, he might have a hundred acres, more or less, but since the Dominion surveyors were thieves and liars to a man, probably less.

"How can I say for certain when I've never yet found but two survey stakes?" he asks with habitual truculence.

"Maybe you sell?" The speaker smiles blandly.

So they want to buy? So that's it!

For how many months has Heggerty harangued his little wife upon the hardship of their lot: "Planted down at the back of beyond in the perishing bush."

How often has he put in futile hours weaving the dreams that will never materialize, the plaints that start always in the same manner with the eternal "If" of the fool?

And now here are these two little yellow fellows smelling after the place. Heggerty thinks: "Well, by God, I'll sell if I get my price." Aloud he says: "This is a damn good layout and don't you forget it. Were you thinking of buying?"

"Maybe," says the little fellow, who seems to be spokesman and arbiter. "How much you want?" The little man, thrusting his hand into his waistcoat pocket, produces a card and bows, German-wise, from the hips, and all the while he is smiling, smiling, smiling.

Heggerty takes the card and holds it in his hand.

"How much I want?" he repeats with a stupid air. "Well, now, that's not easy to answer. I must figger all the capital I put into the place. There's the building, the clearing done, the well I dug."

The little men listen and smile.

"How much?" again asks the spokesman.

"Lock, stock and barrel?" parries Heggerty while, in his cunning head, he is trying to screw himself up to an unheard-of price. "Well, if I was to give up this nice little place – and I don't say I would, mind you, for I'm well fixed here and me wife likes it fine – it 'ud have to be a good price."

"How much? How many dollar an acre?" The smiling face, the unblinking eyes, the wide mouth and the flashing teeth. "You say how much."

Hard folk to haggle with, these Japanese, with their "How much?" "How much?'" all the time. Conflicting emotions crowd Heggerty's mind, and little Joe, looking up at his father, reads that familiar face.

Sure, he wants to sell, to git out of it, out of the solitude, the want and lack of everything, back to a town where there's bars and pool-rooms and dice to be shaken for cigars, and street corners where there's talk. To the city where there's the cinema and newspapers, and things happening all the time.

It is an alluring vision which superimposes itself upon the smiling face of the verdant bush. A pleasant prospect! Heggerty contemplates it unhampered by any shadows of practical problems: how he would live in the enchanted town; how he would house, clothe and feed his family. Who would give him work and, having the chance, what work he could competently perform. These things worry him not at all as he calls up that glowing prospect: the chance of ready cash.

And, pursuing these images of a paradise within reach, there comes the voice of the bush: What now is it saying to this man, speaking by its pregnant silences, the silences that spoke to the first man?

Does it not say: "Heggerty, here, near the heart of nature, you are where you belong. You are but a creature of the past, a primitive man, cousin of the cave man. You have fallen into the twentieth century, but you belong to the days, long gone, when the tribe was the human unit. You are no citizen, for you know not the obligations of that state, nor is your cunning brain adapted to the struggle for life away from me. Heggerty, you had better turn these smiling men away."

All these things did the silent bush whisper to the settler. He hesitated, considered for one moment that he should call his wife into consultation, and decided against it.

"I'll take fifty dollars an acre," he announced, "and not a cent less! No, sir!"

The two little men smile. "We go look about," says the spokesman, and they turn, followed by Heggerty, and scramble over the debris of the slovenly slashing, vaulting great trunks with incredible agility, side-stepping holes, leaping on to fallen trees, running down their trunks like brown chipmunks.

They return. "Your deed good: we buy," says the spokesman.

Heggerty's heart leaps within him, and then drops like a shot partridge. He has sold! And as soon as that thought is grasped by his slow-moving mind, a pang of regret stabs him to the heart. The place, squalid, for all the garniture of nature, slovenly, eloquent of ineptitude, is suddenly dear to him, and he has sold it. He looks down at his little son and reads into those wondering eyes a reproach which is not there.

The voice of the Japanese recalls him: "For thirty dollars," he is saying, "when your title is good."

Heggerty taps himself upon the chest, upon the apron of his stained overalls: "Me sell to you for thirty dollars an acre? NO, SIR!"

The little man smiles: "That is all I pay," he answers, and stands there, a little in front of his companion, smiling like a gargoyle. "Thirty," he repeats, "and too much then."

3.

Thus it was that Heggerty sold his place to the first Japanese to settle in Ferguson's Landing. An hour later the news had spread from one end of the settlement to the other.

Stein had seen the Japanese get off the train and, curious, he had followed them to see which trail they took. He saw them go to Heggerty's. An hour later, he himself appeared in the cutting, stroking his long beard and looking about him with the air of a government official. Yes, he had come to see whether Heggerty could do a job of work for him. No? Then no matter. A good place, and he would be soon getting a plough in, eh?

So Stein got the news first and carried it to Tom Preedy at the depot. And Tom Preedy took it, with the mailbags, to the store and Blanchard broadcast it thence.

To Heggerty, it was a home sold precipitously and impetuously. One more in a series of foolish moves that made up his feckless way of life and which pulled his faithful little wife and children, happily unaware, along the weary road of failure.

Yet that deal in the slashing on that bright spring morning was much more than a mere buying and selling of land. It was a chapter in the history of Ferguson's Landing, a turning-point, an economic and historic landmark.

4.

They talked about the coming of the Japanese consul for days. Old Man Dunn it was who explained the business to the crowd in Blanchard's store.

"It's the Japs' purpose to get this Province by peaceful penetration," he boomed.

Blanchard eyed him askance and limped off, murmuring to himself: "A man who took money out of the store and lived like that."

"Yes, the Japanese were out to get the whole Pacific slope." On and on the voice boomed. Their Island Empire had drunk the strong waters of Western ambition. They had their modern army, their great navy.

"Which, don't forget, has walloped the Roosians.* An' they have their elementary schools: Western civilization grafted on to the feudalism of Nippon," he boomed. "That's why the Tokio government sends her consul up into the Valley. The Japanese settler merely has to locate his place, report to the consul, get it inspected and passed, and his government advances him the money to buy."

This time, for once in his life, the Sage was not striving to convert his audience. They believed him, and they believed him because they knew what he said was true. "In the end they'll get the whole of the productive land of the Province, and what they haven't got the Chinese will have, and if there's any left, why, then the Hindus will have that, and we can clear out."

Old Man Dunn moved off towards the door and sent his last shaft over his burly shoulders: "But don't you forget, when you start cursing these invaders, that not so long ago we stole this country from its rightful owners. We stole it from the Redskins. They didn't people it and neither have we. It's going to belong to the Japanese because they've got the sense to take it."

5.

So it was that Heggerty passed from Ferguson's Landing. There were folk who said it was a good riddance. And these latter backed up their view by pointing to the astounding

"The Japanese settler merely has to locate his place, report to the consul, get it inspected and passed, and his government advances him the money to buy." (p. 93). Crowds at the CPR Station, Vancouver, awaiting the arrival of the Japanese Prince Fushime (1907).

change which, in the course of three months, staggered the settlement.

The Japanese had come in with his little red-cheeked wife and chubby baby. How had he done it? Nobody knew. But in three months from the day the wagon lumbered up the trail with his household goods (upon which rested, like a funeral urn, his cask of *saké*) he changed Heggerty's slashing into a ten-acre garden of strawberries.

Old Stein crept up the trail to look about. He reported that the ten acres was the cleanest piece of ground in the Valley. "Clean as a whistle, and planted in young strawberry plants," he announced.

So it was that the first Japanese came to the Landing, a little smiling yellow man who kept himself to himself. A settler who settled with a vengeance, but who did not mix. Yes, indeed, the Japanese kept to himself. A new family unit in the Valley, but not new human material to be absorbed into a new land. The Japanese it was who absorbed the Valley.

A little man, five foot nothing, who could take a two hundred pound weight lift, and whose arms were knotted with mighty muscles. A little man who, when the *saké* coursed in his veins, would show you the egg of muscle that swelled at the bend of his arm and grin at your surprise. A little man who could use the edge of his hand like a mallet.

He was an object of profound curiosity at first. Stein probed his ways of life with revolting conscientiousness, bringing every new item of interest to the store at the crowded hour. He described how the little man, having got his ten acres of strawberries planted, knocked off for a day and waxed merry on his *saké*. He could be heard singing three miles off.

And it was Stein who solved the mystery of the second building which the Japanese had put up as soon as he took possession – a rough shake shack with its floor a foot above ground. From behind a tree Stein had seen the woman crawling beneath the shack and had noted her purpose.* He had seen the Japanese, yellow and gleaming like a statue of warm marble, step out of that shack. A glistening, miniature Hercules.

Thus Ferguson's Landing learnt that the Japanese was a mighty little man, who took a daily vapour-bath. There were many other things they had to learn of him. For he was to teach them many useful lessons. The first was an economic truth, which is this: that the low standard of living of the Oriental in a white man's country makes him master of markets, a competitor against whom it is not possible to compete.

CHAPTER XI

1.

The busybodies of Ferguson's Landing saw little of the newcomers during the many months. Columns of blue smoke were seen rising into the still air above the bush in the new clearing. Once or twice the voice of the Newcomer floated down the slope. He was calling "Fire!", the warning of the land-clearer about to blow a dynamite charge. "Fire! F-i-r-e!" the voice of the Newcomer drifted over the Valley, and the reverberating boom shook the timber.

When he came down to the store now his jeans were no longer spick and span. The bright blueness of them was faded by the August sun. The elk-hide boots, into which the trousers were thrust, were now darkened and scratched. The once-smart Homburg hat was now shapeless, drooping, and peppered with cigarette holes, burnt there to let the air in.

It was at Blanchard's that the Newcomer struck up a friendship with Old Man Dunn. The two would walk back along the dusty road to Dunn's ranch, now a jungle of lusty grass, bracken, and dock weeds.

Old Mann Dunn liked an audience, but at Blanchard's his neighbours heard him with a veiled hostility. The Sage was none too popular. His views damned him – and so did his neglected place.

"Man never learns," he was complaining oracularly to the slim Englishman who walked at his side. "Every time civilized man, so-called, settles in a new country he sets about ruining it." The old man lumbered along. "He brings all the bad old ideas of the Old World and leaves the best behind."

The two men turned in at the gate that hung upon one hinge and walked through the long coarse grass of the orchard towards the sad-faced house. They sat down on the doorstep, facing the orchard beyond which ran the river. The trees were like old men upon crutches, with their wooden props to take the weight of their too-luxuriant branches.

"Every time white men enter a new land God gives them another chance," he went on.

The old man thumped his two hands down upon his legs: "Think of it! Think of this country! Here there is everything – an ideal climate, mineral wealth, billions of feet of magnificent timber, great waterways, fertile soil – everything. A race of wise men, settling here, could have made of this country a Garden of Eden. It is the Garden of Eden. And what have they done with it?"

The young Englishman returned the old man's enquiring stare with a hint of embarrassment. He was thinking: "Well, and what have you done with it? With this corner, this ranch, overgrown, neglected, this by-word of the settlement?"

The Newcomer said: "You could scarcely expect a race of Platos. After all, one must march by the slowest."

"In the Old World they have inherited their social evils from the days when men knew little of statecraft. And now they are cudgelling their brains how to rid themselves of that rotten legacy. But here, in Canada, they had a clear field. They could have built grand cities and towns." He snorted his contempt: "They will tell you that they have done so; but where in Europe will you find slums worse than those of Old Quebec, Montreal or Winnipeg?"

The old man thrust his beard forward: "Eh? or in Vancouver itself, a mushroom town, built overnight?"

"They've handed their heritage over to the grafter, the land-grabber, the commission-snatcher. They've sold themselves to the big corporation which has no soul and is out for profits and more profits. And their politicians? – Riddled with graft!

"Yes, that's what they've done to Canada. And now the

few men who are thinking clearly are seeing it. Yes, their universities have bred a few thinkers – McGill and Toronto. But the damage is done."

Old Man Dunn turned towards the young Englishman and put a gnarled hand on his leg: "You're starting out to make a home out of the bush," he said. "You look forward to seeing a return for your work and for your investment. If you make this place your permanent home, you will raise your children here. British children, Canadian-born they will be. Well, what are your prospects?"

The Newcomer made a mental note that Old Man Dunn overlooked one factor – work. If one worked one would be bound to make good. Work, say, like that fellow Johansson.

"I know what you are thinking," said the old man, "you are thinking that you will win through by hard work – that hard work always has its reward: Samuel Smiles stuff.* Well, I hope you do. This country needs, more than anything else, settlers from the Old Country. Aye, and from the rest of old Europe too."*

He paused: perhaps he had spoken too freely, perhaps it was hardly fair to damp the ardour of this man just starting to fight the bush.

"When I came here thirty years ago," he went on, slowly and without the passion which had made his deep voice boom as he denounced the evils which had crept into the new land, "I worked hard." He waved his hand towards the field where grazed a Holstein cow. "I cleared twenty acres of heavy timberland; I planted trees and berry bushes. I raised livestock."

He shrugged his heavy shoulders: "Now I do just sufficient to keep me and the wife going. My time is put in reading and thinking – and trying to make folk see the way things have gone and the way they are going. Behind my back they call me The Sage. But they don't mean that to signify that they respect me. No. They think I'm a lazy old man, that's all."

And Old Man Dunn rose stiffly. "Well, let 'em," he concluded. "Let 'em! Little folks, in a little settlement, with little minds and little ideas – when they've got any ideas at all!"

The Newcomer picked up his sack and set off. As he came out onto the dusty road, now pencilled with giant shadows from the inclining sun, the gaunt figure of Johansson came into view. Johansson, swinging his great hands like clubs. Johansson, a day's work done, going to milk a cow, to saw wood, to add a little to that fencing, to do a bit of hoeing. They walked along together in silence.

It was the first of many such talks, talks from which the Newcomer was able to sketch in the life of this rugged old miner until, at last, he saw Dunn clearly against his variegated background.

The dreamy pony-boy in the Yorkshire pit. The old parson who saw in the coal-smeared boy the makings of a scholar. Those long nights in the dingy cottage spelling out the Greek grammar by candlelight. The encouraging words of the old scholar. The dream of Durham University. The mine disaster that took away the bread-winner, and the years in the mine, first as pony-boy, then as hewer.

All this was a matter of time and growing intimacy. In the end the whole pieced together as the odyssey of a frustrated man. The first adventure overseas, the burly young man in revolt against intolerable conditions, seeking a new land; and the fair and slender girl standing beside him on the deck of the emigrant ship.

Yes, all this Old Man Dunn sketched in, bit by bit, casually. "For a time I worked in the lead mines of Nebraska." And he would hold out his hand which shook with an incipient palsy, "Yes, that's why I quit that work: poison. A man can stand it just so long – but no longer."

And that episode when he and his wife had gone south to Florida. Blue skies and golden orange groves, but no market for the fruit. And the ache for the sound of British voices. And then the trek to the North-West.

Failure, in a word. Restlessness, the eternal quest and defeat. And yet defeat without surrender.

"In the philosophy of the Western world," he would declaim, "men worship material success. The how don't matter, so long as a man can steer clear of the penitentiary. What he is, nobody ever asks. They say, 'What's he worth?' That's their criterion in this country. Nobody cares whether he has harmed the community, whether he has fleeced simpletons, worked raw grafts, pushed the country a bit further along the road to damnation. They worship money success and that's all there is to it. Canada has become the land of the commission-snatcher and the back-scratcher. She calls out for workers. What she really means is that she is running short of mugs to rob."

But it was Old Man Dunn's failing that he did not select his audiences. He proclaimed his doctrine (that service was the root principle of any community claiming to be civilized), and he boomed his denunciation of the men who took, but gave not in return, whoever might be listening.

In that way he made a mortal enemy of Carlton Tidberry, MLA, the member of the Legislative Assembly in whose constituency Ferguson's Landing lay. To be called a "no-good grafter" to his face was too much for Mr. Tidberry. It happened to be true.

2.

In August Ferguson's Landing set about harvesting. It was the busiest month of all the year for the folk of the settlement, this month when river, fields, orchards and bush yielded up their spoils. A good August meant a winter without want in the Valley. It meant money laid by, and good pork salted and hanging in the acrid smoke of green alder. It meant a full pantry: bottled fruits and gay rows of jam jars, salmon smoked to a mahogany hue, sound potatoes pitted down, winter cabbages, a sack of wheat beside the iron kitchen stove, and apples in the barn, laid out on dry straw.

A good August in the Valley meant all these things for the rainy season, for the grey months when the sodden Valley drank the rains and the bush answered with its mysterious voice.

It was a good August in the Valley when Mrs. Armstrong disappeared into Vancouver and Kurt Olson returned from the North and fished the river (and came out once more top boat), and the Newcomer got a tiny patch of potatoes in and his woodshed finished.

A good August, yes, so much so that people even forgot about the defaulting contractors who had skipped out without paying and under the heat that poured down on the Valley from the cloudless dome of the sky, with its sun like a fiery eye, the road gang worked out their taxes with pickaxes and shovels and sang ribald songs as they laboured on the growing road.

The air of the Valley stirred no leaf nor blade of grass; the workers moved about in yellow fields that waited the quickening breeze. From the floor of the Valley heat waves quivered tremulously into the still air: they were like the pale ghosts of living flames, like opaque swords brandished by an unseen host.

Only in the eternal shadows of the bush was there cool.

Small fields to be mown by hand, and larger fields to be reaped with the machinery of the Harvesters' Company (bought on the instalment plan – and sometimes lost through non-payment of instalments). Lush orchards, heavy with crimson fruit, and pickers moving in the shade of big straw sun-bonnets, women and children packing the white wood boxes with graded apples and pears.

Raspberries, blackberries, loganberries, red and black currants, and strawberries that ripened to perfection on those sunny southern slopes. Long days of work in heavy, languorous air.

But the evenings felt cool when the day's work was done, and Kurt Olson would perhaps be persuaded to take out his concertina and play in the great kitchen of the Olson place so that Old Ole might beat time with his stick as he loved to do. And Blanchard would lie back in his broken chair, in the little paper-littered room behind the store, and play his wheezy gramophone; while, up at the Reservation, the Old Chief would sit in his shack and drain off his last assignment of hooch, and dream his dreams.

A queer little community of small ranchers they were, these folk of Ferguson's Landing. Why, many of them were so pettifogging that they boasted not even an old hack to take their crops down to the CPR depot.* Instead they trudged the miles of dust-laden road or rough bush trail from the outlying clearings, arms taut on home-made wheelbarrows.

Not hard work, as work is counted in the Valley, but work needing skill, care and close attention to details.

Why was it that the gooseberry crops of everybody failed, blighted by the mildew? Only Fuller knew that, Fuller whose giant gooseberries fetched a big price at Sapperton market. Only Fuller knew, Fuller of the infinite patience; Fuller with the secret of the Valley tucked away in his egg of a head. As for the others, they grubbed up their bushes and cursed the hairy, yellow fruit that refused to grow for them.

So summer passed.

3.

Boys and girls brought up together in a small community may fall in love with each other unawares. The familiar-

ity of childhood masks the emotions that come after adolescence. It is possible to love without knowing it, so subtle
is the transition from childish affection to the love of man
and woman.

It had been like that with Kurt and Lulu. As the children
of a remote settlement they had tramped together to the
school, sat together on the rough plank bench, copied from
each other's slates, swapped toys, fished small creeks together,
romped in the fields at harvest time.

Later they had danced (that was after the hall was built)
and Lulu had learnt to play the piano a little. Kurt had become a money-earner and shyly brought his Lulu presents
– his first nugget (acquired during his first rush to the
goldfields), and a coloured kimono bought in the Chinese
Quarter on Pender Street in Vancouver. Such things as that.

Being a woman, Lulu had explored her emotions first.
Kurt crept into her dreams and her dreams became vivid affairs – sometimes merely absurd, sometimes frightful, always
fantastic, and ever with the face of Kurt before the end.

She built for herself a dream-world for the waking hours
and set Kurt in it. As she went about the house, silent and
self-contained; as she gathered up the fruit in the dappled
shade of the orchard; as she tramped about the settlement,
it was always Kurt who went with her. How slow he was,
that Kurt, with his lumbering body, his broad, short-fingered,
clever hands, his keen blue eyes.

So often had he made love to her in that world of her own
making, so often had she responded to his overtures, that
when the time came for her dream-life to merge with reality,
that surrender, so swift, so easy, in the friendly darkness of the
spring night, there in the straw-scented wharfshed, had seemed
but the most wonderful of many splendid adventures.

But Kurt had changed since then. It was unaccountable.
Sometimes he came along the dusty road in the evening in

his soiled work-clothes and stopped by the broken fence. He talked as though nothing had happened between them, shyly avoiding her eyes. And Lulu, waiting for those unspoken words, was shy too with him.

"Guess your mother will be staying some time down Vancouver?" he would ask, and then he would go through the chronicle of the settlement's news.

"There's been a bit of fire out at X Limit," he would say, or "Your Dad's let this orchard go to hell, ain't he?" or "Dad's carving a wood doll for little Ole," or "Johansson's wife's sick again."

Not lover's talk: no. But Lulu always told herself that this was because Kurt was a shy man, a man who had no fine words. She knew he loved her, and that was all she wanted to know; she could supply the fine speeches in her brain, spinning them through the days, throughout the long nights, sometimes asleep, sometimes lying wide awake, a little afraid of life, with that deep blue square of night looking in at her from the window, and the murmur of the bush, soft and low, sad and melancholy as thoughts of death.

But when August passed and September came, something had to be done. Mrs. Armstrong was back again, a whirlwind drawing to her door the unattached men of the settlement. The sound of laughter came from the white house with the stained walls, and once more the sound of singing after nightfall. In contrast to her mother's vivid personality, Lulu moved about, a colourless figure, hardly noticed by the men.

But if the men saw nothing, the keen eye of Mrs. Armstrong saw everything that was to be seen. The girl was ailing, and there was something on her mind. Mrs. Armstrong hated her as only a mother who has ardour without youth can hate a daughter.

So it was that when the affair could be no longer concealed, she did not spare the frightened girl.

She confronted her one morning when Lulu, grey-faced and trembling, had collapsed into the rocking-chair.

"You quiet girls are all the same," she sneered. "I've seen what was wrong with you for some days. But I gave you a chance to speak first. As soon as my back was turned – shameless!"

Lulu covered her face with her hands and made no answer, rocking herself to and fro. How could she explain? What could she say? She had deceived herself all along, with her amazing power of denying reality, of escaping into her world of make-believe. And now, with brutal words, the truth was rammed home, without mercy, by her mother.

"And who, may I ask, is the father of this coming brat?" her mother continued. She was in a white heat of anger and shot her questions at the cowering girl as she clattered among the dirty dishes.

Lulu had been waiting day by day, week by week, for Kurt to speak. At first she believed she understood his reticence. He was as bashful as she was, she told herself. He would speak tomorrow. She had put herself in his way, craftily, with the deep cunning of a woman in love. She had created opportunities for him. She had made it clear that now she belonged to him.

And Kurt had made no response. Not quite the offhand, friendly Kurt, but a Kurt who held back. A Kurt who would have been glad to cancel the past had that been possible? She wondered. A Kurt who chafed at the present? Perhaps. A Kurt who feared the future a little? Puzzling questions, and no answer to them at all.

She would never reveal his name to her mother. Something held her back. It would be disloyalty and it would be desecration of a secret life she had created to escape her mother's enveloping personality.

"I can't tell you who it is," she answered, "so it's no good cursing at me. If you like I'll go away. Go down to Vancouver to Aunt Annie. She will take me in and no one here need know. I could get work in Vancouver afterwards."

"Yes, of course, your aunt will be delighted to have a young girl in the family way. People always do like that sort of visitor, especially when she's not married."

Mrs. Armstrong abandoned her dish-washing and stood, arms on hips, before the girl rocking in the old chair.

"I'm going to know the name of that man," she shouted. "You're going to tell me if I have to shake it out of your miserable body. Who is it?"

But Lulu made no answer. She had slowly slid forward in the first faint of her life.

Mrs. Armstrong looked at the huddled figure of the girl. There was no pity in her eyes and she made no move to ease her. But her mind was working rapidly, reviewing the men of the settlement whom she knew so well. A moment's thought gave her a list of twelve, and it might be any one of them. She knew the rest and was sure they were safe. Kurt Olson was not one of the twelve.

"Little wretch," she apostrophized the unconscious form. Then to herself: "To think of this, when I had such a good time in Vancouver, too! A nice mess to come back to!"

CHAPTER XII

1.

Vancouver, as any up-and-coming, hundred-per cent efficient citizen will tell the stranger, is the Last Great City of the Last Great West.* And the panegyrist, imbued with local patriotism, will indicate just where his city "puts it across" Calgary, Winnipeg, Toronto and Montreal.*

ENTRANCE TO VANCOUVER HARBOUR

"The magnificent natural anchorage which would comfortably house the navies of the world . . ." (p. 107). Entering Vancouver harbour through the First Narrows: a photo from 1908. On the right: Prospect Point lighthouse, sans Seawall. Note the Union Jack (very significant) on the left.

"Yes, sir, Vancouver sure is the Pearl of the Pacific. Now the Panama Canal is open, we reckon to take a big toll of Montreal's trade.* Our harbour's open the year round. The quickest route, and the cheapest freightage, is what we offer the prairie. Yes, sir!"

And the booster, sitting in his last-word office, high up in towering skyscraper, will gaze, with the eye of a visionary, over the vast harbour below, the magnificent natural anchorage which would comfortably house the navies of the world, towards the soft blue contours of Grouse Mountain to the north.

"Yes, sir, watch Vancouver grow! Lookit here! Montreal is frozen stiff half the year. What's the logical route for the prairie grain? – Why, Vancouver, sure. Open all the year round, a bottle-neck for the grain. The best route because

" 'Yes, sir, Vancouver sure is the Pearl of the Pacific. Now the Panama Canal is open, we reckon to take a big toll of Montreal's trade. Our harbour's open the year round. The quickest route, and the cheapest freightage, is what we offer the prairie. Yes, sir!'

And the booster, sitting in his last-word office, high up in towering skyscraper, will gaze, with the eye of a visionary, over the vast harbour below . . ." (p.107). This photo was taken from the old *Vancouver Sun* tower. Note the North Vancouver ferry in the top centre. Below: the same view in 1994.

it's the cheapest route, now the Panama Canal is opened up."

And, elaborating the claims of his city as against every other port of the Dominion, the Vancouver man (who thinks as a Vancouver man and not as a Canadian) will prove conclusively that this youthful port is destined to become the second port of the Empire. "Yes, sir, it sure is!

"In ten years we shall hit the million mark. Yep! And don't you forget it! Real estate is going to boom right here."

2.

Under the effulgent sunshine of the warm Pacific slope pessimism wilts and perishes. It is the land of the optimist, of the speculator, of the get-rich-quick merchant, of the booster.

The little village on the edge of the bush that Old Man Ferguson saw from his boat has become a city in less than fifty years of feverish transition. It is set on emulating the older ports of the Pacific. It believes in itself, in its future, in its great destiny. Well, Santa Barbara had the fever in the 'eighties. And Seattle and San Francisco that sent forth the Argonauts to the goldfields had it too.*

And now has come Vancouver: young, raw, unsophisticated; arrogant like a lad newly in long pants, conscious of departed childhood and deceived by budding virility into belief in its maturity.

Skyscrapers, shouldered by old frame buildings of discoloured wood, rough streets with wooden sidewalks right next to macadamized thoroughfares, canyons of Portland stone through which surge the unending tides of motor traffic. A railway terminus vast as a Byzantine cathedral, and banks housed more magnificently than any London or Paris can show. Great department stores and insurance offices. Theatres, cinemas and impressive newspaper offices. And,

"A railway terminus vast as a Byzantine cathedral, and banks housed more magnificently than any London or Paris can show." (p. 109). Note the trees of Stanley Park in the background. *Below:* the same scene in 1994 with Canada Place on the right.

"Vancouver . . . the Last Great City of the Last Great West." (p. 106). This poster is typical of the clever blandishments of Liberal Immigration Minister Sifton. One wonders how much such splendid propaganda influenced George and Dorothy to immigrate to Canada.

at the city's door, lapped by the Pacific, the great trees of Stanley Park – the bush, cleaned a little, but unspoiled, a momento of the past.

3.

On an early Autumn morning, with a white mist still low upon the river and the air as yet unwarmed by the morning sun, Lulu Armstrong carried her bag from the old white house to the little depot and took the local for Vancouver. She was alone and as she clambered up the steep steps into the day coach, there was only Tom Preedy to see her go. He heaved her bag up after her and, in his whining voice, said: "If you've time, Miss Lulu, you might buy me a *News of the World,* you can get 'em at the news store on Cordova – if you don't mind." And Lulu promised, for it was easier to do that than to explain that she was leaving Ferguson's Landing for good.

Above all else, Lulu wanted to be alone with her thoughts.

She wanted privacy, just as a wounded animal seeks a secret place where it may lick its wounds unseen. The train, with clanging bell, clattered through the rock cut and swung round the bend of the mist-enshrouded river. Lulu knew every inch of that landscape which unwound itself as the train sped westwards towards the city.

Here and there among the timber she could see shacks and figures moving about clearings. The men in their grey shirts and faded blue canvas breeches, the women in their great white overalls. For the first time in her life she thought about those women curiously. They did all the work of those little homesteads: they cooked, washed, sewed and baked. And, between whiles, they had their babies, suckled them, reared them. Her heart went out to them, for already suffering was working like a solvent at her heart, making her sensitive and responsive to all suffering. Up to now she had been a child, accepting it all unquestioningly.

At Port Murdock, a settlement little bigger than Ferguson's Landing – a port without shipping – the train, bell clanging, slowed down and ran into the station. Through the glass of the window Lulu watched the scene below. A temporary encampment was set on the boards of the depot: a dozen or more families of Indians, oblivious of everything about them, contriving to make themselves comfortable on their baggage.

She noticed that they had divided themselves naturally into family groups. There were a number of women. Some were young, with bright and comely faces. These stood against the station wall, their papooses tightly strapped to their backs. Others were old, immensely old, with the faces of mummies and eyes that no longer sparkled, but were dull and fish-like. Women who had ripened and faded young, women with old faces scarred by a thousand wrinkles, so that they looked like forgotten winter apples.

"They [the women pioneers] did all the work of those little homesteads: they cooked, washed, sewed and baked . . . [Lulu's] heart went out to them, for already suffering was working like a solvent at her heart, making her sensitive and responsive to all suffering." (p.112). Photo: A pioneer kitchen in Vancouver, *c.* 1900.

These too, the watching girl surmised, had known bitterness. Her eyes fell upon an old man, an old Indian with protruding jaw and the expression of a baboon. His feet were naked and deformed and he beat a tin tomato can upon the ground, turning his withered head from right to left. An idiot, brought to his idiocy by fire-water.

Simple Indian folk, waiting to get a train to their reservation. The young men in their flash town clothes smoke cigarettes and talk idly. The women wait, and on their faces is that look of simple wonderment of a child in a strange and perhaps dangerous place.

"Patient people, folk of a fast-dying race which has given place to the white usurper. A people who have lost both land and religion." (p.115). Photo: Quatsino (Vancouver Island) native people gathered for a potlatch.

Patient people, folk of a fast-dying race which has given place to the white usurper. A people who have lost both land and religion. A people who have traded their furs and their freedom for firewater.

Once, they were fierce and merciless on the warpath, splendid people living near to the heart of nature. Now they are besotted refugees in their own land.*

It was the first time Lulu had thought about the Indians at all. They had always been just Indians, thieves up at the Reserve, low-downs, always getting drunk. Neighbours in a sense, but people apart. Now she looked at this group, and pity stirred within her. Suffering had lit the lamp of pity in her heart, and she saw their tragedy: the tragedy of the dispossessed. Sympathy had given her sight.

4.

The train restarted with a jerk and a wrenching of steel couplings. The engine bell tolled mournfully and across the window of the day coach Lulu saw the temporary Indian encampment move like a picture upon a screen.

While her newly-awakened imagination had been stirred by those patient creatures, she had forgotten for a moment her own pressing problem. She had given her pity to the Indians: now she needed it for herself. Not that a trip down to Vancouver was in itself so wonderful. She had often gone with her mother or girls from Ferguson's Landing.

Once she had gone to hear a real opera. It had been a disappointment. She had understood nothing whatever of the mouthings of the singers, and the music had stirred no chord in ears attuned to Norse folk-songs. Once too, she had gone to stand in the crowds which greeted the Governor General. That had been fun, to see a Royal personage. For the rest, her trips to the city had been shopping expeditions after a good year on the river or a lucrative contract had made her father flush.

Now it was different. She was putting Ferguson's Landing behind her for good. Her mind was painfully orienting itself to that bewildering prospect. Vancouver was to be her home, her permanent abiding place. From now on the Landing would be merely a background for memory.

The local wound around the bank of the river, creaking upon the blistered ties that held the metals. A bridge came into view, an arc thrown across the mighty river.* The timber ended abruptly and small farmhouses flashed past, little gaily painted bungalows, each with its golden plot from which streamers of washing flapped a greeting at the passing train.

Thinking of that epoch-making visit to the travelling opera company in the city, Lulu's mind travelled to the songs she loved best, and their singer. How often had she sat in the great kitchen up at the Ole's place listening to Kurt? He would sing in a high falsetto, playing his own accompaniment on the concertina. The old songs of Norway, wistful, sometimes melancholy, melodious always. As she hummed them noiselessly now, forming the words with her lips, the rhythm of the train keeping time for her:

Spinn, spinn, spinn, dotter min,
Morgen kommer friain den.

Yes, Kurt was her knight, like the knight in the old ballad.

Dottern spann og tarar rann
Aldrig kom den friain fram . . . [1]

---

[1] *Spin on, my daughter, while there's light,*
For soon shall come thy shining knight.
On, on, she span with cunning art,
But no knight came to claim her heart.

And that too was like her and Kurt. She had waited his coming, waited for him to claim what was already his, and he had held off, strangely shy, elusive, enigmatic. Yes, like the knight in the ballad, he had deserted her.

The train was running into Vancouver, winding around the curve beside the blue tongue of water that reaches out from the great harbour to lap at the standing timber of the mainland. Wharves with huddled timber buildings and warehouses painted with the names of grain and meat companies, filed past; jetties, broad and blunt, pushed out into the blue water of the inlet; tugs and moored cargo boats eased the itch of steel sides against barnacled wharves. White sails flashed in the sun on the blue water. Lumber-yards, piled with fir and cedar; the scream of buzz-saws, and white-turbanned Sikhs carrying timbers. Over to the north was the humped back of Grouse Mountain on whose lower flank the geometrical terraces of North Vancouver showed like the pattern of a Persian rug.

5.

Lulu became aware of two men sitting across the gangway from her. They were big men dressed in the town clothes of the Valley farmer – ill-cut, ready-made suits, thick, black felt hats, boots like barges. Both rested work-calloused hands on the knees of their trousers. The elder man, whose face was stamped with the scar left by the boot of a lumberjack, was talking:

"Well, sir, I figured it was time to quit. Farming in this Province is a fool's game. And I gotta good price. Yes, sir."

The speaker paused to bite viciously at a mottled yellow plug of chewing tobacco. His companion spat a dark brown squirt of liquid into the brass cuspidor, and held out a hand for the plug. He bit in turn and, comforted, the two resumed their talk.

"Take eggs," went on the first speaker, "time was when you gotta good price for hen fruit. Now you can't sell 'em at all. Have to give 'em away. Yes, sir."

"The Chinese imported eggs have put a crimp on the Valley chicken farmer," said the second speaker. "And it's the same with apples which they git right here in the city cheaper from Spokane, Washington, than they can sell 'em no further off than Ferguson's Landing."

"You done well to sell, I reckon."

"You bet yer."

"Where d'you figger to locate now?"

"States. Yes, sir, that's the country. Got the dough and got the land and got the markets. I reckon to locate in California. Yes, sir."

The train slowed down, ran into the shadows cast by towering warehouses, clanked over rails and slid into the dimness of the great terminus.

The two men rose to take down their hand baggage.

"If you ax me," said the first speaker, "British Columbia is no goldarn good for farming. I've tried the coast and I've tried 'way up in the dry belt and it's no goldarn good at all."

"You sed it," agreed the other; "I've seen the Fraser Valley going to pot this last ten years."

"Me too, I've done with the Valley."

Lulu gathered up her wicker basket. She too had finished with the Valley. But after all, the world was a big place. The Valley was but a tiny corner of it. She felt braver than she ever had since that first moment when, in the solitude of her bedroom under the slanting roof, she determined to face her fate alone, and see her trouble through secretly, as a wounded animal does.

The local came to a halt with a series of metallic jerks. Through the window the long low platform made a picture of teeming humanity, a motley throng: smart townsmen, drummers with big grips, overalled loggers with fat, canvas-covered packs, white-turbanned Sikhs, negroes, Klootchmans, Chinese and Japanese.* Vancouver in miniature. Vancouver, city of all nationalities, the West's racial melting-pot.

Well, Lulu had also done with the Valley, she told herself. Slowly she descended the steep steps of the daycoach to the platform. She turned and hauled her bag down after her. A moment later she was lost in the crowd.

Mrs. Armstrong gave it out that Lulu, after all, was going to a business college.

CHAPTER XIII

1.

The Fire Warden was sweating for he had driven hell-for-leather through the settlement, calling out to all able-bodied men in the name of the law to fight the fire which was raging in the X Timber Limit, five miles back in the bush.

He reined up at the Woods place and boomed his order. By law, all able-bodied men must turn out to fight forest fires.

"I am afraid I would only be a nuisance," Woods apologized, as he came slowly down to the dust-covered rig with its steaming horse.

His voice invited sympathy. "Only last week I had a slight attack: it might come back." He placed a lean brown hand upon his brown shirt. "Heart," he explained.

The Fire Warden retorted with a "Huh," putting into that monosyllable a measure of contempt.

As Woods watched him climb into his rig and slap the reins upon his horse's lathered back, with an impatient: "Gettup, gettup," he smiled a slow smile and turned slowly back to his seat – a low chopping block on the sunny side of his woodshed.

Yes, there certainly was a bushfire somewhere out there. Woods crossed his legs, relit his corn-cob pipe, folded his stringy arms, and contemplated the heavens. A pall of smoke hung over the Valley and the acrid atmosphere stung his nostrils and made his beady eyes smart. Flakes of ash like grey snow fluttered slowly down. The red eye of the sun showed like a warning light through fog, blood-red and blurred. A bad fire.

The parson had no heart disease. He met the urgent order of the sweating Fire Warden with eyes that shifted quickly in embarrassment.

"Ah, a fire, and at the X Limit? I think it my duty to stay and look after the women," he announced. "Yes, that seems to me my obvious duty, much as I should like to come and lend a hand."

The little man had been brought thus abruptly from the depth of his arm-chair, and *Chambers' Journal,* sent out to him by his brother, the Dean, lay opened on the seat of his arm-chair at the page which had been gripping his attention. Moreover, his wife was at that moment making the tea: an unpropitious moment for such a demand.

For the rest, the men of the settlement were hiking towards the distant plumes of dense smoke which billowed up in angry puffs above the dark green of the bush. The torrid air was oppressive, and the silent bush flanking the rough road stood strangely still, like a sentient forest, petrified by fear of an impending doom, it seemed.

2.

The bush in the Valley was tinder-dry, parched by a rainless summer: so that a match, carelessly thrown by a hobo

"... *whatsoever comforting creeds man builds himself to fortify his mortality against the stark cruelty of the material world, the powers of destruction rule the universe.*" (p. 129). *Top:* Aftermath of a forest fire, Vancouver Island, 1920s. *Below:* forest fire just off the Kamloops-Jasper Highway near Clearwater, B.C., August 1994.

'walking the dog' or the unquenched fire of a careless camper, was enough to change the green silences into a roaring furnace of racing fire.

The X Limit was a superb stand of first-growth timber, Douglas fir and red cedar, straight as the columns of an ancient temple, mighty trees that had looked down on the teeming transient life of the bush at their feet through centuries of unchallenged dominion.

The Carlyle Lumber Company had run a spur-line through the bush from their sawmill at Carlyle, seven miles up the river from Ferguson's Landing. There was a clearing in the heart of the bush where the trees had been felled, and the narrow-gauge spur-line, winding its way through the tall timber, debouched into this clearing like a stream into a lake. The tar-papered shacks of the camp, with their clutter of barrels, rusty iron gear, dumps of tomato, salmon and kerosene cans, lay like a flotilla of vanquished ships, rudderless, among the debris of defeat.

It was past noon when the first men from Ferguson's Landing got to the Limit. The bush to the north of the menaced camp was a sea of flames, the fire travelling west. Giant flames lashed upwards against the recoiling canopy of smoke that puffed and swirled above the bush. Upon the ground it ran, darting forward in forays, lapping the dry vegetation as it swept forward in a molten tide. Long streamers of fire lashed at the mighty trunks of the trees, caught the doomed branches, and leaped from them into the air, capped with plumes of black smoke. A loud crackling ripped the silence of the bush like the fusillade of a million riflemen.

The squat engine from the mill had raced madly along the uneven narrow gauge track back and forth throughout the morning. It came now, snorting out of the heart of the timber to the south, its caboose packed tight with passive-faced Hindus.

"A hellofa lot of good to try to stop *that*," said a begrimed logger standing by the tool dump. His face was black and streaked with rivulets of sweat. His shirt, drenched with sweat, was plastered to his chest. "Why the hell they send these damned niggers up, God only knows. We can't do nuttin'. It's a crown fire, that's what it is."

He pointed with a black hand: "See it leapin' along them top branches? Holy Goley!"

A gang of a hundred Hindus was feverishly trenching ahead of the advancing fire. They looked like demons intent on some mystic ritual of the Inferno. From time to time they took fright and abandoned their fireline, running back, stumbling and yelling, their long-handled shovels and mattocks trailing behind them. Then, turning, they formed a new line and went to work digging like frenzied demons.

Far in advance of the racing furnace, the clang of axes rang out above the angry crackling, where men were striving to fell the dead timber across the path of the fire.

For with a crown fire, a fire which travels along the crests of the trees, the only chance of stemming it is to sword-slash across the path of its progress.

The ranchers from the settlement stood around gazing with awed eyes upon the fearful spectacle. Impotent men they were, men without leadership.

The voice of the Chief Fire Warden, loud and angry, dispersed them. "Say, youse guys," he roared as he lumbered, black and menacing, past them, "you ain't paid good money to come and look at it. Get busy."

They took shovels and mattocks from the dump and moved towards the sea of flames.

The air grew hotter still and the sun, inclining to the west, sank slowly down behind the veil of smoke. The fire leapt on, while the fire-fighters fell back gesticulating. It was as though those gestures acknowledged defeat, the defeat of man in a universe of blind and purposeless cruelty.

So afternoon wore on to evening. There was no more to be done. The X Limit, bar a miracle, was doomed to destruction. Already the flames had leapt the gap where the fire-fighters had back-fired.* The blaze was advancing with incredible speed, thrusting its red tongues into the green shadows of the foredoomed timber ahead of it.

But as twilight fell a soft breeze sprang up out of the west. It puffed upon the fire, but it blew the leaping flames back upon the charred remnants of the fir stand. In the gloom lit by the glare of the fire men with blackened faces and singed shirts ran hither and thither. Voices called through the confusion, "Trench! Trench! We've got her under."

The X Limit was saved — saved by a miracle, by a gentle breeze out of the west. Half the great stand was gone, but half was saved.

Night fell, and the bush became a thing of infinite melancholy. It stood forth from the dying flames, charred, defeated — dead. Here and there the black trunks of the great trees smouldered like extinguished torches. Glowing cores of fire ate into the blackened stumps or crackled malevolently in the incinerated undergrowth. It was desolation.

Yet only that morning the bush had been most beautiful, a wonderland of dappled lights and odorous air. The great trees that had risen from a green floor had seemed powerful and permanent as pillars of stone; their immense, fanlike branches outspread as though to bless this gift of universal life, as though bearing silent testimony to the loving goodness of the Creator.

And now had come fire and wiped that loveliness away; and all the comely bush had vanished. Sapless and destroyed, the forest's skeleton smouldered in the evening air.

3.

Solitude — whose gifts are perspective and self-revelation — sifts from the chaff of Time certain pregnant moments, and interprets them.

Strange, but now the mind of the Newcomer was ranging the past, a series of changing pictures. A small boy, rising before the sun was over the rim of the English Channel, looking out from a window towards a pearl-grey sea. A small boy who loved the early morning hour when the air smelled damp and salt and new. What adventure to creep down narrow stairs that creaked beneath bare feet and to un-latch, with a sense of sin, the front door with its red and blue coloured panes. And, once free of the imprisoning house, to rush, fleet-footed towards that sheet of glassy water, oblivious of the sharp pain of flints on calloused soles.

A September morning with no breath of wind. A small boy standing on the shingle of the foreshore, hair a tangled mass, torn shirt and patched blue breeches, gazing out to sea. Watching the sun come up, a majestic molten orb, casting before it golden javelins of light, and unrolling across the cold grey sea a carpet of liquid gold.

Watching, with wide eyes and parted lips, this daily miracle, the boy saw float into the golden haze a dream ship, a great four-masted ship with sails full set. She glided slowly, serenely across the sun and hovered there, ghostly and motionless. A ship painted upon a disc of dazzling light.

He had run down to the edge of the sea where tiny waves curved arched necks and cast themselves upon the shining pebbles of the sloping beach. But the vision had vanished. The great ship lay southward now, a blur in the haze.

A memorable moment, that, because for that small boy it was the birth of the wonder of beauty. Thereafter he sought for beauty, hoping that one more such vision would be vouchsafed to him.

And it was.

4.

Horror had come later, leaving a scar upon his mind that refused to heal. Eight years later. A whitewashed classroom with rows of yellow pine desks, a rostrum, blackboard and yellow bookcases. The sharp crack of bat on ball from the practice-nets outside. A small boy kept in and set to writing lines through a summer afternoon.

"Koran."*

He took the book idly from the shelf, opened it at random and read.

As he turned the pages anger seized him. Fear followed, and horror. Beauty there was in the world, and love, and kindness. But there was also this. These fearful tortures, eternal punishments. So horror came to him, to be stored throughout the years in the chambers of memory. It remained for the bush to teach him the impersonal cruelty of the elements.

Watching that raging fire at the X Limit, the boy grown man sensed for the first time the relentless destructiveness of the blind elements. He tried to square that raging hell of living fire with the infinite pity of the traditional creed.

Those roaring flames, consuming the green earth, defacing the verdant beauty of the tall timber, burnt up his faith. He could no longer believe that a universe wherein such vast forces lay latent and ready to destroy could be governed by the spirit of the Galilean.

That misplaced Koran of the school classroom had revealed the ingenuities of man's sadistic lusts; the bush fire exposed the mercilessness of the Unseen God.

5.

Night had fallen upon the camp, making it desolate. The squat loco had clanked its way down the narrow-gauge line, its trucks festooned with half-naked Hindus. The fire fighters had set out for the settlement, walking slowly, like defeated men, along the uneven ties. Yellow squares showed from the

shacks of the camp where wearied lumberjacks were turning in to their bunks. The Fire Warden remained. Stout and
imperturbable he was, that burly Norwegian.

"We should sleep a liddle by turns," he announced to
the Newcomer, who had elected to stay with him.

"I'd like to see the dawn," the Newcomer had explained.
As a matter of fact, his bank account was overdrawn: the extra dollars would not come amiss! But the dawn promised.

They scrambled over lying logs, made their way through
the squat stumps of the slashing and lit a camp fire, for the
night air had turned chill and no fierce heat breathed on
them now from the charred timber.

In the dimness of the moonless night the bush was a black,
jagged wall about them. Where the fire had destroyed the
timber, charred snags smouldered fitfully; red lights blinked
out of the velvet darkness, high up on the trunks of dead
trees, like lighted windows in high towers.

"Some of them'll be coming down soon," explained the
Fire Warden. "Resin, it kinda collects in the trunks, and when
the fire gets at it, it jus' burns and burns until it has et through.
Then she breaks in the middle and comes down."

The Newcomer turned his eyes from the embers of the
little camp fire and gazed at a great dead cedar into which a
flickering flame was eating. Suddenly, without any warning splintering, the top half of the tree swayed and broke
clear. It crashed to the ground with a boom of a distant gun,
and from the hot earth a constellation of sparks was tossed
up.

With heads nodding upon hunched shoulders they dozed,
and the dancing flames of the fire played over their faces,
making them look by turns sinister, grotesque, mournful,
haggard, pitiful.

When dawn crept up out of the east, the desolation of the
bush slowly revealed itself. Thin coils of smoke rose straight

"He was discovering the hard fact that the felling of a tree is the least part of the labour of land-clearing." (p. 129). Godwin the Newcomer had plenty of difficulty with stumps but the houseowners of this street seem to have chosen to ignore them. Port Moody, *c.* 1910.

into the still air but the great trees, denuded of their foliage, naked, charred and gaunt, stood forth like fantastic relics of a long bygone age – a dead forest, a forest carbonized by time.

The Newcomer shivered, stretched stiff limbs, and rubbed smarting eyes with blackened knuckles. The Fire Warden lay, head resting upon arm, his great bulk stretched out on the ground, bedded on dead bracken.

The fire had come suddenly, filling the whole Valley with acrid smoke, obscuring the blue sky and the golden sun, obliterating beauty, bringing terror. It had raced through the bush, destroying noble trees whose growth had occupied the centuries, and all the tender life of the bush. And it had gone as mysteriously and as purposelessly as it had come.

And pigmy man, with his muddled thinking apparatus, there at the foot of the timber, like a speck beneath a cliff, mutely apostrophized the unanswering universe: why such waste, such futile destruction?

Thus came another memorable moment to the Newcomer. He learnt, there in the stillness of dawn, with the handiwork of the element Fire to confuse him, that whatsoever comforting creeds man builds himself to fortify his mortality against the stark cruelty of the material world, the powers of destruction rule the universe. Blind forces beyond the moral law, beyond pity and reason, and the warm, comforting faiths of men.

CHAPTER XIV

1.

As Johansson had foreseen, the Newcomer came to him about his clearing. It was going too fast; hence, too slowly. He had felled with good will but without method. The result was a clutter of felled alders, with a few second-growth firs, maples and cedars. He was discovering the hard fact that the felling of a tree is the least part of the labour of land-clearing. There remains the stump and the felled tree itself and the tenacious roots of the undergrowth.

"The big stumps'll take blasting powder," Johansson explained.

The two men crossed the slashing to an enormous fir stump. "Ah, you been trying it here, eh?" he asked as he noted the earth about the stump.

It looked as though a strong blast of air had blown up from below and shot away the loose heavy soil. The root was intact.

"How many sticks d'you use to this?" he asked.

"Well, I must have used half a box," admitted the Newcomer ruefully. "Somehow or other all I did was to blow the earth out: the roots never budged."

Johansson did not smile. A man knew a thing or he did not. This man, he had heard at the store, was something of a scholar and therefore must know much that he, Johansson, knew not at all. What was it, after all, to demonstrate to him so small a thing as blasting a stump?

He took the long-handled shovel and dug out the dirt from around the splayed roots. He worked like a man digging for gold.

"Now you can see the lie of the prongs," he explained. He spoke without any hint of patronage, merely like one neighbour assisting another – just as he himself might ask assistance in a matter beyond his own ken.

He took the double-bitted axe, examined the two blades: "Always keep one blade for felling," he counselled, "and the other for chopping roots in the ground. That way you get a blade widout nicks, one you keep good and sharp on the stone."

He sent the steel into the great root prongs, cutting them across. "That helps the powder," he went on. "They're half cut, the powder'll do the rest."

"I've only two sticks left," said the Newcomer, "and that's the fifth box."

"Two's enough," answered the Swede. He was now digging down into the heart of the root, tunnelling narrow shafts under the great stump. He fixed the shining cylinder of the detonator to the fuse wire, nipping the end with his teeth. "Never do that," he advised, "I do it b'cause it's kinda habit, but a few months ago a fellow at Port Murdock blew his head off that way."

He cut the fat oily sticks of blasting powder in two, and placed, in all, four charges in his tunnel ends.

"The real secret is to tamp down good and hard," he went

on. "Get air around the stick and you don't git no explosion to count."

He tamped the soft earth with a pole of vine-maple, adding shovelful by shovelful until he had filled in his holes, leaving only the fuse ends exposed. They were white and sinuous, like pallid, air-starved roots.

He lit the four fuses and the two men scrambled back to the shelter of a big fir. They shouted "Fire! Fire!" as they ran. A ball of smoke puffed up; the explosion came with a rending boom; from the shattered stump a shower of debris sang through the foliage like shrapnel.

That is how it was. To the simple manual task, then, there was technique. One had to know. Knowledge brought results, ignorance failure. The stump, about which coiled thin shreds of smoke, lay torn open with its deep-set prongs exposed, like a vast molar.

"Git fire in that hole and she will burn herself out," Johansson explained.

He had accomplished within an hour what had baffled the Newcomer for weeks.

But when the Newcomer proffered him three dollars, Johansson shook his head. "Keep it," he said, "you'll maybe want it later on."

"But I can't let you work for me without pay," expostulated the Newcomer, "it's worth that to me to be rid of that damned stump. Please take it."

But the Swede shook his head. "Keep it. You'll maybe need it later on," he repeated.

Neighbourly, one must be neighbourly . . . Perhaps if the Englishman wanted a big job done he, Johansson, would take wages like in the ordinary way. But not for a bit of neighbourly help. Johansson's gaunt figure lumbered across the slashing, his huge hands swinging at his sides. He took the downward trail to the store.

2.

"Folk down at Blanchard's were a bit put out," he told his daughter, later that evening, when he had climbed the hill back to his place. "Seems they've been sending down their small-fruits to Sapperton and they've been gitting bills back. Seems like the price small-fruits fetch at Sapperton market, they ain't wort' growing. Seems that arter deducting freight rates and broker's commission there's no money left."

It was not the first time it had happened to the settlers in the Valley. Through the summer they worked in their hardly-won miniature fields, packing the small fruits that grew on ground wrested, yard by yard, from the bush through years of hard, unremitting toil. In the end, after waiting weeks, they were billed by the commission men.

Yet Fuller grew small-fruits – and made 'em pay. Whenever he wasn't cleaning out his long chicken houses, you could see him moving around his berry bushes.

Yes, Fuller grew small-fruits. But he grew only two varieties: gooseberries, which fetched a premium price in Vancouver (he shipped them direct to a department store), and black currants, which he shipped to Calgary, where they were a much-sought-after luxury and fetched a good price. Yes, Fuller was the man: he understood the Valley. He could make anything at all pay.

3.

Mann had sold his brickyard. Blanchard heard of it from Mann himself and passed on the news.

"Twenty thousand dollars, he tells me," Blanchard said as he shuffled along behind his counter, butcher's knife poised ready to descend upon a side of American-cured bacon. "And nine months ago he bought it for nine thousand."

"Yes, and on terms," remarked Old Man Dunn.

"Two thousand cash," added Blanchard.

"The balance over five years," interjected little Tom Preedy.

"There's a feller who understands how to make money," Blanchard's voice was admiration and envy articulate.

"And how to lose it," said Old Man Dunn. "He'll go straight down to Vancouver and play fan-tan in the Chinese joints on Pender Street. He's done that before. A passion for gambling." He shook a disapproving head. "Men like that don't do a country any good in the long run."

Having sliced off a handful of fat rashers, Blanchard cast the limp result onto a soiled piece of newspaper and stuck the point of his knife into the dark wood of the counter. "He's got a new stunt on this time, he tells me." He waited an appreciable second to whet the appetites of his audience for his news. "Oil, that's the new stunt," he told them. "He wanted me to put some money in his company. Don't know but what I might do it either."

Old Mann Dunn snorted. "Oil!" he exploded. "What the devil next do they expect to get out of this blamed Valley? A year or two back it was gold; well, there is gold – that Chinese across the river is getting pay dirt. Works about ten hours a day pan-handling for about three dollars' worth of dust. And now it's oil!"

The old Yorkshireman's voice rumbled like an erupting volcano. "Why the devil don't they dig for diamonds and have done with it?" he demanded.

"Ask me," put in little Tom Preedy in his whining voice. "It's just a swizzle, that's wot it is. I'm a Londoner and I've seen something of the share swindling sharks."

"He argues it like this," explained Blanchard, leaning one elbow on the counter and shifting the weight of his body from his lame leg. "There's oil in California, see? Well, we're on the Pacific slope just the same as 'Frisco. If there's oil there, why not oil here? Sounds logical enough if you put it that way. And he showed me a geologist's report. Seemed kind of optimistic, far as I could make out."

"Well, I'm not taking any," rumbled Old Man Dunn. "Before you can get oil you've got to drill, and drilling's a mighty expensive game. Will Mann drill? No! You see."

"Anyhow, he's formed his company – the Fraser Valley Oil Fields, he calls it.* And he's selling stock – ten cent shares. He's got five million to sell."

"Then let him sell them to the suckers in the city," said Old Man Dunn, "and not try that game on his neighbours."

4.

The Fraser Valley Oil Fields was launched upon a flood of clever advertising. It was unfair to Mann to say that he had put no money into the venture himself: he had – some five thousand dollars in advertising.

The trump card was the geologist's report. True, he was a Yankee geologist, which took a bit of gilt off his certificate, and his qualifications were those of a negro college down south. But the housewives of Vancouver and Sapperton, the streetcar conductors, store clerks, drummers, CPR men and a multitude of other wage-earners imbued with the spirit of the West, knew nothing of the shades of difference between the OK of a McGill professor and that of a gum-chewing geologist from across the line.

Mann's discovery of oil in the Fraser Valley looked good to them. They were seduced first by the high-faluting verbosity of the expert, and secondly by the pictorial demonstration of how the Fraser Valley would look when the plant of the Fraser Valley Oil Fields was bringing up the crude stuff.

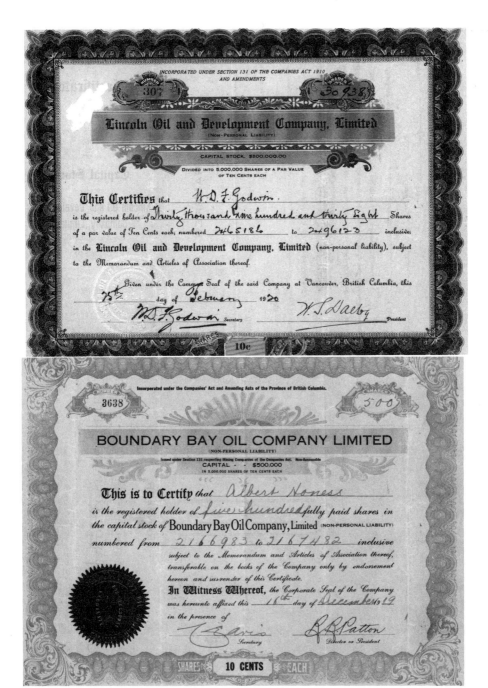

"Those share certificates made happy many small homes in and around Vancouver and Sapperton. They carried conviction to those in whose minds doubts, sowed by sanity, still strove against unreasoning cupidity." (p. 136). Photo: some of these certificates were once owned by Donald Godwin, George's older brother (see biography).

When they called in on Mann in his imposing Vancouver office, there he was, all day long, puffing on a cigar and fussing about the model of his oil wells (It was a working model and had cost him five hundred dollars. Dirt cheap at the price!). Swapping their dollars for shares, they left clutching something rare and fine in the way of the lithographer's art.

Those share certificates made happy many small homes in and around Vancouver and Sapperton. They carried conviction to those in whose minds doubts, sowed by sanity, still strove against unreasoning cupidity.

In less than a month there were no less than twenty new companies advertising oil shares. Within three months the oil boom broke on the coast and Vancouver, dulled a little by the periodic excitement of real estate booms, went oil crazy.

Real estate men pulled down their signs and hung out boards covered with samples of the share certificates of the oil companies in which they dealt.

'Share-butchers' packed their grips and boarded the Agassiz local to peddle oil shares among the rube population.

"Yes, sir, you can buy on terms. Quarter down, balance six, twelve and eighteen months. Sign here." They spieled like this.

Heggerty turned up at Ferguson's Landing one day. He had on a store suit and a collar. "Hell, I guess this ain't such a bad country arter all," he gloated. "I've plunked my bones into oil and I figger to be a rich man inside twelve months. Yes, sir."

5.

The several real estate booms which had hit the West had sent land prices soaring. In Vancouver and Sapperton, and

". . . hard-working Chinese, men who lived on nothing and peddled their produce from door to door, undercutting the storekeeper." (p. 139). Pedlars buying produce on Pender St. (just west of Carrall St., looking east). 1905.

even in sleepy Victoria prices rocketed. Every other man in a white collar was a professional real estate merchant. Men who had built up decent little businesses in hardware, in gents' furnishings, in groceries, in 'Good eats' restaurants and tonsorial parlours, closed down to reopen as real estate men.*

Half the window space on Vancouver's Granville and

"Lots changed hands four, five and six times a day. Men dealt in them as men deal in stocks and shares on the Stock Exchange, dealt in them as men deal in groceries.

Everybody was rich, or seemed so, and every car was crowded with happy buyers being whirled out to see the land they were buying, the land which was to make them rich quick. It was the only business being done in the city."
(p. 139). Pictured: a typical real estate ad from 1914.

Hastings Streets was given up in those days to the display cards of subdivision promotors. Suburbs sprang up overnight, sprang up on paper, that is.

Loggers, clerks, railwaymen, master mariners from the Pacific steamships, carpenters, bricklayers, bank clerks, store clerks: everybody with a few dollars to put up as deposit got into the game.

That was the time when prices in Vancouver touched their top. On Hastings Street and Granville Street, in the business section of the city, dealers no longer talked about blocks: they bought and sold by the foot as they do in London's famous Square Mile of banking houses. Their prices went higher than frontage on Lombard Street or Threadneedle Street.

Nothing had changed in the city overnight. True, it had grown and was growing. But the mad boom was without economic justification; there was no big business to back it.

So it was with the forcing up of suburban land values. Locations which had been farms once, and had become the market gardens of hard-working Chinese (men who lived on nothing and peddled their produce from door to door, undercutting the storekeeper), were snapped up, christened grandly and surveyed into hundred-foot lots.

Grandview came on the market during this boom time and so did many other undeveloped suburbs.* Lots changed hands four, five and six times a day. Men dealt in them as men deal in stocks and shares on the Stock Exchange, dealt in them as men deal in groceries.

Everybody was rich, or seemed so, and every car was crowded with happy buyers being whirled out to see the land they were buying, the land which was to make them rich quick. It was the only business being done in the city.

Outlying shack villages caught the mad fever. Pittsville on the Pitt River (a dump of wooden shacks with a general store, a third-rate hotel and a tar-papered pool room) boldly proclaimed itself a city in the making.* Its real estate boosters claimed that the CPR was about to build terminals in their town. They went so far as to say that the great Angus shops of Montreal, which employed thousands, were to locate in Pittsville.*

Pittsville got itself subdivided over an area which would, with one house to each lot, have absorbed the population of Chicago, Illinois. In the end, the CPR did build, but what they built was a roundhouse for turning their engines around at that jerk-water junction. It took a row of wooden bungalows to house the new staff, and that was all. The Angus shops remained in Montreal where, a moment's clear thinking would have made it obvious, they would remain.

But in the interim, between hysterical optimism and crashing hopes, Pittsville deliriously got itself renamed Port Pittsville and the Provincial Legislature, just as deliriously, consented to charter the place and give to that scattered collection of shacks and shanties the dignity of a city. Pittsville overnight became the City of Port Pittsville. Its purblind citizens proclaimed it the Liverpool of the Pitt River, the Port of the Future, and similar flapdoodle and claptrap to catch the 'easy mark.'* They went about repeating their new slogan: *Watch Pittsville Grow.* Some of them are still watching.

And afterwards?

Afterwards, Vancouver woke up and rubbed its eyes. It had cashed in on future profits and spent the money. It had to settle down to face the economic consequences. Rents soared and real estate men, having returned once more to their lawful occupations, found that they would have to raise the prices of their goods to pay the higher rents. Prices being higher, people spent less. The city passed through the doldrums of her trade history.

The only people who profited were these same land speculators, or those of them who sold in time.

6.

The second time, the sickness returned in the shape of an oil boom, started by no less a person than many-sided Mann of the brickyard, Ferguson's Landing. The whole Valley, still working out its sentence from the last land boom, was ready to be stung again. Every time the local slowed down at Ferguson's Landing, it dropped a number of big fellows in Stetson hats with big cigars on the lookout for oil leases.

It was Mann, however, who had corralled most of the available land on the settlement.

They tried their tricks on Johansson.

He was working on his wood pile, using a buck-saw, one foot on the trestle across which an alder log lay.

"Fine location you got here," said the man in the Stetson hat. "Smoke a cigar?" He smiled and looked about him patronisingly, hands on fat rump, beneath wide coat-tails. "Shure is a nice lo-ca-shun."

Johansson paused in his work, wiped his nose on the side of his great hand, eyed the intruders. Then without a word he resumed his sawing. They left him and strolled across the sloping land of the clearing. Johansson kept his eye on them, and presently they returned. A big man, followed by a small man.

"Say, can we have a word with you, colonel?" queried the big fellow. "A word on important business."

Johansson stopped his saw, pulled it out of the half-cut log, and lumbered towards the shack. "Come inside," he invited. The three men entered the neat, prim little room. They sat down ponderously and the big man opened up.

"See here, mister, we kinder figger this land of yours might – only might, mind you – be oil-bearing. I wanna be square with you – I'm a square guy – Zat so? Eh, Zeitlin?"

Zeitlin, the little man, nodded his head. "Yep," he affirmed, his eyes shooting from his boss to the cold grey eyes of the peasant. "I guess you're OK when it comes to producing the greenbacks."

"Well, mister, as I was saying, this here layout of yours may be oil-bearing – or it may not. But I'm a guy that don't mind a risk. No, sir! Gimme a fifty-year lease on this land to bore for oil and I'll pay you a rent of – " He paused dramatically, screwing up one eye and tilting up his banded cigar. "Gimme a fifty year oil lease and I'll come across with hundred plunks per annum rent?"

He pushed a pudgy hand into the recesses of his coat. "If you've got your deeds right here, I guess we can frame up the lease and git it signed, sealed and delivered right away."

He produced the agreement form, and spread it on the blue and white check table-cloth. Shifting his chair, he inserted a hand in his hip-pocket and produced a worn leather wallet, slipped an elastic band off it and displayed an orderly wad of hundred dollar bills.

The Swede looked blankly from one man to the other. His face expressed frank astonishment and a mild amusement.

"You tink dere's oil on my land?" he asked.

"Under it," corrected the fat man. "Under it, my friend."

"So-o-o." Johansson eyed them. He was thinking: "And they look intelligent fellows too."

"And you pay hundred dollars a year to go scratching fer gasoline?" he asked.

The fat man nodded. "Yep, zat's so. Seems kinda foolish to you, maybe, but I'm an oil expert. See? Been all through this yer California oil boom. Prospects here as good as there, accordin' to geological experts. You see, I'm on the square wid you. I ain't trying to bulldoze you. You've probably got a fine thing here. Maybe, of course, you ain't. I'll take a chanst on it. See?" The cigar went up, the eye went down – knowingly.

Johansson looked from one to the other. Slowly he shook his head. "Dis is a bit o' farming land;" he explained, "it ain't no oil field. I want it to grow things on and for pasture for my cow – she's calving soon. No, I ain't signing no lease."

The two strangers argued the point at length but they were up against something new to them: the firm purpose of a simple single-aimed man. Johansson did not try to argue the point and although a hundred dollars would have been welcome, something in his peasant blood told him that you don't get a hundred dollars as easy as that unless there's a catch somewhere.

Seeing themselves defeated, the two men rose. "Kinda foolish, ain't it, turning down easy money?" said the fat fellow. He waved a fat hand at the meagre piece of harrowed land: "Not much of a living out o' that, I'll say!"

Then he swung round, thumbs in waistcoat-holes, "See here, mister, just why don't you do business? I'm curious."

Johansson scratched his long, thin nose to which the grey powder of his snuff adhered. "Well, I'm sure in my mind there ain't a kerosene can full of oil in der whole Valley," he answered. "And if I was to take your money believing that, I'd be a crook, I reckon."

The fat man whistled between his gold-filled teeth. "A crook, eh?" he said. The whole thing was beyond him.

"And goldarn it if I don't believe the mutt meant it," he laughed as he and his companion walked off. "He turned it down through a disease called honesty!"

Which was a fact.

But others proved less invulnerable against the blandishments of Cyrus P. Donkin.

Little Tom Preedy was at the depot, going over waybills when the strangers descended on him.* He listened with glistening eyes as they talked. "Oil? Sure he had heard all the talk. So they thought there was oil on his ranch? Well, well, perhaps that's why the fruit-trees done so badly."

The strangers looked at each other and nodded knowingly.

Little Tom Preedy saw the nod and interpreted its purport, which was according to plan but not according to *his* plan.

7.

An hour later, hot and bubbling over with excitement, he was heading for home to tell his missis the news. In his pocket was the duplicate lease, fifty years at five hundred dollars a year. Five hundred dollars a year! Why, with what he earned from the CPR he could sit back and live like a gentleman! No more chopping wood: he'd get Johansson in – he could cut six ricks in a day.* No more messing with those damned fruit-trees. They could be cut down. "I own oil lands, oil lands! And an option to swap my rent for shares!" He hugged the wonderful thought. "Some class!"

Mrs. Preedy was less enthusiastic. "Well, you'd better see that you git your money," she said, "and don't you go having nothing to do with them shares. I don't hold with shares."

But little Preedy knew better. "Garn, Ma! You're a woman. You don't understand business. If they find a gusher those shares will be worth a forchun. We'll go back to the Old Country and settle down in London."

Already, in his mind, he was rushing across the prairie on the transcontinental, peering out on the golden wheat fields, but seeing and smelling London. London, the only place in the world to live in.

He actually waxed jovial. "Say, Ma, I heard a good one today at Blanchard's. A chap out from the Old Country was working in a lumberyard. Says a Canuck to him: 'Where you from?' 'London,' says the English feller. 'What, London, Ontario?' asks the other feller. 'Garn! No, silly, London,

England. London, the capital of the bleedin' world!'"

The little man chuckled.

The rot spread. It attacked all that is weak in human nature. It stimulated cupidity, it unfolded visions of ease to the lazy, it seduced the settler reconciled to the hard bargain of the bush.

Half the settlement went oil mad. More than half. Every morning at Blanchard's store the men trooped in, in their overalls and battered hats, to talk oil, where yesterday they had talked crops, weather, produce prices and cattle.

"Heard they've started drilling across the river at Langford," said Fuller. "Set of mugs!"

"Why 'set of mugs'?" asked Blanchard. "You haven't seen the geological report, I reckon, Mr. Fuller. I've got one here."

Blanchard delved under the counter and produced a bunch of pamphlets. The men gathered round, craned necks to read the good tidings. Fuller took the paper, glanced at it, and threw it back. "Yankee fourflushers," he summed up tersely. "Whole thing's a swindle. Worse than the real estate ramp."*

But he was in a minority with Old Man Dunn. Dunn claimed that he did not need any geologist to tell him what he knew already. There was oil in the Valley, but it was all stored in kerosene cans. "They're flat, dishonest grafters," he alleged. "And already they've demoralized the Valley with this talk of oil, oil, oil."

"But they found oil at Okotoks," whined Blanchard, "haven't they? Why shouldn't there be oil in B.C.?"*

Old Man Dunn looked at him pityingly. "Sure, there's oil in Canada. Okotoks! Why, Okotoks is in Alberta! The other side of the Rockies and away to the east!"

But he convinced nobody, for in the West there is something in the air that makes men credulous. They fly to the maddest schemes like moths to a candle, like trout to a dry fly. And they need less playing than the trout!

"There was oil in the Valley, but it was all stored in kerosene cans." (p. 145). Pictured: a typical oil well promotion ad from *c.* 1914.

That year the Valley sent down less produce to Sapperton and no more than ten acres of land were cleared and broken by the plough. The Valley was at a standstill. A derrick reared its head at Langford across the river. News came along daily. They were down five hundred feet . . . a thousand . . . the drill broke. They had sent to Detroit for new machinery.

They had to start again. They'd got indications of crude petroleum. And then the money gave out.

But that one plant had done the trick.

In Vancouver, oil-share dealers pointed ringed fingers to large blueprints of the Fraser Valley and explained the position.

"See here! Right where that white circle is, they've struck oil. How's that? In paying quantities? Well, no, not yet. But they are only a thousand feet down. The big thing is, *they've found oil.* Now, sir, right next to the Langford Oil Lands, right here, is our property, the New Langford Oil Company. I claim that the shares I offer you today at fifteen cents will be worth fifteen dollars six months hence. No bull! This is the goods."

And the money was exchanged.

It was "easier than taking a sucking bottle from a baby and a darn sight more pleasant," as the man who sat down to write out the share certificate tersely put it.

But like every other ramp since the South Sea Bubble, it brought its Nemesis.*

Two years passed and the boom fizzled out. But the harm was done. The Valley had lost virtually two years of its growth. That slow growth of men living cleanly, simply, in the shadow of the bush.

And the bush, impenetrable and enigmatic, looked on. Green and still, it flowed across the Valley, eaten into here and there, but unconquered, unconquerable.

The gambling madness came to an end and the settlers, wiser though sadder men, went back to their axes, their mattocks and their crosscut saws. They were like men after a night's debauch. It had been fun while it lasted but they questioned the value received. The price seemed a little high. The fun of anticipation was rather more than offset by the letdown.

And little Tom Preedy took it hardest of all.

He had chopped down all his fruit-trees, rooted up all his small fruit. His place was six foot deep in stubborn bracken. And he sulkily refused to touch it.

CHAPTER XV

1.

It was two years before the oil boom passed from the Valley, but long before that, it was known that not a single drop of crude petroleum had been raised. Once again the Valley had been stung, just as it had been stung by the land boom which left prices so high that nearly every settler was saddled with such a large mortgage that interest on previous investments amounted to nothing and neither did the wages for long hours of daily work.

Stein declared that the Valley was not worthwhile.

"I am going to live in Vancouver," he declared. "The days of pioneering are over. The Valley has been victimized. There's nothing to it."

That was all right for Stein, who had money. But not everybody could just walk out like that.

Then it became known that Stein had sold to a Japanese.

"That makes five Japanese families in Ferguson's Landing now," said Old Man Dunn bitterly. "A man oughter be ashamed to sell to 'em – it means the ruin of the Valley."

Two years had passed and the aftermath of the oil boom was being felt. Bad luck seemed to dog the settlement. Small fruits were no longer worth growing: they sold for less than the CPR freightage to transport them to Sapperton market, and most of the old-timers had grubbed up their bushes.*

Apples were not much better. The apples imported from

Spokane and Portland were dumped on the Vancouver market cheaper than the Valley farmers could produce them. Even chickens were in disfavour. The price of grain rose as the result of manipulations of the Winnipeg Exchange and the Vancouver market was flooded with eggs imported from China. As these eggs could lawfully be sold as new laid, there was no sense in shipping genuine new-laid eggs in competition.

It was the same with truck-gardening: cost of production rose, markets declined. Not a farmer in the Valley could compete with the Chinese truck-gardeners. Those indefatigable workers had virtually annexed Lulu Island, that flat, fertile delta at the mouth of the Fraser River. It had become like a provincial Chinese village with no inch of it that did not support a lettuce, radish, cabbage or young tomato plant.

There remained the bush. The bush! That fertile source of wealth. And the river, with its salmon.

But, alas, here again the settlers found themselves threatened by hard economic facts. The coming of the Japanese settlers had revolutionized logging. The Japanese, employing Japanese labour, quoted prices that undercut the white workers. They could afford to put a boom on the river at a price that would have been possible to the white worker only if he had accepted wages of around fifty cents a day.

It was the old problem – the racial clash, with all it implied in economic and social conflict.

Five families already in the settlement, and talk of more coming.

As for the river, it presented its own problems. Japanese fishermen and pirate fishermen from American fishing waters took toll of the salmon even before they had properly cleared the open sea. The salmon that escaped those far-flung and busy gill-nets at the mouth of the river came upstream. But the Valley had seen the last of the big years. The days of the big run, when the salmon sped like a mighty glittering army in the waters of the river, were passed.

Strangely, this decrease in output had no corresponding effect on prices. This mystified the Valley men until they realized that the Japanese were shipping canned salmon from Japan at prices which undercut the British Columbian product. The fact that they exported these goods in tins labelled in imitation of those of the B.C. canneries only leaked out later.

Fuller survived the changing conditions. He had saved for many years. "If things get too bad here," he said, "I'll up stakes, sell to the Japs, and go south to Florida. I've been studying conditions in Florida for years. I know what I'll be up against there, and it's a country where a man can make good."

Oh, wonderful Fuller! Wonderful Fuller!

And Johansson too had weathered the storm. His fifty acres were bought and paid for. "If you've a bit of land that's good land," he would declare in one of his infrequent communicative moments, "there's always a living in it. A man doesn't need to buy and sell, he's self-contained, so to say. And with a cow, why, a cow's half a man's living."

By now Johansson's fifty acres were cleared and cropped. Moreover, his cow had calved twice: a fine heifer follows her around the meadow where she feeds on the rich red clover.

2.

Yes, Johansson had prospered. His land is clean as a whistle. Only the Japanese who had bought Heggerty's place could boast so thoroughly cleared a ranch.

There was a neat picket fence all round Johansson's place now, a fence against the intrusion of the bush. Behind the shack stood a byre with steep pitched roof, trim and shipshape.* Hard by was the new barn, four times bigger than the shack. It was full of good fodder. A new chicken house accommodated a flock of a hundred white Leghorn hens who passed their consequential days under the gimlet eye of a haughty cock, inside a wire enclosure. All day long there were sounds from the Johansson place. The clucking of hens, the mooing of the cow, the grunting of the sows. His two sows lay all day in the churned-up mire of their sties, their vast bellies exposed for the convenience of their voracious litters. Berkshire sows of high quality. The litters sucked at those rows of dugs and grew and grew.

A step from the shack stood the timber from the clearing: fire-wood to last a man a lifetime, stacked neatly in cords, like troops in column of route. The biggest wood pile ever known at Ferguson's Landing.

And no more water trouble! The hazel twig had solved that problem! Folk laughed at the hazel twig, but not Johansson. He had gone out, the forked twig tightly clasped in his great hands, walking slowly over his land, looking for water, waiting for his hazel twig to bow down to it.

And it had bowed, suddenly twisting against the tight clasp of those strong fingers, so that when he opened his bands there was the mottled smear of sappy bark left upon them.

He had dug at that very spot, and at thirty feet he had come upon a spring. It flowed through cleft shale, cold and sweet and plentiful. It never failed him now whereas the old well was closed up. The new well being to the north, on the high ground, he installed a zinc tank and a force-pump. Mrs. Johansson had but to turn a tap to get water in her living room. She had even a sink, a sink of tin, neatly made from kerosene cans – a little job done in odd moments by this machine of a man.

A rick thatched, and potatoes pitted, clover; young fruit trees close to bearing; berry bushes, but only enough for his own needs; then great winter cabbages.

It was nothing to Johansson whether there was oil in the Valley or not. The Valley had fertile soil: it gave back what you gave to it. It paid dividends. On fifty acres such a man could live, frugally, thriftily. Nothing came as a gift. No, one had to fight the bush and sometimes the bush fought back. Even so, it was a better master than the city, the city that cheated a man.

There had been that hard winter when the rare silver-frost was seen in the Valley. The rain had fallen and even as it fell, the temperature swooped: the falling water froze upon the branches of the trees. In an hour the bush, white and wonderful to behold, groaned beneath the weight. Before morning many trees cracked and broke with the report of guns, crashing down with their loads of ice. Very beautiful the bush looked with the silver-frost upon it. It was a forest of glass that shone and sparkled.

One ice-laden branch crashed onto the roof of Johansson's shack. It tore away the shingles and left a gap like a shell-hole. That had been a misfortune for it happened during one of Mrs. Johansson's bad spells. The terrifying noise had frightened her and next day she had not left her bed.

From where she lay she could gaze through the jagged hole in the roof and watch the scudding clouds. The face of her man peered down at her, his mouth full of shingle tacks. She listened to his fast hammer for hours. The hole shrunk: by night he had made good the damage.

Johansson was becoming his own master. He could take or reject work as he chose. And there was plenty of work at home. Plenty. No plough had ever turned a sod of that rich soil; he had dug over his fifty acres by hand. Slow, slow labour. But a bit at a time, an hour here, an hour there; perhaps even a day, a whole long day once in a while. But in the end it all added up.

Now the work was done. In a sense, Johansson was a made

man. In a sense too he was a man unmade. He had made a ranch, but he was now a little stiffer in his movements. His back was bent a bit and he knew weariness, aches and pains.

3.

Little was seen of the newcomers. They kept to themselves. They had cleared a patch (no more than half an acre), and had sown it down to red clover. Red clover, always the first crop of the redeemed bushland.

"You sow red clover," Johansson had advised him. "It's rich, is red clover, and the land likes it. Plough it in the following year and then plant potatoes. You'll get a good crop."

The Newcomer's wife was not seen about, not even moving on the new clearing. But the Newcomer hired himself out whenever he could. Sometimes it would be a few days' work at the gravel pit, loading the wagons for the teams. Once he got work away back in the bush. It was so far back that he would set out while it was still night, with the moon to light him along the silent, ghostly trails of the bush. He went off swinging a lard pail containing his lunch: big sandwiches, a screw of salt, apples. And it was night when he came back from the shadow of the trees.

Long and weary days, and a weary man at the end of each. Earning bread by the sweat of his brow, getting down to 'hard tacks,' was the Newcomer. No more grand living, no more long evenings around the fire. That small patch of bush had eaten up his little capital, consumed it insidiously, a bit here for blasting powder, a bit there to pay Blanchard's bills. Tools, lumber for the chicken houses, haulage up the steep and slippery trail from the river. One thing and another. It was all gone.

He was wearing out his dress trousers now, wearing them tucked into his heavy elk-hide boots. His shirt was of faded canvas.

Much better than working animal-like, long hours for a fixed wage of three dollars, he liked to get what he grandly termed "a contract."

Mrs. Woods, for instance, had climbed the trail to the new place one day. A thin little woman, she might have stepped out of a Sussex village high-street, from a rectory or from a manor house. She was prim, proper, dowdy, plain, a colourless little woman. Kindly, but afraid of reality.

She explained that Woods was suffering with his heart and could not prepare the winter's fire-wood. Would the Newcomer do it? She would pay two dollars a rick, the wood to be delivered.

She had thereupon ordered twenty ricks of fir. A splendid contract!

"You see," he explained to his wife as they talked it over after Mrs. Woods had trotted off down the hill, "working on a contract isn't half so heart-breaking as working for wages. You can just go at it, and the more you go at it, the more money you earn. I like that feeling. Wages somehow deaden one. It's like being an animal. I don't think anyone ought to be paid by the hour. It ought to be abolished. It ought to be money for work: more work, more money. That would fix the slackers."

4.

So he would set out with his dog Peter, a big pure-white collie who would lollop ahead of him, turning round every now and again to wave his fan-like tail and then scamper off again into the fringe of the bush, sniffing, hunting chipmunks. A happy dog.*

And the man walked behind, striding along with his little lard pail in one hand and across his shoulder the springy six foot blade of his crosscut saw.

Long days in the silence of the bush, sawing wood. Perfect stillness everywhere. Beauty all around. A symphony in greens and browns. And the smells! Scents of the aged earth. Moist, living smells that touched the nerves and evoked emotions that belonged to a time long, long ago. The smell of the past, the first smells at which the nostrils of the first man quivered.

And there was life in the bush: teeming life. The stillness was broken only by the unexpected sound of falling twigs and the slow drip of water. A nervous chipmunk, scuttling with the staccato jerks of an automaton, brush waving, along some rotten tree stump, peered inquisitively from the tangle of the forest floor at this strange intruder. Holding beech nuts in tiny paws, he cracked shells with incredible cleverness. Marvellous strength of canny teeth.

Everywhere, life and the struggle for life.

By the trunk of a first-growth Douglas fir, from which he was sawing mighty drums of firm, yellow wood, he saw how a vine maple, caught by the fall of that mighty tree, had contrived to thrust out its tenuous branches from its prison. It writhed like a snake from beneath the fallen trunk and curved in graceful lines towards the light of day, victorious over death.

Life, always life, sought against odds. Everything striving to survive.

Half an hour's rest for lunch, and mental calculations. How many more sections of that tree can he saw before darkness falls on the bush ? Peter looks on, head cocked, awaiting his share. He is not disappointed. No word is spoken. It is true companionship: man and dog. Friends. Perfect confidence on either side. Love.

Everywhere, life.

He moves aimlessly, for it is still the rest period, and the frugal lunch is done. He picks up his axe, swings it idly. It comes down upon the dark brown wood of a rotten red cedar.

At the blow, the timber falls apart: red, moist, loam-like. Decayed wood like sand pours out of the wound. The tree is returning to the earth. After how many proud centuries as a giant of the bush, a proud, straight cedar?

He stoops and picks up that humid mould that was once wood. It is wet and gives off a damp, vegetable odour, the odour of decay.

He sits on the rotted tree, and now there springs into being before him an unsuspected city of teeming life.

5.

The red ants have captured the fallen tree and have converted it into a living citadel. A labyrinth of tunnels lies exposed, a complicated and highly organized city.

The ants run hither and thither, without apparent purpose. Little black heads peering this way, peering that way. Bulbous bodies, upon spidery legs, moving swiftly in erratic courses.

Ah! He has raised an alarm, has this Gulliver!

Ants are debouching from those circular doors, rushing hither and thither, lifting minute heads high, waving antennae defiantly towards the vast menace. Some dash forth into the light carrying in their forelegs the yellowish larvae. They describe erratic courses with their treasure, seeking safety with fear-quickened instincts.

Life, and the struggle for life, even here. The menaced generations and their custodians: faithful unto death.

There are the dead, crushed by that idle blow from the axe. Already they are being hurried away by their living fellows, held high in legs no thicker than thread.

Curious, he turns a piece of loose wood and exposes the serried ranks of the ant stable. In each neat cell the pallid aphids stand. The workers are removing them to a place of safety. They race off carrying their cattle in their forepaws, running here, running there. At all costs they must save their honeydew, the sweet honeydew which they tickle so cunningly from their patient captives.

Frenzied, but working to plan. Fearful, but controlled by purposeful wills. A kingdom within a rotted tree. A kingdom menaced, and meeting that menace. An organized community, ruled – by what? Instinct? Intelligence? The blind force of all life to survive? Or a realm ruled by the power of minds housed marvellously in minute, black, shining heads?

Thoughts enough for the afternoon. The shadows deepen and the bush, ceasing to glow with mellow light, becomes dim, shadowy, mysterious.

The saw rips through the yellow fir, rhythmic, two-noted. Beside the trail stands the split wood, stacked in ricks, each eight foot by four.

And the long trudge back to the clearing, to the yellow house with the smoking chimney, to the patient, waiting woman. Eight dollars earned.

Eight dollars!

A small moving object at the foot of the soaring trees. A tiny creature concealed by the vastness of the bush. A man: an ant!

The bush made one think.

6.

When they had come to the settlement his wife had known nothing of the management of a house. She had never cooked a meal, never swept a room, never washed so much as a handkerchief. In the two years that had passed she had learnt much, however.

The table would be set when he clumped the mud from heavy boots and crossed the threshold. The kettle on the stove would be spurting out its homely plume of steam. The smell of cooking food would pervade the warm, cosy kitchen.

"But why have tablecloths when it only makes more washing? Why not American cloth that can be wiped over?"

She is silent as she moves about the range, pouring the water upon the tea, taking, with cloth-shielded hands, the hot dishes from the oven. She is silent because in her own department she likes to do everything in her own way.

She sets her man's meal before him and herself takes her seat. A tired-looking little woman with patient eyes. A heroic woman without heroics. Prosaic, unimaginative, matter-of-fact. But hardened by a vein of unsuspected steel. Something fine.

Bob England had predicted that she would not last six months. "Buried away up there! A bride, too! The fellow's a damn fool," he said to his wife. "Girls from the Old Country aren't used to that sort of thing. She'll whine and make him sell and go down to Vancouver."

But Bob England was wrong: she did not whine.

Consider this supper.

The bread: a cottage loaf with head awry, crisp and brown and light. Her baking, and she taught herself. Another woman would have gone breezily to a neighbour and borrowed in an hour the other's experience of years. Not so this woman. She bought a book and taught herself. Failure came before success.

There is salmon. There is so much salmon on the place that it must be eaten, and meat is a luxury now beyond them. Salmon! God, how they had sickened at the repetition of that dish!

But see what she had made of it, this little woman who, throughout the long silent day, has been thinking of him out there in the bush working, scheming how she shall give him a sustaining meal.

There is white sauce, and the fish is transformed from the familiar flaky pink monotony and tastelessness to a French delicacy! He consumes it rapidly without a word of praise.

She does not mind that. This is what she wanted: that he should feast upon what she has prepared for him.

She pours the steaming tea and passes the big cup across.

He tilts it into his saucer and gulps it down.

"That's good! Good!"

Times have changed. Drinking from a saucer, wanting American tablecloths.

Her mind switches back to the past. She sees his homely face above a white expanse of dress shirt and white waistcoat. White hands, manicured nails. Immaculate. He explains what goes into the making of a perfect Bordeaux . . .

"Why are you smiling?"

"Thoughts." She continues to smile.

Sip, sip. "Amusing ones, eh?"

"If I had a washing machine."

He looks up and studies her.

A washing machine.

She looks tired. Her hair is not groomed. She has no corsets on and the big apron makes her look shapeless.

A washing machine!

His eyes rest upon her hands. Small hands they are, with fingers scarred by a hundred minute intersecting lines. Work-coarsened hands with ill-tended nails. A washing machine!

He gets up and lurches stiffly over to the little pine-wood dresser. He picks up the old German beer-mug, relic of the old days when he was a *realschule* student.* He gives it a shake by the handle. "Only ten cents in the bank," he announces. "But I'll be getting the Woods' money soon. Should finish that job this week."

She is clearing the table.

"How much would one of these things cost?"

She knows that, of course, knows precisely the make she wants, and why.

"You see, with these things you simply heat your water, dump it in with soft soap, bundle the dirty clothes in after, and work the handle to and fro. It saves so much stooping."

"And I suppose we could get one on credit?"

He moves over to the dresser, feeling his pockets with his hands. He frowns, then smiles to himself. He takes the tea canister and from it fills his pipe. It lights up. A smoke of sorts. Better than nothing.

He is in the rocker, his feet in carpet shoes. Canvas shirt open at the neck and old dress trousers, stained and torn.

She is clearing the table with the precision of the worker who has performed the same movements every day for a long time. She is slow, methodical, orderly.

"I'll have to get you to fetch water from the creek, dear. There's only half a bucket left."

Puff, puff.

"Blast the water! I'll have to dig a well."

He gets up stiffly, for his muscles, even now, feel the reaction of ten hours' constant usage. "The devil is that I can't dig a well until I can pay a man to work with me. I'm down ten feet, but I can't throw up the dirt any higher and Johansson says it will probably mean going thirty feet before we get to the shale."

He takes two buckets and goes out into the darkness.

No money, but it is their own place, and the best furnished home in the settlement, with its arm-chairs, chesterfield, bronzes and pictures in oils, its bedroom with the big brass bedstead.

He clatters in with the filled buckets, sets them down, and returns to the rocker by the stove.

"Old Country mail tomorrow."

He says that twice a week, always optimistically, as though

the Old Country mail would yield them letters, newspapers, magazines.

But it never does yield them any of those things.

People soon forget. They are cut off from their old world.

"Go down to the depot and buy a *Saturday Evening Post* off the newsboy on the local," she says. "I'm reading the serial. Take the ten cents from the bank."

He is glad she has suggested that. Yes, that's good. He wouldn't have liked to suggest it himself.

Yes, that is her quiet way – to ask for herself what she wants for him. What time has she for reading? In the evenings there's mending to do. By nine her head tilts forward in her chair, her mouth relaxes and she sleeps.

7.

That winter they took her down the hill. Snow was on the ground and Bob England brought up his sled with the chestnut team. The horses slipped in the mush.

It was the only way to get her down. She could not walk, neither could she climb into a rig.

Bob England put straw on the sled. She huddled upon it, a little woman with wide open, startled eyes.

Twice on the downward trail it seemed that catastrophe must overwhelm. The following sled swung round on the soft snow and collided with a tree stump. But she did not cry out. She merely clutched with her little work-worn hands; her patient face blanched a little.

A week later, down at the hospital at Sapperton, her baby was born. A boy.

CHAPTER XVI

1.

Johansson secured a contract to take out ties for the CPR. Always the CPR were calling for ties and more ties. Three thousand miles of track, and heavy trains, heavy locos, that pounded the track, spreading the metals, splitting the ties. The section gang that lived in wheelless trucks beside the track laboured day after day at their six-mile section of line.

It was like painting the Eiffel Tower: you started at the bottom and when the top was done you had to start all over again. Their work was never finished.

Dark, quiet, smiling Italians they were, men burnt mahogany through exposure to all weathers. Great labourers: contented, thrifty, well-conducted. They sent all their money back to Italy.

And kindly too. They would stop always when they met a child, and their beautiful Neapolitan eyes would shine with tenderness, and their perfect teeth would flash white from dusky faces. They gave the children of the settlement candies. Their foreman was a Norwegian.

Every day these fellows were uprooting ties that had cracked and become unsafe to carry the six-foot permanent way. The clank of their crowbars was heard all day long down the road.

So Johansson got busy when the contract came along and, a month before the scheduled date, had dumped the last load of ties beside the track. They were of Douglas fir, shaped up and ready for use.

That was the largest cheque he had ever had. Mary explained to him how he must write his name upon the back of it in order to get the money. He made a special journey down to the Bank of Montreal, Sapperton, to get the money. Hundreds of dollars – like that! That was money indeed.

He came back with a new store-bought suit, black and ill fitting. A hat, too, for his wife, and for Mary a print dress.

They all dressed up in their finery and inspected each other.

"Well, there's other things I'm wanting," drawled Mrs. Johansson in her slow, tired voice. "Maybe we could spare the money to send to Eaton's Store for a parcel of things?"

"Sure, there's money. What was it you were wanting?"

His voice seemed to say: "Have I not bought you a new hat? Did not the girl in the shop say it would suit very well indeed? What can you be wanting? You have a well with a pipe, a sink, a churner."

But he spoke none of these thoughts. "Sure, you send to Eaton's." It was grandly said.

Mrs. Johansson was at the table, the fat catalogue before her, turning the pages she knew so well. Mary, chin in hands, twisted her neat head to see the pictures. Ladies with wonderful waists, in wonderful corsets, flimsy drawers and chemises. Hats, cloaks, high-heeled shoes, toilette articles.

Wonderful things.

"We might have the newspaper sent to us," Johansson bursts out.

He is standing looking down at his clothes. He looks like an undertaker in them. They fit him nowhere, nowhere at all. But it is broadcloth, and with the black hat for Sundays. The proper thing, because it's what his father had before him. But the suit is cut on American lines: padded shoulders make him look grotesque.

"Yes, we might be having a newspaper."

2.

The newspaper marked an epoch. It stood for more than words can tell. Every day to go to the store: "My paper in?"

Ah, that was something!

The paper was a great success. It changed the evenings. Instead of sitting silent for the hour before bed (save for sporadic little bits of talk about the day's work), the Johansson family found themselves talking of the big world beyond.

Mary read the paper aloud in her clear, toneless voice. Mr. and Mrs. Johansson sat, one each side of the stove, listening with wooden faces.

They read it all, for after all it cost five cents.

"Much of the speech of the British Columbian Member was applied to the Oriental problem of the Coast, which he regarded as a menace, especially the Japanese end of it."

Johansson nods his head. Mrs. Johansson nods her head.

"Instead of immigration being curtailed, it had reached four hundred and one last year.* He maintained that Orientals should not be allowed to enter Canada to become workers in competition with Canadians. There was a Japanese woman to every two men and the birthrate was mounting rapidly. Within thirty years there would be three million Orientals in British Columbia."

A rustle of pages.

Johansson: "That's right, I tink."

Mrs. Johansson, petulantly: "Why don't some of them stop it?"

And Mary's voice again, monotonous, but very clear, in an English tinged with the nasal tones of America.

"Perhaps the word 'toil' is the wrong one to use in connection with the Indians. They work only intermittently, leaving their jobs when they tire of them."

"That's so."

"In British Columbia all Indians are part of four great divisions: the wolf, the eagle, the finback whale and the raven. A wolf never marries a finback. Already the native arts are almost gone and every year sees some change towards what we know as civilizing which will end in absorption."

"They ain't no good."

A rustle of paper and Mary's voice again. "At the Magistrate's court two Hindus were charged with an offence against the penal code. According to the evidence, both men, who worked in the Excelsior saw mill, had been guilty of secreting a white girl for immoral purposes. They were committed for trial."

"Time you was gettin' to bed, Mary. Mother'll read the paper."

The door closes behind the girl.

"Can't figger why they allow the Jap's wimmen in, and not the Hindu's wimmen. Hindus are British subjects, ain't it? If they don't allow their wimmen in they got to expect it, ain't they?"

Yes, the coming of the paper was a great occasion. It had everything one could want. It even told you how to get rid of potato blight, and corns, and it offered you prizes. Yes, the newspaper was a great success.

But Mrs. Johansson did not see a solution to this riddle of the Hindus. Her head had fallen forward on her meagre breast. She was asleep. Her mouth, with its colourless lips, lolled open.

3.

Johansson put down the newspaper and lumbered to the door of the shack. There he stood, casting an all-seeing eye over his ranch. Evening had thrown violet shadows on the bush, the sky was violet-tinted. He admired the trim meadow, now a dim square on the arabesque of the clearing. He admired the new well, the stacked wood and the chicken house. He admired the new narrow, tall smoke-house, like a big privy. He walked across to the stye and there, leaning upon the rail of it, he admired the Berkshire sows. They lay weighted with maternity and eyed him with sullen, pink-rimmed eyes.

Clean sows, because as he would say: "Pigs is clean as other beasts – if you let them be." A big stye, so that it was no vanity to be proud of it. One sow had risen. He watched her rub her swollen flank against the lice-pole. She grunted her relief as the kerosene got to work on the ticks.

Yes. And he admired the cow as he walked over to her byre and smacked her lean and glossy flank. He loved his cow, the cow that was half a man's living.

His simple soul was serene. And, as he returned to the trim shack, he took snuff. His contentment was complete. Soon the rain would come.

4.

The rain beat upon the bush. Far down in the shrouded Valley a light danced in the darkness describing a series of eccentric arcs, like some fire-beetle battling against the steady relentless beat of the downpour.

The squelch of heavy boots fighting the suction of the greedy mud became audible as the light grew, then two figures appeared, the swinging hurricane-lamp throwing their forms into high relief of fitful gleamings. It was as though they had stepped out from a parted curtain.

Their streaming oilskins glistened and with each swing of the flashing lantern their white faces were revealed and blotted out again. They moved like men with urgent business across the debris of the Newcomer's clearing. Then they passed into the bush and were swallowed up. It was as though they had pushed aside the curtain of the night and passed on to the stage of some hidden world beyond.

The rain beat upon the bush. The unseen drummers of the forest drummed. The darkness was alive with sounds.

5.

Mrs. Johansson had been dying for four days. Her suffering never ceased. No woman in the settlement had known anything like that, though all could tell stories. A withered woman, worn out by work, and sapless. Her breasts had long since shrunk, and her bones were brittle. The thing within her gnawed incessantly.

The Swede pushed open the door of his shack and a shaft of light leapt out to meet his gaunt figure. The room was clean, neat and over-heated; its warm, vitiated air rolled towards the two streaming men and enveloped them, invading their senses. Upon the iron stove a kettle threw out a cloud of steam. The stove-pipe reared up like a snake thrusting its black trunk through the boards of the ceiling.

Mary rose from the table. She was prim and demure. From behind round spectacles her grey eyes looked at her father and the doctor with the experience of thirty years but her softly-rounded body spoke of mere adolescence.

From behind those glasses she had watched, with the intelligence of a terrier, the work that her mother performed, year in, year out. This had given her precocious wisdom: she meant to escape, and escape lay by way of those scattered books. In three years she would leave the bush and become a pupil teacher. She might even marry a white-collar man, a man who did not take snuff, spit, or need to hire himself out for three dollars a day.

Her voice was flat and toneless. Since her father had gone for the doctor things had seemed worse. Mrs. Dunn had come but she had quickly departed.

Poor little Mrs. Dunn, with the thin body and darting movements of a hen. She had done what she could and, after an hour, had gone off, tears streaming down her thin cheeks.

Standing by the stove, the doctor nodded. His face was expressionless. Johansson watched it, looking for a signal of hope. In his slow mind the thoughts marched about like convicts round a prison yard.

"Four days, doctor," he said, and his dead voice seemed to carry a reproach to God and an exhortation to this silent man to make good the botched handiwork of the Deity. "Four days she keeps cryin' out in pain."

He became aware of his daughter's voice again. She told him she thought the end had come, and that she had felt powerless. She was alone.

The steaming kettle started to boil over, making of the lid a castanet that clattered furiously.

6.

From behind the further door, which led into the bedroom, came a low, long-drawn-out moan. It was the weak protest of utter exhaustion, the agonized articulation of suffering too exquisite for human flesh. It seemed to come from far away, as though down all the corridors of the ages the flood of pain had swept into this one human frame.

The doctor divested himself of his enveloping oilskins. He stood revealed as a pale young man with a lick of wet black hair plastered to an unhealthily pallid forehead. He moved slowly and with deliberation. His face was expressionless. He busied himself with his bag, opened its wide mouth, took out a glass-stoppered bottle, held it to the lozenge of light from the shaded lamp, returned to his bag, rummaged in its secret places, and brought forth a slender, glittering syringe. Slowly and methodically he adjusted his hypodermic and turned towards the closed door.

The groaning stopped.

7.

When Mrs. Johansson found that she had cancer she had tried to kill herself. She had suffered for three years. Violent sickness racked her. She could not eat and her body became a numb and pulsing ache. She suffered but refused to see a doctor. She did her work, rising early to prepare her husband's breakfast; she did her work and complained only mutely with her eyes.

Johansson said nothing, but he went one day to the store and got from Blanchard a money order for Oslo. He knew what his wife wanted – knew what she was too thrifty to ask for. His daughter had written the letter into which he awkwardly stuffed the flimsy money-order with his big, work-coarsened hands. That money represented twelve days' work – thirty-six dollars.

But he too believed in this patent medicine, this wonder-worker. What did his Swedish paper say of it? Why, it proved things, publishing photographs of the miraculously cured. It would set his wife on her feet again. It would cure her sickness, banish her fears and her melancholy. Things would be the same again. Hope of a cure rose once more in his simple heart. It had been three years since he'd felt any hope at all.

When the parcel had come he had fallen on it like a drunk on his bottle. He carried it under his arm up the steep trail to his clearing. His wife rewarded him with the first smile she had given him for months. She read the instructions with the reverence due to the word of God, and took her first dose. She felt the better for it an hour after, she declared: the pain in her side had let up. "Doctors!" Her voice was full of scorn for them.

She consumed those twelve bottles, one by one. Her face became more yellow, more like dead maple leaves. But she praised the wonder-worker.

8.

The patent medicine had done its work.

The young doctor, finger upon the sleeper's pulse, was puzzled: it throbbed under his fingers, slowly, with little fits and starts, and little frenzied pulsations, dying away as though wearied, resuming its pumping with a slow, dull determination. He searched in the unused chambers of his memory for half-forgotten medical lore, and returned, yawning, without it. He fell back on the pompous sophistries of his craft: low vitality, he told himself; debility. An older man would have said, cancer, wrong diet, overwork – and drugs.

The rain beat its ceaseless tattoo on the cedar shingles of the roof above the doctor's head. He dozed in the heated air.

In the living room, drying his thick socks before the stove, sat Johansson. There was no expression upon his grey face; he was a patient kind of man. With head cupped on arms, the girl slept over her books, the light upon her head, with its pig-tail twisted up and secured with a meagre bow.

At two o'clock the doctor pressed his fingers to the eyes of the dead woman and tip-toed into the living room. He was tired and cold. His journey had been for nothing. He would have to tell this fellow and he shrank from the task.

In a straight-backed chair Johansson slept. His mouth was slightly open, and, at its corners, the snuff tobacco which he sometimes ate oozed in a yellow rivulet onto the stubble of his chin.

The rain beat upon the roof and the unseen drummers of the bush beat upon their drums. The patent medicine had done its work; it had cured the sufferer of her pain.

9.

Death, having had his way, bestowed the useless boon of beauty on the thing tortured and destroyed. The lines, carved by pain, were wiped from that waxen face; the moulding, made by melancholy, had melted to a softness; the old discontent had fled and the tired face was beautiful.

Looking down at the help-mate who had slipped silently from him while he slept, Johansson marvelled at death's transfiguration.

Life, the reward of unremitting toil, the tardy recompense of the brown earth and the green forest, had dried the emotional wells of this gaunt man. His mind moved slowly about the tomb of his emotions. The vast central fact of death escaped him.

It seemed so small an affair after all: a waxen figure, impersonal, remote and very still. A waiter who waited for nothing. Stillness made manifest. It woke nothing in the heart of the man but a vague sense of fear, a repulsion tinged with whispering awe.

What was this effigy of wax, less alive than the loam, than the water of the well, than the bleeding core of the new-felled timber – what was it to him? It was nothing. It was an obtruder who had taken the place of a living woman.

Johansson wanted his wife back. He wanted her about the shack, moving slowly about the hot stove, stirring the stew pot, bending over the washtub wringing the dirt from his sweat-soaked shirts, lying in bed beside him.

Monstrous forms moved silently in the hinterland of his mind, lumbered up from their primeval stamping grounds and threw dark shadows upon his thoughts, pursuing him out of a remote and unremembered past. Racial memory marched to him down the centuries, bearing with it man's unconquered fear of death and death's inscrutability. A cold finger touched his heart.

He wanted things as they had been, and gazing at that shrouded outline, moulded by the red-and-white check coverlet of the wooden bed, resentment against it rose like a gorge within him. This was death looking at him from the closed eyes and waxen face of an image. His wife had vanished utterly.

He wanted to escape to the living, to the girl there beside the dying stove, to the living memories of the woman whose dead body barred the avenues of his mind with the imponderable fact of death.

The dogmas of the Lutheran faith of his youth came back to him but he found that his faith, stowed away in a disused chamber of his mind, had mildewed. It was as dead and meaningless as the still figure upon the bed.

He fled from reality to the refuge of all afflicted, baffled mortals. He sat beside the stove, lean chin cupped in one great hand, and conjured up the hosts of consolation. In some way the dead lived. He had heard it often.

He put reality behind him and walked the fields of fantasy.

10.

The Newcomer had asked him to blow the first-growth stump that barred his back door like a dwarf battlement. It could be done. Four or five half-stick charges, deep down among the splayed roots, tamped carefully: that would split her up. Too near the house for fire. Dig down and chop. It would take three days. Three days, nine dollars. There was talk down at the store of an outfit from Sapperton coming to take out ties for the railway.

He might get a sub-contract as he did before. It had paid well. On contract, he could make six dollars a day. Perhaps a hundred dollars there.

The Newcomer had to have a well. His creek dried up in the early spring. Plenty of water on the slope. At thirty feet. Hazel twig would show. A week's job. Eighteen dollars.

He could do it easy. But the patch by the chicken house would have to wait. There would be no time to spade it over for potatoes.

He rubbed his two great hands together. They were immense hands, hands as big as the hands of Epstein's *Christus.* *Calloused, sinewy, hairless, very strong. He spat upon furrowed palms and rubbed the two leathery surfaces together. Presently he took out his round tin tobacco-snuff box, lifted a pinch to his thin nostrils and sniffed the tobacco into his nose.

It brought him comfort.

11.

Johansson had figured it all out. The stream of life swept him along.

The dead woman had become a living problem. And he had solved it: he could see his way to paying for her funeral. He could pay the doctor: forty miles, forty dollars. Yes, he could do that too, but the potato patch would have to wait.

Outside, a Leghorn cock with bright eyes quizzed the discarded heap of medicine bottles. He stalked off disdainfully, lifting his yellow feet high, stretched his feathered legs, stretched his shapely neck, shook crimson wattles, and gave shrill voice.

He had seen the dawn, the dawn that peered, grey and watery and sad, through the bush. But a dawn nonetheless. He greeted it, throwing his soul into a shrill crow.

And neither the bird nor the man knew the secret of those bottles that had promised life and had rewarded faith with death.

Love and sacrifice had dug a grave between them.

CHAPTER XVII

1.

Things were not going well with the parson. His sallow face wore a set expression of melancholy and the deep furrows which ran from high-bridged nose to coarse mouth seemed to deepen. He frequently complained of the strain of his ministry. But he had found one true sympathizer – Mary Ellison.

He was driving her from the little wooden church back to the old Ferguson Place, her home.

"I sometimes almost feel as though it was sheer waste of time to continue to work here," he complained.

They were driving between tall trees along a rutted trail, as yet ungraded.

He flicked the back of the old mare. "One finds so little support," he went on. "The people seem to be utterly irreligious. Why, last Sunday there were only fifteen people at matins."

Mary Ellison listened in silence, her gentle face expressive of sympathy and understanding.

"I'm sure it must be very difficult," she said. "Even those without rigs could get lifts, you'd think."

The parson's face twitched. "You know it isn't the few miles, Mary, that keeps the church empty. No. First, it's that Presbyterian Church that draws the people. They go to it because they disapprove – oh, I know they do – of what they call my ritualistic practices. The blunt truth of the matter is that the Church of England is not wanted in Canada. Canada is Nonconformist at heart. The Presbyterian Church has usurped the place of the Church of England."

All this was said in a voice which somehow seemed to imply guilt on the part of the girl beside him. Being Canadian born, she felt that she had somehow a part in the disgrace of this defection from Anglicanism to Nonconformity.

"There is only one thing which repays me a hundredfold for my efforts here, Mary," he continued, throwing a glance at the warm face beside him. "And that is the support which I receive from your family."

Mary Ellison blushed. She knew that the word 'family,' being interpreted, meant herself.

Was he a fool to be thus playing with fire? The rig jolted down the rough trail, the mare stumbled, they remained silent. One of those things that cannot be unsaid, one of those declarations, hypocritically masked by indirect statement, which mark definitely the course of friendship's march towards a closer, more dangerous relationship.

He eyed the girl beside him to see what thoughts were passing in her mind and, being unable to divine them from that Madonna face, moistened his dry lips and broke the strain of the silence.

"Yes, it is the Old Country people who support me," he declared, and wondered whether he had made things better or worse.

2.

The Ellison family were a graft from the Old World upon the New. They had brought with them all the class notions of traditional England. Not the England of the cities, but the England of the counties where tradition survives.

They understood perfectly the social scheme which allots to each his place, and approved it. They knew precisely who were their social superiors and gave them an ungrudging deference, without loss of dignity or self respect. Just as they placed those lower than them selves in the social scale and drew the line with care and exactitude.

They belonged to the county life of England and the

social gradations of that peculiar institution were to them something right and proper and immutable. The Socialistic doctrines of the cities had left them untouched and they were sublimely unaware that the whole fabric of their England was undergoing a rapid disintegration.

Father Ellison was Lincolnshire as far back as he could go, which was to the early eighteenth century. In America, he would, of course, have ranked as an aristocrat by right of long lineage. In England he had been a yeoman farmer.* What was he in Canada? That was a question this little old man with the iron spectacles and iron whiskers often asked himself. Things had gone awry in this new land.

"There's no respect," Ellison told his wife. "They don't seem to have a feeling for what's right and proper, all mixing up together. It's a country without gentry, that's what it is, and for my part, I'm sorry for it. Gentry I approve of. It's all in the Book of Common Prayer, quite plain, quite clear."

And old Father Ellison, burdened with a ten-thousand dollar mortgage at eight per cent, and secretly regretting, every long day of his life, the impulse which uprooted him from the heavy clay of Lincolnshire, would go back to whatever he was doing with a sigh.

That the Vicar should show an interest in his Mary pleased and flattered him. The Vicar was an Old Countryman like himself. It was a bond between them, not that he would presume on it to be familiar. But just the same, if the Vicar wasn't too proud to take a meal with them, why then, surely Ellison was glad to see him at their table.

An interesting and sympathetic man.

3.

But this night the Vicar pleaded the preparation of his Sunday sermon and drove off after setting down his passenger.

The truth was, the parson had just awakened to the realization that he was treading dangerous ground. And he wanted immediately to examine himself. The long drive home gave him that opportunity.

He was aware of a profound discontent. Two years ago he had come here full of enthusiasm – and now, well, now he wished he had never come at all.

His memory flashed back to the day that he had gone, full of zeal, to the Clergy House, Westminster, to be interviewed. The great building, the bare corridors, the littered, unmethodical office into which he had been shown, and the slouching figure in dusty black who had greeted him, pipe in hand. He recalled the damping effect it had all had upon him. He had announced his intention to volunteer for foreign service a month earlier; the interview was the result.

For foreign service! There had been something thrilling in that. It sounded heroic, just as a soldier might feel setting out for active service abroad. Foreign service! The mission field! Inspiring phrases!

And what did it really mean? This! Living in a crude settlement among people who seemed to have no time nor inclination for anything but grubbing on their wretched little farms. No theatres, no music, no social life, only a drab monotony and a growing sense of futility as reward.

He thought about his wife and his face darkened. It was an awful test for a man and a woman to be set down in a place like this. He wondered whether Agnes's discontent was really at the root of his own. He thought it over and decided that it was. "Agnes is the sort of woman who should have married a vicar with a comfortable living," he muttered. "She would just fit into that atmosphere. Here she is lost."

She had lately got on his nerves, he told himself. Instead of trying to get her mind oriented to her new sphere of usefulness, she was stretching out, futilely, towards the interests of that other life in England. Her thirst for letters, for instance. That showed how she lived with her mind always in England. She was, he told himself, one of those women that do not grow. He remembered a dozen instances of her extraordinary rigidity of mind.

There had been that rumpus when they had tramped out together to take underclothing and socks to the Heggerty brats. That had been a lesson! But it was Agnes's own fault. She ought not to have 'Good womaned' that daughter of God's own country. He had a flashing vision of the outraged Mrs. Heggerty, hair soft and damp from application over the washing tub, skinny arms bare, face red with indignation, as she had flared out at the parson's lady. "Who's your good woman? Go to hell and take your damned charity with you!" And then, worst of all, the poor little creature had burst into tears.

No, Agnes was not the right woman. She ought not to have turned her back on Mrs. Heggerty just because of that. And her icily uttered: "It's simply disgusting!" had made a bitter enemy of Heggerty too.

Agnes would not fit in. That was the truth of it. It certainly handicapped a man. He remembered the bishop who had given him an episcopal blessing before he sailed. He had said: "In your dear wife you have a sure shield against despair in the life which lies before you." Now wasn't that sort of thing sheerest cant and humbug. As if that old fool knew anything about Agnes at all!

The shades of evening were falling and the old mare stumbled. The bush that lay upon either side of the trail was now full of deep shadows. It was very peaceful but it brought no peace to the troubled heart of the parson.

What was there to look forward to? he asked himself bitterly. Oh, there was no good disguising the truth from himself any longer: his church was empty because he did not understand how to fill it. That Presbyterian, working his two churches, ran constantly between Ferguson's Landing and Carlyle, and kept them both chock-full.

"I'm a damned failure," he told himself, "and Agnes is practically more to blame than I am. The women detest her. Even I've noticed it. She chills them. She can't enter into their lives. And I'm no good with children; never could get at them. What was that bit in Francis Thompson about the angels that plucked one back?"*

Then he came back to the central fact at which his self-deceiving mind had so long boggled. He started to think of Ferguson's Landing with Mary Ellison in the vicarage.

"There's a girl I could pull with: soft and gentle and sympathetic." Her face rose before him in the gathering gloom. "Madonna face," he told himself, "she is like the Sistine Madonna."

He made an effort to pull together his disintegrating moral forces and tears of self-mortification came into his eyes. "If people only knew what it was like to be a parson," he told himself. "If they guessed how difficult it is to keep it up all the time." Then savagely: "But we are only men after all! We can't help our feelings, we can't control our affections."

"It is better to marry than burn," he chuckled grimly. "But suppose one did both?" he asked himself. "Paul said nothing about that possibility."

4.

It was dark when he pulled up at the little vicarage. A light showed from the kitchen. He unharnessed and fed the mare and went in. Agnes was sitting in the rocker, her feet up on the iron stove. She held a novel in her hands.

"Supper has been ready for nearly an hour," she complained. "I do think you might tell me beforehand when you are going to be late."

She got up, and taking a cloth, opened the oven door. "If your supper's spoiled you've only yourself to blame."

She set it on the table. "What has kept you all this time?" she asked peevishly.

"I drove Mary Ellison home."

"But surely it isn't always necessary to do that because she helps in the church?"

"One can't very well drive away in a rig and leave the girl to walk."

"But she walks there, doesn't she?"

"One way is enough – five miles."

"Well, I think it is very provoking to have to sit waiting here after the trouble of cooking a supper for you. You know perfectly well I detest unpunctuality."

"I am sorry, my dear. You shan't have to complain again."

The picture hurt. It didn't bear thinking of. The affair had to be lived through to the bitter end. For a parson there was no way out.

But it was easier to tell himself this than to banish the Madonna face which kept intruding itself.

The thing had to be faced: he was in love, head over heels in love. Besides, there were other things stirring within him, things that made him afraid.

Silently eating his ham and eggs, he scrutinized the face opposite to him. Yes, that woman was his wife. "Until death doth us part." Had he ever been in love with her? he asked himself. Was it possible that he had ever felt for that colourless, peevish woman, that complainer, that weight about his neck, the emotions that the serene face and gentle manners of Mary Ellison evoked in him? Impossible! He had made an egregious fool of himself. It was one of those all-too-common cases of propinquity. She was there. He saw her every day. They had drifted, haphazard, into marriage. That must happen to a number of people, he considered.

5.

At ten they retired to bed. Agnes carried the oil lamp. She never let him carry a lamp. "You are not to be trusted with a lamp," she said. She was mortally afraid of their wooden manse catching on fire and she had a horror of oil lamps.

He rapidly slipped off his clothes and got into bed. He snuggled down with the sheets under his blue chin and stared miserably at the moving figure of his wife. He knew every motion of her nightly toilette. The long period before the small glass, the sharp point of her bared elbow as she moved her arm in the motions of brushing her hair. Her thin face, reflected in the mirror, the eyes staring incuriously at her own image, the white camisole binding her flat breasts, her striped petticoat.

He always watched this undressing. And it always mildly disgusted him for an exact reason he had for long been seeking. He got it tonight. "It's like an old maid going to bed," he told himself, and his memory flashed back to the maiden aunt with whom he had once shared a bedroom during a summer holiday by the sea, when the rented villa had been overcrowded. "Yes, by Jove! That's what it is! Agnes is a typical old maid! Now a woman with the instincts of the . . ." He sought the right word and failed. "Well, the marrying sort of woman would avoid that exhibition. She would have a dressing-gown, or something, so that she did not look unbecoming. Confound it."

That moving arm with its sharply pointed elbow infuriated him beyond endurance.

"Aren't you ever coming to bed?" he snapped.

"I am coming when I have brushed my hair," she answered acidly. "And when I have said my prayers."

Ah, that was a dig at him!

He threw off the bedclothes and fell upon his knees

beside the bed. The stereotyped words jumbled them selves meaninglessly in the chambers of his mind. Images obtruded and jostled them out again. Better to marry than burn, but idiotic to do both! No, that was awful . . . and on my knees! Most merciful Father who knoweth the heart of this thy child. Better to marry than burn, but idiotic to do both.

He passed his lean hands through his thin, dark hair. Oh, Mary, my Mary, he groaned inwardly. Better to marry than burn. Most merciful Father.

It was no use. He rose slowly and got into bed.

Agnes was moving slowly across the room. Her feet creaked. Abominable! Feet that creaked, clicked, like twigs snapping! Corns, too! Horrible!

She was wrestling with her nightgown, flourishing it around herself, struggling with her petticoat beneath the covering garment. Modest Agnes! Oh, modest Agnes!

He watched her fall on her knees and cover her face with her hands. And, curiously, he wondered what words would make up her prayer. The fantastic notion entered his head that she would scold the Almighty. He smiled grimly and covered his face with the clothes.

CHAPTER XVIII

1.

The Newcomer's wife came back from Sapperton at the end of a full month. Her first child had gone hard with her and her labour had been long and exhausting. Bob England was waiting at the depot with his rig to take her back up the steep trail to the new clearing.

She carried the baby in her arms, a white bundle above which her oval face showed. Her eyes seemed bigger, bluer. She was not quite the same woman now as the one who went down the steep hill precariously on the swaying sled. She had experienced maternity, and it had changed her. Suffering seemed to have set a sign upon her: patient, she looked, and very gentle. She bent her head to look into the shawl and drew aside the covering to show the two men a tiny pink face and a clenched hand no bigger than a shell.

Her gentle eyes were filled with a great happiness and a solicitude for this tiny being so dependent upon her.

Her husband helped her climb into the high rig and handed up to her the white, woolly bundle. All the rough way up the hill she kept peeping into that nest of warm wool, glancing shyly at Bob England on the front seat beside her, turning back to her baby.

2.

Everything had been made ready for her homecoming. A great fire blazed from the open fireplace where great gnarled prongs of fir-root spurted vivid flames-from resinous deposits.

She sank upon the chesterfield, taking in with one all-comprehensive housewife's glance, every detail of her home.

"It is good to be back after that awful hospital," she exclaimed.

But she was very tired and for the first time since their marriage she was content that he should wait upon her instead of her upon him.

He was in the kitchen making much noise. She lay back, the baby propped on cushions beside her. Yes, it was good to be back!

He brought the meal on a tray and there, beside the great

fire, the baby by them, they ate their simple food. He was in high humour. "I've made a special omelette," he said, "Omelette Supreme à la Ferguson's Landing. Try it. It's really good, by Jove! Scads of butter, and, shall I tell you the secret? Water instead of milk! Yes."

She agreed languidly that it was good. The warmth of the roaring fire coming after the forty-mile journey had wearied her. He thought she was not so glad to be back as he was to have her back and the boyishness went out of his voice.

Then suddenly: "What about the baby?" he asked.

"Let him sleep," she answered. There was a new note in her voice.

The baby, as though it had been listening, stirred. The tiny shell of a hand emerged from the swaddling clothes and the shell dissolved itself into a pink, five-pointed star.

A thin, puling wail came from the bundle, which stirred vigorously, then the wail changed with startling suddenness into a vigorous bellow.

"I must feed him," she explained. She leaned forward to take the bundle from her husband and, feeling her already familiar hands about him, the baby returned to a peevish hunger whimper.

To the man it was all a marvel: the woman and the child. His woman, his child. He sat watching, fork poised in air.

"Gad! What a hungry little beggar," he exclaimed, watching with awed eyes his wife suckle her firstborn. The baby lay cupped in the crook of one arm. She opened her loose blouse and lifting her full breast with her free hand, drew the baby towards it. The baby burrowed into the white, firm flesh, groping for the nipple, found it, and drew it into his sucking mouth.

She winced.

"Does he hurt?" he asked very tenderly.

"Yes, he does rather. The doctor said I should use alum."

"Alum?" he asked, in surprise.

"It hardens the nipples," she responded, condescendingly.

"Oh!"

In the flickering firelight he watched. The full, heavy breast, the tiny face, one bright eye fixed impersonally upon the face above it, the shell-like hands fingering that whiteness, plucking at it with futile movements, drawing tiny nails down it. "It's rather wonderful."

He is awed and reverent.

She looks at him as one looks at a child and a slow, very gentle smile touches the corners of her mouth. "But it hurts," she said, and bent her head again over the suckling babe.

She is matter-of-fact.

4.

For the women of such settlements as Ferguson's Landing maternity means sacrifice. The bearing of the child is only the beginning. Thereafter the mothers of the settlement must be all things to their babes. And at the same time they must do all the work of the little homes where civilization has brought none of its amenities. The men have still to be fed, and there is washing, always washing, to be seen to. Days are long, but not long enough to complete all the tasks of the settlers' wives who have about them growing families.

For that reason comely women fade after a few years in the new land. For women were never meant to work and rear children at the same time. They do it, certainly, and in every settlement throughout the Dominion you will find such women. But their frame is not designed for such labour and the toll is terrible.

The housework of the city woman is made up of what are, to the wives of the settlers, the minor chores of the day. There is no Chinese laundry for the settler's wife, no telephone for the ordering of groceries. There is no Ford van to call for the orders, no baker to deliver bread.

They must do everything themselves. So, too often, comely women fade and their backs take on an unseemly curve from plucking crying children from cots and carrying them as they go about their kitchens, incessant crying having made physical discomfort and strain a relief for maddened nerves.

Even for women of peasant blood it is not easy. But for women gently nurtured and accustomed to the ease of an Old Country home, it is the test. It is only the women of grit who pull through; the others sink slowly into heart-rending apathy.

5.

Slight and slim was the Newcomer's wife, but she tackled her new problem with a quiet and determined air. Now, in addition to the cooking, cleaning, washing and sewing, she had the baby to tend. Every four hours he must be suckled. His washing alone doubled her work. He cried at night and she had not the heart to wake the man who could sleep through such noise as that.

The washing machine had not materialized yet. The extra fees at the hospital had swallowed the Woods contract money. She washed numberless napkins day after day by hand, stooping over the corrugated washing board, her fair hair in her eyes, her arms working vigorously, her face moist with sweat. A flapping line of washing fluttered in the clearing.

The baby slept well now; his milk agreed with him. He slept all morning beside the stump that was like a sentinel; in the shade of the alders his little basket, a laundry basket, was set.

And when he awoke and uttered impatient cries, there she was at his side, wiping her wet hands upon her pinafore, unbuttoning her dress.

6.

As for him, he approached the miracle of the baby from a different angle. It was a curiosity and a charm, a marvel and a source of extraordinary pride. He would .leave his work under the trees of the uncleared part of his land and stalk across the uneven ground to have another look at this astonishing thing.

There he would stoop over the basket, hands on knees, observing the baby minutely. He knew all there was to know about it: the yellow downy head (with the pulsing fontanelle that always filled him with apprehensions of accidents), the incredibly small and shapeless nose, the pouting wet, red mouth.* But most of all, the hands, so absurdly small, they seemed, such useless little members.

But they could grip! He would poke a finger into that little hand and thrill as he felt the pressure of tiny fingers closing over his; and he would chuckle as he felt the pull of that hand towards that feeling mouth.

"Want to suck my finger, eh?" he would ask, "little beggar! Always at it, aren't you?"

And he would walk back to his work.

It was something to be a father.

7.

When the baby had learned to crawl they put him down in the slashing to feel about for himself. He was a vigorous child and scuttled over the ground on all fours with a sideways movement. They would listen to his chortling. They were so very proud of him.

Then one day when he was able to walk, he disappeared. She had put him out while she washed the bed linen, a heavy task that used up all her strength. And when she came out, calling, shading her eyes with her hand, and looking all about the place, lo! he had disappeared.

She did not panic at first because there was a chance that he had gone right over to the further side where his father was hewing timber.

But he had not, and together they rushed madly about. Calling, calling, calling.

The baby had wandered off into the bush, over the tangled brush he must have gone, picking the white wood-anemones, burbling to himself. And it was near evening.

That had been a terrible experience. He rushed down to enlist Bob England's help; she ran for Johansson and found him away. But Mary came and ran off into the bush, calling in her high nasal voice.

It would have been better if they had not called the girl. She added to their terror: "It was only three years ago one of Heggerty's – little Joe, wandered off just the same."

"Yes, yes, and did they find him all right?" the mother, clenched hands to cheeks, waits with horror-filled eyes, the answer.

It comes: "Not for a week, they didn't." It is a slow nasal drawl. "Little feller was only a hundred yards off, too. Must have walked around in circles. And nobody heard a cry out-er him."

Terror now has her in its grasp. She raises her skirt, and runs forward calling, calling, calling.

And thus calling, she stumbles over something, soft and white, in the dim light of the bush. It is her baby, head resting on chubby arm, asleep, unhurt.

After that they put a little bell upon him. And at such times as he was out and about the clearing his father would stop his work, sawing, felling, building up great fires, to listen: "Hullo, little 'un, all right?" and back to work.

Or he would glance up to see a woman's figure on the

veranda; a woman who remembered, who would always remember, a woman who was going to make sure.

He took a day off to fashion a little cart on rockers to keep the little fellow amused in one place. It was made of cedar, with a little seat and two joy-sticks for the youngster to hold on by.

8.

The coming of the baby had stiffened the back of the Newcomer. There was no turning back now. And yet, consider things how he would, there seemed but little prospect of making a living off those few acres, even when they had been finally won from the bush, cultivated, and brought into bearing.

The truth was, slowly he was coming to see that, whatever he did, there was no decent living to be made upon the place. First of all, he had insufficient acreage. Then the lay of the land (sloping steeply towards the river below, although it looked to the south) was too steep for practical purposes. Then again, as he well knew from going among his neighbours, only two white settlers in the whole of Ferguson's Landing were making a living from their land: Johansson and Fuller.

One couldn't count the Olsons, who worked at many other things. Their finished ranch was but a profitable home with them. It helped out and nothing more was expected of it. It was a home and a headquarters for strong men who fished, mined, or disappeared for spells into logging-camps, there to earn good money against winter's inactivity.

9.

"Perhaps we ought to sell?" he put the question to his wife.

"But where would we go if we did sell? At least we've a roof over our heads here," she argued.

"He knew exactly how Mount Baker gleamed when a faint haze hung over the Valley. It was like a floating island in the sky at those times. It was not hard to see it as a fairy castle, set in the clouds; its white, conical head was easily conjured into a turret of ivory." (p. 191).

"But, damn it, where does all this work lead to? We both work like slaves and, confound it, we get nothing out of it."

But for all his grumbles, he had come to love the bush. It drew him mysteriously—the strange quietness of it, working, day after day, with the bush at the back of him, and below, the Valley with the wide and tranquil river; and far beyond, again, the rolling land that swept, green and dappled, to the violet horizon in Washington State across the border.

He had come to know every detail of that scene and every varying mood of it. He knew exactly how Mount Baker gleamed when a faint haze hung over the Valley. It was like a floating island in the sky at those times. It was not hard to see it as a fairy castle, set in the clouds; its white, conical head was easily conjured into a turret of ivory.

But while the beauty and the solitude, which had given him a perspective of life, called, drawing him, magnetically, to stay there in the bush forever and forever, the other side of him irked to get back to the hurly-burly of civilization – the civilization he yet hated.

They talked their future over many times. And, as is ever the case, advanced not one step towards the solution of their central problem: the education of the boy and the founding of a secure future.

In some way, both felt that they had been cheated. Certainly they had been deluded, listening to the bland talk of the Vancouver real estate men, reading their lying literature which made ranching in the Valley appear as a picnic in the garden of the world.

"But dash it, surely there are other things I could do!" he stormed, walking up and down the living-room while she watched him from the depths of an arm-chair, her two arms resting on her lap.

"What, for instance? You might qualify out here, but how would we live while you were doing it?"

She was very practical. He was all wild schemes. One merely waited: the ideas tumbled into his head, but they tumbled out of it again.

"No, damn law! I don't want to be a lawyer. But I tell you what I do want to be," he paused dramatically – "A doctor!"

She smiled, ever so slightly.

"But, my dear, that's ever so much more difficult; it takes seven years, and consider the expense."

He quickened his pace. "That's where you are wrong. You always jump so to conclusions. Do you know anything about the medical profession in this country? No, of course you don't. Why, there are men who have worked their way through the universities and taken good degrees without a cent of help from anyone. I met a man a week or so ago. He was walking to Port Murdock, and he told me he used to drive a team for the visitors in Banff during the summer months. He got plenty of tips. And he had been a waiter and a newsboy on the CPR. But anyway, that was not what I wanted to say – I thought I might go to the States where you can get a degree in four years."

"And we would live in America?"

"Why not? It's a perfectly good country, so far as I know."

She did not bother to argue. She had learned quickly that it was best to let him talk. Nothing ever came of it. Only a few weeks before, he had been all agog for California. He had bought the American papers off the train and had become absorbed in the real estate advertisements. Orange groves going at two thousand dollars. He read bits out: sun, glorious climate, easy money – you simply waited until the oranges were ripe and pulled them off the trees and packed them.

"Yes, but the Valley sounded like that when we talked to the real estate men in Vancouver," she reminded him.

And that had made him petulant. He had snapped at her.

"Every damn thing I suggest – you throw cold water on

it. Hang it, can't you get enthusiastic?"

But she was very wise. It was certainly true that she never got enthusiastic but she had that abiding quality of seeing a thing through, and keeping him on track as well. Doctoring, orange growing – there had been so many schemes to escape from the penury and drudgery of life at Ferguson's Landing. They came to nothing.

10.

They rattled the German beer-mug and there was money in it, or there was no money. They lived from hand to mouth and once, for a month, they had no meat. They lived then chiefly on bread and potato soup. The subscription to their newspaper having run out, they had to borrow Old Man Dunn's. He lent it willingly, just as he lent his books, or pressed upon them little gifts of butter. "Now the cow's giving us so much milk," he would say, "we've more butter than we know what to do with."

So the Newcomer would thank the old man and pretend it was but a neighbourly courtesy. But he knew well enough Blanchard at the store was short of butter and would give forty cents a pound for it.

Yet, close to nature poverty is divested of its worst horrors. There need be no squalor. Thus it was that these people lived in beautiful surroundings and in a comfortable house although, often as not, they had not a penny piece between them.

There were times when money seemed to have disappeared from the Valley altogether. There was occasional work, but the hirer would offer apples, potatoes or milk in exchange. "Can you do me a day's ploughing?" one would ask. "I'll let you have a couple of hundredweight of best potatoes." Or: "Can you help me with my new well? I'll keep you going with milk for a month or two." Or: "Give me a hand with the roof of my barn and you can take all the apples you can carry away for your trouble."

So, one way and another, they contrived to live, but it was a poor enough living and very different from the one they had expected.

11.

And all the while the bush was getting its grip upon him. There were days when there was not much to be done, or when, disheartened by the slowness of his progress against the heavy timber, he had no stomach to face another day with axe and saw. Then he would go off wandering into the bush. It gave him a strangely sweet sense of peace. And slowly he began to know its many moods.

There were days when the bush was benevolent, filled with transparencies, and patterned with shafts of golden sunlight. Then he would sit on a rotted log and watch the life of the forest. Chipmunks racing with jerky movements up the rugged tree-bark, gripping with sharp claws. The steady tap-tap of a solemn mottled woodpecker. The minute sounds that came from the ground if you put your ear to it: the sound of bracken moving, of bushes stirring, of bent twigs releasing themselves. And above, now and then, the slow sigh of the roof of the forest, stirred by the sluggish breeze.

Many moods it had, and some were sinister. Once he stayed too long and night fell. That had happened in the winter when the bush was all white with soft snow. He had sat for hours in a world of enchantment, a world white and spotless, and then night had come down with incredible swiftness and left him in darkness.

It had been an experience. He had lost his way. For hours it seemed, he wandered, floundering in the dark. He tripped and fell, cutting his hands, and rose and stumbled on, cursing. But he kept his head, and to himself repeated over and over again: "This land slopes down to the river. If I keep going downhill, I must come out in the end."

And he had – just when he was starting to doubt. A twinkle through the dark, and a light – the light cast from his own door into the darkness of the bush.

Blessed relief!

CHAPTER XIX

1.

At the end of his third year the Newcomer had his land slashed and five acres cleared and under cultivation. The original starkness of the yellow house against the green of the bush had been toned by weather to a dull grey. He had marked out flower beds with the smaller boulders gathered while clearing; in summer, flowers adorned the place: simple flowers, such as petunias, stock, begonias, pansies, Canterbury bells.

When they sat together on the veranda in the evening they now looked out at the beginnings of a ranch, and it filled them with a sense of triumph, the sober sense of triumph that comes only after much toil and many fears of failure.

In the evenings when the air stood still they would take their chairs and sit in the open. Below them the Valley lay in shadow, purple in the half light of evening; the river, seen dimly, leaden-hued. Sometimes a cannery boat would pulse upstream. The sound of its engine came up to them like a fast heart-beat, its headlight like a luminous fly in steady flight.

"How the nicotina smells!"

"Yesterday evening the Northern Lights were ever so clear, but you missed that. You were asleep."

"So would you have been asleep if you had been up half the night."

"Were you up half the night? I didn't know."

"Yes, I was. The new baby is at the worst time. He will be better after he gets to six months."

"Why don't you go to bed now?"

His feet are on the new rail and he is smoking a corn-cob pipe, sleeves rolled up, chest bare. His hair is long and rumpled, his arms sinewy and lean.

"Because I like it out here."

Silence. They contemplate the dreaming Valley below. The light of the unseen boat has passed the wide sweep of the river's bend and is fading.

"What are the Northern Lights like? I've never seen them."

He tries to describe them, but cannot. He gives it up, sits fretting at the impotence of the inarticulate who have no words with which to clothe their experiences, and therefore live much alone.

"Have you got that job taking the boulders off the Woods place?"

"No. They have hired those two Hindus from the back. They work together as a team for five dollars a day. Of course Mrs. W. was very nice about it, but it does make one a bit sick when even the white people here don't stick together."

"Personally, I can't see why they don't prohibit all coloured people coming into the Province. They only take the bread out of our mouths."

"I know. By the way, I'm selling all the hens – the whole lot of them."

"You're not! All those pedigreed Leghorns, and when they are laying so well?"

"Well, I am. I got a cheque from the egg-dealer at Sapperton this evening – didn't mean to tell you till morning, as a matter of fact. We only got nineteen cents a dozen for the last consignment."

"Nineteen cents?"

"Yes, so you see its sheer waste of time to keep the damn things."

"I do think it's disgusting. I suppose it's those Chinese eggs."

"Precisely. In this country it's Chinamen, Japanese, Hindus and Swedes, Italians, Norwegians, every other race – anything but the Anglo-Saxon."

"Yes, and the white men who take the money are the commission snatchers."*

"And the gentlemen from across the border with their get-rich-quick schemes."

She rises slowly, yawning: "Perhaps it would have been better if we had cleared out when you wanted to. We can't complain that we weren't warned – old Mr. Dunn told us pretty plainly that it was hopeless."

She passed into the house, leaving him there in the dim, soft light, a still figure with eyes fixed upon the darkening valley. A man with a riddle to solve.

2.

Presently he got up and went down the shallow steps to the little flower beds. He smelt the pale white faces of the nicotina and passed, puffing his pipe, into the twilight.

To the north, the solid wall of the bush stood like a jagged cliff, black against the electric blue of the sky. The stars shone faintly.

As he stood watching, the sky seemed to stir and become alive. The pale stars suddenly dimmed, shining so faintly that they seemed to have put out their lights altogether. The sky opened like a fan and glowed mysteriously. Long spears of light shot up to the zenith and marched about the heavens until the Pole star was scarcely visible and the Pleiades grew pale and wan.

He turned to the south and in that hemisphere of darker sky the stars were marshalling their glittering forces against the opposing north, the north that sought to quench their fire. The fan revolved like the beams of unseen lighthouses, like shafts of great searchlights. Its vivid hues changed as they moved.

The Northern Lights again, the mysterious *Aurora Borealis.*

He turned again to the north and watched, enchanted, pipe in hand, face dimly lit by the heavenly display. So bright was the north now, so alive, that it seemed as though the sun must surely burst from that mysterious region and rout the darkness utterly.

Through the silence of the valley came the clang of a bell and a dim throbbing. It grew louder, clang . . . clang . . . clang . . . clang . . . The earth rumbled, and far below, speeding through the violet gloom, a moving chain of yellow lights winked from the floor of the Valley. The transcontinental roared east towards the Rockies, towards Montreal, towards – England.

3.

Bob England came up the steep trail to the new clearing, smoking his pipe and taking in the new improvements with the shrewd eye of the old-timer. The Newcomer was making chicken crates from cedar slats.

"Sending birds to market?" asked England.

"Yes, selling the whole damn lot."

"To the Chinese dealer?"

"I suppose so. The beggar gives the best price."

"Yes, Chinese are straight – straight as Japanese are crooked."

"Personally, I've about come to the conclusion that a man is a bloody fool to settle in this Valley. But somehow I've come to like it."

England grinned. "You'll go back to the Old Country, just as I did. You'll go back wild with gladness to get there. And for a few weeks you will think it is Paradise. Then you'll do what I did – you'll come back."

"Come back?"

"Yes, they all do. They curse this country and when the first chance comes, they book passage and scoot for home. Then they start making comparisons and the Old Country, with its narrow ways, its cursed snobbery and conventions, starts to get on their nerves – and they come back!"

"I don't believe I would. Not that I don't like this country. I do. I've come to feel it in my bones. The silence, and the beauty, and the freedom. No, the country is all right; it's the way it's run that's all wrong. They make the odds too difficult for the small man. He has to compete with Orientals and he is fleeced by the booms from which he gets nothing but land at crazy prices. The big combines squeeze him, to say nothing of the freight rates, which swallow up most of his mangy profits. It's a fine land for everybody but the producer, if you ask me."

"Oh, well, that's the same all over the world."

"No, it isn't. Its not like that in Denmark, for instance. And the French and Belgian peasants are better off than we are."

"Perhaps they're more competent than you are."

"Perhaps they are."

Bob England cupped his hands and lit his pipe.

"Well, d'you want to sell out?"

"If I get a decent price – yes."

"Well, I think I can get you what you want."

"Right, produce the buyer and I'll sell, lock, stock and barrel."

"I'll bring a man up tomorrow."

"Then you've really got someone in mind?"

"Yep, and he's got the money all right. He will pay cash."

"By Jove, do you really mean it?"

"Yep, I'll bring him up tomorrow."

4.

The prospect of selling made them deliriously happy.

"Think of it! No more slaving away day after day, no more washing for you, no more working like a Dago for me!"

"I shall be as glad as you to see England again but you must remember we shall have little left after paying our passages."

"That's true, and England is far worse than Canada to be hard up in. You can't do just anything at home as you can here."

"No, that's true. I can't see myself hacking up the wood-paving in Piccadilly, exactly."

"Precisely, and we shall have to consider what we should do."

"My idea would be a tiny little place in Sussex or Devon. We could rent a small farm and live quietly. After all, we have learnt the ropes out here. We aren't green any longer. And at home everything is so finished. Why, farming would be like falling off a log!"

"I'd like a little place in Sussex too; it must have electric light – I loathe these oil lamps. And running water – I'm sick to death of fetching water in buckets to wash with. And gas, or at least a decent coal range – wood is infernal."

"You know, we shall reap the benefit of this experience then. Just think! It will be as easy as winking. Not a stone on the land, every inch cultivated. Personally, now I come to think of it, I simply don't understand why farming is considered a played-out game at home. They must be a lazy crew, don't you think?"

"You'll have to change your ways a bit, though. You've let yourself go rather, you know."

"But dash it, how could I help it? I haven't had a penny to buy clothes for three years. Everything I brought out, including my dress pants, is worn out. I'll go to my old tailor. He'll give me credit. Sackville Street."

"And I'll treat myself to the heavenly delight of new clothes too. Now that's one thing we really must blow ourselves on. Clothes! Oh, heavens! How wonderful to feel crêpe-de-Chine again!"

"And to have a hot bath every day."

"And a neat, nice little Sussex maid."

"And all the newspapers and journals."

"Theatres!"

"Books!"

"Dances!"

"People down for week-ends!"

"But we aren't there yet; this man may not buy!"

5.

Bob England had produced his man, even as he said he would. But when the Newcomer saw him, his heart sank. He shook his head. "Sorry, nothing doing," he announced, finality in his voice.

His wife had looked at him with consternation in her great eyes. "What do you mean, 'nothing doing?' If he has the money, what does it matter, if he is Japanese? We are leaving the country."

"Sorry, but that's how I feel about it. It would be so

confoundedly inconsistent. For two years or more I've been shouting that this should be a white man's country. Am I now, just to get out of it, to sell my place – to a Japanese?"

"If you don't sell, somebody else will," put in Bob England. The prospect stood beside him, a little man with a beaming face. "My man likes this place. He is willing to pay your price, and now you go stalling us off. You must be crazy!"

"But surely you can understand?"

"No, I can't understand. I think it's pure moonshine. I know the Japanese aren't much good to us. (It's all right; he can't understand.) But a commission is a commission, and I'm too old a bird to turn ready money down."

He changed his voice to a propitiatory tone: "Besides, if you don't mind my saying so, you ought to think of your wife. Two youngsters now. It's really not good enough. Not the sort of life to let a woman in for."

"But your wife has stood it for twenty years."

"We've no youngsters, worse luck! Besides, my wife is, as you very well know, a Norwegian peasant. That's a bit different. This sort of life is normal for her."

They were all silent for a few minutes, standing there at the front of the house.

"I'm sorry that you won't get your commission, Bob, but that's how I feel about it. I won't sell to anyone but a white man."

Bob England shrugged his shoulders. And when he spoke his voice betrayed his annoyance and disappointment. This sale would have paid his overdue mortgage interest. And now . . .

"Nobody can make you sell. It's a free country," he said. He turned round, made a sign to the Japanese indicating that no business was concluded, and waited until the yellow man's face registered understanding. Then, lifting the peak of his old cap, he walked off.

"Dash it! But how could I sell to that yellow fellow?" the Newcomer stormed.

But his wife merely shrugged her shoulders and disappeared into the house. He saw by the heaving of her shoulders that she was struck down by a bitter disappointment. He followed her into the kitchen where, mechanically, she was adjusting the washing machine. He noticed her fingers, calloused, stained with much immersion in greasy water. He saw the little nails, broken and scored with black lines. He knew from that heaving of her shoulders that she was crying with disappointment.

6.

Why, after all, inconvenience oneself for a mere abstract principle? What difference would his paltry stand make when the Japanese were buying land in the valley every day?

The argument went on inside him as he stood there watching his wife's back.

But if everybody made a stand against these Orientals, then the Valley would not be going to the dogs. There would be work for all and decent prices for produce. Still, how utterly impossible for one man to make a stand! One's wife and children came first. Of course they did! Would the children one day applaud their father for committing a quixotic act that compromised their future?

He wanted the boy to have an English education. To stand thus on principle was perhaps doing him out of the chance of one.

"I'm awfully sorry if you're so upset," he said very softly. "But I can't eat my own words and go back on what I've stood by ever since I came to Canada – that this should be a white man's country and a white man's only."

He watched the heaving shoulders and waited. Her voice

came shakily: "You were perfectly right. Now, will you get me water? Fill the big tub. I've a big washing to do. Oh, and take the two trunks from the bedroom and put them back in the attic."

He passed out of the kitchen carrying the two buckets. The dream of England had vanished. They were back to the old routine, the wheels of their life were turning again.

Thoughts of Sussex had faded, and all that Sussex meant. After all, it was just a phase, this nostalgia for home. If Bob England had not come offering to find a buyer he would never have thought of selling.

He dropped the bucket down the well at the end of a jerking rope and heard the dull splash of it as it struck water.

"No, damn it! I won't sell to a Japanese or a Chinaman or any other sort of Oriental. I won't."

But the next minute his heart smote him and he felt as though he had betrayed his wife – his woman and his children. He inwardly cursed himself for indulging in unprofitable heroics. He half made up his mind to go after Bob and tell him it was all a mistake and that the damned Japanese could have the place. He felt that he ought to return to the subject and explain at great length to his wife why he would not sell to a Japanese. But he shrank from doing it when he once got into the kitchen and saw her going about her work with a face like a mask.

No plain sailing anywhere, he thought. An issue looked perfectly plain, but somewhere right out of the back of one's head came a monitor with peremptory orders.*

7.

When he turned the matter over in his mind he saw that it had always been like that in the past. It had been like that when he had everything set to run away from school.

The school had been near a port and he had determined – so much did he hate the imprisonment of that great red-brick pile, with its walls and its ordered playing fields, the soulless routine of the white-washed classrooms, the hairy hands of the form-master who persecuted him – to run away to sea.

He had saved his pocket money for two months and had written to every aunt and uncle he possessed, asking for money. He had packed the things he meant to take and had fixed the hour for the great escape: the half holiday when, not being down to play for the second eleven of his House, he intended to ask for leave to pass beyond bounds – and bolt.*

Why had he not bolted? It was then, as now, a moral inhibition, a certain spiritual fastidiousness. He had turned back and faced the balance of the term simply because he had envisaged too vividly the feelings of his mother when she should hear of his total disappearance.

He had wept silently as he pictured her anxiety and distress. And the next day, just to show him, as it seemed, the folly of his quixotry, he had got into trouble, yet again, and received a thrashing at the hands of the school sergeant (the headmaster being a clerk in Holy Orders, and too fastidious to handle the switch in person).*

It had been the same old thing when he had become engaged. True, he had a comfortable set of chambers to which he might easily enough have taken a bride. And he might have risked finding some sort of work in London – oh, journalism or something of that sort. But he had refused to take the easy way, because it was the easy way: it had seemed like not playing the game by the woman he loved.

To give it all up and set out for Canada, to start clear and make a home – that had seemed the right thing, perversely, because it was the hard thing.

He asked himself now whether he was not the biggest fool

on earth. Why, he considered, should the easy way be wrong? Why did he deliberately, at every crisis, raise shadowy moral reasons for turning from the course his heart desired?

Yet (so inevitably does a man behave in character), he knew if Bob England returned with a battalion of Japanese, with a brigade or army of Japanese, if he returned jangling bags full of gold, he would refuse to close the deal.

Was it just cussedness, obstinacy? It seemed like it. Who, in God's name, would thank him for putting his puny carcase in the way of the Japanese invasion? Nobody! For the good and sufficient reason that nobody cared!

He thought of all the tirades he had heard from Old Man Dunn, and felt that one man at least would approve his steadfastness. Old Man Dunn would probably find a bit of Carlyle that would make the business plain: he generally trotted out some passage from his hero to meet difficult occasions.* He would go down in the evening and chat with the old chap. They would sit in the tiny living room while little Mrs. Dunn bustled about in the kitchen, or ran about the orchard after her broody hens. They would talk it all over. And he would get his perspective again.

He wondered if Old Man Dunn had any remedy for his wife's bitter disappointment. Or if any man had. Words, words, words. What the devil good were they when it came to the real troubles of life? Just mockery, that was all.

Words were good enough when you were not hurt, a sort of cheap solace for those not greatly needing comforting. They were quack medicine for small complaints, that was all.

8.

They returned to the routine of their lives on the fringe of the bush, and put aside the dream of home. But the sudden prospect of leaving that clearing had made the Newcomer alive to what the bush really meant to him. It had told him that he loved it, and that whatever the future held for them, this episode (if mere episode it turned out to be), would be immemorable. The days and years of life in the finished world, the world of great cities and comely counties, like gardens in their patterned beauty, glided by, leaving no spiritual mark. It was life frittered away on trivialities that left the soul sleeping.

But the bush was different. It got hold of you and made you think, it gave you your place in the universe, taught you the significance and the insignificance of man; it whispered of God.

Hard thoughts to put into words. Sometimes not even thoughts, but only emotions. Could he make her understand? It was worth trying.

It was evening. The day's work was done, the chores finished. He was washed and satisfied by a supper of ham and eggs, hot tea, bread and home-made jam. They sat at ease, as they often sat, he with a book and she with her head nodding over a *Saturday Evening Post*.

"You know, it has not really been futile," he began, continuing aloud the trend of the thoughts which had come between his mind and the printed page of the newspaper.

"It isn't really the waste of life it sometimes seems to be. I shall always feel we have got something out of these lean years."

She regarded him unblinkingly, as though she was hearing him judicially with the intention of passing judgment when he had made an end of it.

"When we came," he plunged on, wrinkling his forehead and floundering for the right words to convey the problem as he saw it, "when we came, we were little, weren't we? I mean our outlook on life was petty and overlaid by the things that don't really count at all.

"I don't think that in England I ever thought straight,

really, though sometimes I tried to. Life was overlaid with so many small things that the great issues were all in shadow. But out here one can see great principles at work. Life sticks out. You know what is real and vital."

Still she listened, and from her immobile face you could not have told whether his words were registered at all upon that secret mind of hers.

He continued, now pacing up and down the room.

"Out here it's just as though we had been able to pick the works of civilization to pieces like a clock. Out here it's a framework, skeleton sort of civilization and one can get at fundamentals.

"And I think seeing clearly has made us grow. I can now see that, if you get down to it, a country must find its level from the average honesty and industry of its people. Out here, for the first time I came to understand that the things we need for life – bread, meat, fruit, clothing, leather, tools – all come from the earth, from the soil, or from under it. In England the soil seemed so remote from the cities and the leisured life of the countryside. There were farmers but they were just – farmers. There were miners – people who went on strike.

"It's astonishing, when you think of it. London: everybody eating and drinking, wearing out clothes, millions of them, living in houses of bricks and mortar, consuming, taking from the earth. And just following professions and jobs which have sprung up like fungi. Giving nothing back to the soil. I wonder it has lasted so long.

"If you think of it, the whole population of the world, all the teeming millions that eat and eat and wear out and consume, the money-changers, banks, insurance offices, commission-men, middle-men, all the white-collar people, are just feeding off the man whose sweat produces the wherewithal of existence.

"And it's funny, when you think of it, that the richest men are those furthest from the soil. The most artificial of all the artificial types that civilization has produced are the money-changers. It looks as though the more useful your work is, the less you get paid, and the reverse.

"After all, what organized community could exist for twelve months without the farmer, the fisherman and the miner?"

She raised her eyebrows ever so slightly. Taking this as a gesture of disagreement he plunged on, feeling for words with which to clothe the thoughts that crowded in on him.

"But they are the real pillars. If you had no farmers, fishermen or miners, the whole thing would crumble and collapse. Those pompous, top-hatted, pot-bellied men who rush about as though the whole of society depended upon their work, are they really necessary? You don't find them in any primitive community. There are none of them at Ferguson's Landing."

He was talking fast now: "And I've come to the belief that there ought to be preferential treatment for the producer of the necessities of life, for the farmer, the fisherman and the miner and so on. They carry society on their backs.

"Look at Johansson, for example. He can barely read and Mary does all his figuring for him when he gets a contract. But he is as close to the earth as a man can be. Look at him! He is a completely self-supporting man. He could survive if Ferguson's Landing were isolated from the rest of the world. He would merely go without tea, snuff and one or two unnecessary things."

She raised her eyebrows again.

"You are thinking of things like clothes?

"Perhaps you didn't know that Mrs. Johansson could weave. She taught Mary too, before she died. They've enough land cleared now to keep sheep, don't forget that. And Johansson can tan too. He could make his own boots. He grows all his own food, even now. And he fishes for himself.

"No! Away back in the bush, up here on this ledge of the Valley, with that wide sweep always before one, over the timberlands, over the river, one seems able to look down on the world and poke about in its machinery."

He paused, his brow wrinkled. It was not easy to put into words ideas such as these. And there was always the feeling that he made no impression on her. He could not guess whether she was sympathetic or vaguely hostile.

"And it's the same with other values too," he went on, talking more to himself than to her, as though thinking aloud. "We have always bothered too much about manners and too little about morals. In the Old Country the polished cad can pass, at least for a time. But it is fatal to be plebeian common. What mucky thinking has gone before that standard!

"Look at Johansson – he belches across the table, picks his teeth, spits and blows his nose through thumb and finger. But consider the man himself! Good God! He is heroic! He has beaten the bush single-handed. He works like a horse. You never see him idle, doing nothing. Yet he will always lend a hand to a neighbour. It's Johansson who starts the bees (volunteer work to the hard-pressed neighbour).

"You remember when that old woman came and tried to start life in the bush, away ever so far back in that slashing? Well, who whipped up a bee to cut her wood? Johansson. Who got up a bee (I gave a day's work) to dig her well? Johansson again. What do spitting and table manners count beside those things? He owes nobody a cent and you never hear him say a bad word of a neighbour. He minds his own business. He thinks and works for his daughter as he used to for his wife. He's a *man*."

He stopped and she rose without a word and passed into the kitchen. He looked after her retreating figure with a shadow of chagrin on his features.*

She said so little. What was she thinking, this woman so close and yet so remote and unknowable?

She neither agreed nor argued. She would never take up a challenge of an argument, never express an opinion.

He continued to walk up and down. Of course one had to remember the futility of words. How she worked! Always, early and late. And she never complained. She never asked life to grant quarter. She faced facts, never tried to get round them. A heroic little woman!

But still, talking did help. It was one of the oldest ways in the world for getting at solutions; the Greeks knew that. You tried a theory on another mind, and hey presto, it weathered the encounter – or crumbled on the rock of fallacy. You cast out the old idea and took in the new one. Like that you grew.

And she had baffled him with her silence, as she always baffled him. If she would only argue, dispute, challenge! But she never did. Her silences seemed to challenge, though – it was as if she could not bother to set him right.

From the kitchen came the rhythmic sound of the wooden handle of the washing machine. His conscience smote him. So much work to be done, work that no amount of thinking would accomplish. He passed out into the clearing and made his way towards the standing timber. Work, that was it.

CHAPTER XX

1.

Old Man Olson sat in the warm sunshine beside the door of his son Axel's low, rambling farmhouse. Before him, dazzlingly bright in the summer sun, lay the Valley with its undulating tracks of timber, green and vivid, and its shining river that seemed to have changed from water to quivering mercury.

Fowls pecked at the earth by the old man's feet, cocking absurd heads with bright and watchful eyes. From the open doorway came the voices of the women and the clatter of pots and pans. High voices, laughing chatter, with snatches of old songs, that took the old man's memory back to the days when Kurt was a toddler, riding his knee and listening, gleefully, to those same old folk songs of Norway.

Times had changed and things were not as they were. The old man's heart was heavy as he turned over in his slow mind the changes he had witnessed since the early days. The young people had changed. They were no longer content to work hard, to save, and to rear up big families. No, the city attracted them with its gew-gaw pleasures. One by one, they went away, coming back only to flaunt their fine clothes and to talk of things of which he knew nothing, nothing at all.

Thus Lulu had gone to Vancouver. The girl had never so much as come home to visit her mother and the old friends of childhood. Heggerty, the no-good messer, had betaken his family off. Easy money, that was it. They all sought easy money, despising the toil of the bush.

Even Kurt, not content to fish the river and earn good wages building for newcomers, had to leave him and go north again. Madness! That was what it was. If one wanted proof of it, why, then, there it was: Kurt home again from the North and without a dollar for the hardships he had borne. No, for his trouble he had gained nothing, had even lost, since his right hand now lacked the index finger, amputated after frostbite.

The clatter from the great, low kitchen continued. The women were making jam, stirring the big stew-pots upon the crackling stove, their sleeves rolled up, their skirts tucked about their middles, their faces moist and shining from the heat. With big wooden spoons they skimmed off the pink, bubbly scum that rose from the dark-red, simmering preserve. Hot work, but when winter came there would be, row upon row, the sweet fruits of summer.

The old man was sad, sad because Kurt his favourite, had come back changed. He had asked him, that first evening when he returned from the North, would he not play a bit as of old: for his old father, maybe? Then, for little Ole, who danced so prettily in his clumsy, nailed boots?

But Kurt would not play. He shook his head. A silent man, a man of strange moods. They could make nothing at all of the man from the North, sitting there silent, his face a mask of grief.

2.

"Reckon Kurt must be in love," suggested Mrs. Axel to her husband, "he's that queer in his ways."

But Axel dismissed the idea. Sitting with his vast bulk upon a hard wood chair, his two legs spread, his fat freckled hands upon his knees, he stared at his raw-boned wife with the bland eyes of a great child.

"Aye? In luv, you tink?" He had a vast respect for this shrewd woman, and some reason for it.

Whenever there was a big business at hand, she it was who directed his policy. She knew he needed her protection, with his slow wits and cocky self-assurance, his simulated cleverness, his transparent cunning of a peasant.

She would go on with her work as the men sat around the kitchen table talking business and passing the square-faced bottle from one to the other. But she would have her eyes open, oh, dear, yes!

And when they were gone, and her husband was still uncommitted, he would look over to her, his moon face flushed with the warming spirit: "Well, how is it to be?" he would ask. "Will I sign the contract, Freda?"

And she would stop in her activity and straightway make answer: "That one from the city, de one wid the wall-eye, you watch him, Axel. You git what he promised in writin'. Maybe, the young feller up by Johansson would make the writing for you; they say he's somethin' of a lawyer."

And Axel, full of self-importance, would nod his big head gravely, as became a man talking over matters of high import; a man listening to advice, and weighing it – and good advice at that.

3.

So now, he listened with respect.

"In luv, you tink, Freda? Now, who would he be in luv wid in the settlement, and him away all this time? Kurt ain't a particular man for the wimmen, and up nort' there's only hookers."

But Freda held to her view.

"I guess I can tell," she persisted sagely. She bustled about, a woman who made much noise in the domestic operations, for a kind God had made her without nerves. She even bore her many children with little more fuss and bother than a cow that calves.

And Axel watched her and turned the matter over in his mind.

"In luv, well, maybe . . ."

4.

But once Freda had gone down sick with a miscarriage at four months. It had happened shortly after a visit from Mrs. Armstrong, but the two occurrences had never linked themselves together in slow Axel's mind as a coincidence with sinister implications.

That business had alarmed even Axel, however, for it wasn't natural for anything to go amiss with raw-boned Freda.

He had walked down to Old Man Ellison. Old Man Ellison was used to stock. He might be able to suggest something.

But Old Man Ellison had thrown up his work-stained hands in horror.

"What! a miscarriage, and you don't go for the doctor at Port Murdock? Heavens alive, man! Good gracious me! Dear, oh dear!"

It had shocked him dreadfully, it seemed.

But jovial Axel had laughed his deep belly-laugh. These Old Country folk, what a fuss they made!

He said: "I've had cows miss on me, Mr. Ellison, many a time. It's nuttin' serious. Doctor, doctor, for a little thing like that!' And off he had rolled, chuckling and thinking of other matters – of his latest contract in the bush, of the road grant, of the new gravel pit.

And, sure enough, the woman had been up and about two days later, and none the worse, so it seemed.

And Axel, the wiseacre, told the tale of Old Man Ellison's alarm, told it with relish. "Maybe they don't know that the old Bohemian woman, out Carlyle way, just goes in from hoeing when her time comes, does her business and comes out when she's washed her baby. Maybe they don't know dat!"

And he laughed his deep belly-laugh. You could not teach Axel anything about women: he thought they were just another sort of cow, but with intelligence. He allowed that.

5.

Now he turned this matter of Kurt over in his slow mind. There was, sure enough, something wrong. But could it be because the fellow was mushy on some bit of a girl?

But Axel knew better than to ask questions of Kurt. "Leave him alone," he counselled, as he got up from his chair and clumped towards the door where the old man sat in his sad reverie. "If he's in luv as you tink, Freda, I guess he maybe marry the girl, or forget her. He'll git over it, one way or de odder, I reckon."

6.

When Lulu went off without a word to him, Kurt took it as a sure sign that he had disgraced himself and was not to be forgiven. Therefore, he had gone north again in search of gold. "If I make good," he told himself, "I'll come back and ask Lulu to marry me."

He had heard in Blanchard's that Lulu was to return to the business college on Granville Street, in Vancouver, from which she had been brought home by her mother to help entertain the shingle-bolt outfit. She had left without a word to Kurt; she never even wrote him a message.

He had reckoned he might be back around the same time as Lulu would return from the coast. But ill-luck had pursued him in the North. His claim was a washout; frost got his finger. Time went on. When he did return he was broke and bitter. But he had not forgotten Lulu. She moved about in the dream realm of his life, a remote, unattainable figure; unattainable, even though she had surrendered to him.

But that brief, mad hour in the shadows of the wharf house, amid the bales of straw, with the scent of the spring night about them, that intoxicating moment when she had given herself to him, no longer seemed real. Whenever he thought about Lulu, it was of the girl who played with him as a child and later had been his companion on fishing trips, his partner at dances. That night had been an experience apart, a turning away from the main stream of life. It refused the setting of the prosaic pattern of their normal lives, dissolving into unreality.

The Lulu of their passionate hour was gone, lost in the other Lulu: the Lulu of quick laughter, long silences; the Lulu who sang, who made flies for trout-fishing; the Lulu who once teased him, pulling his unkempt hair.

7.

When Kurt stepped down from the local onto the low board platform of the wayside depot, Lulu the dream-woman who had shadowed him in the North became at once intense and alive. From the river-banks the bull frogs croaked; there was a scent of the earth on the air, humid and loamy. A faint odour of decayed fish came to his nostrils. The past rose all about him.

"So good a year with the salmon," he thought, "that they spread them on the land for manure!"

So, while he had been suffering in the Yukon for nothing, the men at home had made the money he so badly needed, out there on the broad river, dragging up the salmon in their flashing thousands.

He turned away from little Tom Preedy (anxious to be friendly, inquisitive to know how the miner had fared) and walked quickly along the familiar, dusty road towards the house with the stained white walls.

"If it ain't Kurt Olson!" Mrs. Armstrong exclaimed. "Come right in, Kurt! It's real good to see you back again."

All smiles and invitation, she was, there in the cluttered kitchen, in petticoat and camisole, standing by her stove, her face flushed with heat, her hair disordered.

Yes, she flashed at him with dazzling smile, and there was no mistaking the genuine pleasure that lit up her handsome face as she pushed a chair towards him.

Things had been dull with Mrs. Armstrong. There had

been no men around the house for a long time, and she was hungry for a man. The virility of Kurt Olson, moreover, had always stimulated her easily excited imagination. He was very attractive to her because she realized that she could exercise upon him none of her practiced wiles.

"What about a drink?"

She bustled to the cupboard for bottle and glass. "You must overlook my dress," she apologized, smiling alluringly. "Last thing I expected was to see you of all people."

He eyed the curves of her thighs, emphasized by the short striped petticoat that she wore; he noted the firm curve of her full bosom. And he found her rather repellent.

He dropped his bulk wearily into the chair, resting his hands on his knees. His face was tanned to a mahogany hue and his miner's clothes were bleached by the glare of northern days. He looked shabby and soiled.

He watched her for a moment, then: "Say, Mrs. Armstrong, where's Lulu?" he asked abruptly.

She swung about, bottle and glass in hand, and eyed him shrewdly. Was this the man?

The thought flashed through her brain. But no, it could not be. Why, Kurt and Lulu had played together ever since they were nippers. Besides, hadn't she herself, once or twice, made it pretty clear to Kurt that she might not be unkind, and hadn't he turned her down? The fool! No, Kurt wasn't a man for the women.

"How's that?" she parried. "Sure. Didn't you know? Lulu is settled in Vancouver. Guess she went away around the same time as you did. Doing fine, but she don't write – not much."

Kurt shuffled his feet, his bronzed face twitching. "Why, d'you mean she don't come visiting oncet in a while?" he asked. "Say, Mrs. Armstrong, she ain't married, is she?"

She slowly placed the bottle and glass on the table,

smoothed down her petticoat over her hips with two pressing hands, stroking the fabric voluptuously. She was scrutinizing Kurt's face, trying to read his thoughts.

"No, she don't come visiting, Kurt," she answered slowly. "You see, Lulu got the bug for the city pretty bad. Discontented she was, and crazy to get education and go into business."

As she spoke, she watched like a cat the effect of her words.

Lulu's migration to Vancouver had passed without a whisper of scandal. There must be no scandal now: what was this great fool going to do?

It was awkward.

8.

Soon after Lulu had gone down to Vancouver, Mrs. Armstrong had received word from her sister that the girl had given birth to a still-born child. Two weeks later came another letter saying the girl had disappeared.

"So much the better," thought Mrs. Armstrong, as she read the agitated words of her sister's message.

Since then, whenever anybody asked after Lulu, she told the same lies. The girl had disappeared. Well, good riddance to a trollop! Girls as ignorant as that should behave. She had no patience with it. If you couldn't be artful, why then you must take the consequences.

She had come to hate the memory of Lulu.

The voice of Kurt brought her back to the present.

"Give me Lulu's address," he said. "I'll be going down to Vancouver. Maybe I can take her to a movie."

Just as she feared! She would have to think quickly. At all costs, Kurt had to be put off. Disaster was threatening, but long practice in the art of lying saved her.

At random, she invented a story to turn him from his purpose. "Say, Kurt," she began, speaking slowly, and with simulated sorrow, "what I'm going to tell you may hurt a bit. You know what girls are, crazy creatures with their fancies, kinda taking off in a huff. Well, Lulu had a crush on you, Kurt. Why, I never could find out."

Kurt quivered and a deep flush spread over his troubled face. She was talking again, more quickly now.

"I guess she was a bit soft on you, and when you never made no response, she got kinda peeved."

She tossed up her tousled head: "Anyway, she sure had a crush on you. It would be no good going down to Vancouver."

She waited a moment, watching the effect of her words. "Anyway, she said to me before she went: 'I want to live my own life. I'm fed up with the folk at Ferguson's Landing. Let me cut loose.'"

She took the cork from the bottle and tilted the amber liquor into the glass. He watched the pungent liquid spinning in tiny, oily eddies within the glass. Then he met the eyes of the woman, and the two regarded each other silently, with a fixed stare of embarrassment, hostility, mistrust.

"Then Lulu ain't visited home since she left?" he asked. "And you, her mother, ain't tried to find her?"

He rose, his eyes cold upon this woman whom he suddenly realized he had always detested.

She stood, returning his gaze. At all costs this great fool must be kept silent. If not, in spite of all her scheming the story of Lulu's baby would come out.

Shrewdly she judged that Kurt would keep the story to himself. It was the only way with such a man.

"*Lookit* here, Kurt," she began. "I got to tell you the truth, and you got to keep it to yourself." She was speaking rapidly now. "Lulu got into trouble. Had a baby. Still-born. We haven't heard of her for two years. I've never found out who the man was. She wouldn't tell."

"A baby?" he whispered. "A baby, you say? Lulu had a baby?"

Slowly he got up and stood like a somnambulist, repeating the single word. Then, slowly, a tear gathered in his eye and dropped, bright and glistening, down his tanned cheek. He stood there shaking, the tears in his blue eyes. Then slowly he turned and walked towards the door.

At the door he turned: "I'm going to find Lulu," he said. "I'm going to hunt until I do find her. I'll never rest until I have found her. And when I have, I'll settle with you." He turned and disappeared into the twilit orchard.

The woman whistled softly as she watched him disappear, his feet slashing the long wet grass, as he strode towards the road. Then her eye fell upon the untasted drink poured out for him. She snatched it from the table and drained it at one gulp. She saw it all now. Kurt was the man!

9.

How could a man with such a business on his mind talk with his folk? How could he play for the old man, or for little Ole either?

Sitting in the hot kitchen with the old man in his accustomed corner, his brother Axel in the rocker, the children playing on the scrubbed floor, and Freda seated before a pile of thick woollen socks, Kurt was so numbed by the blow he had received that he was oblivious of the curious eyes which were secretly watching him.

When little Ole plucked at his sleeve he did not even push him off. It was his mother who said: "Ole, Ole, don't go a-bothering your Uncle Kurt. I guess he's tired. Leave him be."

Next morning, with as little warning as he had given of his return, Kurt disappeared again.

He had started upon his quest.

CHAPTER XXI

1.

It was at that hour when twilight falls like a cloak about the city and the Chinese Quarter becomes a place of shadowy mystery.

Kurt drifted eastwards, mingling with the silent-footed spectres that flitted, mothlike, along the ill-lit sidewalks of Pender Street East.

Now and then the glare of a garish chop suey joint painted a yellow patch upon the darkness; otherwise the street was in shadows, with silent houses whose shuttered windows showed dimly, like the closed eyes of dead men.

For a week Kurt had wandered the streets of Vancouver in his quest for Lulu. He moved along, scanning the faces of the passing girls, and every girl ahead of him he invested with the personality of the lost Lulu, hurrying on only to turn and glimpse the face of some stranger.

At nights he slept in an hotel in Water Street. It was a dismal place, with a sordid rotunda where slept sailors from their ships, and loggers come to the city to drink the earnings of months of toil in remote lumber camps. They sprawled in rows on leather-backed chairs, heavily-booted feet thrust out, inert arms hanging down. Shining brass cuspidors, stained with tobacco juice, stood by each somnolent form; and, behind the counter, the hotel clerk with glassy eyes played a game with the bedroom keys, thrusting them into their locker holes, taking them out. The atmosphere was stale. It reeked of cheap cigar smoke and spirits.

2.

The quest of Lulu had become a fixed and unalterable

purpose with Kurt. Wherever she was, whatever had happened to her, he must find her.

He had patrolled the broad thoroughfares of the city throughout the busy hours of the day, walking first Hastings Street, then opulent Granville Street with its white, towering buildings and big fashionable stores.

He tramped far beyond the red-brick pile of the Canadian Pacific Hotel until the skyscrapers dwindled and the street's splendour faded. Here, among the negroes of that quarter, Kurt moved in the shadows of the shabby old frame buildings of an earlier Vancouver.

Many girls like Lulu passed him: slight girls with lithe limbs and swinging steps. He peered at every face.

Thus he walked the city's ways, rubbing shoulders with men of all nations: sturdy little men from Nippon, slant-eyed Cantonese, lean Red Men – Siwash and Klootchmans – huge broad-nosed smiling negroes from the States, drifted northwards from prejudice and the doubtful heritage of the Emancipator, dignified Hindus from the Punjab, Sikhs, turbanned and bearded, lumbermen, redolent of the timberlands, massive, impassive Swedes, swarthy Italians.*

3.

So it was that he came to the Chinese Quarter and halted uncertainly beneath the flaming sign of the Dragon. A Chinese theatre: it would do. Anything would do to ease, for a while, the pain of his despair.

He passed within, taking from the Chinaman, whose parchment face was framed by a small window like an old and time-mellowed picture, the flimsy ticket with its sprawling Chinese characters.

At first he was aware only of the jingling orchestra upon the raised platform, where figures went through the

"... opulent Granville Street with its white, towering buildings and big fashionable stores." (p. 223). *Top:* corner of Granville and Hastings, looking southeast, 1907. *Below:* the same view in 1994.

"Kurt moved in the shadows of the shabby old frame buildings of an earlier Vancouver." (p. 223). *Top:* A view of Christ Church Cathedral and the West End, probably taken from the old Hotel Vancouver. *Below:* approximately the same shot, taken in 1994.

Top: Corner of *"opulent Granville Street"* and Georgia in 1910, looking north-east towards the Hudson Bay Company (still there, as the 1994 photo below illustrates).

pantomime of the play – of that, and of the fetid odour which rose from the immobile, silent audience. The fantastic scene closed about him like a dream, and sitting back, he gave himself up to its spell, understanding nothing, not caring to understand. A white face in a sea of yellow faces.

And always the play went on, without climax or anticlimax, incoherent, meaningless, without design. The smoke-laden air, the stench, the discordant din, and the high-piping voices of the doll-like players.

The little figures moved like puppets, their sumptuous robes a blaze of colour, shifting against the drab background of the theatre walls hung with incongruous, blatantly Western advertisements.

Sleep fell upon him and, head upon chest, Kurt dreamed of Lulu. He awoke with a start, coming back painfully to reality, and pushed his way out into the dim street.

Night had fallen and the city was in sombre shadows. Shafts of light from shuttered windows cast arabesques upon the sidewalk. Figures shuffled through the gloom.

He turned westwards, crossed Hastings Street East where the electric streetcars roar down a canyon ramparted by skyscrapers, and made his way towards the waterfront.

Crowds thronged the sidewalks, some passing along with preoccupied faces; others with alert, eager eyes, like men with great expectations. Young men, with soft felt hats and smart ready-made Americanized clothes, toothpicks stuck jauntily in mouths, turned, with their girl-companions, into the brilliantly lighted facades of picture houses whose walls flared with lurid posters.

Men from the mines clumped along in heavy-studded boots, big packs giving their figures the illusion of deformity: they were like gnomes, like Nibelungs.* Spindle-legged boys carrying bundles of the *Saturday Evening Post* ran shouting their wares; idle men loafed at street corners, talking from

"... rubbing shoulders with men of all nations: sturdy little men from Nippon, slant-eyed Cantonese (...) dignified Hindus from the Punjab, Sikhs, turbanned and bearded (...) massive, impassive Swedes, swarthy Italians." (p. 223).

Top: Italo-Canadians' triumphal welcome to the Duke of Connaught, 1912. *Below:* same scene today. Note clock in Sinclair Centre.

-9. B.C. Canneries. Hindu unloading Salmon. J.D.J.

Top: The Sikhs (erroneously referred to as "Hindus" in the early years of British Columbia) played an important role in forestry and fisheries.
Below: Oriental immigrants disembarking in Vancouver harbour, 1910.

the corners of their mouths, laughing, spitting expertly into the road.

4.

Kurt made his way down to the waterfront. Before him, the night-enshrouded harbour, pricked here and there with the red and green lights of unseen ships, lay like a sable garment, spangled with rubies and emeralds. Beyond the water, to the north, the contours of Grouse Mountain marked the sky-line like a sleeping Nubian woman, there beside her discarded garment softly voluptuous, inviting.*

Above, the dark firmament was spangled with stars and smudged with wisps of sable cloud that drifted, like the discarded feathers of some fabulous bird, through the high air.

The wharves, amorphous shapes in the gloom, were silent now, and the great ships lying alongside raised tall spars and riggings, like skeleton spires, into the sky. Behind him Kurt saw the jagged outline of the city silhouetted against the night sky, punctured by a thousand patterned light-points. A fiery mist hung above the city; a low murmur came from its heart.

Somewhere in this darkness Lulu lived and breathed for Kurt never contemplated the possibility that she might be dead. He never speculated that she might have drifted from the city, might have crossed the line into the States, so sure was the instinct which told him that Lulu was in Vancouver, was near him, needed him.

At night he sat sleepless in his hotel bedroom, a bleak, oblong room with a single bed of soiled linen, a fixed washbasin, a let-in wardrobe and a chair. It smelt of stale tobacco and unclean humanity. The window, draped by sad curtains, looked out over the narrow street and framed the large pricked-out lettering of an electric sign.

When he lay wide awake in bed, the winking sign danced, a fantastic ghost, upon the patterned wallpaper beyond his bed.

5.

One day, as he wandered the city streets, Kurt met Heggerty. The little man was slouching, with humped shoulders, along the crowded sidewalk.

"Yep!" he admitted. "I'm down-and-out. Nothin' doing in this darn city. Can't even get work on the roads, and there ain't no building going on now the oil boom's bust."

The defeated little man poured into the indifferent ears of Kurt the story of how he had sold his ranch up at Ferguson's Landing for a mess of shares that proved to be worthless. His wife was sick too and he had lost another youngster.

At first scarcely listening, Kurt gradually took notice of the tragic story as the whining voice unfolded in nasal, oath-soiled sentences. He looked at this man, and pity for him eased his own trouble.

Poor little devil! The soiled overalls, the battered hat, the three days' unshaven chin, the burst boots, tied with string; most of all the eyes, with their reproach against a Fate that knew no mercy and gave no quarter to the weak and foolish.

Poor little devil!

"Come and have a drink."

Heggerty's eyes lit up.

"Say, now you're talking!"

They passed the swing-door of a saloon and stood against the long mahogany counter, feet firm on brass rail. Kurt ordered whiskey.

An hour later they left the saloon, and both reeled as they stepped into the crowded street.

6.

This chance meeting with Heggerty was the first crack in the resolve of Kurt to find Lulu. He still continued his crazy hunt but he seldom passed a saloon door without entering it.

And in the evening, instead of continuing his quest, he sat in his bedroom with whatever chance companions he could muster from the hotel rotunda below.

They sat and drank raw whiskey from the bottle; they argued, quarrelled, bragged of their exploits at sea, in the bush, in the mining camps of the North.

Now and again, they wept drunken tears upon one another. Hard luck, whiskey, and self-pity made them lachrymose.

It was at one of these debauches that Kurt, for the first time, heard himself telling of his quest. His listener, a hard-bitten sailor, whose pock-marked face was lit by two vivid blue eyes, and whose hairy ears were adorned by gold rings, heard him out with a smile of contempt on his weathered face.

"Say, Bo," he jeered, "you are some kind of a boob, ain't you? Searching the city for a wench that's slipped, and you haven't tried the red light district! You are some guy, I'll say!"

Sobered by this coarse speech, filled with self-loathing for his betrayal of this most sacred secret to this sottish sailor, Kurt sprang at the man with an oath.

Together they crashed to the floor, sending the bottle, from which they had been drinking, flying against the white porcelain washbasin, where it smashed into a hundred fragments and spilled its contents, filling the room with the biting smell of raw spirits.

Neither man fought by any rules for both had learnt to fight where rules are unknown.

Once or twice, in logging-camps, and once in the North, Kurt had fought. He had always remembered the advice of an old sourdough: "If you fight out here, get in first and get in how you can."

He did so now, kicking and biting and gouging at the blue eyes of the drunken sailor. A fury possessed him. He felt that he had further soiled Lulu by talking of her; he felt that this sailor's ignoble suggestion had sent her down from the heights to the lowest depths; he felt that he had been party to the profanation of his holy of holies.

He struck and struck again.

Both men were streaming blood when the hotel clerk, used to such fracases, followed by a group of jubilant loafers, burst into the bedroom and hauled the gasping antagonists apart.

7.

When he awoke next morning, Kurt realized that he was sliding downhill, and sliding rapidly.

He was no nearer finding Lulu and he was making efforts which had become merely mechanical. Half the time now, when he patrolled the city streets, he forgot his purpose. His mind was besotted and self-pity was fast unmanning him.

Once, reacting to the sinister suggestion of the sailor with whom he had fought, he stalked Alexander Street, the place of brothels. But he turned from the first windowless house, with its evil red eye, in disgust, the blare of a mechanical piano ringing in his ears.

To seek Lulu there was to dishonour her. He made his way back to the lighted streets with rage in his heart.

Kurt had but little imagination: but such as it was, it served to torture him. He envisaged, one by one, the many catastrophes which might have overwhelmed Lulu. And from these evils, conjured up by his disordered mind, he came back always to the central tragedy: the birth and death of their baby, Lulu's loneliness, her agony, her silence which had separated them. Or was it his silence which had spawned this wretchedness?

Tramping with a face of melancholy the ways of the city, he alternated between frenzied searching and bouts of drinking during which he became first a garrulous driveller, and then a raging beast.

Among the many desperate devices he employed was a telephone search of the city. Day after day, starting with A and working through the directory to Z, he rang up enquiring for Lulu Armstrong. But nobody knew the name.

"But wasn't there a Miss Armstrong with you some time since?" he would ask, and when the answer came over the wire, as it did with monotonous regularity: "Say, you got the wrong number," he would bang down the receiver with an oath.

During this time Kurt heard little of affairs at the settlement. But one day as he sat reading the *Daily Province* in the hotel rotunda, he saw a headline across the front page: "Father of Oil Ramp in City Coop."

He thus learnt that Mann had been charged. And later, when Mann came up for trial, he read the details of the flotation of the twenty-odd oil companies, by means of which the swindler had ruined so many valley settlers and Vancouver people of their savings.*

But the sensational news, luridly set forth, interested Kurt but little. He was now a man of one idea, his slow mind following the single track of his purpose with the inflexibility of the mono-maniac.

He became addicted to talking to himself, and would become suddenly conscious that, as he tramped the hot pavements, he was, by this eccentricity, drawing the attention of passers-by. When he talked thus, it was always to the Lulu whom he pursued, the Lulu of memory, already an idealized, ethereal Lulu.

"Why didn't you help me, Lulu, to say what was in my heart? Why did you go away, my little love? Didn't you understand, girl, that I was just waiting for you to give me the lead? You see, I thought, maybe, what happened that night should be forgot. It seemed up to you to give me the lead. And you didn't. That was why I went away, Lulu, went up north, to make a pile for you and me."

In this way he eased the ache of his heart.

He had grown thin, and pallor showed through his deep tan; with his beard, which he had allowed to grow, he was a different man. It was brown and full. He took no trouble with himself; every day he became more and more like a hobo.

8.

One day, as Kurt wandered listlessly along Cordova Street he saw the familiar figure of the Old Chief coming towards him. The two men stopped.

"Well, what you doing in the city?" asked Kurt.

"Me? I come down to see Indian Agent," replied the old Indian, his copper-coloured face wrinkling into a thousand minute lines, like an ancient parchment.

"But the Indian Agent is at Sapperton, you old stiff," said Kurt.

The Old Chief smiled again: "Well, maybe, I come to try get a little drop of something too. Very thirsty in the valley."

Thinking to hear some news of the Landing, Kurt told the old fellow to come with him to his room where he would give him whiskey. The old Indian's eyes glittered at the prospect and together they set off for Water Street.

9.

They were sitting side by side on the bed, drinking whiskey raw. The spirit had already galvanized the old man into artificial animation. He was talking and wagging his head:

"Everybody tink Indian damn fool," he complained. "But that all wrong. Indian know many tings. More than you know.

"Everything Indian best. White man spoil goddam country. No good."

The old man raised the bottle to his lips and gurgled the burning spirit down his corded throat. "Indian God, best God," he announced in a tone of conviction. "We know how God made birds and beasts. Yessir. White God, not much good – got killed. See? Indian God still skookum, yep, Indian God jake.

"In time my great-great-grandfather, Great Indian God make all animals. He call birds, they come flying, from bush, from prairie, from mountains. Great God say: 'You go 'way and be father all bears, you go 'way be father all moose. Every bird, he say, you make father animals.'"

The old fellow chuckled, showing his toothless gums.

"Next day – you listening? – come one bird too late. God say: 'Now you come too late, bird. You kin go 'way and be father all coyotes.'"

The old man put out a stringy arm and touched Kurt upon the shoulder. "You know a coyote never, never sleep? Now you know why: coyote afraid of being late next time."

The old man grimaced his cunning:

"Yessir, that way our Great God make bison, buffalo, horse, cow, sheep – all goddam animals."

Kurt listened apathetically. The whiskey was making the Old Chief, generally so secretive, loquacious.

"Same way our God make man. Yessir. I tell you real story. Not white man's bunkum, no squaw's ribs, nossir.

"Long time before my great-great-grandfather, Great God make first men."

The old man blew a cloud of tobacco smoke through his withered blue lips, eyed the whiskey bottle covetously, and resumed his discourse:

"Great God take t'ree little loaves, yessir, and put 'em in his oven to bake. One got burnt, that was Black man. One no dam good, not baked at all, that was White man. One, ah! one baked just nice, that red man."

The Old Chief paused: "That why red man best. God bake him right, yessir." He wagged his senile head and stretched out for the bottle a lean paw, like the hand of a mummy.

He had escaped his Catholicism like a snake that sheds its skin.

"Maybe I know plenty wot happen at Landing?" he went on mysteriously. "You remember murder at the store, maybe? Who did that murder? Everybody say: 'Can't tell.' Old Chief can tell."

Kurt pricked up his ears. The affair at the store – wasn't Mrs. Armstrong connected with that business in some way?

"Well, Chief, if you know – shoot," he invited. "I sure would like to hear that story."

The old man smacked his lips and his small eyes glittered: "One day – that day – I go down after dark to the orchard behin' store. I go to steal apples and maybe a chicken. See?

"Blanchard was playing his tinned music, and I crep' up under the window to watch, for I hear much laughter and I tink: where laughter, there whiskey.

"Well, sir, there they was having a hellofa time. Mrs. Armstrong, she was sittin' drinkin', and there was Blanchard, sittin' drinkin' and there was some other stiff sittin' drinkin'. That was the feller they found with a bullet in him.

"I seen the whole ting. Blanchard, he went out, and other feller, he start making up to Mrs. Armstrong. Presently, Blanchard come back from store. Very mad, Blanchard. He limp across room and swipe other feller with bottle. The other feller pulled his gun. Yessir. Mrs. Armstrong she jump up and knock it outer his hand. Blanchard grabbed it, other feller sprang at him, Blanchard fired. Then Mrs. Armstrong run off. Fine goin's on. God's truth, she run back to her house skeered outer her life."

The old man paused.

"Say, d'you know, Mrs. Armstrong, she gits credit at the store, all along? That's why. Old Indian no dam' fool, no sirree."

Kurt shook the old Indian's hand and told him to get out. He had heard enough. He wanted to be alone. His head swam from the raw spirit he had consumed; the garrulity of the old Indian had become unendurable.

At the door, the old man turned and looked down at the massive figure of Kurt on the untidy bed. Plainly, he was loath to go, to leave this crony, to abandon the alluring spirit. He dallied to make small-talk, there by the door; to gain time, to get another little drink. Kurt, bemused, scarcely listened, lying back, eyes closed.

But what was this breaking in upon his consciousness, like the clang of a gong on half-awakened ears?

The Old Chief was talking of Lulu. Kurt sat up with a jerk: "Lulu! what did you say? Lulu!"

"She came back home, ain't I bin tellin' you?"

There was astonishment on the old fellow's face: a strange man, this Kurt Olson!

Kurt took the afternoon local for the Landing.

CHAPTER XXII

1.

Excitement in the settlement: Johansson has bought a Ford. He goes clanking up and down the steep trails with it, the thick mud slimy beneath whirling wheels that can find no grip. He uses it to transport his few remaining needs – flour by the sack, bran for the hens' mash, things like that.

It is an old Ford, true enough, but it goes. The fenders (from which, long since, the black, shiny enamel has flaked off, so that they are pitted with yellow rust) are crumpled and loose; the battered body, with its torn seat-covers, weather-faded hood and cracked windscreen all proclaim the age of the vehicle. But it goes. The grinding of its gears can be heard from Stein's prim ranch to Bob England's place.

Johansson crosses the trail at the edge of the Newcomer's place with pride. He presses one enormous boot upon the pedal and, his brow furrowed by thought, makes the change down. Driving his own Ford, is Johansson, the first motor car to appear in the settlement.

The Ford marked an epoch in the growth of the place, in its transition from the old, early days of the bush (when there were only ox teams) to the modern settlement with its CPR depot, its church, store, wharf and grain-barn.

But Johansson had not bought this amazing vehicle out of pride. Whatever else he is, Johansson is a simple man, thinking always of practical things. There it was: the settlement had a need and Johansson was the first to see it. It needed transport so he provided transport for it.

There were new people as far back as five miles in the bush now. How were they to bring in their gear, their household junk? Hitherto, horse-teams had done the work, lumbering slowly along the deep-rutted trails, sometimes overturning.

But there were not teams enough in spring when the hillside clearings were ploughing and every team was forespoken till early June.

The Ford solved the problem. It had cost Johansson one hundred and fifty dollars. A lot of money. But it quickly recouped him for his outlay. The Ford was a paying proposition. The lads of the settlement cheered derisively when they met the gaunt man, sitting sternly behind the clutched steering-wheel, driving along the rough new roads.

Every day now, instead of going forth on foot to work long hours in the bush, or on the new roads, or on the land of his neighbours, Johansson set out to fetch from the wharf-house bales of odorous straw, soft sacks of wheat, oats, bran and meat-meal that the Sapperton boat brought up-river to the settlement.

Five or ten cents a sack he charged for delivery. Not much, it is true, but it mounted up, and folk paid cash. Very soon Johansson had learnt to understand the mechanism of his machine; he tended it with the same thorough care that he lavished on his cows, his pigs and his hens.

The Ford solved a pressing problem for Bob England too, for he had sold his team, Frank and Gert, and had no horses on his place. The mortgage interest must be paid. All Bob England's supplies now came up the steep hill by Ford.

All week Johansson worked, part time on his own place (now finished and trim as an old-world farm), part time upon his new transport business. Sometimes, in his slow mind, this tardiness of luck, this prosperity that came too late, stirred wistful regrets: his wife was dead, and alone, the salt was gone from life, the triumph from hard-won victory.

2.

The settlers had got together. The seeds, sowed laboriously in the early days of Old Man Dunn, were bearing fruit.

Ferguson's Landing was starting out to fight the middle-man, that unseen octopus that sucked in with prehensile tentacles the meagre profits of the Valley farmers.

The ranchers now clubbed together and bought their grain by the car-load. They had their Co-operative Association.* It saved them many a hard-come-by dollar; not, it is true, that they could fight the Canadian Pacific Railway with its prohibitively high rates. That was beyond their power. But even so, the co-operative scheme was a great success; they owned their own warehouse, the dark, yellow building by the track, to the making of which each man had contributed his share of labour.

They forgot Old Man Dunn, Dunn the Sage. Yet it was Old Man Dunn who had sown the seed of this idea, years ago, when it was no uncommon thing for the old man to be scoffed at as a 'goldarned Socialist.'

There was, too, talk of a second store. Blanchard seemed more obliging nowadays. He did not press for payment. He smiled on everyone.

The settlement, it is true, had been severely shaken by the collapse of the oil boom. But it faced the future with quiet courage.

The boom weeded out the weaklings.

Little Tom Preedy, full of plaints, inefficient in his work at the depot, had been threatened with dismissal. When he crept from his dark little office now to chalk up on the black-board the arrival times of the trains, he spoke but seldom, nursing his grievance in silence. But when he spoke it was always of the oppressive methods of Big Corporations and the Tyranny of Big Finance. "Grinding the face of the pore, that's wot it is," he would whine. He contrasted the Old Country with British Columbia and found everything in Britain's favour.

"Why don't you clear out, if you don't like the country?"

Old Man Ellison asked him. But Tom Preedy had no answer.

He is broke, is Tom Preedy, with only his meagre pay to live on. His ranch is neglected. The fruit-trees, grubbed up when fortune seemed in sight, lie dead and withered where he had flung them down.

And the little man has other troubles too. Mrs. Preedy has become the prey of frightful headaches. The doctor merely shakes his head and talks of the bad time of life. Mrs. Preedy talks of ending it all, so miserable is she. She can cook no more and the little man now muddles about the stove, whining at the hardship of his lot, intent on his own unhappiness, regarding the suffering of his withered wife as a grievance against her.

So the settlement goes.

3.

A strange life in which good comes out of evil – it was the bickering of the mission parson and his wife, and the rapid progress of the man towards a dangerous intimacy with Mary Ellison that eventually proved the turning-point.

It happened thus: one day, when Agnes had been more than usually acid, the parson's misery reached its peak. He was love-sick for the girl with the Madonna face.

He met her as he strode along the road, neat in her simple dress, demure and smiling, her great eyes soft with love. She read his moods as one reads a book. It was understood between them that they were tragic lovers, the characters in a romance centering about the conflict of love and duty. Her sympathy was mostly silent but it spoke none the less clearly for that.

When he left her, it was with a desperate need to get away somewhere alone, to think, to wrestle with this temptation. He decided to go down to Vancouver.

He returned to the vicarage, changed into grey flannels, donned a non-clerical collar, and took the local.

As the train sped through the silent Valley, he examined himself: his life, his failure to make good, the misery of his marriage, the hunger of his heart.

When the train ran into the shadowy terminus he was convinced that he should never have entered the Church at all. It had been a terrible mistake.

Yet the idea had been planted in him as a boy and, boy-like, he had accepted it. Looking back now on those early days at school (and later at Trinity College, Dublin), he saw himself as a supine, purposeless puppet, jerked hither and thither at the bidding of wills stronger than his own.

Overshadowing all those early memories loomed always the austere figure of the father he had never known, the dead father who had become a hated tyrant dominating him from the grave.

"Your father would have wished you to follow his own sacred calling," his mother was always saying. "Your father disapproved of smoking." Or "Your father, my boy, was a Christian gentleman; that is my ambition for you, too."

Why, for example, could he not fill his church? Why did the settlers tolerate him, and no more? Why was he unhappy in his home, with his wife – that wife selected for him by his scheming mother (he saw that plainly now). Teeming questions, for which he found no answer.

In the city, lonely and unhappy, he wandered the crowded streets, wrestling with the problem of his life. He turned into a cafeteria and passed along the counter with its steaming dishes and white-aproned attendants. He selected food automatically, ate it unawares, lost himself in a dream.

All afternoon he wandered, wrestling with his problem. Night fell, and he arrived at the station to find the local gone. For a while he toyed with the mad idea of cutting himself loose from his old life with Agnes, the Church, and the hated settlement. He would just go away somewhere and make a new life in some new land. Other men had done it. It wasn't as if Agnes loved him. He thought of Mary Ellison. He feared the future.

Thus, in his unhappiness he walked the city's streets, a little man with shuffling steps, bottle-shouldered, weedy, turning over that desperate resolve in his mind.

But in the end he told himself there was no escape. For even in a new land, self-unfrocked, emancipated, he would not be free: he would take his memory with him, and it would poison all his days.

One carried one's hurt in the heart: there was no escape from that.

4.

He found himself in an unlighted street, a thoroughfare of stagnant pools, and patched and sagging side walks. In the deep shadows figures slunk by, men with hats pulled down over faces dimly seen. Now and then an auto with vivid head-lights bleaching the mire of the road bumped and creaked over the rutted way, slowed down, stopped. He saw the red points of cigars and heard laughter. Sinister in the darkness shone red lights above impassive doors.

Suddenly he understood that chance had brought him to the red light district.

He had discussed the social evil many times, in and out of the pulpit. Once he had preached on the theme when taking holiday-duty for a brother cleric in Vancouver, at a time when the civic elections were being fought on the issue of an open or a closed city.

He had preached on 'Our City's Shame.' It was on a big board outside the church. A little blatant, perhaps, a bit like the Salvation Army, but this was Canada. Punch, and so forth: 'getting messages across.'

Curiosity stung him. He was in mufti.* Was it only curiosity? Of course. One should face facts: one should learn life. One should see things for oneself. So one side of his mind told him.

Looking back afterwards, it seemed as though his hand had gone to that electric bell without his volition. He stood there in the gloom, the glow from the red lamp falling upon his soft hat, upon his lined face.

The door opened silently: he stepped inside.

5.

He was sitting on the bed struggling with a shoelace. The girl was smiling down on him with a slow, exaggerated, mechanical smile. She was young and pretty.

The room contained a big bed, a dressing-table, a Mission rocker, and wash-hand stand with jug and basin. Thick curtains masked the place where there might have been a window but where, as it happened, the wall was bricked up.

The hands which fumbled with the shoe trembled. That was why the girl smiled; understanding there was in that smile, and a sad wisdom.

It said, quite clearly: Not an old hand, and a married man. One of the ones who are ashamed always after it is all over, one of the emotional ones who haven't the guts to sin without whining about it.

The little man, unconscious of that smile, fumbled with his shoes. The swollen veins of his scrawny neck made in his ears a thudding music, so that it was as though his heart was pumping beyond danger-point. And one had to talk, too. One had to *say* something.

He looked up from the close contemplation of his absurd

problem. "Queer place to live in," he suggested. "I mean . . ."

Then, for the first time, he really looked at the girl. Downstairs, after that spiritual struggle which had left him shaking like a man under fire, he was coming to his senses again.

She smiled at him in a businesslike way – waiting. He considered her depravity and wondered, vaguely, that her eyes should look so frankly into his without hint of guilt or sense of shame. They were like the eyes of a child, perfectly candid, friendly. Even her painted mouth seemed soft. It looked babyish, with its slight droop.

He stood up. A feeling of revulsion had wiped out desire. A surge of pity swept over him.

"You are not an ordinary sort of bad girl, are you?" he blurted out. "I saw it as you stood there downstairs with those others; you don't belong to this sort of life. You are only a child."

"What sort of guy are you, anyway?" she asked resentfully. "First, you behave like a rube, then you come up here and preach at me. I know your sort. Just because you feel the beast that you are, you work off your cheap emotions by being mushy, don't you?"

Sitting on the bed, he listened to her tirade with parted lips.

"Do you think I don't know your sort?" she continued, her voice rising with her anger. "Cheapskate! Want to get a new sort of thrill. That's about your speed! You make me tired."

She turned and snatched up a soiled kimono, thrusting her white arms into its wide sleeves. "Well, if there's nothing doing – get!" she shouted. "You're wasting my time. I'm not here for my health."

Then, hard upon her anger came tears; her mouth quivered, and he saw it and was touched by pity for her. He felt a lump rise in his throat.

The close room, with its atmosphere of vice, the haunting phantoms of a thousand depravities, oppressed his spirit and choked his lungs. He felt the hot tears rising, felt the tickle of their progress down his cheeks.

She was speaking again: "Some men are brutes, and we know how to handle them. Just animals, they are. Well, we give them what they want. And they pay. And go. Some of them, like you, aren't content with a girl's body – they want to go poking around in her soul. You want to dig up things and make me miserable, don't you? Cheap little beast!"

6.

That house had been her only home for two years. She seldom left it. Sometimes, for days, she never dressed herself entirely. She was often drunk. Not because by drinking you could forget. That was sentimental rubbish. But because the men wanted to drink, and one had to drink with them: there was the commission.

Elderly men liked her. Prosperous citizens with fine homes on Shaughnessy Heights, or out in Point Grey. It saved something from cracking inside them; they told her so. Well, why not? They paid well for the privilege of being themselves sometimes. "It don't matter what you do in front of these girls, no, sir! They ain't like ordinary women-folk, no, sirree!"

Frank animalism no longer nauseated her. She had acquired the protective trick of shutting her essential self off from her mechanical parodying of love.

And then, once in a while came some weakling fool to go through the pantomime of remorse; some soft fool getting sentimental, talking about reform, or danger.

7.

"It's my business to understand men," she went on, "and I understand them pretty thoroughly. You bet I do! I wasn't in Cranbrook for a year for nothing."

Cranbrook was a mining town near the Crow's Nest Pass, notorious for its vice.

She was calm now, speaking with a contempt that smote him to the heart.

"In the ordinary way, I hand out the kind of guff they want. Some, like you, want a bit of sentiment. Well, they get it, see?"

She laughed a hard little laugh.

"I've about five stock stories, and I hand 'em out to suit my particular client. There's the story of the brutal step-mother who drove me from home. I give that to Mr. Family Man to think about. Then there's the story of a hard-hearted father who wanted to force me to marry a rich old guy – it tells how I nobly refused and set out to earn my own living.

"Cinema stuff, but it suits the sentimental ginks. I finish it with a shrug of the shoulders. They understand every time: I was seduced by a bad, wicked employer." He was sitting, listening with an expression of intense pain upon his face. It was his first contact with reality and he shrank from it appalled.

She was speaking again in that hard voice of hers:

"Then there's the story of the brute who drugged and seduced me – that tells how I was too frightened to go home and drifted down, down, down. And that's movie stuff too, all right.

"I give that to the guy who likes something sensational and dramatic so he can put himself in the role of the villain and enjoy a good time.

"And that ain't all. No, sir. There's the hot-air story of the nasty young man who seduced me under promise of marriage and vamoosed. I hand it out to prospects that look like easing up with a fat wad."

He was looking at her now with a set expression on his

lean face. Lust was dead in him. He wanted above all things to get out of this room, out of this house, out of this vile street. He wanted to get away from this girl, this awful girl whose words lashed him and hurt because he recognized that they were stark, cruel statements of a part of life, a hidden, dreadful, shameful part that he had never realized in his petty, artificial world of make-believe.

He said: "My God, I'm sorry! My God, I'm sorry!"

He extended a thin hand: "I never meant to exacerbate your feelings. The truth is, I felt ashamed of myself, and sorry for you. We seemed, all of a sudden, just two human beings, divested of all the pretences that make up daily life as we live it. I felt you were the first woman I had really and truly looked at. I felt real, and you seemed real too because we were neither of us playing at pretence."

She heard him in silence, picking up a cigarette, striking a match upon the sole of her high heel. Her manner softened.

"Suppose we swap our real stories?" he suggested.

She shrugged her shoulders: "Go on, then, you can tell me about yourself."

He braced himself as for an effort, his two hands clasped between his legs, his head low upon his narrow chest. He looked little and black and insignificant. She noticed that his hair was thinning at the top into a little tonsure.

"Have you ever tried to realize what it's like for an ordinary man to take a priest's vows?" he asked her. "Of course not. Nobody has! They sit on us when we fail but they never give a thought to what it means to have to pose as morally superior to other men. They treat us as though we enjoyed an immunity from the lusts of the flesh. Well, we don't, I find. I don't mind telling you, it's a difficult business."

She slid down beside him on the bed, her anger gone, her interest roused.

"Go on," she said.

"Year after year, can't you understand? Suppression. A parson's human, after all, but he must never own up to it. He must always pretend that being good comes easily to him. Well, let me tell you – it doesn't. You've been hating these fat fellows who come to you from their comfortable homes to, well – to let off steam. But you are wrong. I can understand how they feel, I can sympathize with them – now. Men are animals underneath. Every one of us. Our morality is artificial. Necessary, perhaps, but unnatural."

"But what about marriage?" she put in.

"Marriage?"

He looked up at her and a deep colour spread over his face.

"You guessed, then?" he asked.

She laughed. "I know a married man directly he locks the door of this room," she answered, contemptuously. "Sure I know you're married. I could tell you what your wife is like."

He looked at her, incredulous: "You could?"

"Yes."

"Well, tell me."

She inhaled deeply the smoke of her Caporal cigarette, leant back upon her elbow, and gazed at the ceiling. Then, in a slow, reflective voice:

"She's a thin woman, I think, with thin emotions. When she married you she did it because she saw that not to be married left a woman out of the swim of life. Marriage was a sort of – a sort of charter to be treated as a woman of importance. It showed everybody that she could get something."

He winced.

She continued, blowing straight spirals of smoke into the air and dispersing them with an idle finger into tattered cloudlets.

"But she is a sensible woman and realizes that in this world everything has a price: she submits to you like a good wife because for some reason she can't understand, the Church sanctions such vulgarity.

"She tries to hide from you the fact that she loathes it, all of it. And she is barren. I mean, not only barren physically, but barren in her soul. Probably if you could see her as nakedly as I can see you, you would be looking at a cruel, heartless, judging sort of woman. Underneath she despises you. You irritate her every day of your life and her only compensation is that you cut a figure among the other women whose husbands aren't in the exalted position of a Bible-thumper."

She paused. "Well," she queried, "is it a good portrait?"

He looked up, self-possessed and calm.

"No, it isn't," he answered. "But I will tell you what you have done. You have made me see clearly. Yes, if that is how my wife feels inside, and perhaps it is, then what must her life be like? Why, it must be worse than mine! D'you know, I've often felt that I had missed something . . . something big, something – well – redeemed. It's hard to talk, isn't it? It's strange, us sitting here, in this place, talking like this, talking, like human beings. Showing each other our souls."

She shrugged her shoulders and turned upon her side. "Which is worse," she asked, "tell me this: which is worse, to be one man's harlot, or to take all comers?"

"One man's harlot?" he repeated dully. "What do you mean?"

"Being a tart is giving yourself for money, isn't it? Well, giving yourself for a home seems to me about the same thing – if you're not afraid to think straight."

They were silent for a while.

The foundations of his orderly life seemed to have crumbled under him. He had always slid around hard facts: he had a putty mind. He loathed himself.

He spoke again:

"But if you can see things so clearly, can't you see my point of view? Can't you make some allowance for my having so far forgotten myself as to be here, in this house?"

She nodded her head.

"Don't be a poor fool; of course I can. It's the undersexed wives who provide us with clients. They don't know it, but they do. I don't blame men. They can't help their natures."

She stretched forward from the bed and took another cigarette, placed its brown end to the glowing tip of her burnt stub, and sucked in the fire.

"There's another story I could tell, but won't. Yes, I will tell you. I wasn't seduced, or drugged or anything like that."

She shook her head, throwing herself back on the bed and gazing up at the ceiling.

"I loved a man and gave myself to him. I thought he would marry me. Well, he didn't. It was just the usual sort of thing. Appetite and satisfaction – that's the truth about most so-called loving, so far as men are concerned."

Her voice was bitter.

"So I cleared out. I've drifted here for several reasons. I could have kept myself easily enough. I could have gone as hired-girl on a farm or could have got a job in a department store – anything like that. But I'd always hated that sort of routine life. I'd had a pretty good dose of it ever since I was a kid."

For a moment she became silent, swinging a silk-stockinged leg over the side of the bed.

"I guess when my feller let me down something died inside me; I had wanted him. He passed me up. I turned cold."

She gave a hard little laugh.

"I guess my heart's a stone right now," she concluded.

From below, the music of an automatic piano started up *Alexander's Ragtime Band.*

He was troubled by her confidence:

"But, look here, can't I get you out of here? You can't go on like this. Think of the future, when you lose your looks and . . . and are old."

She looked at him with anger in her eyes.

"Go on," she sneered. "Go on, rub it all in. My God, man, what a damned fool you must be if you imagine that I never think about that! And what, may I ask, are you prepared to do? Will you take me on as hired girl in your parsonage? Will you hand me the cash to start a bijou milliner's shop? Will you vouch for me among respectable folk? Pshaw! You damn well know you won't!"

She got up from the bed and passed her hands through her hair.

"No, we've both blown off steam and you must go. You're interfering with business."

She crossed to the mirror and lifted her oval chin towards the glass. With deft fingers and in a businesslike way she applied a touch of rouge to her cheeks and pencilled in, adroitly, blue lines in the shadows of her great eyes.

"You trot along," she said, "and put that wallet away."

"Please," he pleaded.

She shook her head, making her hair swing out in a golden mop that caught the light of the red-shaded electric globe.

"Nope! Now run along back to your wife, and parish and your church, and be a good little man in future."

He moved slowly towards the door, fumbled at the handle and stepped out. He crept silently down the thickly carpeted stairs, and the music of the automatic piano blared up at him from behind a closed door. He stood in the hall, finger to lips, heart beating. The girl was no longer in his mind. He was thinking "Suppose someone from the settlement should see me here! My God!"

A silent wraith slid out of a recess and touched the heavy chain of the door. A yellow face turned towards him and two expressionless almond eyes looked into his. A long, tapering yellow finger beckoned to him. He was out in the dark street again, breathing, like a man come to the surface of the water after too deep a dive, the air into his hungry lungs.

He turned and ran.

8.

In the Agassiz local a stout, homely woman with a large mole and kindly eyes could make nothing of the little man who sat with grief-stricken face turned towards the velvet darkness of the night.

"Trouble, there's trouble everywhere," she sighed to herself as she watched with eyes made kind by understanding.

She passed the next two hours constructing in her mind theories as to the nature of her fellow-traveller's troubles.

He had lost a child; he had been to see a brother in the Provincial Penitentiary; he had lost all his money in this oil ramp; he had buried a wife.

She thought of many things but she did not hit upon the truth. She was watching, had she but known it, a man who wept because he had lost nothing at all, a man who wept because he had found himself and, having found himself, was praying in his heart the first real prayer he had ever sent up to the inscrutable mystery.

"Pity me, oh Lord! Pity me! Pity her, oh Lord, pity her!"

CHAPTER XXIII

1.

Father O'Reilly was an old man who had put in forty years in the West; a wise old man, with a charitable and understanding heart, and a cassock powdered with dandruff. He had fat, soft hands and carried them locked over his sagging paunch.

He told the mission parson many stories of the old days when the Catholic Church had shown her vision and foresight on behalf of the Red Indians. "Everywhere you go," he remarked, "you will notice that the Indian Reservations are finely located and on the best land. That is because the Church secured that land for them."

Yes, it was true enough. The Catholic Church had looked well after these converted natives, regarding them as her especial wards in a land where every white man's hand was against them. She did not suppress their customs nor did she interfere with tribal laws.* She merely grafted Christianity on to their lives. Gave them Christ in place of their fabulous deities.

The mission parson had come into contact with Father O'Reilly one day when he had gone across to the Indian Reservation to put in an odd hour with the Old Chief. The parson was all for knowing all that could be learnt of his people, as he now thought of them. Of course the Indians and the breeds were Catholics to a man. But that did not matter. To be neighbourly – Christian, that was the thing. So he came, smiling and friendly, talked to the old man, to the women, patting the heads of the children, giving them candies and good advice.

Everybody marked the change in him. When he drove about the settlement in his old rig he had a smile for everyone. He started to organize bees; he blessed the harvest by giving a hand with the hay-making instead of forcing upon a hostile congregation a medieval Feast of the Rogation.*

He took to entertaining Father O'Reilly when O'Reilly came to take service at the dilapidated Catholic chapel once a month (Father O'Reilly had a parish which ran into several districts along the valley. A vast parish, bigger than an English county).

They avoided theology by mutual pact.

"I'm beginning to get the western idea," the mission parson told him. He had bought a bottle of 'Perfection' whiskey, for the old priest liked his toddy, saying: "All good things come from God. Use them but don't abuse them."

"No, it has not been easy," he confessed. "At first, frankly, I hated this rough life, just hated it."

Father O'Reilly quizzed the little man. "Rough life?" His blue eyes twinkled. "Why, this is not what an oldtimer like meself calls a rough life, my friend. When I think of the old days. Rough!"

And Father O'Reilly clucked his tongue and wagged his ponderous head.

"Oh, you mustn't think I'm complaining. We've blessings here, indeed we have. But after the polish and refinement of the Old Country – you know what I mean, don't you?"

But Father O'Reilly had but dim memories of the Old Country. He had always been poor and overworked in the early Dublin days. And now his heart was in his work; he had put thought of self away. Comfort was when his corns behaved and the children learned their catechism without trouble – comfort to body, and comfort to soul.

He smiled benignly: one had to have patience with a Chechahco.* He would learn in time.

But the mission parson needed a confessor and rushed on blindly. "I've been guilty, you know, of uncharitableness. I looked down on my parishioners – yes, I did! I'm ashamed to say it, but there it is. And now I'm sorry for it. My eyes are opened. I can see them as they are: the hardness of their lives, their courage, their staunchness. They are magnificent."

Those old enthusiasms! How well the old priest knew them. They came hot from the heart, but they passed, and something took their place; that something was quieter, more steadfast, and abided.

"They have so little pleasure," the parson hurried on.

"Pleasure?" interrupted the old man. "What should they want with worldliness? Pleasure and happiness! Different things, my friend. One loses the one by seeking the other."

The mission parson nodded.

He found it difficult to give words to the things in his heart, yet he needed to talk. And one side of him, the side of the son of his mother, felt a little ashamed of hob-nobbing thus with a Papist. Somehow he had slipped into the position of an inferior, of one sitting at the feet of a teacher.

"I find there is so much about life that I do not know," he went on. "And only slowly am I finding things out. All my old ideas are in the melting pot."

Father O'Reilly nodded. "That means growth," he answered. "Things go, but others come in their place. Opinions are like linen, to be changed now and then."

"Charitableness, don't you think?" suggested the little man. "That seems the central thing."

The old priest nodded. "Charitableness, yes. That can never take you far wrong."

Suddenly the little man looked at the fat priest with closer scrutiny. He was old and he looked tired.

"You must be looking forward to going home," he suggested, "after forty-five years in the Mission field."

"This is my home," the old man told him, "and I have no other." It was simply said, in a quiet voice. A mere statement of fact, uncoloured, laconic.

"This is my home." Like that.

They were the best of friends, these two, and there after many were the intimate exchanges between them.

"Old Father O'Reilly is the sort of priest one could confess to," he told Agnes enthusiastically.

Agnes looked at him with a new-born curiosity. He was changing. Not so long ago he said things about the Catholics that were dreadful. And now he praised a priest!

She said: "Yes, perhaps you are right. A sweet old man but oh, how dirty!"

2.

They were going to bed. The simple little room with its varnished-board walls and Mission furniture was dimly lit by an oil lamp.*

He was thinking: "Wonderful, really wonderful, how other people change when one changes oneself. Agnes seems a different woman now. Gentler, softer."

And she had, indeed, noticed the change in him. He seemed to think now of all the little things he might do for her and he complained no more when things went wrong. He seemed to have found a new courage, a new strength.

She had married him because she had seen the fate in store for old maids in a Dublin suburb, the pathetic women of such localities as Blackrock and Monkstown. They withered with the years, lonely and forlorn. Nobody wanted them, and in her heart – that heart she found it so difficult to show – Agnes wanted to be desired. But somehow her heart seemed pasted over with prejudices. She wasn't herself at all, really, but only a collection of other people's notions, littlenesses, narrowness. And she felt that all that was passing. She felt a change.

He watched from the bed as she brushed her hair before the mirror. Presently, raising himself on one elbow, he said:

"Agnes, you know, you have rather pretty shoulders."

She paused, her brush held against her sleek and shining hair. In the mirror he saw her eyes reflected: they looked back into his. They seemed to ask a question.

"Really, you have, and 'pon my word, I'm ashamed to say

I never noticed it before. Very pretty, white and soft, and in this light they shine."

"Are they?" she asked, and the glass reflected her slow smile. "I like to hear you say that."

Ah, wonderful, really wonderful, how people change when one changed oneself. Agnes. A different woman, a creature gently flowering, responding to a kind word, warming to a hint of love. And life was hard for women. It was hard when they were good. And when they were bad? – No, not bad: when they sinned – strayed. Terrible, then. Were they ever bad? Weren't they made bad by men?

He felt a yearning and a desire for her. Poor Agnes! What chance had she had? None. The real Agnes was like a thing in a cocoon, waiting to break through and see the world. The cocoon was the casing of environment and they had imprisoned her in it from earliest childhood.

Her mind too, dormant and unquestioning, accepting the order of things as final. And now, all at sixes and sevens, in a world where everything was different.

He must help her to grow, and he would struggle for emancipation himself. They must grow together, side by side, helping each other like travellers along a weary road. Comrades, that was the idea. Could he get at her mind? Get near to her, probe beneath that surface and discover the real woman beneath?

Was there a real woman? What had she in common with that other woman? Yet they were essentially the same: both women. But Agnes was overlaid with 'lady'; that was what was so frightful. The artificial had crushed and swamped the primitive in her. Every action she referred to some outside standard. She never dared to be herself. But perhaps she would now, now that things were different with them.

She was struggling with her white nightgown, an amorphous figure, fantastic in the yellow light of the lamp. A writhing, distorted shape. Like that – like her life, like their two lives.

She came towards the bed and he forgot to listen for the creak of her feet which tortured him at other times. He watched her now, wonderingly, for her eyes were bright, and she seemed to him at that moment transfigured, like a woman who came to him for the first time, and came shyly, timorously, hedged about with a sort of virginity.

Full of wonder, she seemed, as at something unexpectedly found.

He put out his arms to her and she crept into them, lifting up her face to him to be kissed; returning his kiss in a new way, shyly passionate, softly maternal.

Small and insignificant they looked in the big bed.

Outside the bullfrogs croaked, and the chug-chug of the gasoline boat of a night fisherman, drifting the river, came through the open window. And another sound, indefinable, weary, ageless: the voice of the bush, a sighing and a lamentation.

CHAPTER XXIV

1.

August again, and the Valley heavy in the heat. No wind, no breeze even, and the great river a belt of shining silver in the sun. Green everywhere, except where the first leaves of the maples are yellowing, and on the ordered pattern of the hillside the little wheat fields lie like fragments of amber glass upon a green carpet.

The sweet smell of new-mown hay is in the air. As far as the eye can see, a cobalt firmament roofs a quivering earth. Not a cloud against that burnished dome, only on the southern horizon, the dead volcano dreaming against the burning sky.

Down along the old road, very near Old Man Ellison's place, the road-gang, hacking at the hump in the road, grading with the big team that was once Bob England's. The sweating chestnuts strain, snorting loudly, and the great scoop, like a giant's shovel, catches its point in the hard road surface and pitches the steerer. Its two handles come up as it overturns and threaten the arms of the Newcomer, throwing his weight down upon them.

Overhead, the great trees giving shelter from the sun, here and there dappling the road with cool dim patches. Five bronzed, lusty men using picks against the surface, singing in unison:

> *"Darling, I am growing old,*
> *Silver threads among the gold . . ."**

Good singing it is, each man taking his part, throwing his soul into the words, into the mournful melody.

In the tangled undergrowth, in the bush, there is sweet moisture. A tiny spring dances its downward course. Singing as it goes, it drops over a mossy shale stone, a dwarf cascade, to the ditch, and thence flows through the old culvert.

They will be making a new culvert when the crown has been cut from the road. A culvert of great rot-defying cedar planks, a little tunnel beneath the road, and that road hereafter will be easier for cattle and for horses.

Easier, too, in the years to come when the valley is close-settled and engineers come to macadamize the road which was once a trail.

But these road-makers will have passed on by then and nobody will give a thought, as automobiles speed down the highway, to these singers of today, the settlers of the Landing.

Building a culvert on Baker Road. Since 1878, every man over 18 had to work two days a year on the roads, or pay a $3.00 levy.

"[When] engineers come to macadamize the road which was once a trail (. . .) these road-makers will have passed on (. . .) and nobody will give a thought, as automobiles speed down the highway, to these (. . .) settlers of the Landing." (p. 261). Photo: workmen building Baker Road (240th St.) in Haney, 1912.

"Dinner! Dinn-e-r!" Noon, and the road boss's voice. He is way down the road and his voice travels through the air, into the bush, like a bird of sound.

A welcome sound, a blessed word: dinner. The men drop tools and move towards the shade of the bush, to their coats, to the little pails which contain their simple meal. An hour's respite, a blessed hour of rest.

2.

When their money had given out, the Newcomer had said to his wife: "I can always make a living out here. After all, anyone can labour, given ordinary strength. It doesn't require knowledge. There's no technique to a pick or shovel."

Now, with aching back and aching arms, he moved stiffly

"... the low rumble of the stirring city heard from the silence of the Temple ..." (p. 266). Photo: the Temple Bar, London, 1910. On the left you can see the entrance to the Bar.

to the grateful shade. He took his lunch alone, clambering a little into the bush, crushing down bracken and forest flowers, sprawling by the little spring.

He had been wrong, of course. Even manual work required skill. Amazing discovery! Yes, there is technique to the simplest manual action. There is no unskilled work. There are merely unskilled workers.

In the cool darkness of the tin are sandwiches, carefully packed in buttery paper, fragrant and moist. He takes one in a soil-stained hand and bites into it. Bread and meat, and water from the spring. A simple meal.

No, manual work was very skilled, very skilled indeed. He considered his pick. At first he had grasped it and swung it high, lustily, eager to show his strength. And that had been all wrong. There was gravity, friend gravity, which helped. One merely raised one's pick and let it drop. No need of an arduous downward tug: gravity did that, the road surface split under the steel nose with no other force than the weight of the unwieldy tool. Something learnt.

Shovels too. Tools of infinite variety. What ease to shovelling when the edge of the tool was sharp! What misery, when it curled like a lettuce! One learnt. Slowly, laboriously. But one learnt.

From his coat pocket the Newcomer took a slender volume as he lay there in the friendly damp softness of the lush bracken, wearied limbs relaxed.

It was *Elia* that he read. It took him back, as did no other book, to England, to that other life, that other world, now no more real than a tale remembered.

"*. . . What a collegiate aspect has that fine Elizabethan hall, where the fountain plays, which I have made to rise and fall, how many times! to the astoundment of the young urchins, my contemporaries, who, not being able to guess at its recondite machinery, were almost tempted to hail the wondrous work as magic . . . Fantastic forms, whither are ye fled? or, if the like of you exist, why exist they no more for me? . . .*"*

3.

He could hear the fountain now, the fountain in the old, leaf-strewn court where the pigeons walked with confidence and the old plane trees cast their shadows. Sometimes it played, and sometimes came a porter and shut off the stream. That always disappointed the idlers resting at the midday hour. They would be there now: that is, if England was really true, and not merely the shadow of a dream.

Queer, the evocative power of words, little wriggly things. Symbols, yet much more: magicians that conjured up the past and things forgotten, flooding the mind with memories, stirring emotions dormant and forgotten. And sounds: with them it was the same.

Talking water. Water splashing from the fountain. Water singing through the bush, dancing over shale boulders. Water lapping under the bow of a boat; the drowsy monotone of little waves breaking upon golden sands in summertime; the mournful clang of bell-buoys over grey, troubled waters; the haunting, eerie hoot of foghorns across slow-heaving, leaden seas.

All sorts of talking sounds. The rustle of the skirts of the great trees in the heat of noon, in the darkness of night; promises and menaces, light and darkness. The first twitter of early-awakened birds heard between sleep and waking; the low rumble of the stirring city heard from the silence of the Temple;* the chime of distant bells; the lazy cawing of crows, flapping along, languidly, above the trees, under a summer sky; the beat of horses' hoofs on turf, insistent, purposeful; the argument of strong machinery; the plaintive ascending wail of great buzz-saws in pine-scented lumberyards.

Sounds, sounds with magic to awaken the sleepers from the chambers of the house of memory when, like grey shadows, forgotten things open wide fast doors and emerge into the light, and glow again with brilliant colours so that the days of the past troop by, gay and full of remembered sweetness. Sounds.

Voices down the road. A stirring, champing of bits, the clank of iron.

The dinner hour is over.

4.

Down in the low, rich land beside the river a patterned market garden displayed its ordered comeliness. A blue-robed figure beneath a great straw hat moved along the green rows, stooping to pluck a lurking weed, marking each growing thing with patient almond eyes.

Three times has he sown turnip seed, and three times the fly has consumed the tender leaves. But by the fourth sowing the fly was gone, the crop survived germination, and the first thrust from dark to light. Now it is growing apace. There will be a fine crop. But the white settlers, cursing the blight, sowed only once. Later, they will buy from the Chinaman because he alone will have turnips for sale.

Away down in the Delta, Lulu Island is overcrowded now. Chinese labourers, having endured their long period of servitude as indentured workers under the Boss Chinaman who paid their head tax for them, must seek for land further afield.* There is no place at all on fertile Lulu Island. They come therefore to the valley and here, with the infinite patience of their kind, they raise great crops of vegetables, tomatoes, small fruits and strawberries. So little do they require to live on, that they can sell very cheaply at Sapperton or Vancouver. And every year the settlement itself offers them a widening market for their truck.

There are eight of them now growing garden truck, while the Japanese make strawberry gardens, as it were, overnight.*

But the white men work upon the new roads, eating up the government grants like locusts. Defeated men they are, for they cannot make a living from their land. They think in wages, sometimes going up into the mountains of the mainland to sweat in the smelting works at Trail and Kaslo, coming back to their little ranches with their wages. But more often selling out and moving into the city to join the amorphous, floating population which does what it can, how and where it can, for a living.

So the process goes and the valley, green and fertile, lovely in its summer dress, and in winter soft with kindly rains, passes from the white to the yellow man.

5.

Yet Johansson has survived and flourishes. When taxes fall due, he does not apply to work out the debt upon the road: no, he pays, pays out of the little store of dollars which he now keeps, strangely enough, beneath the soil of last year's Christmas tree that stands in the corner of the tidy living-room. He merely grasps the withered evergreen and lifts it, mould and all, and, lo, beneath is the snug wad of green dollar bills. He pays his taxes thus, does Johansson.

But as he moves his arms these days a twinge of pain shoots along. Like a hot needle it is. He vaguely wonders what can be amiss. Once he could take a lift of two hundred-weight. But not now. So it is well that he has his Ford (Child's play! Guiding a machine, pushing down on pedals . . .). But this man has no memories of play – he has worked since he could remember.

How does Bob England manage?

Johansson often wonders that. From his place high on the hillside he can see right over the bush to the England place. There is Bob, pipe in mouth, doing chores aimlessly, or strolling, hands in pocket, through his garden. He talks of making a tennis court.

But Bob England has no goad to urge him on. True, he is in debt: always has been, always will be. But, once a quarter comes that Old Country letter with its bank draft to save the embarrassing situation. Remittances keep Bob England going. They have saved him (or have they damned him?).

6.

Old Man Dunn at the store, his red face radiant. Very important. Bursting for an audience. Living already in the future. For weeks he has been poring over timetables, writing letters in his shaky hand to the CPR agent in Vancouver, reckoning up the fare, figuring the cost of living in old Yorkshire. "Oh, yes," he says, "I'm going this time, sure enough."

"Well, Mr. Dunn, I'll believe it when I see you board the train," laughs Blanchard. "I've heard you talk of going back to the Old Country now for ten years." And he smiles his twisted smile that is neither friendly, nor yet unfriendly, but something in between.

Old Man Dunn going back to an Old Country which ceased to exist twenty years ago. Old Man Dunn living in a sweet illusion which will dissolve in bitter reality. Old Man Dunn dreaming of an England that has disappeared. Yes, full of certainty that it will be all the same after these long years of exile. Nothing changed; Old England. The place where he was born and where he hopes to die.

How many years of parsimony have gone to make this great venture possible? How many little luxuries has he foregone? How many coveted books have had to go no further than a review read, and a mental note that at some future time would come the pleasure of reading it? And little Mrs. Dunn? What things she has done without, and no word of complaining!

"Yes, we go early next month, Mr. Blanchard. We go directly we get the first payment on the place."

His voice is confident, assured. Always before, something had intervened; but this time – No!

"Then you've got your deposit, Mr. Dunn, I take it?" Blanchard is politely curious, no more.

The old man nods his great head, his little eyes are

dancing with excitement: "We have that, and the agreement signed by all parties. There's but a few things to be fixed up now: the hens and the cow. Do you know anyone who is wanting a good milch cow?"

Blanchard considers the matter, carving-knife in hand: "A Holstein, ain't she?" he enquires. "No, I don't know of anyone, except maybe Johansson. He might buy. He's got the grazing now. He might be glad of her."

Johansson bought the cow and led her up the hill and turned her, with a slap on her lean flank, into the meadow by the tall trees. A good cow, but not a cow to compare with the first cow he bought.

Old Man Dunn met Fuller on the road and told him his great news, word for word, all over again. And Fuller nodded. Not one for words, Fuller was a man preoccupied with his own urgent affairs.

"I have every bird trap-nested now," Fuller said as he turned to go into the new co-operative grain store.* "Make 'em earn their keep – that's my motto."

For Fuller, Old Man Dunn's future, his past, and his present held no interest whatever. His mind was filled with thoughts of laying hens.

And little Mrs. Dunn? Ah, hardly believing yet, hardly daring to believe. That old, old longing to be appeased at last: the sight of Old England after the long years, the sights and scents of old Yorkshire with its teeming cities, its rolling, scented moors.

Tramping the four miles back to his ranch, the Newcomer looks in on Dunn. He does this often. To borrow a book – ostensibly: but really to talk with Old Man Dunn.

The old man is not yet back from the store.

Mrs. Dunn greets him with her quick smile of welcome.

"Say, wait till I've given these birds their mash and I'll come right back and talk with you. You've heard, haven't you? No? We've sold. At last! Yes, we're going back to the Old Country." Her kindly little face, moulded into those lines by years, aye, by a lifetime of kindliness, beams upon the dust-stained man. She sets down the bucket of mash, there on the rickety steps of the old ranch-house, and gathers herself for speech.

"Yes, we're going right back next month. Yes, to Yorkshire." Confidentially: "Do you know, I haven't seen England for forty-two years? When you have been that long away you'll know what home-sickness means."

When the little tasks are done (those little daily tasks which call for patience, faithfulness and courage), she comes into the house and sets before her guest a glass of milk fresh from the cow. Warm and frothing, scented it is. He drinks it and it is good to his dry throat. Milk, a homely drink, after all. Warm from the cow, with bubbles upon it, from a woman smelling of the byre.

Far ahead of the flying transcontinental, little Mrs. Dunn is speeding east. Indeed, she is already in England, that England she left forty-two years ago when it was a bold woman who would wear bloomers to ride a bicycle and Queen Victoria's photograph (with John Brown in attendance) might be seen in every photographer's window.

Rapidly she moves about her orderly kitchen, preparing the evening meal, chatting as she works.

"Do you know, I can recall seeing Francis Thompson when he was a young man?" she says.* The mental image of the dead poet crystallizes in her memory where it has lain like a garment put away, forgotten, and now unexpectedly recovered. "He wore such short trousers, all frayed – and of course then we didn't know that he would be a great man one day. Poor fellow! I used to feel sort of sorry for him. He always looked so forlorn. How he must have hated his medical studies."

On and on the little woman ran. Such is the power of joys anticipated, such is the tie of native soil. Calling, calling, calling the wanderers back, beckoning them from the four ends of the earth, never leaving them at peace to plant new roots, to forget. And, having reclaimed them, giving them nothing. Worse: shattering illusions.

She sets the little table, moving with her quick, darting motions, a dozen and one things on her mind, and yet that mind free to reconstruct the past and conjure up from it a radiant future. She is living in England already, tasting the pleasures that will so soon be hers. The Newcomer sits, elbows on knees, watching her as she bustles about. It makes him home-sick, almost. Francis Thompson: how queer to be seeing here a woman who watched the poet tramp a city's pavement in outworn clothes.

And then, heavy feet and the booming voice of Old Man Dunn. He does not live now in this crazy house; no, he is but a man who waits a little while to depart upon a journey. A long journey, and one he will take very soon. "You've heard?" he booms. "Yes, my dear fellow, we are going home."

8.

Foot ease, the big boots discarded and grateful toes astretch. And hunger reasserting itself with the smell of food. He takes his boy upon his knee and dandles him. He does this every evening when he returns from working as a hired hand and the little fellow has come to look forward to the game. Later will come the bath: wild splashings and shouts of laughter as Daddy tickles him and pats his pink and shining rump.

But food first.

"See what you think of this." She sets a big bowl of soup before him. He tastes it. "Great!" he tells her. Then, without more ado, he falls to, drinking his soup with relish, with the relish known only to manual workers.

"D'you know what it's made of?" she asks him as he finishes.

"No idea. What?"

"Nothing but vegetables: potatoes, artichokes, carrots, onions, turnips and a little milk." There is pride in her voice. "I invented it!" she laughs. "You know we haven't had meat now for a fortnight."

He frowns at this for it is like an indictment which charges him with inability to provide. As he munches his bread-and-butter he frowns. He is working now, working long days in the heat. For what? Not for money, but just to pay off the taxes he cannot pay in cash. He will be as hard up when it's done as he was at the start. "Is it a fortnight?" he asks. "Good Lord!"

The baby is in bed, but the elder boy sits in his high chair beside his father. He bangs with a spoon upon his tray and invites his father to a game. But the Newcomer is preoccupied this evening. He is thinking of Old Man Dunn and how, in a few days, he will see him climb into the transcontinental. Ought he, too, to have sold? He girds at himself: quixotic fool!

9.

The Valley and the bush were beautiful but they lived in the shadows. For him the horror of failing to provide was a daily torture which rose to desperate fear at times. And with her there was always the fear of adding to the problem. The idea of another child haunted her and she thought of it often. To live again those long and weary months of physical discomfort, to face again the pangs of labour, the months and years of toil for the baby and the child.

But neither spoke of the troubles which weighed them

down. There was, indeed, nothing for it but to go on working. This they did, stoically, doggedly, with a sort of fierce pride which turned its back upon the fact of their failure.

"Under this system," Old Man Dunn had said, "the harder the work, the less the reward; the manipulators and exploiters make the money. There's so many parasites that decent folk can't live any more."*

In the city, down in Vancouver, he might, true enough, make an easier living. He considered it, sitting back in his chair, tilting it back and gazing at the ceiling where the boards were shrinking, leaving gaps that oozed amber coloured tears of resin.

But the bush beckoned him back from his defection. He would hate the city, its heat and its scurry. If one was poor here in the Valley, yet was one free in a sense. One sold one's body but one kept one's soul. That was only a fine phrase. Moonshine! Oh, the beauty of these silent places that called and called. These silences that spoke, this solitude that let you grow. Why should he leave it?

He looked across the little table at the still face of his wife. How patient she was! What pluck was there under her strangely quiet, enigmatic personality. And his eyes fell upon her hands, so small, so work-stained, ingrained with minute black lines from the peeling of many potatoes, from much immersion in dirty water.

Then he saw her against the background of her old life. A quiet, uneventful life running smoothly along the orderly years. The low, creeper-covered house, the big rose garden. Callers and calling; the buying of clothes; the discussion of neighbours. Small talk, dances, garden parties, small talk again. A narrow horizon with character dormant, waiting for the test, waiting for a chance to grow. Fine material going to waste. A journey without a definite bourne. Just a waiting for middle age, for old age. No design, no purpose.

An aimless, futile life. The life, even so, of how many Old Country girls?

No, better the want and hard work of the settlement than that stagnation which leads inevitably to the warping of womanhood and the atrophy of the instincts. Better in the end, because they meant growth, development and a deepening.*

CHAPTER XXV

1.

Two courting blue jays upon a low dead branch of a fir tree. The comedy of love. The dance of the mating season, the foolish cock making this absurd exhibition of himself to win his passive, critical-eyed mate-to-be.

"Them jays is terrors," says Kurt, lying, head upon arm, there beside Lulu in the shade of the forest. "Gee! Look at that feller, jazzing around for all he's worth like he was a pink-tea expert."*

The cock-bird, in the love frenzy of spring, is advancing with mincing steps along the branch towards the huddled hen. He utters his hard metallic note, pirouettes, retires, struts. Every movement says: "I am a fine cock. Just look at me, hen. Could you give yourself to a finer cock? You know you couldn't. Do you not thrill at my fine purple shades, at the sheen of my curved black neck, the lilac, brown and white of my breast?"

Cunning and brazen and purposeful he is. And the watching hen, for all her passive air, is intent upon the business too. Spring and mating time: she must soon be about her business.

"Down beyond the Trunk Road I'll be building, Lulu," says Kurt. "A good piece of land, some slashed and a bit cleared, too. Guess I won't buy lumber, but'll build us a real log house." Lulu smiles and nods her head.

"Sure thing," she says. Then, after a pause: "What about water? Plenty of water?"

Kurt nods. "Yep," he answers. A laconic man, little given to long speeches. But a Kurt who now has his Lulu secure, a Kurt who means to keep her now.

The blue jays are past the first stages of courtship and, oblivious of the two creatures below them, are fulfilling their purpose, mating there in the sun-dappled forest, in the fragrant air of a spring morning.

"I'll fix a force-pump with my old gasoline engine from the boat." It is Kurt. Scheming, practical Kurt.

Lulu does not answer him. She is thinking. What is she thinking? What does a woman think about when she is beside the man she loves, alone with him, on a spring morning, with life and love ahead and the bitter past wiped away?

She slowly turns her head, and leaning over her man, puts her soft lips to his.

2.

The marriage of Kurt and Lulu was like all other settlement weddings. There was the service in the Mission Church (it was to the Mission Church that the Lutheran Norwegian settlers went, when they went at all). Then it was the wedding feast with Old Ole at the table's head.

What joy in the old man's eyes! Kurt, the well-beloved. Kurt the masterful, the clever. No longer in the shadows, but quietly radiant. A bridegroom!

"Like it was us all over again," exclaims raw-boned Freda. But Axel, slow-minded, matter-of-fact, merely grunts. "Huh!" he says, "ain't different from any other sorter wedding, I guess."

Little Ole now can do as he will with his uncle. He is on his high knee, a little flaxen figure between the bridegroom and bride. A symbolic figure, a sign and a portent.

There is much to drink, more to eat. Loud laughter, and the coming and going of great Freda bearing the steaming dishes. As the feast wears on, as the folk warm up, there are coarse jests, jests that bring a bridal blush to Lulu's cheeks, a cloud to her thoughtful face.

And now there are tears in the old man's eyes.

"Tears at such a time?" chides Axel, his son, whispering the complaint in Freda's ear as she bustles about the fire. "Why is father sad today?"

But Freda – obedient, patient, kindly Freda – pushes the great fellow away. Men! What are they if not stupid creatures who understand nothing? That the old man should cry! One cried, sure thing, when one was sad but one cried too when great happiness filled the heart.

Off they go in the rig, old shoe and all, and other rigs follow to see to it that all on the local know of the affair (if rice, jests and flushed faces can tell the story).

3.

They cannot tell their thoughts, these two; they cannot cleverly probe their emotions. But they are content as they are. They are together and it is enough.

There is sympathy between them. They speak without words. She knows the contrition of his heart and, looking at her slender figure, there beside him, he remembers the baby that died.

Like a woman bearing upon her brow the triple pointed diadem of love, understanding and knowledge, sympathy steps down into the dark valley of sorrow and suffering. Her hands are healing hands under whose touch the troubled heart is stilled. Her voice is as a precious unguent poured upon open wounds. Her bosom is for the weary a sanctuary, fast closed against pursuing loneliness and despair.

Slowly the local steamed into the twilight of the vast terminus.

Kurt rose stiffly. "Well, I guess we've just about time to catch the Seattle boat," he said.

They had decided against Vancouver for the honeymoon. Lulu moved after him. She felt suddenly tired and old.

4.

The doctor put it this way. "You see," he said, "postmortems show that nine people out of ten who die of something else have tubercular lesions on their lungs. They probably get it before they turn five, and their untainted young blood fights off the fungous parasite. The lung is damaged and eaten into but it heals. We call the process calcification."

The Newcomer listened apathetically. Somehow or other his mind slid away from this revelation. He was absorbed by the picture above the doctor's desk, and was distracted by sounds of the busy life below in the general store penetrating the thin boarding.

"In most cases those early-healed lesions never break down. Sometimes they do. Yours has. Some strain put upon the system which was too great for it; wrong or insufficient food – anything."

The Newcomer caught a word here, a word there. But his mind was focussed upon the picture – the physician in his mediaeval gown who bent over the dissected body and told of its marvels to the eager students gathered around.

Now, if one cut open his chest, as that surgeon had opened up the forearm of that dead man, there would be a pink lung disfigured with a scar, a scar from which blood oozed. Curious and rather horrible.

Three dollars – a day's work. A handshake, a kindly word. Malt, rest, no strain.

That was what he said. And he said it (Oh, irony!) as he calmly took one whole day's wages for the information that physical strength, the last weapon of a poor man, was gone.

The doctor's place was three miles from Ferguson's Landing and the nearest way was along the track of the CPR. The Newcomer took it. Three miles back made six miles in all, and that after a long day's work.

What should he tell her? Or should he tell her? As yet she knew nothing of the blood that he had spat up after trying to lift a weighty log. He considered the matter. There was no money. Suppose he gave up manual work without explanation? She would think he was a quitter. Somewhere (Was it in some story in the *Saturday Evening Post*?) he had read 'God hates a quitter.' It had helped him once or twice. If only Old Man Dunn had not gone off. He could have given wise counsel. Now there was no one.

It was dark and from the river banks came the now-hated croaking of the mating bullfrogs. How he hated that noise: insistent, monotonous, unending.

When, tired and melancholy, he reached the ranch, he feared to meet that patient woman, his wife. His problem remained.

By the flower-bed, where the night air was scented with the nicotina he loved so well, he drew off his heavy boots. His wife often slept in the rocker. Well, let her sleep. He would creep round to the kitchen.

Treading lightly in stockinged feet to the window, he peered in. The room was empty. Before the dying fire hung, upon a clothes horse, a line of babies' garments. Shadows danced upon the walls. The room looked snug and homely. On the table, ready set for him, he could see food. A pain pierced his heart, a pain compounded of love and tenderness, as he considered the thought which had left nothing undone for his creature comfort.

He crept silently down the steps, drew on his boots, and turned his back upon the house. Over the rim of the bush a pale luminosity showed in the night sky.

From far off he could hear the bullfrogs croaking their two-noted spring song devoid of joyousness and melancholy as a threnody. *Cric, cric, cric, cric.* Or was it, *Wan-Ik, Wan-Ik?* A throaty croaking, maddening, deadly, down there in the swampy places where they bred, unseen, beside the mosquitoes.

No other sound broke the stillness of the spring night. The Newcomer stirred. In his heart was a vague emotion, indefinable; a sense of mystery; a surging of a life-long yearning.

And in the great river itself the strong, clean salmon were returning after four years in the open sea to the places of their spawning, themselves to spawn in turn and die. Four, five, six hundred miles up the great stream, silver-sided, purposeful, leaping impossible cataracts, buffeted, bruised, moving in response to the great impulse to reproduce and die. *Cric . . . cric, cric . . . cric:* otherwise, silence.

Just what had he expected from this change from the Old World to the New? And just what had he got? An old longing still unsatisfied. Peculiar that tonight his mind should hark back to the past, conjuring up the dead days so vividly.

For a moment the clearing in the bush was blotted out and the frogs became silent. From the dim chambers of memory trooped forth the procession that had been his life.

He was looking down from a high cliff. He felt his fingers gripping the soft, cold chalk; in his boots his toes were curled the better to grip the narrow, perilous ledge. The pain of taut and tortured muscles maddened him and the scream of outraged parent birds was in his ears. Below, the sea broke in a curving line of white foam upon the yellow sand. Then the smooth surface of the egg and the ascent, slow and arduous, the egg secure, pressed by his tongue against the roof of his mouth. And the fury of the white birds whose generations he imperilled.*

Other pictures flashed up. Those long years of monotony that had been his schooldays. The bare white-walled classroom, the drone of the master's voice through the long summer afternoon and his own dreams, strange figments of imagination, jumbled with the remembered horrors of that haunting *Koran* – oil boilings, nameless things. Visions of high galleons, golden seas, mahogany-faced men and green isles under tropic skies.

What had he been seeking then? High adventures? Romance? Perhaps.

Then the years when he had gone, with the regularity of an automaton, through the routine of a city clerk's drab life. Was the impediment lack of courage? God knows he had hated the life. He had worked, paralyzed by some dimly comprehended inhibition. Fear, perhaps. Circumstances.

He saw the long, overcrowded train draw up at the dingy terminus, and the debouchment of those swarming units that went to the making of the world's financial heart. Little, self-important molecules bent upon reproduction in unending cycles of time, working for the next generation, preoccupied, blind.

Pity surged into his heart and something akin to anger against the scheme of things.

He moved slowly into the moonlight and the majesty and mystery of the night held him in thrall. A great pain was in his heart, a great longing. He was lonely, but not so lonely as he had been in that narrow city thoroughfare where the tide of men's voices rose and fell and with it the tides of men's fortunes. Shorter's Court: how very remote it seemed!*

He made his way to the edge of his little garden, passed among the great stumps, thinking of them as cowled and hooded spectres mocking his bewilderment, his loneliness. He passed under the shadow of the fringe of the bush into the enchantment of the primeval. Under his heavy boots twigs snapped and the fronds of ferns waved protesting fans; they too, would live; they too sought immortality, looking darkly upon death and annihilation.

He sat upon the crumbling ruin of a once mighty cedar, now a world peopled by swarming, purposeful black ants. The moonlight filtered through the tall trees, patterning the underbrush. Vine maples, like fountains petrified in play, glistened, wet with the cold night moisture. And from the distant river, the bullfrogs: *cric . . . cric, cric . . . cric* – or was it *Wan-Ik . . . Wan-Ik?*

Yes, he had always been seeking! But what? He became suddenly aware of a sense of expectancy, vague longings, dimly comprehended, crystallized into clear thought and concrete desire, no longer nameless.

All these years he had been striving for One-ness. A strange change had come from within, without impulse, without volition. Only it had come, and with it he was uplifted upon the wave of a great emotion. He cast himself upon the earth, his arms outstretched, his work-calloused hands digging into the soft mould of centuries of rotted leaves. He thrust his face into the earth and its strange, sweet odours intoxicated him. He knew the mood of the moon; he heard the breathing of the earth. He was listening to a great silence and it was speaking to him, saying things to his troubled soul.

So it had come at last. Adventure. Life. Yes, it was One-ness with all these. Isolation was but blindness, the sleep of the senses. This was community with God. Holy Communion. The ecstasy increased. He heard God moving among the trees. His face was in the moon; the trees were nothing but His fingers uplifted in benediction and the incense of His temple was this sweet smelling earth.

The ecstatic uprush of emotion crowned his life with one divine moment. Then it was gone. But he knew.

He stood up and to his nostrils came the acrid smell of smoke. A glowing heart showed plainly through the tangled undergrowth of vine-maple. A smouldering fire in the slashing! Yet for a moment he had the strange illusion that a bush burned from whose glowing heart peered forth the face of God.

He moved out into the clearing. A coil of smoke rose into the still air above the dim outline of the bush. He shivered and gathered himself together.

Adventure? Yes! Now he knew: it was the experience of the spirit, it was the search after God; it was the true vision of the unattainable; it was proud submission. And from that glowing heart of fire came again the illusion of an unearthly light, white and blinding. A vision of God in a burning bush.

He moved to the house, an empty man. Creeping along the veranda, he peered through the bedroom window: the lamp burned. Within reach of his arm, in the great bed she lay, the baby in the crook of her arm. Her head was thrown back, her gentle mouth was slightly opened. Weariness sat, like the insignia of her abiding steadfastness, on her brow. Then, at the slight noise the baby moved, raised a round head, releasing the breast from which he fed.

He fixed two blue, incurious eyes upon the face at the window. A spray of milk, as from a fairy fountain, spurted upon the tiny face.

EPILOGUE

A blaze of August sun baked the city, stifling the crowds that laboured along the deep canyons of the streets, where the air, petrol-tainted and stale, hung like a miasma, devitalized and fetid. Men, straw-hatted, with belted trousers and white, soft shirts, mopped brows; and women, in gauzy summer garments, made for the ice-cream parlours whose vivid signs flashed bright in the sun, or paused under awnings to gain a momentary respite from the implacable golden eye.

Into the burning sky the tall buildings of the city rose, white and gleaming, their countless rows of windows catching the sun's light and flashing back little blinding flames. Mighty ramparts, towers and pinnacles soared up and etched against the cobalt sky the simulacrum of a fairy citadel.

But mere ferro-concrete and steel, granite and stone after all. Vast temples of commerce dedicated to the God Dollar, yet planned by men pursued by dreams of beauty. Dignified as monoliths, and as rich in promise of strength and time-defying permanence.

At the fringe of the city the vast harbour lay like a disc of lapis lazuli, mirroring the sky; across its burnished surface the shipping moved, a phantasmagoria, remote, unreal, yet vivid. A picture without tone or atmosphere, tropically stark.

To the north beyond, Grouse Mountain raised its emerald green hump against the skyline, with North Vancouver climbing its lower slopes in ordered array of shrill streets and intersecting avenues.

The Newcomer paused at the top of Granville Street to mop his sweating face. He wore the old overalls in which he worked about his place. They were sun-and rain faded, patched here and there, threadbare.

The decision had been made at last: he had come down to the city to sell.

He watched the stream of cars sweep past, and their glittering nickel fittings dazzled his aching eyes. All about him flowed the tide of the city, urgent and unresting. Men and women of all nations, old and young. Tired feet, aching at each step, trod the burning stone sidewalks; the old went slowly, elbowed by the young, the vigorous, the purposeful.

Should he try the Hastings Street places, or Pender Street? He decided for the former. Pender Street always wore an air of dishonesty. It looked third-rate and just a little furtive. It drew the share-butchers, the tin-horn real estate men, the cheapskates.*

The Newcomer paused before a large plate glass window across which sprawled, in self-assertive gold letters, the legend:

ANGUS FERGUSON
REAL ESTATE: OIL LANDS: INSURANCE
NOTARY PUBLIC

Ferguson! Queer to come on that name here and now. But perhaps an augury of luck.

He passed into the cool shade of the high-ceilinged interior. A mahogany counter ran the length of the office and behind it, at little yellow, fumed-oak tables, girls in flimsy summer attire bent neat heads over clicking typewriters. Blueprints adorned the walls, maps of new subdivisions of the ever-growing city. In one corner stood a steel safe, defiant and challenging.

The man who came from the mystery of the inner office beyond was stout and urbane.

He had a round, pink, freckled face, red hair, and beneath two bushy brows a pair of shrewd grey eyes.

A slight change came over his face as the Newcomer stated his desire to sell, and not to buy, land.

One took down particulars of land for sale. Something came of it, or something did not come of it. But a prospective purchaser was a bright hope, a fish on the hook, as it were. There he was, right here in the office. It was up to you to get busy and make him buy. Salesmanship. Hope was not eclipsed until the prospect went out the door. Besides, what one said did not matter. (And one could say much – especially when the prospect happened to be a diffident, shy sort of hay-seed.) It was what you wrote down that mattered. Mr. Angus Ferguson was always very careful what he wrote down. Caution, he would declare jocularly, was his middle name.

"Well, sir, I'll sure take particulars of your little dump," he announced, drawing a form towards him. "There ain't not much demand for Fraser Valley properties right now but if any man can find you a buyer in this city, I guess you are talking to him right now."

Mr. Angus Ferguson placed his arms firmly upon the mahogany counter and smiled. He was pleased. He was prepared for a little talk – a little chat about Ferguson's Landing.

"Ferguson's Landing, eh? Wal, wal. And how's things at the Landing?"

The Newcomer admitted that he had come in just because of the name across the window.

"Say, that's not strange after all," said the fat man. "There's a bunch of Fergusons in Vancouver, and some more in Victoria. We're an old family, yes, sir. Why, it was my grandfather who gave his name to Ferguson's Landing. Yes, sirree."

"The place is still there," the Newcomer told him. "The people who have it now are called Ellison but it's always known as the Ferguson Place."

The Newcomer had heard stories of Old Man Ferguson.

He had a clear picture of the old pioneer in his mind: a sturdy Scot, hard as nails and dogged as a Highlander is dogged.

Now he looked with curiosity at what the third generation of that hardy race had produced, and he saw a soft and flabby man, slowly chewing gum and exhaling a sickly odour of the tonsorial parlour. A man with fat, pink hands set off by carefully manicured nails. A man with a taste for flashy ties and a mouth made conspicuous by many gold fillings.

"Aren't any of your people on the land?" the Newcomer asked. "I would have thought it was in the blood."

Angus Ferguson waved away with one hand the obnoxious thought of the land and everything it meant to him.

"The land?" he sneered in a voice of disgust. "Nix on the land! The land's for the easy marks. For the newcomers. No, sir. Give me the city, where there's somphun doin'. Every time. Money to be made. Yep. Money. Sure, I'm out for the dollar. Why not? Ain't everybody out for all he can get? You bet yer."

"And are none of your people on the land now?" the Newcomer asked, curious.

"No, sir, not one. I've four brothers, and all doing fine and dandy. There's Sandy, he's salted himself down – oil. Built him a fine house 'way up Shaughnessy Heights. Don't need to do any more work. Donald, he's partner in a law office and a smarter lawyer you won't find on the Coast. He reckons to stand for the Provincial legislature. Yes, sir."

The fat man glowed with satisfaction. "Wal, I've listed your ranch," he concluded, "and if anyone can find you a buyer, I'm him."

The Newcomer returned by the evening local. In the soft light of evening the city breathed again, fanned by a soft breeze from the Pacific that bore away the tainted air.

As the train drew out, it ran with clanging engine bell into the shadows of the waterfront, and blood-red fires yawned like dragons' mouths out of the gloom against the nebulous background of lumber yards and refuse dumps. Over the dreaming harbour a thin mist, like a floating scarf of gossamer, veiled the winking lights of the northern shore. In solemn procession, the huddled buildings of the harbourside slipped furtively past. Swinging lanterns held by unseen hands made signals: red and green stars floating in the gloom. Far out, by the Narrows, beyond which the open ocean waited, a bar of brilliant light glided across the purple water of the harbour as the Honolulu boat put out.

Night fell and the train cleared the city, fleeing from that heaped constellation of winking yellow lights that was Vancouver. It drove straight for the heart of the bush, the immemorable bush that had ceded for a time a little to that parasite, man, and watched, incurious and patient, the birth of the city and its growth.

The eternal forest would witness in the fullness of time the city's passing, its decadence and death. The forest, invincible and cruel, would claim back its own and stand triumphant at the last, rooted fast in the shattered masonry of a forgotten city.

THE END

Notes

(I) A SHORT BIOGRAPHY OF GEORGE GODWIN

Foreword (p. xxi). *Maple Ridge, a History of Settlement* (by Sheila Nichols *et al.*) contains several passages commenting on farming as a lost cause in the Whonnock area in these same years:

"(. . .) Where are the farms that the pioneers so bravely struggled to win for us out of the resisting forest? Not a single large farm flourishes in Whonnock today, in spite of all their efforts, and their visions of fruitful fields and orchards seem rather faded as the suburbs creep ever nearer" (p. 50).

"These early farmers cleared the land, grew vegetables and fruit, kept cattle and hogs, and built a home. They were able to sell (and trade: ed.) some produce and dairy products but found it difficult to make a living exclusively by farming" (p. 36).

(II) THE ETERNAL FOREST

p. 4. **Sapperton.** On the eastern fringe of New Westminster, Sapperton dates from the Fraser River Gold Rush (which started in 1858). Sapperton is named after the Sappers, i.e. the road workers of the Royal Engineers. Sapperton formally joined New Westminster in 1889.

p. 6 (a) **Ferguson the mariner** is probably based on a real person, although Godwin has altered a few facts to suit his purposes as a novelist. The first Ferguson in the Port Haney area was Hector McLean Ferguson who was born in 1854 and arrived in Port Haney in 1878. (In 1849 the only whites in the Fraser Valley lived at the Hudson's Bay Post at Fort Langley.) Ferguson married Mary Stevens (1880) and they built a small log cabin one mile east of Haney. They had six children: Archibald, Hector, James, Mary (McDonald), Isabel (Selkirk) and Catherine (Mullins). By the time the fifth child was born, the Fergusons had a thriving farm and an eight-room house. Ferguson "the mariner" was important in the community as reeve, justice of the peace and police magistrate. He and his wife Mary lived for 50 years in Haney. Ferguson died in 1931; his wife in 1948. There are several place names in Maple Ridge which honor the Fergusons. (Mrs. Isabel Selkirk and Mrs. Isabel Byrnes in *The Gazette,* 28 May 1948).

There was a "Ferguson's Landing" in Whonnock near the bottom of 269th St. Nearby was a general store which burnt down in 1911. It is unclear whether Godwin used this store or Carlton's at Port Haney (or both!) as a model for "Blanchard's." On the map (p. xxxii) I have assumed that Port Haney was the inspiration behind "Ferguson's Landing." Godwin's house might have been just south-east of 98th Ave. and 269th St.

The fundamental importance of farming is one of Godwin's favorite ideas. It will be developed in later works like *The Land Our Larder* (Acorn, London, 1939).

(b) The Agassiz-Vancouver section of the CPR railroad (see map) was completed in 1887.

p. 9. **Newcomers:** There are many parallels between the Newcomer and Godwin himself. See Godwin's *Journal*, items 19, 20, 22, etc. and Mr. Woodcock's Introduction. "Newcomer" and "Chechahco" are used synonymously.

p. 10. Godwin uses the term "Cascades" and "Rockies" more or less interchangeably.

The boom which Bob England refers to is doubtless the boom of 1912, the year in which a great influx of immigrants gave a boost to the lumber and construction industries. The economy downturned in 1913 as the demand for lumber plummeted. George and Dorothy Godwin's timing was unlucky because they arrived in Port Haney/Whonnock (i.e. the "Ferguson's Landing" area) in late 1912-just in time to experience the 'bust' phase of the boom-bust cycle. The area was still badly depresssed in 1914 when Rev. A. W. Collins of Whonnock wrote: "Nearly all the people (in Whonnock) are simply making a scratch living and have not a cent to bless themselves with." (Quoted in *Maple Ridge, a History of Settlement,* p. 47, op. cit.) See Mr. Woodcock's Introduction for other economic influences.

p. 18. **"Great Last West:"** by "Great Last West" Godwin probably means "Last Best West," a phrase coined by Laurier's Immigration Minister Sifton (in power from 1895-1905) to present the Canadian West as the land of opportunity to prospective immigrants. Sifton was spectacularly successful at finding immigrants and Canada's population rose from about 5.3 million in 1901 to 7.2 million in 1911. In British Columbia the decade 1901-1911 saw a considerable increase in immigration from the Orient. Here are the statistics for B.C.'s Chinese, Japanese and East Indian immigration from 1871 to 1911 (note the increase in numbers in the 20 year period just before the Godwins' arrival).

	Chinese	*Japanese*	*East Indian*
1871 - 1881	4,350		
1881 - 1891	8,910	0	
1891 - 1901	14,201	3,516	
1901 - 1911	19,568	8,587	5,195 (all of Canada)

Anti-Oriental feeling among whites culminated in the the infamous 'riot' (read: provocative invasion) of 1907 in which whites marched on the Chinese and Japanese quarters of town, breaking windows and assaulting people. There was also the shameful business of the *Komagata Maru,* the Sikh-bearing vessel which was quarantined by the Canadian government at great cost of life to its passengers. The racist attitudes in Ferguson's Landing are probably typical of those held by most whites in those years (See Mr. Woodcock's Introduction).

Here is a typical newspaper comment from the 1900's: "Just at the moment when the good effects of Chinese exclusion are beginning to be experienced, it would indeed be the height of folly to throw open our doors to a fresh influx of coolies." (From the *Nelson Daily News*, 14 May 1907, as quoted by Dr. Patricia Roy in her excellent *White Man's Province, British Columbia Politicians and Chinese and Japanese Immigrants, 1858-1914*. UBC Press, Vancouver, 1989.)

For the "Last Best West" see Jean Bruce's book of the same name (Toronto, Fitzhenry and Whiteside, 1976) and the photo in *The Eternal Forest*.

(b) Like most writers of his time Godwin somewhat imperially liked to refer to Canada as "the Dominion." As most readers know, over the years the word "Dominion" has become unfashionable and has lost ground to "Federal." The Canadian government itself officially discouraged the use of the term on October 1, 1947.

p. 23 (a) **Gapes:** a disease common among the feathered population. The telltale symptom is a tendency to acquire a stupid 'gaping' look. Hence the name.

(b) **Drummers:** commercial travellers or salesmen. A term of obscure origin. First recorded use: 1839 (USA). Probably connected to the expression "to drum up business."

p. 25. It is interesting to compare this description of Stein's place with the description in Godwin's *Journal* (entry 20).

p. 27. **Henry George** (1839-1897). In his main book, *Progress and Poverty* (1879), George proposes his "single tax" idea, arguing that only land and buildings should be taxed because landowners made an unduly large profit from increased property values. George thought it unfair that non-property owners should languish in poverty. The single tax idea would raise sufficient revenue to meet all government costs; it would also make income tax unnecessary.

p. 30 (a) **Chechahco:** see note to page 9.

(b) **"dress for the simple evening meal"** i.e. 'put on the Ritz.'

p. 32. (a) **patria potestas:** the absolute power of the male head (the "paterfamilias") of the Roman family. This power theoretically included even the right to put to death any family members if he so desired. A law fortunately honored more in the breach.

(b) **praetor:** Roman magistrate, next in importance to the consuls. Important during Republic after which they lost much of their power.

(c) *Lex Talionis:* Roman law by which an injury is righted by appropriate compensation, not by vengeance. According to the *Twelve Tables* (451-450 B.C.) the state looked upon punishment as its own prerogative.

(d) **Riparian rights:** the rights of holders of waterfront property to full use of the water provided they don't infringe on the rights of the public to basic uses such as navigation.

(e) **Scrolls** made from parchment or papyrus were in use in Rome from the 7th century B.C. to the end of the Empire.

(f) **Capitol:** one of the seven hills of Rome. The Capitol was a civil and religious center.

p. 33 (a) **Justinian:** Roman emperor from c. A.D. 482 to 565. His *Institutes* were an attempt to codify and rationalize the Roman legal system. Technical legal passages such as this probably were written during or after Godwin's legal studies at the Middle Temple in London (early 1920s?) although there is some evidence that Godwin had already started studying law before coming to Canada. One gets the impression that he is bored by many aspects of legal training; this might go far to explain why he dropped law for freelance journalism.

(b) **The Temple:** refers to the "Middle Temple," ancient residence and place of study for barristers on the north bank of the Thames, just west of the current financial district. (The Middle Temple dates from the 14th century and takes its name from the famous Knights Templar of the Crusades.) It was at the Middle Temple that Godwin read for the Bar and it was there that he narrowly escaped death when the ancient buildings were bombed by the Luftwaffe in World War II. Godwin wrote a book on the Middle Temple (see the list of his books). These references to the Middle Temple and to the "dry reading" of Justinian indicate that Godwin wrote much of *The Eternal Forest* after returning to England to study law.

(c) **Surrey:** Needless to say, this is the original Surrey in London, England, and not Canada's fastest growing city! See footnote to pages 265, 266 and the photos of the Temple Bar.

p. 37. **'Mission' furniture:** a style of furniture with a plain, square look; usually constructed with thick slabs of dark brown wood.

p. 39. **boom:** see the note to p. 10.

p. 42. **Langford:** i.e. Fort Langley. See map.

p. 45. (a) **Kanaka:** a native of the Hawaiian Islands. This term is neutral in Polynesian but usually pejorative in English. Kanaka Creek flows into the Fraser River about a mile east of Port Haney (Ferguson's Landing) and lends its name to an attractive provincial park at the edge of the river.

(b) **Rocker:** a box-shaped wooden contraption used to extract gold from river and stream water/sand/gravel, etc. For more details see *The Best of Canada West*, Barlee, Vol. 1, p. 77.

p. 54. *The French Revolution* by Thomas Carlyle (1795 to 1881) appeared in 1837.

p. 55. 1913 was the last year of twenty years of stupendous salmon runs. See *Maple Ridge, A History of Settlement*, p. 36.

p. 60. **Carlyle:** Godwin's pseudonym for Ruskin, 7 miles up the river from Port Haney ('Ferguson's Landing'). See map.

p. 68. Until as recently as 1953 the 'Indians' (native people) of British Columbia were forbidden by law any alcoholic beverages.

p. 70. See *Journal,* item 27.

p. 76. **Staggered mare:** a mare who has "the staggers" has an injured tendon which causes one of the rear hooves to strike against the horse's stomach. Also called "string-halt."

p. 77 (a) George Godwin's own ideas on religion are quite unusual. See entries 29-35 of his *Journal.*

(b) **Ealing:** a suburb of West London.

p. 82. **Suckers:** probably catfish or oolichans.

p. 82. **Chuck:** river; salt chuck: the ocean; skookum chuck: rapids (river) or fast tides (ocean). Terms of Chinook origin.

p. 93. **Roosians:** A reference to the Russo-Japanese War (1904-5). The Japanese did beat the Russians soundly, destroying the Russian fleet at the battle of Tsushima (1905).

p. 95. A Japanese steambath or *o-furo* "was located in a small building separate from the house. The bathtub was made of thick wooden sides with a metal bottom under which a fire was burned to heat the water. A smoke stack went up the back." *Maple Ridge, A History of Settlement,* by the Maple Ridge Branch, Can. Fed. of University Women, 1972. p. 19.

p. 98. **Samuel Smiles** (1812-1904). Author of several books on the lives of 'great men' (Wedgwood, Stephenson, etc.). Smiles advocated hard work in order to achieve success.

p. 98. **Old Country:** Britain.

p. 102. **hack:** a cart.

p. 106. (a) **Last Great West:** See note to p. 18.

(b) **puts it across:** i.e. "beats hollow, beats the heck out of." (c) **The Panama Canal** opened unofficially on August 15, 1914.

p. 109. **Argonauts:** The orginal Argonauts were the Ancient Greeks who were led by Jason on a quest for the powerful golden fleece. The miners of the 1848-49 California Gold Rush were also referred to as Argonauts. The goldfields referred to here are probably those of the Klondike.

p. 115. See the *Journal,* item 19 for a similar entry.

p. 116. **Arc:** probably the 1904 bridge over the Fraser River at New Westminster, downstream and on Lulu's left.

p. 119. **Drummers:** traveling salesmen. (b) **Grips:** suitcases. (c) **Klootchmans:** correctly used, this means native (Indian) women. A Salish term. Godwin seems to use it for men as well.

p. 123. **Back-fire:** When firefighters 'back-fire' they light a controlled fire in the path of a forest fire. The theory is that by creating a band of charred earth, the forest fire loses momentum when it reaches this area.

p. 126. *Koran:* Many strange books turn up on the shelves of English private schools and it is probably typical of Godwin to have ferreted out this unusual tome. As he remarks in his *Journal,* his chief diversion (and survival strategy) at public school was to read voraciously whatever he felt like reading.

p. 134. **Fraser Valley Oil Fields:** Within two years of the Alberta oil boom B.C. followed suit in 1914. There never was much oil found in B.C. but some people did indeed make millions of dollars selling shares (see the photo of the newspaper ads and stock certificates). There were at least four companies involved: The British Columbia Oil Company (capitalized at $1,000,000. and with shares selling at 25 cents), Northern Oil Co. (with shares going for $1.00), Boundary Bay Oil (I have no information available) and, right next door to Port Haney (alias Ferguson's Landing), Pitt Meadows Oil Wells Ltd., whose main well was called Patterson Wells.

It is interesting to note that even a respectable magazine like *The B.C. Magazine* was responsible for generating a lot of misguided optimism as to the potential of oil development in B.C. Here is a quotation from 1914:

"There are at least half a dozen distinct areas in B.C. which are to be developed as the sources of rich oil deposits. (. . .) R. C. Johnston (. . .) says in The Daily Oil Gazette *(Vancouver based) and in the* Daily Province *that petroleum will undoubtedly be found in certain areas near the coast line of B.C. The possibilities of oil at Pitt Meadows had long been a dream of optimistic Vancouverites. (. . .) considerable money was spent in this field long before the Alberta oil boom.(. . .)*

The Pitt Oil Wells is backed by a number of B.C. men whose names have always stood for progress and honest development. (. . .) At Pitt Meadows there are natural oil strata and surface indications that far exceed many of the eastern fields. (. . .) The head driller (at Patterson Wells, Pitt Meadows) was practically certain oil in large quantities would be secured. It does not need the efforts of an advertising man to convince the average laymen of the value of oil on the coast."

Sounds like high-toned flap-doodle to this hayseed! In view of the BCRIC "ramp" of the late 1970s one can never rule out the possibility of officially abetted scams.

p. 137. **Tonsorial parlours:** a wonderfully grandiose way of saying barber shops. There actually was a "tonsorial shop" in Haney; it was owned by a Mr. Leggatt (see *Maple Ridge, A History of Settlement,* p. 20).

p. 139. **Grandview Slopes:** the area from Charles Street on the north to 5th Avenue on the south and from Boundary Road on the east to Nanaimo Street on the west. For further details see *British Columbia Magazine,* Vol 8, No. 2, Feb. 1912.

p. 140 (a) **Pittsville** is probably a pseudonym for Port Coquitlam.

(b) **The Angus workshops** was/is a huge operation based in Montreal and owned by the CPR. Its main function was/is to repair and overhaul rolling stock.

p. 143. (a) **Way-bill:** invoice, list of goods being shipped.

p. 144. **Rick:** about half a cord.

p. 145 (a) **Ramp:** "obtaining profit fraudulently by the unwarranted increase in the price of a commodity" *(Oxford Dictionary).*

(b) **Okotoks:** William Herron bought land at Okotoks in 1901 then expanded his holdings into the nearby Turner Valley. He lacked the capital to do his own drilling but in 1912 he went into a kind of partnership with Calgary Petroleum Products. They started major drilling in January 1913 and the operation was very lucrative.

p. 147. **South Sea Bubble:** Infamous promotional scam of 1720. The South Sea Company promised its shareholders wonderful returns on their investment just as soon as Britain won the war with France (the War of the Spanish Succession) and granted the company a lucrative trade monopoly. Alas! it never happened quite that way. Britain won the war but the South Sea Company never made much. The real losers were those who were taken in by all the promotional hoopla, paid very inflated prices for the stock and lost a lot of money.

p. 148. **Grubbed up:** i.e. pulled up and then dug under.

p. 150. **Byre:** cow barn.

p. 154. **Peter** is in the *Journal.* See entry 28.

p. 159. **Realschule:** German public school about the equivalent of the Canadian junior high school.

p. 164. For immigration statistics see footnote to p. 18.

p. 173. **Christus:** A reference to *The Risen Christ* sculpted by Jacob Epstein (1880-1959). Completed in 1920, this powerful work shows an angry, alarmingly modern-looking Christ (his hair is short and parted) pointing to one of his crucified palms. The statue is 86 inches high and the hands are indeed very large. See Richard Buckle's *Jacob Epstein, Sculptor* (Faber, London, 1963). Details like this suggest that Godwin must have written *The Eternal Forest* sometime in the 1920s.

p. 176. **Yeoman farmer:** one who owns his/her own small farm.

p. 179. **the angels that plucked one back:** the allusion is to Francis Thompson's *The Hound of Heaven* (stanza 4):

I turned me to them very wistfully;
But just as their young eyes grew sudden fair
With dawning answers there,
Their angels plucked them from me by the hair.
'Come then, ye other children, Nature's – share
With me' (said I) 'your delicate fellowship;'

p. 187. **Fontanelle:** the soft, boneless area in a baby's skull.

p. 197. **Commission snatchers:** real estate agents, brokers of farm equipment and similar middlemen.

p. 204. **monitor:** a senior pupil in school who has the duties of keeping order.

·p. 205 (a) **second eleven:** i.e. the second cricket team.

(b) **switch:** cane, rod, etc. (for punishment).

p. 206. **Carlyle:** see note to page 54.

p. 210. See *Journal,* extract 24.

p. 223. (a) **Klootchmans:** as mentioned (p.119), native women.

(b) **The Emancipator:** Abraham Lincoln.

p. 227. **Nibelungs:** in German mythology the race of dwarfs who owned a magic ring and a hoard of gold. Godwin was fond of Wagner (see *Journal,* extract 16).

p. 230. **Nubian woman:** presumably because Grouse Mountain looks dark (like a Nubian: i.e. someone from the Sudan) and voluptuously rounded.

p. 234. **Flotation:** the selling of shares to raise money in order to start a company.

p. 241. **Co-Operative Association:** "A group of local farmers banded together about 1912, buying shares in a carload of feed. This venture grew into a successful feed business, known as United Farmers (. . .)." *Maple Ridge, A History of Settlement,* p. 16.

p. 245. **In mufti:** 'out of uniform' i.e. without clerical collar.

p. 255 (a) **She did not** (. . .) **tribal laws:** Untrue: Native languages were usually forbidden, potlatches outlawed, etc.

(b) **Feast of the Rogation:** Christian feast celebration geared to ask God's blessing on the harvest.

p. 256. **Chechahco:** Newcomer, greenhorn. See note re p. 9.

p. 258. **'Mission' furniture:** see note to p. 37.

p. 261. (a) **Silver threads among the gold . . .:** A song by Harold Danks (who wrote the music) and Eben Rexford (who wrote the words). It dates from 1873 and goes like this: *Darling, I am growing old / Silver threads among the gold / Shine upon my brow today / Life is fading fast away; But, my darling, you will be / Always young and fair to me.* (b) Godwin is working on the roads because "a bylaw providing statute labour was passed in 1878, by which every man 18 years and over must work two days a year on the roads or pay $3.00 tax." (*Maple Ridge, A History of Settlement,* p. 109).

p. 265. *Elia:* a book of essays by Charles Lamb (1775-1834). This particular essay is called "The Old Benchers of the Inner Temple." For Godwin's connection with the (Middle) Temple see the note to p. 33 (b). Lamb's association with the Inner Temple was through his father who had worked there as a clerk and it was at the Inner Temple that Lamb first met Coleridge. Being both Romantics, Godwin and Lamb share more: nostalgia for childhood, cult of eccentricity, interest in things bizarre, delight in solitude, nature and beauty, etc.

p. 266. **Temple:** i.e. the Middle Temple. See note to p. 33.

p. 267 (a) **Indentured workers:** It was common for brokers from China ("Bossmen") to import Oriental labourers by paying their head tax (a special fee exacted from the Chinese) to the Canadian government. Once in Canada, these Chinese immigrants had no choice but to hand over a large percentage of their wages to the "Bossman" and they remained indentured to him often for an extended period of time.

(b) According to the authors of *Maple Ridge, A History of Settlement,* the Japanese settlers of the Lower Fraser Valley were almost forced to become outstanding fruit-growers because so many other occupations were closed to them. See *op. cit.* p. 63.

p. 270. **Trap-tested:** the hens had been trained to enter on their own the compartment where they were to lay their eggs.

p. 271. **Francis Thompson:** see note to p. 179.

p. 274. See *Journal,* extract 35.

p. 275 (a) See *Journal,* extract 34.

(b) **Pink tea expert:** a person who frequents "hen parties," i. e. parties for women only.

p. 281. See *Journal,* extract 6.

p. 285. **Shorter's Court:** a reference to the financial and banking district of London where Godwin worked before emigrating to Canada.

p. 285. **Share-butcher:** presumably travelling salesmen who sold stocks.

EXTRACTS FROM GEORGE GODWIN'S *JOURNAL*

Editor's note: George Godwin's eldest son, Dr. Eric Godwin, sent me this *Journal* in May 1994. It arrived at a timely moment, just when I was putting the finishing touches on *The Eternal Forest*. The journal is dog-eared and faded. Many words are crossed out and illegible and the dates are helter skelter. Some pages have mysteriously gone missing and one can't help but wonder what secrets they might have contained. It is a curious little book whose odour of musty rooms and steamer trunks conjures up a world long gone.

For clarity, I have divided the *Journal* into two distinct sections. In the first (1-17) I have put Godwin's recollections of his early years: the untimely death of his father, the close rapport he established with his mother, the wild youthful days running around the cliffs and beaches of Port Reculvers (in Kent), the falling out with his wild elder brother, Dick, and finally, the sad and lonely days at boarding school. (George didn't hesitate to accept Friday canings as the price that had to be paid for reading books of his own choice and generally ignoring the syllabus.).

Extracts 1-17 show some of the key influences of Godwin's formative years and reveal the main aspects of his nature: his extreme sensitivity, intuitive imagination, acute powers of observation, and above all his tendency to question everything in his effort to understand, whether it be the death of his good friend Captain Rogers, the inexplicable cruelty of some of his peers (and of himself, as he sadly discovers) or the stupidity of having to play that game which he detests: cricket.

The second section (18-38) contains extracts from the Port Haney (i.e. "Ferguson's Landing") phase of Godwin's life. These extracts are more varied. There is a poem about the bullfrogs of Port Haney, iconoclastic thoughts on religion and society, and Sherlock Holmes-style observations on his neighbours. In such extracts we can see already in embryo *The Eternal Forest*. Godwin is busy writing down his impressions of people and institutions in this eccentric New World society that he has chosen to test his mettle in. He is also, as usual, at tempting to sort out the mystery at the core of himself.

Perhaps most important of all, he is giving us the keys to various enigmas in *The Eternal Forest* itself (the reason why the horrified Corley scurries away from the Newcomers' place, the autobiographical reason for that scene with the aurora borealis and the nicotina). Altogether, the *Journal* is a fascinating record of the private thoughts and observations of a writer.

A. CHILDHOOD AND YOUTH (1889-1904)

(1) When I was three years old my Father died. I have only two distinct recollections of him. I remember on one occasion bursting open the door of the

dining room to find my Mother and Father sitting there talking. I received a sound whipping for breaking in on them so violently. I thought my Father a hard man then but now, in the light of experience I can think more kindly of him. At that time I had but one sentiment towards him: fear. What could a little child know of the jaded nerves and irritability of an overwrought man suffering from cancer?

My Father died in London while we children were away at Port Reculvers in Kent where we had a country house. We spent the summers in Kent and the rest of the year in our suburban London House in Highgate.

(2) My brother Dick *(see photo: ed.)* was 18 months older than I, fair and sturdy, and lacking a complete set of front teeth (he fell from the esplanade at Port Reculver and struck his mouth on a breakwater). To Dick I was always "Slippy," his faithful servitor, his abject admirer. Dick was my first hero if not, alas! my last. Wilful, wild Dick! I believe that he was never really tamed; instinctively he turned toward the open places of the world. Streets and offices were not for such as he. Men like him belonged to the times of Elizabethan England.

His vices were pronounced. He lied shamefully and taught me the art. He led me into bad company with street boys and schooled me in fighting with them by thrashing me himself quite frequently. In common with his kind he was a strange admixture of contradictory characteristics, a human boy and later a manly man. He did things that in later years I may have despised him for but I never lost my affection for him because he possessed the one quality that compensates for many weaknesses: he was always generous, amazingly openhanded and beneath his turbulent nature there beat the heart of a woman.

(3) By my Father's death my Mother was left with the responsibility of looking after a family of eight. On my eldest brother Bert fell the task of replacing the head of the family and whilst yet in his teens he became a man of affairs. He took what Fate gave him with a quiet patience and for many years was accepted as the breadwinner as a matter of course. The fact that my Father's premature death entirely altered the career that was Bert's by choice, became entirely forgotten and he came in for a torrent of unfounded criticism from those very people whom he had served.

(4) From the night nursery to my Mother's room was across a landing. A scurry of bare feet and I would be in bed beside my Mother, with always the demand: "Mummy, tell me a tale!" Oh, those tales! They were always touching and moral. Love triumphed ever. Tears would rise to my eyes, a lump come in my throat. And my Mother Welsh, with Huguenot blood in her veins, would be as affected by the pathos as much as myself. Often we would cry

together but I was never happier than during morning hour with my Mother.

From my Mother I learnt in simple language the stories of The Bible and The Lord's Prayer, which I did not understand. Jack the Giant Killer, Red Riding Hood and Hansel and Gretel were certainly more vital things to me than the Deity I was taught to pray to, but I reverenced what I did not comprehend because my Mother reverenced such things. Hardly should a little child feel with an understanding heart for the Man of Sorrows. The story lies dormant throught the immature years, but in later life, when sorrow is a reality and suffering a part of life, the tragic tale of old shines out from the mind with a new and poignant meaning:

"The seed, the little seed
We planted in the dark
Has risen and cleft the soil.
And thrusting forth a thousand arms
It rushes to the sun."

(5) Port Reculvers lies on the coast of Kent where the Straits of Dover are so narrow that in clear weather the white cliffs of France can be seen, like the steadfast sails of a motionless ship. To the west of the town shelved the sloping cliffs (. . .). The land had been converted into miniature Alps by the aggressive waters; the erstwhile estates of Earl Godwin lie fathoms deep and many hamlets rest beneath the waters. This was our chosen hunting ground and it was here that my brother Dick and I would spend long summer days.

(6) In our code scorn of fear was the principal tenet. To admit the hazard would have been unforgivable and, if in the secret heart of either of us fear lurked, the more would its existence be given the lie by foolhardiness.

Together we climbed and scrambled (up the cliffs). Now it would be Dick who, lying full length, would lower me to some cranny in search of gull's eggs. Oh, the wild heart beatings on those occasions! Below, the surf breaking in a long white line upon the shingle, and sending up its rhythmic music. The face of the cliff glistening in the sun, the nest all but within reach, the voice above counselling: "Steady, Slippy! How many of them are there? Can you reach?" And then what heart beats! The slow, slow stretching out, the balance regained, the throat of Slippy beating as with Thor's hammer. (. . .) Then the pull up to safety again, generally with the spoil a yellow sticky mess in my pocket. How the gulls wheeled and cried maledictions on the despoilers! What did we care for the heart of a mother-gull? An egg? We had no hearts then."

(7) At the west end of the seafront lived Captain Rogers, our staunch friend and ally in wrongdoing. The retired skipper of some windjammer, the old

man conducted a "Bathing Establishment," an occupation that enabled him to watch through his telescope the passing ships bound for the four corners of the earth. Captain Rogers, the staunch friend of my youth! He was a figure who stood for the romance of strange places. We boys were lured to the unknown by his tales. In Dick and me he engendered a Wanderlust that led me to bush life on the Pacific Coast and Dick to the wild places of Africa where the skins of lions and the tusks of elephants took the place of the crushed yellow sporting trophies of earlier days.

(8) In the Captain's dinghy we would push off from the beach at dusk. Then in our imaginations we sailed a pirate junk. Dick was the Pirate Captain and Slippy the bloodthirsty crew. Out to where the white yachts were riding at anchor we would pull. Silently we would draw alongside and the faithful Slippy would clamber up the bowsprit and creep down the deck to peer in at some party of card-playing yachtsmen. Sometimes a quick retreat down the bowsprit stays would be the result of discovery, then away from the Revenue Cutter to some other strange craft riding peacefully at anchor where the sinking sun shed long streamers of golden ribbon along the water.

We were never caught at a pirating but had we been, I know that it would have been just so much more evidence of the necessity for our going to school. What did our elders know of Truth and Romance? To us, the boarding of a merchantman, armed to the teeth, was an exciting and commendable business. But boys keep these things to themselves unless there be an understanding heart like the heart of old Captain Rogers. My sisters regarded such exploits as outrages, just as they did when we painted the rabbits green, but neither of these worthies had the imaginations of artistic temperaments.

(9) When the fate that hovered over us in those days finally descended and we were packed off to a preparatory school at Glenrock in Sussex (I must have been 8 or 9), I received a letter one day from my Mother telling me of Captain Roger's death. I was isolated with measles and alone at the time. Looking out over the housetops to whence the sea was whipped white by the March wind, I thought for the first time of death. It meant that old Captain Rogers would never look through that telescope again or pinch my leg and ask had I good thick knickers on. Do you wonder that I cried? That was my first sorrow.

(10) It was about this time that Dick developed a liking for the town boys. One evening he and I quarelled. (I forget what it was about – we quarelled so often but always made up directly we got our wind again.) It was in the evening. Dick together with a number of tradesmen's messenger boys was playing some game on the way home. What started us I have long since forgotten but the result I remember vividly to this day. We fought. There before

those boys he beat me (not that I didn't put up a good fight) but he beat me as he generally did.

Filled with shame and rage (shame that I should have been beaten by my brother before those townsboys and rage that my brother should have done it) I ran home as fast as ever my feet would carry me. There was one fixed resolve in my mind: I would kill my brother. Arriving at the gate I crept silently in and through the garden to the woodshed. Taking a long and heavy piece of wood I crept back and took up my position behind the gate pillar. There I waited, choked with sobs of rage and with hate gnawing at my heart. It became dark. He was afraid to come home, I felt sure of it, but I waited on. He would come through the gate and then I would hit my hardest.

As I look back on that evening that I so nearly became a Cain I am convinced that thoughts of consequences never entered my head. That the law possibly would have considered me doli incapax *(i.e. so young as to be incapable of deliberate criminal malice, too young to distinguish clearly between right and wrong: ed.)* I neither knew nor cared. My moral training was obliterated by the primal passion that convulsed me. My brother came in that night through the stables so that in my conscience remains only the knowledge that once in my life I have lived through the mental phase of murder.

So, before I was near my teens I knew something of the emotions, having experienced virulent hate with a desire to kill, overwhelming sorrow, and then and until the end a profound love for my Mother.

(11) One day, having had some little sickness, I was permitted to go for a walk on the esplanade. Once there I sat down to read a Robin Hood story. Presently there came along a tall person wheeling a cycle. He sat down beside me. Now, although I loathed going to church on Sunday and generally was sore put to it to get through the service, I had a childlike reverence for this surpliced priest. He was not, I thought, as other men.

This tall man spoke to me and enquired of a good hotel where lunch might be had – he knew far better than I – but that was not a matter for a small boy to see through. I told him of an hotel, a big one on the Parade. Then he flattered me by telling me of a recent visit he had made to the Holy Land. The Holy Land forsooth . . . With the insidious cunning of a Jesuit he suggested that I ask permission to go out with him that afternoon. He would have a bicycle for me; I could say that he was a clergyman my father knew; I knew him, did I not? If permission were granted it was arranged that I should go to the hotel after lunch and he would hire a bicycle and we would ride out to the old Castle some 4 miles away. He would like to see it.

We rode out to the old castle, the priest and the boy. At the "Castle Inn" we left our machines and walked along the high cliff. There the man of God did that which set me running to the Inn, terrified. He caught me up, that wily priest, and with soft words silenced me and back at Glenrock sealed my silence with as much sweetmeals as I could carry.

And so while I was child I became contaminated by one who, by profession, followed the lowly Nazarene. I wonder: do such men ponder the saying of Master Christ that it would be better for him to cast himself into the sea with a millstone about his neck?

(12) Saint Lawrence College stands some two miles inland from the Kentish Coast. I was eleven when I left the sheltered preparatory school to follow Dick (who had already been there for a term) and my chum, Jack Drake. The preparatory school which I just left had been conducted on the lines of a home and the Principal, who boasted no degree or other pedagogic qualification, made up for this shortcoming with a large-hearted nature. I was sorry to leave this school with its homelike life but I hankered to follow Dick and my chum.

(13) I speedily found that hopes of my brother and chum were ill-founded. They had formed new associations and this first day at school marked the opening of the gulf between my brother and myself. What we had in common as small boys, we had in common with all small boys: fishing, swimming, smoking cigarettes. But now I found myself faced with what may be called a clique. However much Dick might have wanted me to be one of them, the others were of a different way of thinking, which was as well, as it turned out.

Dick's friends enjoyed a certain notoriety as a gang of boys whose chief amusement was the organised tyranny of those weaker than themselves. New boys were their favorite game. Dick's predisposition towards the townboys of Port Reculvers manifested itself again when he selected the hectoring, ragging element at school as his associates. So it came about that we drifted apart.

The first few days were miserable enough and often I wished myself back at the little school where the scholars sat at one large table with the Principal and his wife. My chum Jack had found new friends too and this defection hurt more than that of my brother.

So it was that I faced the miniature world that a public school is, alone. My advantages were few, my drawbacks many. I found that among so many I was shy, almost afraid. I lost confidence in myself and often had difficulty when answering a master to refrain from tears. Possibly I was suffering acutely from that malady, homesickness. And homesickness like seasickness too often is regarded as the subject of jests.

In any case, my sensations were mostly of a disagreeable nature. I longed for privacy, and there was none. The end of the day was to me one round of tortures, discomforts, and embarrassments. I realized vividly enough that the only way in which I could hope for peace would be to tackle my most aggressive tormentor and beat him but how was this to be done? The tormentors took care always to select those smaller than themselves.

I was the only new boy in that dormitory and I had to furnish the evening's entertainment. This varied from evening to evening. Sometimes I would be bundled into the clothesbasket and once the lid was on the game appeared, so far as one could judge from the somewhat confined quarters, to consist of well-sustained efforts to break every bone in my body. Towel-flipping, superfluous cold douches, and the sousing of my bedclothes varied the programme.

(. . .) That I was eventually left unmolested I can only attribute to the fact that it was discovered that I could tell stories of Robin Hood and his merry men and variations on the romances of Jules Verne.

(14) Yet for the sake of truth I have to record that a year later, knowing as I did the misery of it, I took my part, cowardly little brute, in battering other new boys. I recognize it for what it is: a significant sidelight on the inherent cowardliness of men generally. Nothing can be easier than to strike the weak, to follow with the mob, to point the finger of derision at the splendid few who scorn the wisdom of their generation. Men do these things and boys do them too. The boy is the father of the man and a school is the world in miniature.

(15) The hours of school were so many hours of blank inertia. I was too unhappy to pay much attention. I had no desire to learn the subjects that were taught, or rather, to learn them as they were taught. I therefore closed my mind to the voice of the master and in a world of dreams awaited the ringing of the bell. I surreptitiously consumed many books, mostly exciting stories of adventure. I seldom lost my place at the bottom of the class, except in English, History and Scripture when I contested the other end. And as the Saint Lawrence system prescribed corporal punishment for mental ineptitude – even when it often enough was the ineptitude of the master – I regularly came in for a caning on Fridays. Such was the price I paid for the consolation of private readings.

(16) My other consolation came with the evening chapel service. I sang in the choir and would find consolation in the music. The words of the Te Deum conveyed some vague promise to me of a future compensation for present ills. The poetry of the psalms stole over me; I found a sensuous enjoyment in the volume of the organ music. I was anything but religious but those services were to me at that time what the music of Wagner came to be some years later. They took me to the verge of the unknown, quickened in me hitherto unknown emotions, and intensified a longing, hardly recognised by myself, to love something. In these moments of emotion I ached to pour out a love – how, or upon whom, I knew not, but this knowledge would come later.

(17) In the family council it was decided that I should go to Germany for

a year or two while I came to some conclusion about my future career. I had
to do something some day, and at sixteen that day was getting nearer. A
brisk breeze was blowing down the (English) Channel when my Mother, my
sisters and myself went out with the steam packet from Dover. As we stepped
aboard I looked up to where the Castle stands on the high cliffs and remembered the days when I fought mock battles over the downs.

During my stay in Germany I was introduced to Siegfried, to Parsifal, Lo-
hengrin, the Legend of the Holy Grail and the mythology that Wagner uti-
lized so wondrously. Those were happy days. I had no work to speak of and
was free to amuse myself. The country ablaze with colour was a joy always.
The wide shiny streets so clean, so prosperous looking (. . .). *(There is surprisingly little about Germany in Godwin's* Journal: *ed.)*

B. THE CANADIAN WEST (DEC. 1911 TO 1916)

The journal extracts pertaining to life in Canada were not arranged by Godwin in thematic or chronological order. Also, only about half of them bear
precise dates so for clarity's sake I have rearranged them under three headings:
(I) descriptions of people (extracts 18-21); (II) home life (extracts 22-28); and
(III) thoughts on life and religion (extracts 29-38). I have tried to respect
chronology wherever possible.

Section I contains the originals of some of the portraits which the reader
will find in *The Eternal Forest* (Johansson, Stein and the band of Native people on the railroad platform are all there). **Section II** reveals many affinities
between Godwin's experiences and those of the Newcomer in *The Eternal Forest* (delight in swinging the axe, joy in the changing moods of Mount Baker,
exasperation at the nightly chorus of bullfrogs, etc.). **Section III** gives us useful information about Godwin's views on religion and other aspects of life.

PORTRAITS

(18) The Norwegian (1912)

He has only one eye but its exceeding brilliancy more than makes up for
the deficiency. He greets one with the charming frankness of a person who
addresses an equal. He has laboured thirty years with his hands through all
the seasons. Perhaps that is why even now his eye has the brightness of youth.
Working side by side in the same trench we became acquainted and here under the July sun I learnt something of his history. Born in Norway, he sailed
the North Sea in tramp steamers bringing cargoes from his own land to Grims-
by. Then, thirty years old, the exile to the the Land of Promise. He is not sour
or disappointed after these thirty years of labour. He has a wife and seven chil-

dren and they are content to live in a shack. No material comforts. If you were to tell him you admired him he would hardly understand. It is by the unremitting labour of such as the Norwegian that we have changed the face of this vast continent.

(19) **Aboriginals** (New Westminster, April 28, 1912)

Oblivious to everything that is transpiring about them, some dozen or more families of Indians are contriving to make themselves as comfortable as possible upon a Railway Platform. I found the temporary encampment in full swing about three o'clock and on returning about five o'clock they were still there.

They seem to have divided themselves naturally into family groups. There are a number of women, some young with their babes, and others old, immensely old. I know not whether they, like the women of Southern Europe, ripen and fade rapidly, but Time has scarred their old faces with a thousand wrinkles so that they have the appearance of winter apples. An old man sits apart. He seems more beast than man. His jaw protrudes to a great length beyond his nose, which feature is squat upon his face, giving him the appearance of a baboon. A close inspection reveals two naked, deformed feet. He is an imbecile and beats a tin can upon the ground to rhythmic time. He mutters from time to time and rolls about his blood-shot eyes.

The younger men are clad in civilized fashion, lending an odd contrast to the multi-coloured apparel of their companions. These young men seem to be intelligent and able to look after their more unsophisticated companions. For the older ones and for the women it is an occasion. The women have a look of simple wonderment mingled with infinite patience.

The children cry; the Old Man continues unceasingly his rhythmic tap tap tap on a metal drum; the young men shout to one another in a tongue strange to the White Man, but through all, the sublime tranquillity never fades from the features of these patient creatures. These are of the dying race who have given place to White Man. He has taken from them their land. He has given them his religion. He has taken their furs and has traded them for Fire-Water.

(20) **The busybody** (Whonnock, November 27, 1912)

He has one master passion: an overwhelming desire to manage the affairs of his neighbours. This passion is, like most, a vice. Imagine for yourself one of those old portraits of the Dutch master, Van Eck. Long face, sallow complexion, the beard brown and patriarchal. The brow is narrow and the eyes below it set too closely together. These eyes give the face a mean effect. They never rest, but move hither and thither furtively, avoiding a fixing. (. . .) A certain distinct personality is revealed in his dress. He affects a wide-brimmed soft hat which harmonizes with his features and a capped cloak which hangs loosely from his tall figure. I have never been able to make up my mind as to whether his style of dress is an affectation or is purely accidental. He is never without his venerable umbrella.

His little house gives the same impression of order divorced from beauty. It stands upon a clearing of some two acres, looking towards the east; below, the Fraser River winds away to the ocean, dividing once to flow past a wooded isle, and rejoining later to curve majestically towards the south-east (which locality they name the elbow of the river). Away upon the skyline the mighty Rocky Mountains *(sic)* range north and south, natural ramparts, with the volcanic peak of Mount Baker eternally snow-white, like some castello, keeping guard.

The little house watches over this scene and its inmate watches over the dwellers of the adjacent fertile hills and valleys. The house is plain and not a little mean in appearance. It is, as are all country buildings in the West, built of timber. A little oblong house, high-roofed, without a single architectural adornment, even such as should grace the most simple countryside dwellings. It is unpainted without and within.

The living room, which opens off the front and only door, contains a cook-stove, its hideous pipe ascending up through the ceiling. On either side a wooden powder box does duty as a receptacle for fuel, one for kindling wood the other for split pine logs. A broom stands primly against the wall. There are two tables, both covered with green ornamental oil-cloth, and on each stands a common oil lamp of glass. There are four cane chairs and a wooden cupboard. This completes the owner's furniture.

But this I remember: a small bookshelf, a glance of the contents of which leads to idle speculation on the mind of the owner. A copy, in paper cover, of Henry George's *Poverty and Progress.* An early novel of Charles Reade. Marcus Charles' *For the Term of His Natural Life* and a miscellany of Australian and Canadian newspapers and magazines, these last being of the cheaper variety. Some are years old and quite yellow with age.

The bedroom contains a rough, hard wood bed, another small table with an oilcloth covering, a cane chair, a row of clothes pegs, a tin trunk. This little house, like its owner, has an oppressive air of precision. That is the dominant note from the time we unlatch the little gate, trim and neat, with its dexterious (sic) little wire fastening of the owner's devising, till we cross the two acres denuded of all vestige of trees, and now hard with stubble, till indeed, we come upon the owner himself.

Imagine him at work in his woodshed. He is sharpening a woodman's saw, which he tells us is an Art. Neighbours from all around come to him with their saws to be sharpened. He rests a moment, then selects from a prim little case another implement, and re-commences to reset the saw. "Yes!" he has quite a name as an expert in this matter. "Do you know how to sharpen a saw?" he queries. "No!" Ha! Well, he will tell you. Also he tells you he was up at our ranch yesterday – this comes as a surprise. "Yes! You do not understand saws," he continues, touching the tool as another man would place his hand upon a child. "No, it is blunt. You use it barbously *(sic)*. Bring it to me and I will sharpen it. You need not pay me but if someone comes to you, twenty years hence,when you are as versed in wood-lore as I, sharpen his saw for him!"

"I also notice the way you are clearing your land," he continues, gaining unconsciously the manner of a French *magistrat d'instruction,* although as a matter of fact he hails from Schlesweg-Holstein, from whence he fled at the time of the founding of the Federation.

"I will come tomorrow and show you how it should be done. Your axe? Is your axe sharp? What weight is your axe? How much did you pay for it?" Here, right before his eyes is a Newcomer, a Chechacko, someone to whom he can play the role of grand philosopher and friend and alas! although the old fellow does not realize it, play the part of a great and intolerable bore.

(21) "Caste and character"

When first I met Jackson-Woodville he must have spent thirty four of his sixty years in the Dominion, yet the fetters of his caste still hung close about him. Thirty-four years is a considerable length of time but J.-W. might have landed in Montreal yesterday for all the change that has come about in his narrow, limited outlook on men and affairs. He still views the spacious world through the little window of class prejudice. Contact with men of all kinds and conditions has availed nothing.

The seed was sewn in a county rectory, at a public school and in a university, and it has indeed flourished. He will remain convinced that an English Gentleman is, by natural right and beyond all question of doubt above all his fellows. J.-W. would divide mankind into two great and ever-to-be-separated classes: (a) those of his own class and in this category he includes others who qualify for special reasons: (the introductory remarks are telling): "So-and-So. Nice people. Father is Ambassador to Whaloobollo." Or: "Thingamee. Fine shot, Thingamee. All round man. With me at Balliol."

On the other hand, should the subject come under the second category of less distinguished mortals, J.-W. will use a very different kind of introductory remark: "Honest little fellow, Hobbs. Great worker." Or: "Very decent man, Boggs. He gets through more work than any man I know. Wife's no good. Etc."

II. LIFE IN WHONNOCK/PORT HANEY

(22) "The Simple Life" (Whonnock, February 1913)

There is not even a well. A little creek gives a supply of crystal water. After a week or two it becomes quite natural to draw the water from the creek as it is required and to carry it in buckets to the house. In the winter days the lit-tle trail down to the creek is muddy, but even the mud becomes familiar and inoffensive.

There is no coal or if there be any it is as yet unmined so that for us at least no man need spend his days in darkness hewing forests of other times. Our fuel is around us, and when we require warmth (which we always do dur-ing these winter days) the trees give it to us. Before a fire is possible some tree must be hewn down, sawn into lengths, split, and stacked by the fireside. And so as winter wears on there is a clearing in the bush and lamentations among the bleak, gaunt trees.

The general store, which embraces the post office and performs the func-tion of a bank, is about a mile distant. Here the ranch produce (in the shape of eggs) can be traded for other necessities so that even money itself becomes, in a great measure, indispensable.

All day there is no sound but those of the countryside – the hens celebrate another egg with loud rejoicings, the rooster lifts up his voice melodiously. Out among the trees the resounding axe may echo merrily in the distance, punctuated by the groaning crash of some Giant of the Forest. The little wood-pecker hammers on the bark of the birch until you wonder that the strenuous little fellow does not break his sturdy bill. With nervous little jerks, like some furry automoton, the chipmunk eyes you from some mossy stump, and bolts at the first sign of animation in the stranger.

From the valley the shrill whistle of the locomotive is thrown about among the hills, the rumbling grows louder but never more than a metallic mur-mur, then departs. But that does not concern the folk of the countryside. The train travels by us, but its main business is with the city, where men live close-pent and walk upon hard stone and hear all day the multitudinous noises of the city.

To us each day yields fresh delights. Routine there is: there is the little creek to visit, the trees to fell, the flock to feed, and a multitude of other tasks, but each has its delight. The glorious swinging of the axe: Is that work? Well, I suppose the town dweller, flaccid and sluggish, would so regard it, but to me it is sheer delight. The open sky, the chasing clouds, pure and sane employ-ment, while over the river and flung along the Eastern Sky lives the mountain range, eternally white and silent – these help us to a better adjustment of our ideas of the value and importance of things and bring us a little nearer to the eternal verities.

(23) "Mid-April Poughing" (April 20, 1913)

Under the high blue sky of Spring
Where the breeze blows a tender caress
And the air comes sweet from the mountains

And there's naught of the city's stress
Here with the breeze upon my face
And my feet in the furrow wide
I'll tune my heart to the Song of Spring
And little I'll need beside.

Out in the open spaces
Nature doth hold her sway
Over the hearts of her children
Who walk in the narrow way.
Turn your backs on the Market Place!
Follow the call of the Wide!
And health you'll have, if little else
And naught shall you want beside.

(24) A Regret (Whonnock, April 1913)

It is, and will be always, a cause of deep regret and disillusionment to me that it is necessary to descend to the ground floor in order to speak with D. She will never come up any higher and it is in the upper rooms that one can see the stars. And communication between the upper and lower is quite intolerable because there is no common language between the two. So long as D. remains below, to her only the dross of me will be known. All those little imperfections of character must go unforgotten, unoverlooked, simply because she cannot share with me my longing for these bright stars.

(25) My home (psalm)

My home looks towards the South, over endless stretches of timber. The river flows before me, a broad grey-blue band of shimmering water cutting across a green setting. The green of the firs, austere and brooding, and the laughing green of the meadowlands upon the river banks.

The sky is intense blue. Full of poised clouds. It is high summer.

Not long ago everything looked barren and Nature appeared as the Sphynx, albeit without the beautiful face of a woman. That of a hag rather. But even then the quickening had taken place and now the womb of Mother Earth has brought forth in abundant measure, pressed down and running over. . . Prodigal and lavish! The land laughs and is glad.

The breeze murmurs among the Six Sister Firs on the west side of my home – the six symbolic ones that I see standing against the skyline when I return home by way of the river. At those times they stand for much to me: home, wife, the sweetness awaiting the returner. They are gently swaying me back to it all. It is high summer. The land laughs and beholding the beauty of it the heart is indeed full of gladness.

(26) **Mount Baker**

(. . .) Away upon the skyline the mighty Rocky Mountains (sic) range north and south, natural ramparts, with the volcanic peak of Mount Baker eternally snow white, like some castello keeping guard.

Epigram

They named you Mount Baker.
That was a misnomer:
Your name should have been
Jungfrau or Snow Queen.

(27) **"The Bullfrogs' Serenade"**

On a light Spring night
When the moon is bright
There's a nocturnal mad parade
'Tis the Bullfrogs' serenade.

From all around
Comes the mystic sound
From ten thousand swollen throats.
Over the still night air it floats.

Numberless fancy sets
Of Bullfrog castanets
Are clashed upon the green
By those players all unseen.

All night long they play
Until the pink of day
Shews in the ripening west
And then they go to rest.

And the air at dawn
As 'tis lightly borne
Down from yonder hill
Is all serene and still.

(28) **"Peter my Collie"**

Dear Peter of the true and trusting heart,
Though mind may make me other than thou art,
There sure lurks behind those bright brown eyes

Some doggy-soul, though folks say otherwise.
Come! Waggle up to me! Come! Tell about
The doings of the day! The glorious route
Of other dogs, sleeps in the sun
Snaps at the flies, the gorgeous romp and run.

Oh, how you begged your supper: pretty head
Aslant, ears cocked, just dying to be fed.
And how you raced away to chew your bone,
Obedient to doggy law to eat alone!

Sleep well, old chap, and dream your day at last.
'Don't bark unless you feel you have to, please –
It always wakes the Boy up in a fright.
Another pat? Alright! Lie down! Good night!

III. THOUGHTS ON LIFE AND RELIGION

(29) The Established Church is like a bat making a great commotion, but blind to everything around it.

(30) Sincerity is an expensive luxury.

(31) If Christ came to save the world his mission proved futile. If he be God indeed let him come again. There are, as yet, no signs that the Kingdom of God is at hand.

(32) **The Ballad of Despair** *(extracts only; undated. As stated earlier, not all the entries are dated. On the margin of* The Ballad of Despair *Godwin has written "To the Dwellers in the Dark Valley." – ed.)*

The Ballad of Despair

It is not from the present trial
That the soul shrinks back in pain;
It is not with a coward's heart,
But with a throbbing brain
That knows full well in its pulsing hell
That the Past comes not again. (Stanza 1)

Such is the Hell wherein we dwell
Whose loves are in the Past.
As mariners cast upon the sea

Cling to a broken mast
We drift upon the Sea of Life
Tossed by each stormy blast. (II)

'Tis the memory of what has been
That leaves its present sting –
The wistful thought of other days
That knew not suffering.
When Hope was like a golden Lamp
And the Season ever Spring. (V)

We do not know that blest relief
For those alone may weep
Whose hearts though wounded
Yet have Faith, tender and strong and deep.
We cannot weep – our only Faith
Is one long unending sleep. (X)

And though to live be bitter-sweet
We do not wish to die –
To close our eyes for evermore,
Never to see the sky
Of summer, when the great white clouds
Like galleons ride by. (XII)

And yet we cheat ourselves with Hope!
Do lilies bloom again?
Yet some believe they only dream
When the worm is at the brain.
Ye Gods! The vanity of man
Who thinks to live again. (XVI)

For most men live by Faith alone
That they shall live again;
Their only Anchor in this Life,
Their Anodyne for Pain
That when the Angels' trumpets sound
The earth shall not enchain. (XVII)

But not for us such simple faith
In the God who gives no sign;
For us there is no Sacrament,
No God in the bread and wine.

The Nazarene comes not again
Let men think Him divine. (XIX)

And if Christ died to save Mankind?
Full many a Saint has died
With words of Faith upon the lips
And with a Spirit that defied
The very fire of the Christians' pyre
But never the Lord replied. (XX)

Through countless years the human race
Plays out its tragedy;
But the Lord remains forever mute
Silent eternally;
The enigma of two thousand years,
O mystic one in three! (XXIII)

So many Saviours men have had
Besides the lowly Jew;
So many prophets among men
We know not which be true.
We know alone that Pain is old
And Hope forever new. (XXIV)

We know alone that with False Hopes
We stanch the present pain;
And even as we cheat ourselves
We know that soon again
Despair will seize the aching heart
And Logic seize the Brain. (XXV)

A spell of years most sorrowful,
Little of Joy, much Pain –
This we believe . . . and then a sleep,
Dust unto dust again.
We cannot hide from Truth with lies.
Despair is all too sane. (XXVI)

(33) "**De Profundis**" (November 1914)

There is no better stimulant than a complete lack of Sympathy to brace one up when the Pale Figure of Hope grows misted to the vision; when Failure like some Monster mocks at us and the only thing that seems real is the Hostility of the world.

(34) The best way to test one's inherent strength is to turn your back on the older effete civilisation and try your hand in the new world.

(35) The whole fabric of modern civilization rests upon the labour of the Farmer and the degradation of the Harlot. Yet the one class is neglected, poorly compensated, and bears the burden of the day for a mere subsistence, whilst the prostitute bears the moral burden and is likewise outlawed. On the other hand we see those who produce nothing but live by systematic plunder, growing rich and justifying existing conditions by prattling on about the Survival of the Fittest.

(36) The Academic Dreamer

You're an academic dreamer, let me tell you good and straight.
You spend your life in dreams that don't come true.
Why don't you collar hold of life and leave those things to Fate?
You'll be a damnsite richer if you do.
I tell you life's a compromise – just take things as they are.
Quit dreams and see things as we others do.
Leave all this crazy hitching of your wagon to a star,
This dreaming of a dream that can't come true.

I'm an academic dreamer and I'm happy in my dream.
All your talk of life and wealth just leaves me cold.
There's something rather low in it; there's something rather mean.
There's finer things in life than grubbing gold.
I'm in that small minority that's looking for the dawn
And it's little that I care for all you say.
The East is waxing crimson with the shimmer (?) of the morn
And in the dark I'm dreaming for the Day.
(Originally published in *Vancouver World,* December 16, 1913).

(37) The Ballad of Burnaby Gaol (February 1914)

The Ballad of Burnaby Gaol
In Burnaby there lies a Gaol
And on someone lies the stain
Of human blood, for in that Gaol
A miner lad was slain;
Was left untended there to die
Upon a bed of pain.

He did not die as some men do
Choked by the deadly gas,
He wasn't hauled out of the pit
A scorched and blackened mass.
In Gaol he lay, where night and day
He heard the wardens pass.

He heard them tread with feet of lead
Upon the Prison floor.
Both day and night without respite
His agony he bore.
And there he died who had defied
Majestic man made Law.

Three hopeless days of suffering,
Three nights of endless gloom
He lay and waited silently
Within his Prison tomb;
Waited for those that never came:
'Twas thus they sealed his doom

He saw the Sun glance fitfully
Along the Prison wall;
His memory bore him swiftly
To days beyond recall.
He saw the dusk of even come,
The final darkness fall.

No doctor came to tend to him;
No woman raised his head.
Only the Prison Guard was there
Standing beside his bed, or
Pacing along the prison floor,
Pacing with feet of lead.

The friends who sought to comfort him,
His father grey with years –
They turned away that cursed day,
Unmoved by Parents' tears;
Left him without the prison gate
Kenneled by nameless fears.

And all should know that this was so:
A man was murdered there.
A man was left to wilt away
In fetid prison air;
For two-and-seventy hours was left
Without a Doctor's care.

For he who fights for God-given rights
Must suffer at men's hands;
And he who scorns the Right of Might,
They tighten fast his bands.
And all should know that this is so
In this, as other lands.

(This poem appeared in The Vancouver World, *Feb. 6, 1914. In recent years there have been instances of this kind of neglect manifesting itself in the Vancouver City Jail. Plus ça change, etc.: ed.)*

(38) **Little Grey Mother** (October 18, 1914)

Little grey Mother, why do you weep
There by the hearth where the long shadows creep?
"Their chairs they are empty; my sons they are gone
Heard ye no bugles this morning at dawn?"

Little grey Mother, now wipe you your eyes.
Oh, quicken your heart and stifle your sighs.
"'Tis highly you speak to the woman who bore
The sons that are gone to come back nevermore."

Little grey Mother, your lot is to wait
There by the fireside both early and late.
Guard you their chairs til thy sons do return
And watch you the fire that it brightly may burn.

The stench from the trenches poisons the air.
The battered, the dead and the dying are there
And scattered amongst them, so pale and wan
The three sons who answered the bugles at dawn.

OTHER BOOKS BY GEORGE STANLEY GODWIN

1. *Cain or The Future of Crime,* Paul Kegan and Co., London, 1928. 108pp.
2. *Columbia or The Future of Canada.* Paul Kegan and Co., London, 1928. 95 pp.
3. *The Disciple* (a play in 3 acts). Acorn Press, London, 1936. 88 pp.
4. *Discovery (The Story of the finding of the World).* Heath Cranton, London, 1933. 96pp.
5. *Empty Victory,* John Long, London, 1932. 288 pp.
6. *The Great Mystics,* Watts and Co., London, 1945. 106 pp.
7. *The Great Revivalists,* Watts and Co., London, 1951. 220 pp.
8. *Japan's New Order,* Watts and Co., London, 1942. 32 pp.
9. *The Land our Larder.* The Story of the Suffleet Experiment and its significance in war. Acorn Press, London, 1939. 127 pp.
10. *Marconi (1939-45), A war record.* Chatto and Windus, London, 1946. 125 pp.
11. *The Middle Temple: the Society and Fellowship.* Staples Press, London, 1954. 174 pp.
12. *The Mystery of Anna Berger,* Watts and Co., London, 1948. 226 pp.
13. *Peter Kurten. A study in Sadism.* Acorn Press, London, 1938. 58 pp. Reissued by Wm. Heinemann, 1945.
14. *Priest or Physician? A study of faith-healing.* Watts and Co., London, 1941.
15. *Queen Mary College (East London College).* An Adventure in Education. 1944. No info. available. 209 pp.
16. *Vancouver: a Life, 1757-98.* Philip Allan, London, 1930. 308 pp.
17. *Why Stay We Here?* P. Allan & Co. London, 1930. 320 pp.

According to Whitaker's *Books in Print,* 1994, all of George Godwin's books are out of print.

PHOTO CREDITS

All the photos but one of the Godwin family have been generously supplied by Mr. Eric Godwin. The photo of Dick Godwin was available through the generosity of Mrs. Jill (Godwin) Jahansoozi, Dick's granddaughter.

The photo of James Godwin surfaced through the kindness of Rev. Stephanie Godwin, George's sister Maud's daughter.

Most of the photos accompanying *The Eternal Forest* are the property of the Historical Photographs Department, Vancouver Public Library (VPL).

Douglas firs on Vancouver Island Highway (front endpaper): VPL 3718.
View looking north from Fort Langley to Maple Ridge (Whonnock) and Golden Ears (p. 11): Fort Langley Centennial Museum.
Giant cedar of the rain forest (p. 12): VPL 4159.
Port Haney, 1908 (p. 20): VPL 7228.
The Thames with Tower Bridge, 1908 (p. 34): courtesy of B. T. Batsford Ltd., London, England.
Visit of the Japanese Prince Fushime (p. 94): VPL 3010.
Entrance to Vancouver harbour (p. 107): VPL 7718.
View of Vancouver from the Sun *Tower* (p. 108): VPL 4704.
CPR station, Vancouver (p. 109): VPL 2910.
Woman pioneer in old Vancouver (p. 110): VPL 13015.
Portrait of Coast native people (p. 114): VPL 14082.
A burnt forest (p. 121): VPL 4007.
Houses with stumps in front (p. 128): VPL 7041.
Chinese vendors, Pender Street (p. 137): VPL 7234.
Mount Baker (p. 190): VPL 2052.
Granville and Hastings (p. 224): VPL 6776.
View of Christ Church and West End (p. 225): VPL 8605.
Granville and Georgia (p. 226): VPL 7743.
Italian triumphal arch, 1912 (p. 228): VPL 2009.
Sikh fisherman (p. 229): VPL 13138.
Ship of immigrants, Vancouver harbour (p. 229): VPL 3024.
Douglas firs (back endpaper): VPL 2569.
Road crew in Haney, 1912 (p. 263): VPL 13063.
Haney, culvert under construction (p. 262): VPL 13064.
Temple Bar, London, 1910 (p. 264): with thanks to the Wilson Collection of the University of Aberdeen.

All other photos used in *The Eternal Forest* are the property of Godwin Books.

ALSO AVAILABLE FROM GODWIN BOOKS:

Italian for the Opera
by Robert S. Thomson

150 pages, illustrated, soft cover. This is a book for those who wish to delve deeper than the 'quick fixes' supplied by surtitles.

"Singers and teachers of singing cannot afford to be without this excellent text." – Dr. Richard Sjoerdsma, Editor, U.S.-based National Association of Teachers of Singing *Journal*).

Hot Tips for Real Estate Investors
by Robert S. Thomson and Aqlim Barlas

84 pages, many illustrations, graphs. Explains clearly in the context of Ms. Barlas' actual transactions (6 houses, 8 condos) how to use comparables, how to negotiate, how to evaluate prospective tenants, how to borrow on your equity, etc. "As a practical guide this book hits many targets" *(The Vancouver Province)*. "Pearls of wisdom" (*The Vancouver Sun*).

The Eternal Forest
by G. Godwin

HOW TO ORDER
To order *Italian for the Opera* send $12.95 plus $2.00 postage to P.O. Box 4781, Vancouver, B.C. V6B 4A4. For *Hot Tips,* send $8.95 plus $2.00 post. For *The Eternal Forest* (hardcover) send $29.95 plus $3.00 post. Cheques payable to "Godwin Books." GST paid by us. U.S. customers: deduct 10% from Cdn. total price.

GODWIN BOOKS (established in 1993) is so named in honour of George Godwin, the author of *The Eternal Forest*. If you have a promising manuscript, send us a 1-page outline with a self-addressed stamped envelope. Or fax 604-682-5640.